A JURY

OF HER

PEERS

A JURY OF HER PEERS

JEAN HANFF KORELITZ

CROWN PUBLISHERS, INC. • New York

Published by Crown Publishers, Inc., 201 East 50th Street, New
York, New York 10022. Member of the Crown Publishing Group.

Random House, Inc.   New York, Toronto, London, Sydney, Auckland
http://www.randomhouse.com/

CROWN is a trademark of Crown Publishers, Inc.
Printed in the United States of America

Design by Deborah Kerner

Library of Congress Cataloging-in-Publication Data
Korelitz, Jean Hanff
A jury of her peers / Jean Hanff Korelitz. — 1st ed.
I. Title.
PS3561.06568J8   1996
813'.54—dc20   96-4241

ISBN 0-517-70061-1
10 9 8 7 6 5 4 3 2 1
First Edition

To Deborah Michel,
constant reader

We are the Furies still, yes,
but now our rage that patrolled the crimes of men,
that stalked their rage dissolves—
we loose a lethal tide to sweep the world!
Man to man foresees his neighbour's torments,
groping to cure his own—
poor wretch, there is no cure, no use,
the drugs that ease him speed the next attack.

Now when the sudden blows come down,
let no one sound the call that once brought help,
"Justice, hear me—Furies throwned in power!"
Oh I can hear the father now
or the mother sob with pain
at the pain's onset . . . hopeless now,
the house of Justice falls.

AESCHYLUS,
The Eumenides
Translated by Robert Fagles

A TEXTBOOK

SCHIZOPHRENIC

Sybylla had given all of her change to the homeless guy at the foot of the courthouse steps, a classic urban specimen with a grin of syncopated black teeth and a sign that read IF YOU LIVED HERE, YOU'D BE HOME NOW. It had seemed like a good idea at the time, she thought grimly, trawling the chaos of her purse for a coin and churning up only ancient ATM receipts and filth-encrusted Tums. An outraged Yuppie huffed nearby, but she stood her ground in front of the corridor's only pay phone and snarled whenever he edged too close. At last, an inside jacket pocket yielded one quarter, smeared with something that looked like chocolate—she hoped it was chocolate; it seemed unladylike to sniff—and she slapped it into the slot, her fingers jerking at the archaic rotary dial.

Steiner, as might have been anticipated, was not pleased.

"Why are you calling me?" he asked testily. "Why aren't you sitting in my office talking to me?"

"Sorry, boss." She sighed. "They wouldn't let me go."

"Sybylla, far be it from me to impede you in the exercise of your sacred civic duty, but do you have any idea how long you're going to last in voir dire when they find out you're a public defender?" His voice was thick with sarcasm. "You're not exactly the image of fair and impartial, you know."

Sybylla straightened. "I resent that. I'm as fair and impartial as the next guy."

"Yeah. And I spend my weekends getting out the vote for Pat Buchanan."

"Hey," she complained, "you think I didn't try to get out of this mess? I've been calling up all week, but the voice just kept telling me to hit the pound key and stay on the line. So I thought I'd drop in this morning and show my ID or something and head on over to the office, but the woman just took my jury-duty summons and told me to sit down."

"And you did it," he said in disbelief.

"No, I raised hell, like a good lawyer. But she just kept pointing to this little notice on her desk: 'We are not authorized to grant deferments or exemptions.' Like she was one of those deaf people on the subway who hand out the cards. It was her answer to everything I said. So then I screamed some more, thank you very much, and I got a little handout to mull over. From the *Village Voice*. An article about this prospective juror who left One Hundred Centre Street without authorization and how he got arrested in his office and jailed for three days. It gives me a really warm, confident feeling to know the police are protecting me from dangerous criminals like that."

He was quiet for a minute. "Syb, I'm serious. You've got to get out of there."

"Look, what's the rush? Is one of our clients about to confess to killing Jimmy Hoffa?"

"What's the *rush?*" he howled, and Sybylla winced. She'd had the unenviable experience of witnessing his second heart attack the year before. Now, every time Steiner got excited—and he got excited a lot—she visualized the chambers of his heart shredding like toilet paper. "It's just everybody and his mother got arrested last night."

"So?" she said wearily. "Why is last night different from all other nights?"

He paused. "If you really want to know, one of them was Trent."

She let it register. "*My* Trent? My Trent from last summer?"

"The same. The one you thought was most likely not to get arrested again, I seem to remember."

"So sue me." She sighed. "Look, I can't leave here. Not for a couple of hours, anyway. They just called my name for a voir dire, so I'll have to wait till they dismiss me; then I'll go straight downstairs." She checked her watch, itchy to get to him.

"Not downstairs," Steiner said shortly. "Bellevue. I couldn't wait for you, Syb." He cut her off before she could work up too much indignation. "I wanted to, but the cops on duty were practically begging me to move him out, and I couldn't reach you. He screamed all night. They said it was like a banshee on amphetamines. Kramer was on arraignments this morning, so I just let him do the appearance, and he went with Trent for the seven-three-oh exam. Don't worry," he said sarcastically, "it's still your case."

"How'd he do on the seven-three-oh?" She was ignoring his tone.

"He was pretty consistent. He didn't know the day of the week or the month of the year or the President or his own name. They moved him to Bellevue about an hour ago, so you'd better get over there as soon as you can." Then, through the telephone she felt his mood change, the anger dissipating. "It's bad, Syb."

Sybylla frowned. Trent was hardly a pillar of the community, but he wasn't remotely heinous. He wasn't capable of anything bad. Not *bad* bad. "Tell me," she muttered.

"He stabbed someone," Steiner said. "A child, Sybylla."

Behind her, the Yuppie sputtered with rage. She leaned against the phone and closed her eyes. "Allegedly," she said, half to herself.

"What?" Steiner yelped.

"Allegedly stabbed someone. And calm down."

She heard his low laugh. "Okay. But just be warned. He only— allegedly—did it in front of a crowd, and he was still holding the weapon when the cops showed up."

She shook her head. "That doesn't sound like Trent at all." She sighed into the answering silence. "So what's the official version, then?"

"The official version?" Steiner warmed to his task. "Vicious, violent homeless wandering the streets, helping themselves to the fruit of our honest toil. The official solution is that it's time to consider just packing them all off to some army base in Jersey so we can walk the streets again. The official moral is that we've been patient and tolerant enough, but now it's time to retake Manhattan."

"Whoa." She shuddered. "You sound just like Andrew Greer. Whose side are you on, anyway?"

"I keep forgetting. I try to remind myself: we're the good guys. We're Legal Aid. The DA, he's the bad guy. I think I've got it now."

"That's the spirit," Sybylla said. "Now look, I'll get out of here as soon as I possibly can; then I'll go straight uptown."

"Fine," he said absently. He had already moved on.

She relinquished her place before the phone and made for a patch of wall beside the courtroom door, assuming the same long-suffering posture as that of her fellow prospective jurors. Each of them had been snatched from their daily lives with the offer of a few dollars' compensation and the stern reminder that civilized society began with a jury of

5

your peers, and each of the good citizens in the corridor looked about as excited by those inducements as Sybylla herself was. Tired faces scanned the grungy tile floor; bored hands twitched around newspapers and crossword puzzles and knitting. A few pairs of eyes were fixed impatiently on the nondescript gray door before which their assigned court officer stood guard, but most of the others seemed almost comatose. Attack of the zombie jury, she thought grimly. The rush of anticipation they had each felt when their names were called in the central waiting room had faded now as that purgatory gave way to this one: no closer to the diversion of actually hearing some testimony, no closer to the possibility of being released to the wide world beyond the courthouse at 100 Centre Street. And the courthouse itself, she reflected, was surely the most charmless government building in all of Manhattan, surpassing even such paragons of nondesign as the Department of Motor Vehicles and the passport office. The floors were only a dim shade of their former selves, which in turn had been a nothing-to-write-home-about muddy gray, the walls were battered beige, and the aroma suggested a mixture of filterless Camels and underhydrated urine. It had all been bad enough before hearing about Trent, Sybylla thought. Now, the thought of him in some dingy cell at Bellevue proved maddening.

What she recalled most clearly about Trent was the particular impact of his smallness, so marked that one thought inevitably in terms of stunted growth—not an unreasonable assumption, given the man's history. He was rough but unaccountably pleasant, an occasional thief through whom the will to survive moved strongly, and while he had no discernible wish to better himself and no ambition to get off the street, he had managed not to get himself addicted to anything more nefarious than food. Indeed, he had treated Sybylla to more than one vehement lecture on the danger and pity of drugs. In another life, she remembered thinking last summer, he must have been a missionary.

It had taken three months for Trent to get the trial he'd insisted on, not bad for the glacially slow Manhattan criminal court system, but a long time to hang out in jail waiting for a chance to prove you haven't done anything. She could have gotten him out right away if he'd agreed to plead guilty to the assault with which he'd been charged, but he'd been adamant and she'd had to accede to his wishes, and anyway, everybody knew that was how the system worked: plead guilty and go free, or insist on a trial to prove your stated innocence and spend more time in jail waiting than you probably would have served if you'd been convicted. By the time the trial date finally rolled around, the prosecution's posse of witnesses had dwindled to one astigmatic woman and the victim himself, who remembered nothing about the events in question except, he told the perplexed jurors, the smell of burnt vanilla. The jury took thirty-five minutes to let Trent go. All in all, one of your average illustrations of equal justice.

Like most of her colleagues, she made it a habit not to ask her clients outright if they were guilty. Guilt was between a person and his Maker, and besides, it wasn't her job to judge a client, merely to make sure that those who did judge him were given the opportunity to see things as fairly as possible. And that, she knew, was the only possible rule to follow if you had to get through the day as a public defender.

Upholders of the American way, stalwart supporters of the Constitution, flag-wavers from sea to shining sea, all of them seemed to screech to an ideological halt when confronted with the labors of Sybylla and her comrades. Principles like the presumption of innocence, the right to a speedy trial with an impartial jury, and a reasonable bail, they all sounded great when intoned with a James Earl Jones solemnity, but nobody seemed to want to apply them to actual citizens accused of actual crimes. If you get arrested, the vox populi seemed to say, don't go looking to the Constitution for protection—the Constitution is for law-abiding folks.

Sybylla smiled sadly down at the traumatized linoleum. It was true: they'd never promised her a rose garden. Not her professors in law school, who'd rolled their eyes when she announced her career intentions, not her friends, bound for high-profile clerkships or wildly elevated salaries in corporate firms, certainly not her father. Even Steiner, who was in many ways the lawyer she admired most in the world, had given her some painful advice when she returned to her office disillusioned after one of her very first trials: don't expect to be thanked—*ever.* The guilty ones don't give a shit about you—they just want to get the hell out of the building after they've been acquitted—and the innocent ones tend to think of you as just another part of the nightmare. They never want to see your face again.

But still, for reasons frequently obscure to her, she pressed on, and with a kind of defensive honor about her profession. Once, in a DA hangout near Foley Square, when Sybylla had overheard a raucous ADA announce to his friends that Legal Aid had three approaches to trying weak cases—wailing, moaning, and yelling—she made a point of accidentally jostling the guy on her way out the door, dumping his drink over his expensive leather shoes. She wasn't a whiner. She was simply an attorney who combined hard fact with a sensibly measured appeal to compassion. Her job was to make sure the witnesses saw what they said they saw, that forensics proved what it said it proved, and that the police weren't making up the rules as they went along. The strategy had proved remarkably effective over the years. Though a large number of Sybylla's clients were indeed convicted, her acquittal rate was more or less on a par with Legal Aid's overall—about 60 percent. A kid whom the prosecution had painted as viciously indifferent to human life would look like a brutalized and abandoned child by the time she rested the defense case, and that, in her view, was no more than he deserved. So why didn't she feel at least *marginally* happy about what she did for a living?

Absently, Sybylla began to rub the palm of her left hand with the thumb of her right, a habitual motion. She was plagued by smears of black ink on her writing hand, the residue of her favored felt-tip pens, which she went through at the rate of four a week. Like stigmata, she thought now, the humor eluding her. The truth was that she felt herself nearing a personal saturation point for misery, since she seemed to have the bad habit of absorbing other people's. And there was plenty to go around, she reflected. On this narrow strip of land alone, the sheer density of the stuff—the homelessness, the craziness, the disease and violence, even the upmarket angst so appealing in Woody Allen films—felt so overwhelming that Manhattan's very moorings seemed to buckle under all that weight.

She looked up, meeting the gaze of one of her fellow jurors, a husky type in a Rutgers sweatshirt who was running his hands over his rolled-up *Post* in a charmingly salacious gesture. *Lovely*, Sybylla thought, frowning at him as dismissively as she could, a response she gave to most displays of male ardor, even ones decidedly less revolting than this.

Of course, she disbelieved all empirical evidence of her own physical appeal—nothing unusual there for the postfeminist woman, Sybylla thought ruefully. From her mirror, she might glean the absolute evidence that her skin was in fact both pale and clear and that her deep red hair curled to its own rather lyrical design, but other elements stood out to her as far more forceful. To wit: the tiny ridge in the middle of her nose—the aftereffect of a teammate's ill-judged goal attempt during a high school soccer game—the inescapable reality of her thighs—which evidently retained every single bite of ice cream she had ever ingested—and, most glaring of all, the curious pucker in the lobe of her right ear, as if some mad scientist had entered the hospital nursery to mark with a medieval instrument one particular batch of newborns, in preparation for a lifetime of data collection. As physical deformities went, Sybylla knew, the notch in her lobe was fairly mild, but the thing made her self-conscious nevertheless, and over the years she had fallen into the habit of letting her hair cover it and eschewing earrings, which might call attention to it.

Mr. Rutgers, disconcertingly, continued to arouse his newspaper manually.

Given this state of affairs, a little sarcasm was downright refreshing.

"D'you mind telling us how much longer we're supposed to wait?" the Yuppie from the pay phone seethed, directing his displeasure at the court officer. "Some of us have *lives*, you know."

The officer straightened, smiled, and prepared to exercise a little authority, but abruptly—like a spell—the mood broke. Behind him, the door cracked open and the phrase "Let 'em in" was uttered by unseen lips in the room beyond. Thwarted, the officer scowled into the smug face of his adversary. Then, defeated, he held back the door and Sybylla surged with the crowd of her fellow prospective jurors into the courtroom.

CHAPTER

T W O

—⁓—

Well now, she thought. This was getting interesting.

Seated at the prosecutor's table with one corpulent arm slung over the back of his wooden chair was Andrew Greer, known to the dedicated soldiers of the Legal Aid Society as the face behind the office dartboard, and to the citizens of greater Manhattan as the current caped crusader at

One Hogan Place, the DA's office. The man's outsized form was the first thing you noticed about him, but oddly, it was apparent from the way in which Greer carried his body and the way in which he dressed it that he either didn't know he was big or he simply refused to believe it. Sybylla watched him twist in his seat to survey the rows of potential jurors, then turn back to resume his banter with the judge, who was trying hard to be blasé about having the DA in his courtroom. Greer's shirt was gapping between the buttons, and his belt—she could see when he stood briefly to scan the back of the room—had had a hole added to it in order to accommodate a growing waist. Despite a friendly, if disingenuous, smile and the ready ability to look very, very concerned and sound very, very distressed, Greer was probably going to need the talents of James Carville *and* Mary Matalin if he wanted a real shot at being elected governor. That, it had often been whispered, was his dream.

His presence at the prosecutor's table implied that the case at hand had a high profile. Greer personally presided over only one or two trials a year, reserving for himself the plummiest, most shocking crimes, those guaranteed to add luster to his PR profile as the man ready, willing, and able to Liquid-Plumr the crime-clogged streets of New York. Automatically, Sybylla turned to the defense table to see if she recognized the defendant, but the apparent candidate, a slender black man with a closely shaved head and an inexpensive checked jacket, was unfamiliar. Still, she pitied him. To be personally prosecuted by Andrew Greer was to be hung, drawn, and quartered in the press. It would almost be worth trying to get herself onto the jury, she thought, if only to throw that sanctimonious bastard a curve.

As she watched, the chair beside the great man was pulled back and the unmistakable torso of Wendell Burkowitz, the biggest jackass in the DA's office, flopped down into it. Sybylla winced in embarrassment. The summer before last, somewhat the worse for a few drinks at The Recess around the corner from the courthouse, she'd let Burkowitz plant a margarita-sweet kiss in the vicinity of her left ear. She had a feeling that kiss was going to come back to haunt her today.

The judge had been conferring with his bailiff. Now he turned to the defense table. "You need a few more minutes, Mr. Larkin?" he asked, his voice testy. "Or can we get going already?"

Ouch, Sybylla thought, following the judge's gaze, and in spite of herself, she began to smile. She hadn't noticed the defense attorney before, and now she wondered why not. He was decidedly adorable, for one thing, with an oddly crooked mouth and tight ringlets of black hair cut short in an almost sweet attempt to look like a serious grown-up. He wore a blinding array of Brooks Brothers finery, from the pair of perfectly creased tan trousers to the slender blue pinstripes of his shirt, and he looked woefully out of place in this grubby courtroom. But if he felt his own incongruity here, Sybylla thought, he was doing a pretty good job of keeping it hidden. Indeed, his attention was devoted solely to his client, toward whom he leaned, speaking softly. Sybylla noted the respectful expression and the kindly tone of his indistinguishable words, the reassuring hand tapping his client's shoulder—his left hand. A left hand without a wedding ring.

She'd never seen him around the courthouse, but that didn't mean anything. Lots of uptown boys asked for pro bono cases like this one when they wanted a taste of what they'd once thought lawyering would be like. This guy was probably used to a more refined version of legal practice, one involving vast support staffs and wood-paneled offices and long, soggy lunches, with somebody's gold AmEx tossed thoughtlessly onto the bill at the end.

"Mr. Larkin?"

He looked up and nodded. "Yes, ready, Your Honor. Sorry for the delay."

At the front of the room, the court officer faced them and began reciting names. She tensed in anticipation of more delay, but her luck was holding and she heard the name Muldoon—mispronounced, though the man looked Irish enough to know better. With a sigh of relief, she got to her feet and moved forward to take one of the last places in the jury box. An instant later, a dense female body with a bright red head bumped her arm as it took the seat beside her.

"Excuse me," Sybylla said automatically, despite the fact that she was the bumpee, not the bumper. Then she looked up and, instinctively, gathered her arm closer to her body, gripping her elbow so hard her nails made crescents in the skin. She couldn't quite say what accounted for the jerk of her movement, what feature or element made the woman whose body posed, motionless, only inches from her own so profoundly disturbing. She looked average enough, blank and middle-aged, with waxy white skin and hair an abundantly untrue pomegranate color; her clothes—a heavy dark skirt to midcalf, a white shirt buttoned to the chin—were unremarkable. Her only extraneous adornments, Sybylla noted, stealing additional furtive glances, were a cameo too large to be real and a red AIDS ribbon whose shade nearly matched her hair color, clipped to the collar of her blouse with a safety pin. The woman sat, inert, gazing forward. Her mouth was slack. She appeared to notice neither the bump with her neighbor nor the pleasantry that followed it.

It was her stillness, Sybylla decided suddenly. Most people, after all, betrayed their thoughts with a grimace, a little smile, even a blush, but if this woman was thinking, she accomplished it without a single outward show—no flicker, no expression. Indeed, she appeared so placid as to seem almost catatonic, though beneath the blankness there remained the faintest echo of beauty. She'd been a pretty girl, Sybylla thought suddenly. Then, unaccountably, she thought of Annie and her throat grew thick.

To exorcise the image, and her own foolishness besides, Sybylla unzipped her handbag and rummaged self-consciously, finally finding (and brushing the lint from) a roll of Life Savers. Squaring her shoulders, she turned to the woman beside her. "Like a mint?"

The woman's head turned. Sybylla watched her eyes, a little watery, slowly and deliberately meet Sybylla's own, then travel down to the hand, the gaping bag, the roll of mints. Her sigh was barely audible. "No thank you, dear," she said.

Sybylla relaxed. There was nothing wrong with this woman. Just a hint of something unusual in the body language, and maybe an unfortunate choice in hair color, coupled with anemia. Nothing to write home about, only part of the vast array of humanity you see in the big city. She felt the adrenaline drain from her body. You moron, Sybylla told herself. You're losing it.

The judge leaned forward. "Ladies and gentlemen," he intoned, "what we are about to experience in this courtroom today is the bedrock of our democratic society. You, as good citizens, may be called upon to sit in judgment on a fellow citizen, who has been accused of a crime. We presume him to be innocent, but it is the job of Mr. Greer, to my right here, who represents the people"—at least the judge didn't identify him as the DA, Sybylla thought sourly—"to convince you otherwise. To my left, Mr. Larkin has been appointed to represent the accused."

It was all she could do not to shout her objection. Sybylla made a point of requesting that judges not refer to her as "appointed" council. To a savvy juror, *appointed* stood in sharp contrast to *retained,* which meant financial solvency. *Appointed* meant financial hardship, which many people outrageously equated with guilt. It also usually meant Legal Aid, and jurors' negative feelings about Legal Aid tended to mirror those of the public at large. Mr. Larkin, evidently new to the game, hadn't picked up on it.

"In order to make this important process fair to everyone," the judge went on, "both attorneys must be convinced that you, as potential jurors, are capable of being impartial in this matter, that you know neither the alleged perpetrator nor the alleged victims, and that you understand the profundity of what we are doing here."

As he paused, Sybylla looked over in Larkin's direction, but her gaze was waylaid at the prosecutor's table. Burkowitz was grinning at her, and not in a friendly way, either.

"We are about to begin the phase of the trial known as voir dire. This means, literally, 'to see, to say,' but for our purposes, you may think of it as a question-and-answer period. The attorneys here, each in turn, will ask you questions to help them decide whether you would, in their opinion, be an impartial and effective juror. Each attorney has the right to excuse potential jurors 'for cause' if there is an outright circumstance that precludes your being an effective juror—if you have been the victim of a crime similar to the one the defendant is accused of committing, for example. In addition, each attorney has a limited number of peremptory challenges, which he need not justify to the court."

She caught herself smiling. Though the judge certainly made the process sound intelligent and fair, Sybylla had seen too much in courtrooms just like this one to cling too tightly to an ideal. Jury selection? More like deselection. What was about to happen here wasn't a process of choosing twelve good men and true to do their duty; it was each attorney's determined attempt to get rid of any and every prospective juror likely to vote the wrong way. The lovely Mr. Larkin would be trying like hell to weed out the law-and-order folks, the people who made sure their wives and daughters were armed, anyone whose fear of crime and violence was so extreme as to direct their judgment. And the odious Mr. Greer would be trying to get rid of anyone who looked too soft: no liberals or anti–death penalty crusaders, nobody who corresponded with prisoners or looked as if they might belong to the ACLU. Far from being only about getting at the truth, jury selection was a cagey art that seemed to demand mind reading and mind control in equal parts. Potential jurors lied a lot, Sybylla knew. They lied to get on the panel if they had the time to spare and thought it would be diverting to sit in judgment on the luckless person in the defendant's chair, and they lied to get off for a blinding variety of reasons. Sometimes, too, they lied even when they thought they were telling the truth.

If she kept her ears tuned, Sybylla thought, she'd be able to glean a good bit of information about the case at hand. No decent attorney, after all, would let a voir dire pass without taking the opportunity to plant a few favorable seeds in a future juror's mind. "If you were to hear evidence that a man under severe stress had had an episode of temporary insanity when he saw his wife with another man, would you consider that evidence with an open mind?" "If you heard expert testimony to the effect that traces of one person's blood were found in another person's car, would you be persuaded by that?" Voir dire wasn't just a means of stacking the deck; it was a trial run, if you will, for the trial.

She shook her head. We have traveled far indeed from "a jury of his peers," she thought, a little ruefully. Now it was all a joust, really, presided over by instinct, which could not be learned, and luck, which could not be depended upon.

"Do any of you have any questions?"

The gravelly voice brought her back.

"We will now begin with the voir dire, and we'll continue the process until a jury is agreed upon and impaneled. Mr. Greer, you can get started."

"Thank you, Your Honor," Greer said with discernible humility, intent on massaging the judge's ego.

It was a rape. Greer began at the other end of the box, with the woman in the number-one seat. Moving quickly but with care, he easily found a man whose sister had been sexually assaulted, a man whose college roommate had been accused of date rape, a woman who had worked at a rape crisis center, and an outraged senior citizen who responded to Greer's first and only question by stating, "I just wanna say, I read about this case, and you better believe I got an opinion." Greer, with a smile, moved on. Larkin didn't ask the man a thing.

The first few jurors who appeared to earn his approval—a newsstand owner, a hardware store employee, a man who owned a Baskin-Robbins franchise and begged piteously to be excused—also parried the defense attorney's rather less probing questions without turning up any active or latent tendencies toward vigilantism, but Sybylla felt fairly certain that the fourth, a retired radio repairman who appeared to snarl each time he glanced in the defendant's direction, would earn one of Larkin's peremptory excuses. Other prospects seemed equally unsuitable to both sides: people so angry about having to do jury duty that they might rush to the wrong verdict, people too dull to truly comprehend evidence, people who just appeared downright nuts. They would all go when it came time for the challenges.

An hour passed before they reached the red-haired woman beside her. Sybylla eyed the clock. If this went on much longer, the judge would recess for lunch and she'd have to come back and waste more time this afternoon. Her calf twitched in frustration and bitterness.

"You are"—Greer consulted his list—"Miss Rowena Martin."

The woman nodded gravely. Her bright hair seemed stuck in place. Sybylla couldn't help but watch, overcome once again by curiosity.

"And where do you live, Miss Martin?"

She lived with her sister, near Lincoln Center. She had retired from teaching due to a chronic illness, but she still tutored in a literacy program. She was not married. She had never been married. She had no children. She had never been a victim of a violent crime. She felt that people who committed violent crimes should be rehabilitated. If they could not be rehabilitated, she conceded, they should probably be removed from society.

Bye-bye, Miss Martin, Sybylla thought. That nice Mr. Greer has a perempt with your name on it.

"Thank you." Greer smiled and took his seat.

Across the room, Larkin stood and faced the jury box. "Hello, Miss Martin," he said. The woman beside Sybylla nodded slowly.

"Do you understand that, as of this moment, my client here is innocent?"

"Oh yes." Her voice was without inflection, a queer flatness. "Innocent until proven guilty. That's important."

"Do you understand that, as a juror, it would be your job to sift through a great deal of information, some of which would be opinion and some of which would be fact? It would be your job to delve into some pretty emotional subject matter and find the truth. Could you do that?"

"Yes," the woman said. "A verdict is too important to be arrived at by any other means. I wouldn't want to be judged on purely emotional grounds."

Sybylla suppressed her frown. What a chatterbox Miss Martin was turning out to be, not content merely to answer the question, but insistent upon adding a constitutional platitude of her own to the pot. She turned to look again at the strange woman who sat to her left, rapt and utterly focused on the young man across the room.

Too young for you, my dear, Sybylla started to think, but then, abruptly, she began to understand: Miss Martin wanted on. She was trying hard to say what she thought Larkin wanted to hear.

"Miss Martin," Larkin said, "if you sat through a trial and felt convinced that the defendant was not guilty, and then you found during deliberation that your fellow jurors disagreed with you, would you stick to your opinion? Or would you let yourself be convinced by others' opinions?"

She went still, her eyes half-closed. The image that jumped into Sybylla's mind was of a machine on overload, shutting itself down. Almost imperceptibly, a whiff of her earlier adrenaline began to percolate through her body, but before it could really take hold, the woman spoke.

"I would stick to my own opinion. If I thought I was right, I wouldn't be swayed."

Larkin gazed at her. Unlike his opponent, he had chosen to remain at his desk during voir dire, which reinforced the jurors' visual image of the handsome, nicely dressed and groomed young man beside his undeniably scruffy client, as if some of Larkin's likable qualities might rub off on the accused. Now, across the room, Sybylla read intense confusion in his expression. Something was wrong with this woman, and Sybylla saw that Larkin saw, but he was evidently as unable to identify that thing as she herself was. She was just, somehow, wrong. But wrong enough for him to use up one of his peremptory challenges?

"Thank you, Miss Martin," he said quietly.

"Thank you," the judge said, turning to Greer again, but Greer was loading files into his briefcase. "Mr. Greer?"

"I apologize, Your Honor," the DA said. "I have an unbreakable meeting due to begin in five minutes. I'll be leaving the remainder of the voir dire to my colleague, Assistant District Attorney Burkowitz. He has received my instructions on those jurors we've already questioned."

The judge bristled. From anyone else, Sybylla saw, such behavior would not have been tolerated.

"Very well." His voice was tight. "Though while this trial is in session, Mr. Greer, I hope you will be able to clear larger blocks of time."

"I intend to do exactly that, Your Honor." Greer practically bowed. Then he turned and left the room.

The judge sighed. "All right then, Mr. Burkowitz."

Grinning, Burkowitz made a show of consulting the notes Greer had handed him before rising and waddling over to Sybylla. When he stood before her, his smarmy face only inches from her own, she had at least the small consolation of knowing that her remaining moments in this nightmare were numbered. She would take the first opportunity to announce she was a PD, then she would get the hell out of here and uptown to see Trent. But Burkowitz played it for all it was worth, shifting his weight from foot to foot and thumbing his file. "Sybylla Muldoon."

"Yes," Sybylla hissed.

"What an unusual name you have."

Was that a question? she thought blandly.

"I'd like to know a little about your name," the slimewad said.

The judge leaned forward in his chair. "This isn't *The Dating Game*, Mr. Burkowitz. Save it for later and move along."

"Where do you live, Miss Muldoon? Is it Miss?"

"Ms.," Sybylla spat. "I live on the Upper West Side."

"And have you been called for jury duty before?"

"I have," Sybylla said. "In college. I was excused."

"This is a rape trial, Ms. Muldoon," Burkowitz said, emphasizing the *Ms.* "Have you been a victim of sexual assault?"

Only by jerks who've had too many margaritas, she wanted to say. "No. I haven't."

"Do you believe when a woman says no that she sometimes means yes?" Burkowitz leaned forward, so close that she could smell the cheese Danish he must have consumed fairly recently. Margaritas or no, she could see that that summer evening had not been forgotten.

"I certainly don't. When a woman says no"—Sybylla couldn't resist leaning forward herself—"she usually has a very good reason for doing so. Any man who isn't an outright idiot will take her at her word."

Burkowitz surprised her by grinning. "Many thanks, Ms. Muldoon."

At the far table, Larkin rose, a little unsteadily. Sybylla could read his confusion. "Hello, Ms. Muldoon," he said.

"Hi." Sybylla, abruptly shy, felt her cheeks get hot. This isn't *The Dating Game*, she scolded herself. Remember?

"May I ask what your occupation is?"

She sighed. It was almost too bad. Here she was, about to be excused, just at the point where she might want to linger a minute or two.

"I am a public defender," Sybylla said. "I work for the Legal Aid Society of New York, at Eighty Lafayette." She glared at the ADA. "As Mr. Burkowitz well knows."

He had been leaning over his table, looking down at the paper between his hands. Now his head snapped up, his gaze latching onto Sybylla's with a mixture of anger and disbelief. She couldn't help it: she shrugged.

"Don't look at me," Sybylla told him. "I tried. They wouldn't excuse me."

From the corner of her eye, she watched the judge turn to glare at the smirking ADA. "Is there anyone else in the jury pool known to you personally, Mr. Burkowitz?"

He shook his head, choking down his laugh.

Larkin sighed and ran a hand lightly through his curls. "Your Honor, I'm ready to proceed with challenges for this group of jurors, whenever Mr. Burkowitz is."

It was over very quickly. A moment later, Sybylla had been thanked for her time and was climbing past the demurely covered knees of Ms. Rowena Martin, making her way out of the jury box along with eight or nine of her fellow prospects. "Thank you, Your Honor," she said, an automatic reflex. Then she shouldered her bag, indulged in a last, somewhat regretful glance at Mr. Larkin, and left the courtroom.

Outside, the dingy corridor was crowded with weeping mothers, disgusted siblings, and antsy kids—in some cases, the entire families of the defendants whose cases languished in the bewildering system. Some faces on their first visits to 100 Centre Street registered fear; others had been here before and expressed only weariness. Sybylla averted her eyes. Most of her colleagues could leave it all behind them at the end of the day, but this was a skill she had never remotely mastered. Even after these many years in the trenches of Legal Aid, she couldn't manage to navigate the hallways without wincing.

Uptown, she summoned her most entitled New Yorker demeanor to present herself at the ward desk on Bellevue's nineteenth floor. Past the gray armor of the ward door lay the jail unit that functioned in the hospital, a separate city-state within the system, but one that nonetheless shared the cheerful off-white decor and aromatic delights of Bellevue's other floors. Sybylla had been here before, mostly for commitment hearings held in a makeshift court in one of the rooms, but she always felt somehow compromised in this liminal environment, her power to affect her clients' lives thwarted by this incursion of the medical world. Today, the entire ward was awash in the atonal force of a single persistent screaming voice. Automatically, Sybylla moved to cover her ears, but she quickly noted that few of the police and hospital personnel who inhabited the ward were so moved, having evidently grown inured to the noise. She wondered at the sheer lung volume capable of producing such an assault of wretched and wrenching sound.

Watching her approach, the officer on duty swung his clipboard around with a long-suffering expression.

"Jesus." Sybylla shook her head, writing her name and Trent's on the sign-in sheet. "Sounds like something from another planet." She gave the man an ingratiating smile. "I don't know how you can stand it."

He was scanning the form. "Oh, I wouldn't worry about us. You're going head-to-head with the guy."

It took a moment. She stared at him. "You're . . . That's him? Are you sure?"

He grinned, enjoying it. "You seem surprised."

"I . . . Jesus, I can't believe it. *Trent*."

"Old friend?"

"Uh . . . there was an assault charge. Last year. He was acquitted."

"Naturally." The man raised his thick eyebrows. "Nobody's guilty anymore, right?"

Sybylla shrugged. "Oh, I don't know." She wasn't in the mood to argue civil liberties with one of New York's finest.

She hoisted her briefcase. "Any chance of a room?"

He smirked. "Why not? They're your eardrums. This way."

Sybylla followed him down the grimy corridor, occasionally stepping aside as orderlies or officers or both moved past with their cargoes of sputtering and writhing or shuffling and silent patients. Passing one of the rooms, she caught a fast glimpse of one of her colleagues from Legal Aid. He was leaning forward in his chair across from a heavy black man whose head was densely covered with dreadlocks and who pounded the table with his fist.

Room two seemed barely large enough to accommodate its two spindly chairs and a battered Formica-topped table. Sybylla sat heavily and hunted out a working pen from her purse, and in that small moment, the screaming seemed to stop. In its place, Sybylla heard only the low buzz of her colleague's reassuring tones through the thin wall, and in those tones, she heard the unmistakable rhythms of their common supervisor. As attorney in charge of the Criminal Division, David Steiner had served as a mentor many times over to the young lawyers who passed through Legal Aid. They might stay four or five years—as most did—or for all the years of their working lives—as only a few of the truest believers did—but it seemed impossible to work with Steiner and remain unaffected by his compassion, his skill, or his magically reassuring way of speaking to frightened men and women. Sybylla herself could not now escape the certainty that she was his devoted acolyte, though when she first began to work under his tutelage, she had consciously tried to resist thinking of Steiner as what he was so clearly becoming: a father figure. She already had a father, she'd reminded herself all that first year, and yet Steiner, who thought she was wonderful, capable, motivated by only the most admirable of qualities, gifted, and the best possible catch for all the single men in the city, had seemed at that time to be much more of a father than Dermot Muldoon, who could barely bring himself to utter the words *public defender.*

Footsteps brought her back. The officer was pushing open the door with his hip and guiding into the room a slight, hunched, and droning person who wasn't Trent. The person's drone was like a low guttural buzz from deep inside, an electric pattern that made his fingers twitch. His eyes never left the floor. The man's stench was considerable, and Sybylla instinctively made an effort to breathe through her mouth. The officer was pulling back the chair on the other side of the table and pushing the person down by his thin shoulders, but he began to vibrate roughly under the man's hands, breathing a low repetitive syllable that sounded like "ha" from the back of his throat, like a woman learning to pant in a childbirth class. "Ha ha ha." He bounced, his eyes unfocused. Sybylla tried to speak, but her throat was too busy remembering to breathe, and she could only shake her head no, this wasn't Trent. They had brought the wrong man. Trent didn't look anything like this. He was fairly well groomed for a street person, and he had some intelligence, even a little wit. In fact, Sybylla had even known him to demonstrate actual charm on occasion. But—Christ—he was *normal.* He could speak and listen and look you in the eye. This person, this vibrating, sputtering psychotic, was the kind of poignant but untouchable person you glimpsed in alleys or in the alcoves of the Port Authority. "I'm sorry . . ." she started to say.

But then the man lifted his eyes. Sybylla heard her own gasp.

"God." She stared, drawn down into the remembered green of his eyes, looking for the person who used to live there. "God," Sybylla said again. "What *happened?*"

The man who had once been Trent reached carefully, delicately across the table and took her hand. Like a lover, he brought it to his scab-covered lips as Sybylla watched in a trance. The officer moved forward to intercede, but she shook her head no. Because Trent was going to say something. He was opening his mouth to tell his story, to explain what it meant. She leaned forward, drawn irresistibly into the pull of his gaze, as he separated her thumb and forefinger, spread open the web of flesh between them, and bit down with an unimaginable hunger.

CHAPTER

THREE

"**Y**ou should have come to me first," the doctor snapped, pressing gauze into Sybylla's bloody fist. "You people think Bellevue is just like the pens, that you can just go waltzing in to see your clients here, but you forget they're not in the pens for a reason. I'd never have let you in to see Trent without an orderly, at least. They didn't even have him in restraints!" He glared at her as if that, too, was her fault. "It was extremely stupid of you."

Not much of a bedside manner, she thought, setting her jaw against the pain as he poured iodine over the wound.

She was perched on the only chair in the minuscule office of Dr. Bruno Turturro, Trent's psychiatrist of record, and was now in the process of bleeding over his once-white carpet. Discarding the soaked gauze pad, he pressed a clean one against her palm and began to wrap dressing around her hand. "Was it one bite, or did he get more than one into you?"

"One, I think. Hard to tell. Everybody was screaming and I was pretty distracted. I think he sort of bit once, then"—she glanced at him guiltily—"chewed."

Turturro perched himself on the edge of the desk. He was a few years older than she, she thought, tall and bony, his dark hair receding. The office lay behind one of the nondescript doors along a dingy offshoot of the main corridor artery. It was jammed with books and heaps of files that leaned like the Tower of Pisa and overflowed from the desk onto the floor.

"You must have your own system," Sybylla commented, eyeing the clutter to distract herself from the intense throbbing in her hand. "I'm sure you know exactly where everything is."

"Oh, right." He frowned. "What did you say your name was?"

She told him, and he smiled suddenly. "That's unusual. Kind of pretty."

She nodded. "Thank you."

She groped around for whatever professional detachment she still had on reserve. "About Trent. You have time to talk to me a little about him?"

He frowned. "Of course, if you really feel up to it." Reaching down to a pile at his feet, he plucked the top file and opened its red cover. "We did the intake downstairs in Emergency. He's been up here for a couple hours now, pretty much the same."

"So you know what's wrong with him, then."

Turturro smiled. "Sure I do. It's not a difficult diagnosis. Paranoid schizophrenia. He was hallucinating actively when he came in, and as you just saw all too clearly, he's still hallucinating. He talks to thin air; he's fearful, nonresponsive. Classic stuff. No mystery here."

"I think there is," Sybylla said. "I've known Trent for some time. When I last saw him during the summer of last year, he was as sane as you or I."

"Could well be." He leaned back against the wall. "I wouldn't doubt it."

"But what would have caused such a sudden change in him? Why would he be normal a few months ago and totally whacked out today? Listen, the Trent I knew was just a street person. He wasn't a saint or anything, but stabbing a kid just wasn't . . . I can't believe it."

"You don't want to believe it," Turturro commented.

"Excuse me?" she said, taken aback.

"You don't want to believe it. Even in light of what just happened in there. That's interesting."

She shook her head, resentful of the unsolicited psychoanalysis. "No, no, you don't understand. He just wouldn't."

"Look, Ms. . . ."

"Muldoon."

"Muldoon. You know what percentage of our patients come from the street? A good sixty or so. I'm telling you, living rough in this city could make a crazy person out of anybody in time. The abuse these people face from one another, from the weather, from every criminal who sees them as an easy target, it's unimaginable. People view the homeless as an opportunity to indulge illicit fantasies. You get someone with a secret dream about harming a fellow human being, guess who he picks? How aggressively are police going to pursue a case when the victim doesn't have an address? Plus, you've got the everyday stuff—exposure to the elements, erratic and unnutritious meals, lack of substantial human contact, poor hygiene—it's a recipe for disassociation, I'm telling you. If you spent a couple months on the floor of Grand Central Station, you'd go nuts, too."

"But it isn't that. I know all that, but Trent's been on the street for ten years at least. Why now?"

"Dunno." Turturro shrugged. "Maybe a cumulative effect, hitting him all at once. Maybe he started to slide after you last saw him, and this was the culmination. Have you talked to anyone who knows him?"

"Not yet. There is one person. I haven't been over there yet."

"Another homeless person?"

Sybylla nodded.

"Well, don't count on getting much out of him, either. Listen, I hate to fall back on truisms, but these things happen. It's a big sad city. Lotta people."

His nonchalance irked her. "You don't sound terribly compassionate."

Turturro's gaze had wandered to his tiny grime-streaked window. Now it snapped back to meet her own. "Oh, listen, I couldn't do this job without compassion, any more than you could do yours. But I'm practical, too. Your friend is going to need long-term care, and people out there"—he nodded at the window—"are going to need long-term protection from him. My compassion or lack thereof won't have the slightest effect on those facts. And there are ten more Trents who are gonna come through my door when they move this one on out to Kirby Psychiatric Center, and I've got to worry about them, too. So you'll forgive me if I'm restrained with my compassion, all right?"

"All right." Sybylla sulked. She knew he was right.

"So. It's a matter of incompetent to stand trial, am I right?"

"I suppose." He shrugged. "That's your end, but probably, yes. I don't see Trent suddenly being able to help you defend him." He paused and frowned down at his folded arms. "I'm sorry I can't help you more, but if I were you, I really wouldn't waste your energy looking for rational explanations about why this happened. People go nuts all the time, as far as I can tell." He shook his head. "Sometimes, what I see all day, I wonder why *more* people don't go nuts."

"So that's it? Just generic New York crazy person? That was your whole examination?"

Turturro looked at her squarely. "I can assure you, Ms. Muldoon, that we gave your client a thorough exam on his admission here, both physiological and, to the extent that it was possible, psychological. There was nothing in the results to challenge a diagnosis I was quite comfortable making after the first ten seconds in a room with him." He snapped open the file and read in a terse voice: " 'Patient disoriented and unresponsive. Erratic flailing of limbs. Apparent aural and visual hallucinations, simultaneous. Trunk and extremities marked by lacerations, evidently self-inflicted, with exception of left upper arm. Absence of track marks. Palpation for broken bones and masses, negative.' . . . Blah, blah, blah," he said, skimming the rest. "I'm telling you, there're no red flags here. He's a classic case." He shrugged at her. "Sorry I can't give you something more exciting."

She frowned and considered the gauze dressing. A tiny stain of blood was beginning to soak through. "What was that thing about his upper arm?"

"Oh"—he reopened the file—"that. He had a fairly recent-looking scar, which, on palpation, had a hard disklike shape below the skin. I got an internist to take a look at it. He gave some local anesthetic and opened the site, and we found a little implant of some kind."

"What do you mean?" She sat forward in her chair. "*What* kind?"

"Don't know. Haven't had it tested yet. It's not a type I'm familiar with, but I'm not really up on this stuff, and there's a lot of them in trials right now. And you know, lots of homeless people take part in the double-blind studies. Haven't you ever seen those ads? Healthy male subjects needed to test new smoking-cessation aid? Or cholesterol drug? It's easy money for these guys. Easier than collecting cans. Trent maybe got himself into one of those programs for some extra cash."

"You seem pretty unconcerned," Sybylla commented. "Couldn't this disk, or whatever it is, be responsible for his mental state?"

"Oh"—he smiled patronizingly at her—"I doubt that very much. The FDA would never permit a drug with that potential to be tested on people. Even homeless people."

"But you will have it tested, won't you? You'll find out what it is."

"I suppose." He sighed. "I'll write myself a note to send it to the lab. But I'm telling you, it isn't this, whatever it is. Your guy's a textbook schizophrenic—that's all there is to it."

"Look"—Sybylla stood up—"would you mind if I took it myself to get tested? I could get it done faster, maybe. Then you wouldn't have to deal with it. And I wouldn't have to bother you again." Turturro looked doubtful. "I hate nagging people," she said helpfully.

Evidently, the doctor hated being nagged.

"You'll send me a copy of the report," he said sternly.

"Right away." She nodded, trying not to seem too eager.

"It's not exactly protocol."

"That's why I'd appreciate it all the more."

Turturro sighed deeply. "I have to get to rounds." He paused. "All right." He opened the file and quickly found the plastic envelope stapled to a form. Inside, the object was roughly the size and shape of a quarter and made of a waxy white material. It looked like a bar of Ivory soap, worn down to the nub.

"Don't handle it too much, even through the plastic. Don't let it get too hot or too cold. And I want the report as soon as you have it. *And* the implant back."

"All right." She slipped the envelope into her bag. "Thanks."

"Waste of time, if you ask me."

I didn't, Sybylla thought. She got to her feet.

"And you go downstairs to Emergency. You need a tetanus shot."

She stared at him. "You've got to be kidding."

"Not at all. You need a tetanus shot. And get them to look at the bite again. Dressing wounds isn't my forte. If it's still bleeding, it might need a stitch. And if I were you, I'd ask for some Percodan, too. That thing's gotta hurt." He gave her a little shrug. "It can be kind of busy down there. Hope you didn't have any plans for the afternoon."

Oh, nothing special, Sybylla sighed, remembering the three court appearances she had scheduled. She had already wasted her morning on jury duty, she thought with resignation. She might as well waste her afternoon among the urban wounded, her fellow casualties.

"**D**oes it hurt?"

Steiner held her bandaged hand carefully between his palms, examining it with a clinical curiosity. Still light-headed from the Percodan, Sybylla shook her head.

"It did, though. Like hell."

"And you thought lawyering wasn't a contact sport."

She smiled and took back her hand. "Not me, boss. Remember Rafael Ortiz? I got this lovely capped tooth from him." She tapped with the edge of a fingernail, which had a little half-moon of blood under its rim.

"Yeah." He nodded, trying to match her jovial tone. "And that guy who came straight to the office when he got out of Rikers, just so he could ask you to marry him? He ended up trying to brain you with a copy of the penal code, I seem to recall."

Sybylla sighed. "You know what he said to me when he calmed down? He said I was the first person who'd ever treated him with respect, and I made the judge act respectful even though he was convicted. He couldn't get over that. He thought it must mean I was in love with him or something."

"Well, what about that kid whose mother was up for possession? He gave you a black eye, didn't he? I had your father on the phone over that one."

Sybylla looked down. The incident still embarrassed her.

"It got me out of a date, I remember. Some jerk brother of this girl I knew."

"Why was he a jerk?" Steiner said.

"I don't know. I canceled the date, didn't I?"

"And never rescheduled."

She shrugged.

"And this strikes you as normal behavior, Sybylla?"

"You're sounding more and more like my father, you know that?" She got up from her desk and went to the window. The glass was streaked with city grunge and the view was negligible, but she had waited five years for this window, laboring in the maze of cubicles in the large room outside of Steiner's office. She pressed her injured hand to the chilly pane and felt the cold through the dull throbs in her palm. "I could tell he was an idiot."

"Listen," Steiner said, "I don't mean to pry—"

"Oh, pry anyway," she tossed over her shoulder.

"But when's the last time you were out on a real date?"

She turned around and faced him. "A real date. Like dinner and a movie kind of date?"

He nodded.

"Come on. Look at this." She waved her hand at the stacks of files speckling her floor, marking the colorless carpet like clusters of rune stones. "You know how many cases I'm carrying now?" He raised his eyebrows. "Nearly a hundred. They're like a blur to me, but to the clients, I'm the only thing standing between themselves and Rikers. I'm supposed to have a romantic dinner for two? I can barely get to exercise class often enough to keep my thighs from colonizing the rest of my body."

"Your thighs are fine," Steiner objected.

She ignored him. "And don't forget, if I don't get home to Great Falls every month or so, my father reports me missing. Besides," she muttered, taking in Steiner's disapproving gaze, "I don't exactly feel romantic these days. By the time I'm finished here, I just about have it together to get myself home."

"That may be true," he said quietly, "but if so, it's your doing."

"Yes?" Sybylla took in his deeply set dark eyes, the heavy eyebrows over them. "You wish to enlighten me?"

He sighed and shook his head. "We've discussed this before. I think it's wonderful, the job you do. I think you're a fine lawyer."

"And yet you say it in such a way that it sounds just the opposite," she said sardonically.

"All I'm saying is, you don't *have* to be this involved. You take it so to heart. I'm telling you, Syb, it'll shorten your life."

She sighed. "Spoken like one who knows."

To her surprise, he only nodded. "I think you're right, you know. *My* heart would be better off today if I'd been less like you when I was younger. I was out there on the front lines, making it up to every client who never had a decent education, or a nurturing parent, or a single vision of what a good life looked like that wasn't some plywood set on a TV sitcom. And guess what? They couldn't have cared less. For this, I got a divorce, a lifetime aspirin habit, and an intimate acquaintance with the grim reaper."

Sybylla looked out the window and nodded, her eyes on the dark figures moving through city twilight hunched against the frigid early spring wind. Just when she'd thought it might be safe to retire her winter coat, it looked like snow. Horrible, dirty New York snow.

"So why are you doing it? Nah." He wagged a finger at her. "Don't give me the usual lines. I just about wrote them myself."

She smiled at him, a little absently. Her own upbringing had been privileged: the handsome home in the leafy, moneyed suburb, the limitless educational horizon, from prep school to college and beyond. There had been only one black child in her kindergarten class, a bright girl who loved story time and hung at their teacher's elbow. She was the recipient of a wealthy Washingtonian's largesse, and this allowed her to ascend each day from her slum—they were called that then—to Sybylla's own pastoral grove, where kids learned computers and Suzuki violin. The next year, though, the little girl was gone. Sybylla always wondered what became of her.

Why was she doing it? The answer, if she had ever had one, appeared to elude her now.

"Syb," Steiner said, shocking her by reading her mind, "you can't fix the world. Hey, it's a news flash—you can't even fix a little bit of it. When we die, it'll be just as rotten for people as it was before. The whole shebang: wars, torture, starvation, intolerance, senseless violence. Take my advice and find something for yourself. I don't think the good Lord puts us here to be entirely miserable."

She tried for a light tone. "I'm supposed to listen to you? You're a diehard atheist."

"You know," Steiner said, fixing her with a particularly penetrating look, "I sometimes think you feel you've never met a truly guilty defendant. You just see the abuse in their childhoods, the misery in their lives."

"Sure." Sybylla nodded. "I think I can admit to that."

"But I don't feel that way, you see. I think there actually are some guilty people who should be punished for what they've done. I just see my job as keeping it fair for everyone. I want the rules to be the same for everyone, is all."

Sybylla shook her head. "*Et tu,* boss? I thought you were the last of the red-hot liberals."

"I am," he said wearily. "I think we should have a compassionate society, but I think being a good Legal Aid lawyer means making sure the defendant gets the best possible defense and everyone plays fair and square. It doesn't mean just getting them off. Look," he said, cutting off her imminent outrage, "our allegiance isn't to the defendant; it's to the rules themselves. The defendant is just the beneficiary of that allegiance. It isn't that I don't want you to care about Trent. Christ, you may be the first person on the planet who ever did care about him, and it's a testament to your humanity that you do. . . ."

She held up her wounded hand. "Don't patronize me, okay?"

Steiner looked taken aback. "I'm sorry. You're absolutely right." He started again. "It's not that I don't want you to care about Trent, but you've got to care about the law even more. You've got to. Otherwise, there's no way to see clearly through all this human tragedy—you know?"

Sybylla leaned back in her chair and closed her eyes. She felt the exhaustion ascend her body, toes to shins to thighs to torso. She wondered vaguely if she would ever be able to move from this position again.

Beyond the open door of her office, she could overhear the chatter of her more sensible colleagues leaving for the day. Ordinarily, Sybylla would now be just settling in with paperwork, but the past hours had conspired to produce this surreal immobility. There had been an odd déjà vu about her sojourn in Bellevue's emergency room, a taste of the pointless and frustrated boredom she had endured only hours earlier in the corridor at 100 Centre Street. She had spent a full three hours trying to get semicomfortable in her molded plastic chair and keeping pressure on her aching hand as, in the very laudable priorities of triage, knifing victims and choking kids were rushed past her into the treatment room, but finally she had collected her tetanus shot, her very delightful warning that an AIDS test might be in line, and her personal mother lode of three whole Percodans. Then when she finally emerged onto the hospital's front step, gulping the cool air and hoping for some respite, it was to discover that the day's notable and exciting events were far from over. In the parking lot, a gaggle of journalists clustered, their cameras and microphones at rest. A blond head turned, a finger pointed, and suddenly they streamed in Sybylla's direction. Not to the person behind her, either.

Was Trent really so important? Sybylla stood, awkward and dazed as they pressed her. Then, finally and with a flash of unwelcome understanding, she remembered the victim—the little girl. All afternoon, talking about Trent, encountering Trent, wondering over Trent, she had never once thought of the person he was accused of harming, and now her blinkered doggedness rushed in to haunt her. Grimly, Sybylla understood that she was about to make her television debut. She quickly hid her bandaged hand in her coat pocket. She didn't want any of Dermot's New York cohorts ringing him up about it.

"Syb," Steiner was saying, "why don't you let this one slide? Let me reassign Trent to somebody else."

"Not a chance," she said quietly.

Steiner was serious. "You don't need this. You've gone well beyond the bounds of duty. Let me give it to someone who'll bite him back."

"No. Besides, everyone else here's as overworked as I am."

He got slowly to his feet and stretched, his worn tweed jacket tightening across his back. "I've hired a few more hands. Did I tell you?"

Sybylla reached for her coat, carefully sliding the heavy sleeve over her injured hand. "No, you didn't. Where do you find these willing victims?"

He held the door for her as she collected her briefcase and switched off the light. "You'd be surprised. I get twenty resumés a week, you know. It's true." He smiled, taking in her surprised look. "Kids out of law school who want trial experience—they need look no further than the nearest public defender. Hell, we throw them out there the first week. A few are coming right from school, but one's from uptown. He said he was tired of white-collar crime. Let me take that," he said, reaching for her heavy case. Sybylla surprised herself by letting him. "I hope this isn't work." Steiner groaned, feeling the weight. "Haven't you heard anything I've said?"

Sybylla smiled, a half step behind him as he made his way through the office. "Every word, boss."

"I mean it."

"*Okay,*" she said gruffly. "Let's drop it."

Outside, the evening had settled in a chilly bleakness. Sybylla and Steiner made their way down Lafayette and crossed Foley Square. At City Hall, crowds were swelling into the subway station, packed and somber, their heads down. From the corner of her eye, Sybylla watched a hopeful panhandler approach them. "Sorry." Steiner waved him away.

"Yeah, man," the guy said mournfully, "*I'm* sorry."

She sighed, feeling the chilly air sink into her lungs, and looked up at Steiner.

"Heading home?"

He shrugged, sheepish. "Tonight's my night to tutor. I'm going uptown."

Uptown, translated, meant Harlem. She shook her head at him. "After that lecture, too. You're such an old softy."

"Yeah," he told her. He had once been terrifically handsome, Sybylla thought, with great bushy hair and a black beard, but she knew this primarily from photographs; today, his face was lined and his heart attacks had left little color to his skin. There were few vestiges of that early eagerness and charm. Her favorite photograph of Steiner, the one fossilizing in a plastic cube frame on a shelf behind his desk, showed him and two friends in Greenwood, Mississippi, during Freedom Summer. They had driven south from the University of Michigan Law School, hooked up with CORE, and spent a couple of months providing on-the-hoof defense for the "outside agitators" who had flooded the state in those steamy, dangerous months. On Steiner's face, and on the faces of his comrades, Sybylla saw the pure happiness of utter unambiguous conviction: right was right, with no gray area to muddy the waters. If only it were still that easy to believe in the cause, she thought. If only we didn't have to work so *hard* at believing.

He walked her down into the subway station and they parted for their separate trains. On the Broadway express, the mash of human bodies rocked against one another as the car hurtled north underground, and Sybylla closed her eyes, trying to drift. There was a complicity among the passengers not to acknowledge one another, their uncomfortable proximity, their odors. Eye contact, if accidentally made, was swiftly broken, and no one interrupted the odd silence of screeching tunnel sounds. Sybylla had purposely used her injured hand to grip the bar over her head, as if to advertise to any potential mugger that she had already sustained her quota of damage for the day, but the car was so jammed that a mugging seemed unlikely—violence required a certain freedom of motion. Even the hard-luck panhandlers and a cappella singers knew enough to avoid this kind of crunch.

Compared with the fetid smells of the subway, the air felt sweet when Sybylla hit street level and headed over to Columbus. The avenue was lined with gourmet stores and sweater shops, little holes-in-the-wall jammed with expensive leather shoes, and teeming restaurants where they charged fifteen dollars for a plate of pasta. Happy hour was well underway and the bars were packed with jovial Yuppies knocking back margaritas. Entering her local Korean grocer, she gave Mr. Ko a nod and headed for the salad bar—that refuge of the single urban woman—and squeezed between two executive types with her plastic tray. She also picked up a cup of chicken soup and a stack of sardine cans, some for her cat and some for Annie's, and a pint of Ben & Jerry's Coffee Heath Bar Crunch, the bane of her thighs.

The alley was narrow and crowded with trash cans from the Mexican restaurant on the corner. She had to make her way around a white van that someone had parked illegally, blocking the entrance, but she found Annie in her usual spot, tucked far back beneath the overhang, a heavy blanket over her knees. The figure under that blanket might have owed its bulk to obesity or to layers of clothing, but Sybylla did not know which; in all the months she had looked after Annie, worried about her and brought her food, she had never seen the woman upright or less clothed. Once, Sybylla had asked if Annie wanted to see a doctor, but the query was met with such a polite refusal that she had never asked again. Everybody had a right to privacy, even if they lived in public.

"Hi," Sybylla said. "I've brought you some soup."

"Hello, dear," Annie said. It was one of her lucid days, Sybylla noted. They were rare indeed. "That was thoughtful."

Her manners, Sybylla often thought, would not have been out of place in an English tearoom. She wondered how this Annie, so refined and courteous, would react to the other, more predominant Annie if she ever learned of her existence. That jittering disconnected woman would cause her immense pain. The black cat curled, purring, on Annie's lap.

"And some sardines. He likes sardines, doesn't he?"

Annie nodded. Sybylla handed over the bag. Then, noting the thick gnarled hands folded over the blanket, she asked, "Would you like me to open a can for him?"

"No, no," the woman said. "I can manage."

Sybylla stood, feeling awkward. There seemed to be nothing left to say. She found herself looking nervously away from the woman's pleasantly smiling face. "Anything else I can get you?" She shrugged finally.

The woman shook her head. "No thank you, dear." Sybylla turned away, murmuring a good-bye, and left the alley.

Her mailbox in the building lobby was crammed with restaurant fly-ers, a Learning Annex catalog, offers for three or four preapproved credit cards, and one legitimate postcard from a former colleague at Legal Aid who had burned out after four years of rapists and child mo-lesters and was now hitchhiking through Asia. The card showed a Buddhist monk in front of a monastery in Thailand and claimed that Linda had paused in her journey to "center herself." Sybylla snorted.

As the door to her apartment swung open, two of her senses were as-sailed by aggressive adversaries. One of these was her cat, Gideon, shrieking his put-upon outrage as he stood vigil by his empty food dish and didn't even bother to come over and say a proper hello. The other was a glass of milk, set down sometime in the days of yore and now gen-erating an unbelievable stench that pervaded the apartment, making it impossible for Sybylla merely to follow her nose and find it. She put down her things, forked some Science Diet into Gideon's bowl (he wouldn't get sardines until he worked up a little affection for her), and popped another painkiller for her hand, which had begun to ache again. The answering machine held only a message from her father, wanting to know when she was next coming down for the weekend, his tone so skill-fully modulated that it confirmed Sybylla's long-held notion about Irish Catholics holding a worldwide lock on the non-Olympic sport of guilt in-ducement. She sighed, emptied her salad onto a plate, and headed for the bedroom, steeling herself for her television debut.

It came up abruptly—or so it seemed to Sybylla—with a sensational little graphic of a child in a dress and the bloodred graffiti: CHILD STABBED. Chuck Scarborough was grim. "It happened yesterday," he in-toned. "A child, little Amanda Barrett, was getting off her school bus only a block from her East Side home when a man jumped from the shadows and brutally stabbed her. Today, she lies in critical condition at Mount Sinai Hospital, having undergone hours of surgery to sew up the slashes in her face and abdomen. The police have taken into custody a homeless man who goes by the street name of Trent. Several witnesses have come forward to say they saw this man run out of the Eighty-fifth Street entrance to Central Park and attack little Amanda, stabbing her viciously for no reason at all. News Four spoke earlier with the assailant's

[Buzz! Sybylla thought. You forgot to say 'alleged'] Legal Aid attorney, Sybil Muldoon."

"That's *Sybylla*," Sybylla growled.

She winced when she saw herself, pale and grimy in the unflattering afternoon light. Her voice, when it finally emerged from that funny-looking head, was queerer still as it asked for calm and made the illogical claim that the system actually worked. And then, thankfully, it was over. Scarborough moved on: to a power outage on Long Island, a little boy who found and returned a wallet full of cash, a lost basketball game. Sybylla watched to the bitter end, restraining herself from flipping to another channel and having to see herself again. When the newscast ended, she swung her legs over the side of the bed, intent on a long, steamy bath, and her eye fell on the framed photograph atop the bedside table: a young couple, their arms casually around each other's shoulders, their gazes not quite meeting that of the camera. It was the only photograph Sybylla had seen of her parents together, and, in fact, one of the very few photographs she had ever seen of her mother. As a little girl, she had often stolen into Dermot's forbidding (and forbidden) study to contemplate these two faces, framed on his huge oak desk among the books and manuscripts and heaps of correspondence. When Dermot found her so occupied one day, he had not scolded her; instead, in a rare moment of paternal sensitivity, he had had a copy of the photograph made for his daughter. Now, twenty years later, it was the single object that defined home for her—where it was, she abided.

Dermot looked so uncharacteristically carefree here, she thought now, holding it to the light of her bedside lamp. There was no churning of concept, no ideology, and no precedent, just a pretty young girl who smiled in his embrace. Sybylla looked closely into the girl's expression, so like her own but for the glittering and irreducible intensity in her mother's eyes, which, over the years, had both intrigued and perplexed her. She sometimes wondered whether Nuala Heaney Muldoon's early death had somehow sealed the largely cerebral character Dermot had ultimately developed, or whether her father might otherwise have remained more like the jubilant young man in the photograph, but of course there could be no answer to that.

Sighing in anticipation of her bath, Sybylla got heavily to her feet, but as she did, one of those feet touched something cold. The thing fell softly, with a muted thud, and abruptly the carpeting beneath her bed was flooded with a putrid stench, the kind that even the most aggressive carpet cleaner seldom succeeds in excising. Sybylla groaned aloud. A final misery for a truly miserable day, but at least she knew where she had stashed that damned glass of milk.

CHAPTER

FIVE

—◊◊◊—

For the next few days, she kept the strange little object that had been removed from Trent's arm in the drawer of her bedside table and said nothing about it. Steiner, Sybylla thought, was too busy to be bothered with matters promising to be as irrelevant as this one did—at least, that was one of Sybylla's justifications for keeping it from him. The other was that if her boss knew of the disk's existence, he would insist on following appropriate channels with it and sending it to the city labs for analysis, which would only take months and, more likely than not, end up with the damn thing misplaced. Steiner wouldn't approve of what she was going to do. Under the circumstances (she was thinking of his heart, she told herself), it was simply better not to tell him.

On Saturday morning, she slipped the little plastic envelope containing the disk into a gym bag with her workout clothes and headed over to Broadway for her weekly appointment with the "Iron Maiden." It was a sad state of affairs, she had often thought, when one classified as one's chief personal indulgence not pedicures or silk lounging outfits but an hour's descent into muscular hell to the tune of blaring, indecipherable rap music in the company of grunting fellow madwomen. Sybylla's chosen poison was step class, which had surely been designed by a devotee of Herr Leopold von Sacher-Masoch. Sybylla hated it, but she was enslaved by what it did for her thighs. As long as she ate Ben & Jerry's ice cream and expected to fit into her clothes, she had a pact with the Iron Maiden, the howling dominatrix who masqueraded as an exercise teacher.

Exercise class was also an excuse to see Sushila Patel, with whom Sybylla had once shared a New Haven apartment on the cusp of Ye Olde

Yale and the inner city. They had found each other through the housing office, entered into a perfectly genial living arrangement, and found to their mutual surprise that they were becoming friends. It was a question, perhaps, of leisure more than outright compatibility: Sybylla was toiling so hard in law school and Sushila in the chemistry department that neither woman had much time to pursue a social life.

Not surprisingly, the friendship had atrophied somewhat once the two women collected their degrees and headed for Manhattan, dwindling first to a monthly brunch, then a rare evening meal. They did, however, belong to the same health club, and both showed up regularly for Saturday-morning class. Patel was now an associate professor of chemistry at NYU. She had always loved a good mystery, and she had always been discreet. Sybylla was counting on both qualities now.

The gym's stink of sour sweat hit you when you opened the door on Broadway. Weights and machinery clanked mercilessly in the large room as men and women alike paused in their exertions to check out the newcomers. (It didn't do to have a body too impressive here; exceptional form drew unwelcome attention from the men and bona fide snarls from the women.) Sybylla headed for the desk and had her card punched, then descended the stairs along the back wall, where a door led to the aerobics room.

Patel was sitting on the floor by the water fountain, her Lycra-encased legs extended before her. She was reading the "Weekend" section of the Friday *Times*, and she didn't look up as Sybylla took the patch of carpet next to her. "Hiya," she said, nudging her.

"Oh." Patel peered over the top of her paper. "Hi yourself. You're getting pretty famous, girl."

"Really? What have I done?"

She smiled. "That guy, your client. The one who st—" She glanced around, then whispered, "the one who stabbed the little girl. *You* know."

"Susu," Sybylla scolded (Patel had acquired the nickname at prep school), "you know better than that. We don't know that he's guilty."

"The paper said so."

"The paper is interested in selling papers."

"I suppose." She shrugged. "Anyway, I saw you on the news. What happened to your hand?"

Caught in a door, Sybylla told her. "Listen, I've got something for you. Something I need your help with." She found the little envelope in her gym bag and passed it to Patel.

"An Alka-Seltzer," she said. "How thoughtful."

"I'm pretty sure it's not." Sybylla laughed. "It came from my client."

Patel peered at it. "Some new street drug?"

"No, no." Sybylla shook her head. "He didn't give it to me. I mean, it came from him. You know, *out* of him."

Her friend made a face and pinched the corner of the envelope between two fingers. "You're kidding. That's gross."

"I need to find out what it is. Can you help me?"

Patel looked at her. "Don't the police have labs for this kind of thing?"

"Sure, of course," Sybylla said. "It's just that I'm not sure I want the police to know about it yet. At least not till I find out what it is myself."

"When you say 'out of him,' do you mean he passed it in his stool?" Patel held the disk up to the light.

"No." She shook her head. "It was implanted. It was here." She raised her arm and pointed at its underside. "They found it when they examined him. I mean, they found the incision and they felt it under the skin, so they took it out. They don't seem particularly concerned about what it might be. But I'm concerned. I want to know, and I want to know how he got it and what effect it might have had on his mental state."

Patel sat up. "Let me get this straight. We're talking about your famous client, right? The Wild Man guy?"

Sybylla nodded, wincing at the moniker the tabloids had assigned Trent. "I'm beginning to hate that name."

"And you think this thing somehow made him stab the little girl?"

Sybylla took a moment to convert the question into acceptable language. "I'm concerned about whether this thing might have had some unknown impact on my client's alleged act, whether it contributed to a state of diminished capacity that resulted in injury to the little girl."

Her friend grinned at her. "In other words, like I said, you think this thing somehow made him stab the little girl."

Sybylla shrugged. "Well, yeah. Will you help me find out? You'd have to keep it a secret. I don't want anybody to know about it."

As she had suspected, this was the clincher. Apart from chemistry textbooks, the only reading matter Sybylla had ever seen Susu consume were Agatha Christie novels.

"All right. I'll run a few tests, see what we come up with. You need it soon?"

"Yeah." She felt guilty for asking. "I kind of do."

Her friend grimaced. "And I've got midterms this week."

Sybylla sighed. Past Susu's head, she watched a thickset man clomp down the stairs and lean heavily against the wall. He opened a muscle magazine and studiously turned the pages as if its revolting pictorials of pulsing thighs and arms held the secret to life itself. After a moment, Susu faced her. "All right. Look, I just can't get to it for the next week, but I'll try to have it for you as soon as I can."

Sybylla nodded. "That'd be great. Nothing will be happening with Trent in the immediate future, I can tell you that right now. His shrink thinks he's pretty much out to lunch, so the case is sort of a nonstarter. Still, I really do want to know what that implant is."

Patel frowned at the object. "It could be any number of things, you know. Was he part of a medical study, by any chance?"

"Trent's shrink mentioned that, too. No, I don't know."

"Because there are lots of implants in development right now, largely because Norplant's been so successful. You know, that's five years' worth of contraceptive hormone in these little rods the size of matchsticks. See, when you take a drug this way, on an internal time-release system like you get with an implant, you end up using a much smaller amount of it overall because you avoid first-pass effect."

"First what?"

"First-pass effect," said Patel. "It's what happens when you take a medication by mouth. The first place the drug goes is to the liver, which takes a big bite out of the dosage because that's its function, to detoxify the body. So by the time the drug gets into your circulation, it's been vastly reduced. Therefore, in order to get the correct dosage into your system, what you're in effect doing is overdosing to compensate for the liver. When you use an implant, the drug goes right into the circulatory system, bypassing the digestive tract and the liver, so you end up using a fraction of the amount of the drug. That's better for the body, and it can also be cheaper to manufacture, so it's an attractive option for pharmaceutical companies." She leaned away as a woman in sweats ducked to use the water fountain.

"Pretty soon, diabetics will be able to use them for insulin, and people with heart disease will get nitroglycerin implanted. I've heard they're also working on nicotine implants for smoking cessation. And they're already in use for some kinds of cancer—prostate, for example. The implant delivers a hormone that turns off production of LH, which stimulates the testes to make testosterone. It's like a chemical castration."

"Lovely," Sybylla said.

"Yeah, but the big potential is for when you can't rely on the patients to medicate themselves. This new TB, for example. Lots of times the people are also mental patients, or they're narcotics users. They take their medication until they feel a little better and then they stop because they forget, or they can't be bothered, or they don't want to see the doctor. But the disease is still active and still very infectious, so you get these people wandering around, and they don't look sick, but they're infecting the rest of us."

"Like Typhoid Mary," Sybylla observed.

"Yup. But that was just one person, remember, and this TB is running wild. An implant would be a reasonable alternative to the civil liberties problem. You know, how do you make somebody take their medication without having to imprison them? And the same principle might work for certain psychotics, too."

"Really?" Sybylla said. "How so?"

"Well, you know there are some drugs that can alleviate certain kinds of schizophrenia, right? Like Prolixin. You give Prolixin to schizophrenics and sometimes they become functional. Theoretically, they could lead productive, harmless lives if they stayed on the medication, but when you release them, what usually happens is that they stop taking the drug, and then they end up back in the hospital. Only maybe they've done a little damage in the meantime. But if you could implant an antipsychotic drug, and the patient didn't have to be responsible for maintaining the medication, then it's possible for him to live out of the hospital without being a danger to the community or himself."

"How does the implant work?" Sybylla asked. "Does it just dissolve over time?"

"Sometimes. Depends on how it's made. Some implants are made to be completely absorbed into the body, but others dispense their dosage of the drug without changing shape or size. That's to make them easier to remove." She glanced at the disk. "I don't know which this one is, but I should be able to tell when I analyze it."

"It looks like it's wax or something."

Patel shook her head. "I doubt that. Sometimes they make them by combining two liquid chemicals, like polyglycolic acid and polylactic acid, along with whatever drug the thing is going to release. The two liquids then become a solid and make up the body of the implant." She slid the envelope into her purse, then folded up her paper and put that in, too.

"The shrink at Bellevue said not to let it get too hot or too cold, okay?" Patel nodded absentmindedly. "And I need it back, too. I mean, I told him I'd give it back to him when I was finished with it."

"No sweat." She was stretching, her hands clasped over her head, her back straight against the wall. "Oh God. I don't know if I can deal with this class. Why did my mother give me these fat genes?"

"Listen, I appreciate this," Sybylla told her, ignoring her friend's complaint. Susu was still wearing the same size she'd worn at sixteen. "Really."

"No sweat. It'll be fun. Nice change of pace from lecturing all those protodoctors. Showing them how to turn on a Bunsen burner. So tell me, what's the poop on this guy? He just totally bonkers or what?"

"Looks that way," she said vaguely. Across the room, the thickset guy no longer seemed interested in his muscle magazine. Sybylla shifted her legs as the eight o'clock aerobics class let out, releasing a horde of glistening bodies into the waiting area.

"So what's up with you, anyway? You seeing anybody?"

Sybylla grimaced. "What, like since the Carter administration? No. I only see my delightful clients and my cat, who hates me." She shook her head, morose. Then, unaccountably, she thought of the defense attorney from her morning on jury duty, and she felt herself smile.

"You lie," Patel shrieked in glee. "You are committing the cardinal sin of holding out on a girlfriend! I can have you reported to the Ms. Foundation for this infraction!" She got to her feet and shouldered her gym bag.

"I only wish I were holding out." Sybylla got up, too. "Hey," she said, smirking.

"What?"

"Don't look now. *Susu*. Didn't I just say not to look?" She was whispering. "You have an admirer."

"Oh yeah?"

"Guy with the muscle magazine. I've been watching him. He keeps looking at you."

Patel shrugged. "Not my type. Call me crazy, but I like a man with a discernible neck."

The Amazonian figure of the Iron Maiden brushed past them and Patel turned to enter the steamy exercise room. She peered back at her friend. "Ready for the abattoir, my dear?"

Sybylla slapped her right thigh as if it truly were a side of meat. It gave a discreet but significant jiggle and she glared at it. "Evidently so," she said.

C H A P T E R

S I X

—⁓—

Legal Aid attorneys liked to say of the New York County grand jury that it would indict a ham sandwich, if said ham sandwich were presented thus to the jurors by the DA's office: "Ladies and gentlemen of the grand jury, we have reason to believe that the ham sandwich, taken into police custody on suspicion of armed robbery, committed the crime of which it is accused." *People of the State of New York* v. *Trent* posed none of the taxing philosophical challenges of a ham sandwich, however; indeed, to Sybylla, the thing looked depressingly straightforward. Already, four independent witnesses—including the driver of the school bus, who had been only a few feet away—had come forward and given statements to the police, and the apparent weapon—a blood-drenched surgical scalpel—had been requisitioned from Trent's fist by the cops, who'd arrived within a minute or two of the attack.

The indictment came down a whopping thirty seconds after it was presented to the grand jury, as regular as a commuter train under Mussolini: assault in the first degree.

Uptown, the press held a vigil at Mount Sinai, filming the little girl's family and her friends from the Brearley School ducking in and out of the Klingenstein Pavilion as if they were film stars entering and leaving Spago. Seizing on the Barrett family's wealth and player status (Barrett senior was a financial consultant with a Fifth Avenue office; his wife sat on the board of the New York City Ballet), the press leaned hard on the theme of American dream smack up against American nightmare.

Trent, in this interpretation, emerged as a wild man devoid of any human feeling, with the possible exception of envy. A street creature, a representative of the new breed of feral homeless who had come to view the citizens of the city as a perpetual roster of prey, he had made his print debut with a slightly fuzzy mug shot spattered across the cover of the *Post* and HERE'S THE MONSTER! for a headline.

He had caught the wave, all right. For years, fury had been building against the homeless, who no longer seemed content to panhandle their dinners politely and subserviently without subjecting the good citizens of the city to bodily harm. The age of the single neighborhood schizophrenic had ended abruptly when the laws directing institutionalization of the mentally ill changed, and the streets flooded with men and women marching to very different drummers. Soon enough, each intersection and side street had its resident psychotic, and even pedestrians with street smarts enough to avoid eye contact and be ready to run like hell fell victim with increasing frequency. A tourist was stabbed on the Staten Island Ferry, a lawyer was murdered near his West Village apartment, and a former Rockette was set upon as she walked her dogs.

But even in this sordid terrain, Trent had broken some new ground. The attack he was charged with seemed so random, and its victim so innocent. The little girl's beauty (her yearbook picture was quickly located by all three network affiliates) was of the lithe, graceful, and gloriously blond variety, and her disfigurement was so unprovoked that the entire city stood up in outrage. If Amanda Barrett, who was wealthy, whose family had power, who lived on a shady street of brownstones off Fifth, could have her head sliced open like a piece of sashimi with no warning at all, then things had really gone to hell. In earlier times, the cry might have gone out for a dragon slayer; as it was, the concern of the people fell on the ears of his twentieth-century equivalent—the DA.

Sybylla, for her part, viewed her infamous client with a mixture of bafflement and pity. He seemed to her a man who had simply walked out of his own body and taken off for parts unknown, leaving a sublessee whose references he had not bothered to check: an angry man who muttered and twitched and made no sense.

Such were her thoughts on the Monday following the grand jury verdict when a copy of the indictment wound its way through the system and landed in her still-tender hand. She had spent the morning preparing a defense for one of her regulars, a thief named Cleve Rivera, and she was already in a fairly malevolent mood.

Over the years she had known him, Rivera had shopped the streets of Manhattan as if they were his own private smorgasbord, helping himself to the objects of his somewhat whimsical desires. His prevailing passion, however, was the classic gold necklace, and for once, Cleve had failed to gauge the resistance of a specimen correctly, leaving its rightful owner with a permanent scar-colored necklace and a good deal of indignation.

Rivera had been in and out of the shelter system for years, making his erratic and nasty living during the day, when he was supposed to be out looking for work, but Sybylla had had hopes for him. The previous year, Cleve had been hired by one of the relief agencies, delivering food and blankets to people on the street and transporting the rare person who actually wanted into the system to one of the shelters, and with his job as collateral, Sybylla had gotten him bail. More likely than not, however, bail would be the last of her magic tricks; with the victim out for blood, her office mates as witnesses, and the permanent smiley face inscribed on her neck, it looked likely that Cleve was facing some time, and she had told him plainly that he was not to expect any miracles.

So all things considered, she wasn't entirely distraught when Cleve showed up for his court date that afternoon and summarily eschewed her services, announcing with evident disdain that some new friends— dealers, obviously, Sybylla thought—were helping him out with money to buy, as Cleve put it, "a real lawyer." So much for the faith of the indigent defendant in his nation's system of public defense.

"You might have called," Sybylla said crossly, shoving his file into her briefcase. "You're not my only client, you know. I've wasted the whole morning."

"Watch it, bitch," Cleve said, his voice dark. Evidently, he was not used to even this benign degree of chastisement. "You watch your step; might be a body behind you."

"Gee, thanks," she sneered, turning away. "I hope you'll be just as considerate of your 'real' lawyer."

He yelled after her, drawing the attention of the lawyers, the witnesses, the defendants and their accusers, the cops waiting to testify, the bailiff sneaking a smoke beside the men's room. "You watch your step, bitch. You got some trouble coming your way, you don't take care!"

"Wonderful," she muttered to herself, walking through her avid audience (some of whom, she now realized, recognized her from television stardom) and heading outside.

Pissed as she was, the unexpectedly free afternoon did afford her an opportunity to visit Bennis, possibly the only person in the city who might reasonably shine some light on Trent and what had happened to change him so. Fueled by this rush of optimism, Sybylla checked her watch and stopped at a pay phone to call her office. Then she made for the subway station and headed uptown.

Not that there's any particular urgency, she chided herself. As far as she knew, *New York* v. *Trent* was headed for the great gaping limbo that opened between mentally ill defendants and the criminal justice system. If Trent's schizophrenia was as entrenched as Turturro had implied, there was little to suggest that he would ever pass a 730 exam and be deemed competent to stand trial, so that was that. More likely than not, the case would wither on the vine, its victim and its defendant both consigned to houses of the sick. In time, the city and its outraged populace would move on to other outrages and the so-called Wild Man would become a footnote of the crime-ridden nineties.

Except ... except ... The message had landed on her desk in the harried moments before she'd left her office a few hours earlier, hand-delivered by the manicured fingers of Rachel, the office receptionist ("Too hot to languish at my station, babe"), its generic pink "While You Were Out" transformed by the content of Rachel's patented scrawl: "Andrew Greer will see you re Trent, Tues., his office, 10:00 A.M."

But why?

And why so abruptly, as if there were some urgency about it?

Sybylla climbed from the subway station beneath Bloomingdale's and made her way east, stopping to pick up a carton of cigarettes and a six-pack of Coke—a hostess gift, of sorts.

She found Bennis in the exact position she had last seen him in the previous summer, his back to the great concrete support of the Queensboro Bridge, his arms folding a bottle of Thunderbird to his chest, and his pet pigeon, Davis, nearby, tied by a string around its leg. Sybylla had never forgotten that pigeon. On the earlier occasion, she had watched it try to take wing three, four, five times, always reaching a few feet in the air before Bennis tugged it back to earth and spoke harshly to it. The amount of companionship a pigeon could offer was small, but Bennis evidently felt it adequate to justify the cruelty of Davis's captivity. The bird was certainly given ample food, and Bennis liked to cover it when the air got cold, but there was no disguising Davis's wish to rejoin its own kind. The sight of it flapping hopefully skyward had so distressed Sybylla that night that she had briefly considered an anonymous call to the ASPCA, but ultimately she had let the matter pass. Even for an animal lover like herself, it was difficult to anthropomorphize a creature so hopelessly brainless as a New York pigeon, and the affection of a homeless man was one of the better justifications for ill treatment of an animal that she had come across in her time.

Around Bennis was strewn the entirety of his worldly goods—an array of cartons and garbage bags stuffed with God only knew what, and an aged mattress heaped with pieces of rug and torn blankets and sheltered with heavy plastic sheeting. Though the Queensboro Bridge was a gathering point for the city's homeless, its core group of tenants was as firmly ensconced as residents of any Park Avenue co-op, and while he was not exactly house-proud about his dwelling, Bennis had a tendency to view it with a proprietary glare. Through an alcoholic haze, he observed passersby, oglers, and the rare visitor with the defensive suspicion of a plantation owner who believes there are Yankees nearby.

From half a block away, Bennis watched her approach, his face blank. When she was close enough to speak, she hoisted the cigarettes and smiled. "Hey, Bennis. Brought you a present. Remember me?"

He nodded, pursing his lips.

"The lady with the name," he offered.

"Sybylla. I'm Trent's lawyer."

"Yeah." He smiled slowly. "Man, they talked about you for months around here."

"They did?" She perched cautiously on a carton that didn't look too filthy. She had offered Trent a lift uptown after his acquittal and, somewhat against her better judgment, had been persuaded to linger a moment, watching an impromptu celebration spring up around the returning Lazarus. Though declining the numerous open bottles that were on offer, she had been moved by the surreal display of festivity against a backdrop of shanties, litter, and crack vials.

"The only ladies come down here is from the city, or the mission downtown. They talked about you for months."

"That's nice," Sybylla said vaguely. "So, Bennis. How's Davis?"

He looked calmly at the pigeon. "Okay, I guess. He eats; he craps. He don't try to get away no more."

What a surprise, Sybylla thought.

"I brought you a present. Camel's your brand, isn't it?"

For the first time, he showed some animation. Entire cartons of pristine cigarettes didn't come Bennis's way terribly often, and with a feverish thank-you, he shoved the package into his ratty bedroll, out of sight.

"And some Coke." He was less thrilled by the Coke, but he grudgingly accepted it, even offering one to Sybylla while he stuck to his Thunderbird.

"Bennis," she said, "I'm here about Trent. I guess you figured that."

He looked east toward the river and sighed. On the pavement by his side, she had already spotted the folded *Post,* with the bottom half of Trent's face and the word MONSTER! exposed. She nodded at the paper. "I see you've read about it."

Bennis shrugged. "I heard what happened a few days ago. Some guy came down and told us. We chased him outta here."

"Why?" Sybylla asked.

"He wanted to get into Trent's stuff. He was saying how Trent wasn't gonna be back for a while. We figured he made the story up." Bennis shrugged. "I guess not."

"Bennis, has Trent been doing drugs?"

The man smiled ruefully. "Nah. Trent was always giving those crackheads a bad time." He gestured at a few vacant squats farther down the row, their tenants most likely off in search of fixes. "He didn't do drugs. He wouldn't even drink with me."

"Well, do you have any ideas about what might have caused this?"

Bennis leaned his head back against the concrete, closing his eyes.

He was so dissipated that his chronological age, whatever it might have been, had long ceased to be of any use in determining his life expectancy. The broken blood vessels over his cheeks, the red-rimmed eyes, the blackened teeth—all bespoke a body in fierce, headlong deterioration. His liver, lungs, and heart were racing one another to the finish line.

"He didn't do it," Bennis said in a gravelly voice.

Sybylla sighed. "You know, I'd like to believe that very much. I really would. But if I'm going to be of any real help to Trent on these charges, I also need to be practical about where he stands. There were witnesses, Bennis, and people held him down until the cops got there. I've got to find something to hang a case on."

"What are you asking me?" he said harshly. "You want me to say he was crazy or something? Go down to that court there and say he didn't know what he was doing?"

"I'm not asking you to do that," Sybylla said carefully. "I only wondered if you could shed any light on this transformation. You're his best friend. You saw him every day. Did you notice anything?"

Bennis shrugged. "Don't ask me. Ask the people he was with."

"What are you talking about? What people?"

"He wasn't here," Bennis said. "He left months ago. I haven't seen him all this time."

"All this time?" She still wasn't getting it. "How long ago?"

"Before Christmas," Bennis said. He reached for a filthy piece of wool and covered the warbling pigeon against the cooling evening. "I went over to the liquor store. I'm on my way back, just up there to the end of the block"—he pointed—"I seen him getting into one of them city services vans. They was making him get in."

"And this was before Christmas? You're kidding. He just up and left?"

"So they say," Bennis said darkly. "Me, I don't think so."

Sybylla leaned forward, trying to meet his eye. "What do you mean, Bennis?"

He shook his head. "He was the only one here at that hour, see. Except for Paul"—he gestured at the end of the row of squats, where a small figure was huddled beneath a heavy blanket—"but Paul's not too together, you know." He leaned forward to confide in Sybylla, his pores wafting Thunderbird in her direction. "Up here." He tapped his temple.

Her breath held, she nodded.

"Did Paul say anything about what he might have seen?"

"Him? Nah. I'm telling you, the guy don't talk to people the rest of us can see. Besides, he's mostly under that old blanket. Like now. He gets up maybe once a day, to eat or whatever. He didn't see nothing."

"So Trent went to a shelter," Sybylla said thoughtfully. Abruptly, Bennis grinned, affording her an unenviable view of his decaying mouth.

"*Right.* Like Trent would go to a shelter. He lived *here.* His friends was here and his stuff was here. He wouldn't go to no *shelter.* You know what those places is like?"

Sybylla nodded grimly. "But maybe he just felt like a change. You know, have a shower, clean up a bit. They came around, found him in an agreeable mood, and he went off to have a meal, see the doctor, whatever." Bennis was shaking his head. "Look, it's possible. Who knows what happened after that. Maybe somebody offered him a job, or another place to stay. Or a ticket to Cleveland. Christ, I don't know."

"No," Bennis said simply.

"Well, then," she said, exasperated, "you obviously have a theory about what happened to him. So what is it?"

The man leaned forward, conspiratorial. "They took him," he growled. "That's what I think. I think they took him without him wanting to go. They had ahold of him, I'm telling you. I saw it"—he pointed at the top of the street—"up there. They made him get in. He'd a never gone on his own."

Sybylla shook her head. "Bennis, you know that's not how they work. They come and ask you if you want to go to the shelter, but they don't make you if you don't want to."

"They *took* him," Bennis spat. "They musta. Otherwise, why ain't he here? They took him and did this to him!" He snatched up the newspaper and rattled it at Sybylla. "That ain't Trent."

Sybylla got carefully to her feet. All in all, she considered herself lucky to have gotten as much sane information from him as she had. From here on in, though, it was clearly turning into paranoia city. Social Services vehicles did not go around snatching street people from their squats and imprisoning them in shelters.

"Well, Bennis, thanks for your time. I know you want to help Trent."

"Damn right," he muttered, absently stroking his pigeon, who flinched at his touch.

"I'll do my best for him, I promise."

"Damn right."

"Enjoy the cigs." She started to turn away.

"He ain't coming back," Bennis observed.

Sybylla didn't disagree. Not guilty by reason of insanity was about as high as she was aspiring at this point, and contrary to what the public seemed to think, that didn't mean a ticket back to the streets. The best Trent could hope for, in her view, was a lengthy tenure on Wards Island, snug in the maximum-security Kirby mental-health facility. Trent wasn't going to see his friend for years, and it looked unlikely that Bennis would last that long.

"You tell him," Bennis shouted. "You tell him for me. You tell him I got his stuff safe, okay?"

"I'll tell him," Sybylla said. Davis fluttered plaintively under his blanket. She turned and walked away.

CHAPTER

SEVEN

OLD SPICE RAPIST CONVICTED
—by Jonas Sanderson,
New York Post staff reporter

Larry Randolph Jackson, known to New Yorkers as the Old Spice Rapist, was found guilty yesterday in a Manhattan courtroom of four counts of rape and four counts of aggravated assault. Charges resulting from three additional rapes are still pending.

Over a period of eighteen months, Jackson terrorized women in apartment buildings on or near Central Park West between 86th and 96th streets, often managing to evade doormen and other security personnel in these prestigious buildings. He would gain entrance to apartments by claiming to be a member of the maintenance staff and, once inside, rob, rape, and beat his victims. Virtually all of the women reported to police that the man smelled overpoweringly of Old Spice aftershave.

A break in the case occurred last summer when one of the victims spotted her assailant leaving an Upper West Side movie theater. Police said she followed him to his car and wrote down the license plate number. Subsequently, she and five other victims successfully picked Jackson out of a police lineup. Police said that a search of the suspect's Washington Heights apartment revealed evidence linking him to several of the crime scenes.

Jury foreman Wade Jones, a newsstand owner, said that while there had been some initial dissent within the jury, those advocating conviction had proved immovable. Although, at one point in the daylong deliberations, a hung jury had been a real possibility, jurors favoring acquittal had been persuaded by one juror in particular to relinquish their positions.

New York district attorney Andrew Greer, who prosecuted the case, called it a victory for New York's women and a tribute to the courage of the victims. Greer, who was present in the courtroom for the verdict, also expressed satisfaction. "Thanks to this jury," he said, "there is one less element of risk in New York tonight." The DA's office plans to ask for a life sentence without possibility of parole.

Jackson's attorney, Sam Larkin, maintained throughout the trial that the victims' identification of his client was undependable and that the subsequent lineups were improperly conducted. An appeal on those grounds is planned, he says.

"Why don't you just take it?" the woman snapped, folding the paper noisily and thrusting it at Sybylla.

"What?" Sybylla turned guiltily to look at her.

"You're practically in my lap, you realize that?"

"I'm sorry," Sybylla said, blushing. "I didn't mean to. I just . . . I was sort of following that case, you know?"

"Save it," the woman said, grunting to her feet. It was Sybylla's stop, too, but she waited for the woman to get off first, lingering for a moment to let the morning crowd fill the space between them. Above ground, the air was laced with a tantalizing hint of spring. Sybylla made her way up Centre Street, moving among the anonymous crowd of city employees en route to the corridors, offices, and cubicles of their working lives. Sybylla had often wondered why government offices insisted on being quite as dreary as they were. Even the Marriage License Bureau, which had no excuse at all, was downright depressing, and the offices of the public defender were truly the land that Martha Stewart forgot; Sybylla had never known even a houseplant to survive there. The crusty linoleum got a nightly pass with a dry mop, and the toilets were full of foamy blue liquid in the mornings, but the place had no comfort and even less charm.

She had made her peace with this, and she was usually too harried for it to even register much, but visits to the DA's office were a particular thorn in Sybylla's side. The mere fact of meeting an adversary in his or her own office was a concession, and therefore disheartening, but the stark contrast in work space always made Sybylla envious, and envy made her weak. Stepping off the elevator at One Hogan Place was like Dorothy stepping into Technicolor when her house landed in Oz: faux but colorful Persian rugs underfoot, the faux mahogany receptionist's station, even the faux blond receptionist herself—all seemed so animated. Adding insult to injury was the fact that even the lowliest assistant district attorney had his or her own little office, with his or her own desk, shelves, and, most critical, *window*.

Ordinarily, she'd have planned to meet a legal adversary in the courthouse, grabbing a bench or even a bit of standing room to talk over a pending case and maybe do a deal, but Sybylla wasn't about to haggle with Greer. He was waiting for her now, the receptionist said, if she would like to have a seat.

"He's waiting for me, so I'm supposed to wait for him?" Sybylla asked.

"Just have a seat." The woman smiled.

You're not a real blonde, Sybylla felt like saying.

Greer must have been waiting very impatiently, because he kept *her* waiting only fifteen minutes. Then a minion was sent out to fetch her. Sybylla fished in her briefcase for a pen as she walked. She didn't really need a pen, but fidgeting for it made her less nervous. The minion pushed back the heavy wooden door for her and stood with his back to it, waiting for her to pass. Sybylla made a point of smiling at him as she went by, an effort to avoid seeming too interested in Greer.

She might have saved herself the trouble. Her adversary sat in a lush leather seat, swiveling in small rhythmic arcs, doodling on a legal pad in black ballpoint, and talking on the phone. Not talking. Campaigning. Habitually, he reached up, his pen snapped between two fingers like a cigarette, to comb back no-longer-existent hair from his forehead. With so much simultaneous activity, he never met Sybylla's eye as she took a seat and set down her bag.

"If I have a mission," the man was crooning, "it is to see the streets of this city return to the safety they enjoyed when I was a boy. When I grew up in Far Rockaway, you could go anywhere in the five boroughs and not have a moment's fear. I'm not one of those skeptics who feels that the New York of our childhoods is lost forever. I believe that with good tough police work and an effective follow-through on the part of the court system, we can, to a large extent, return to a more livable city."

Greer paused, listening; then he touched one chubby finger to his lips and began again.

"Yes, I would agree with that. We haven't yet found an appropriate means of dealing with the problem, but this office is definitely going to be a part of the solution, I can tell you that. Homelessness is a symptom of a larger illness in our society, but there is no reason that homeless citizens must present an added risk to inhabitants of this city."

This is all for my benefit, Sybylla thought. He had probably waited till the interviewer called before sending his assistant for her. Clearly, he wanted her to hear this.

"My immediate plans?" he was saying. "Immediate, as in, before the election next year?" Greer laughed. The laugh lived in his nose, and it was mirthless. "Well, *immediately* when this interview is over, I plan to meet with my opponent on the Trent case. A Miss Sybylla Muldoon." He glanced up at her for the first time, paused, then gave her a brief spasmodic smile. "*Ms.* Muldoon, you'd better make that. Legal Aid. Yeah." He chortled, as if it was funny. "Courtesy of the city, that's right. Nah, there's nothing new on the case. Nothing for your ears, anyway." He laughed loudly. Then, abruptly, his voice took on a tragic tone. "Yes. She's out of intensive care, at last. Thank God. But she looks terrible. I shudder to think about that poor little girl asking for a mirror, I really do. The parents are camped out up there, total wrecks. Nah, you better ask the doctor that; it's not my field. Okay? What?" He listened for a minute. "Well, look, it sounds great. Put it in the mail to me, okay? I'm hanging up. Yes, thanks to you, too."

The phone settled into its cradle with a loud crack, and Greer lurched forward across the wide expanse of his desk, hand outstretched.

"Ms. Muldoon, it's a pleasure," he boomed. "I don't think we've met before."

"But we have," Sybylla said simply, noting the flash of distress that crossed his face. He did not like to forget a constituent. "At a party for my father about ten years ago." She smiled briefly at his blank expression. "When he was named to the D.C. Circuit Court of Appeals."

It was pleasant to watch him blanch. "You can't be Dermot's daughter," Greer insisted, a little fiercely. Then he summoned a great, hearty, and utterly disingenuous smile. "Yes, I see it now. Couldn't miss all that red hair. Christ, you're probably smart as a whip."

"Possibly," Sybylla said, declining the compliment.

"Dermot never mentioned he had a daughter at Legal Aid."

What a shock, she thought. "I wouldn't expect you to remember."

He was looking past her to the doorway of his office. "What? Oh, coffee?" he asked. Sybylla asked for tea, just to be ornery.

"Herbal, if you have it," she added, hoping they didn't.

"What a mind your old man has," the DA mused, sinking back in his chair, which groaned its protest. "If we ever get him on the court, he'll make a superb contribution."

We? Sybylla thought. "The court?" she said.

"*The* court. The ultimate court."

"Oh," Sybylla said. "Yes, I suppose he would."

"Might happen, you know," he went on. "Far from impossible. I can't think of a more credible choice myself."

"Hm." Sybylla nodded, unsure of how to react. "Mr. Greer, I'm sure you have only a limited amount of time to spend with me, and I want to make sure we cover whatever it is you feel we need to cover." She swallowed. The DA, though clearly unused to having meetings wrested from his control, quickly adjusted. In an instant, she was no longer the daughter of an old friend who happened to be a legal lion, but his lowly opponent on a walkover case—a walkover case that happened to be a pot of political gold.

"Of course," Greer said gruffly. "I assume you've seen a copy of the indictment?"

"I have." Sybylla nodded.

"Your client, I understand, is still under observation at Bellevue."

"He is. I believe the diagnosis is schizophrenia," she said with studied naïveté. "Naturally, I'll be asking the court to leave him where he is. His doctors are pretty emphatic as to his inability to understand the charges or assist in his own defense, and there's been no significant change in his mental state that I'm aware of."

"Schizophrenia," he mused, shaking his head.

"According to his doctors, yes."

The DA smiled. "These are the doctors our city is providing for his care."

She ignored the sarcasm. "I can't think of anyone else who would be qualified to judge."

Greer slowly folded his arms behind his head and gave her a studiously sober frown. "I must tell you, Ms. Muldoon, that the minute your client recovers to the extent that he can meet competency requirements—and with the superior psychiatric care we are providing for him, I have every confidence that he *will* improve—I intend to push for an early court date. I think it's important that we don't let this fester any longer than it has to. I'm sure you understand that this case has become symbolic for many. What your client allegedly did is the ultimate justification of the fear our citizens live in. It must be made clear that even if we can't prevent this violence we will still be swift and thorough in response to it."

Another minion came in with a tray. Sybylla sadly observed the tea bag swinging from her saucer—chamomile.

"I think it's only fair to tell you something else, Ms. Muldoon, and that is that I won't be offering any pleas in this case."

She sipped her awful tea and gave him a cool look. "I wouldn't dream of asking. Last year, as I'm sure you've discovered, my client spent three months at Rikers because he wouldn't plead out on a felony he said he didn't commit. Three months in jail, Mr. Greer, just so he could leave with a clean record. Believe me, if Trent ever does recover sufficiently to understand what's happened to him, he'll want his day in court."

"What's happened to him," the DA mused. "Is that really how it appears to you? That something has happened to him? When a little girl's life has been destroyed? It's all principles on your side of the fence. Civil liberties, right? Well, let me explain something to you, Ms. Muldoon. Here's something we get a good look at in this office. Crime causes real pain—real pain to real victims. And plenty of it would never happen in the first place if the system did what it was conceived to do and removed offenders from society. Citizens who are not criminals deserve the opportunity to live peaceful lives."

"Fine. But there's real pain on the other side, too, you know. There's neglect and abuse and hunger and abandonment and fear."

"I hope you're not implying that some crime is excusable." Greer shook his head.

"Not excusable, perhaps. But understandable."

He smiled tightly at her. "Your heart is bleeding all over the table, young lady."

Sybylla stared at him, momentarily speechless. Then she set down her tea cup with a very unladylike clatter. "Listen, I know how you and your office feel about us. We get our kicks from interfering with the wheels of justice. We mess up all your hard work by insisting on acquittals for people who aren't guilty. And Trent *may* be guilty. I wouldn't know, and I'm not in a position to judge him, any more than you are. But I can tell you this. Something has happened to him since last summer. Some very profound transformation has occurred, and I haven't got the first idea what's behind it. But I promise you, when I *do* find out, that change *will* become a cornerstone of his defense."

He was shaking his head in wonder. "Amazing. I thought your species was extinct."

"A few of us left," she said lightly. "We breed in dark places and hide our young." Past his desk, the window ledge was laden with picture frames covered in flowery fabrics. A woman's choice, clearly. The pictures were of two teenage boys and a little girl in a First Communion dress. Greer and his wife, a brown-haired woman with plump cheeks and two demure chins. "My kids," she heard Greer say. "Lemme show you another picture."

Out they tumbled from the large manila folder he took from behind the desk. They were clinical and raw: delicate blond hair yanked out in chunks, skin scraped from a cheek, the lurid glow of deep bruises, and—worst of all—the gut-clenching shock of those cuts, crisscrossing a face that might once have been angelic but would never be so again. Even with the best plastic surgery money could buy, she would always carry what had happened to her smack across her face, for even strangers to see. Sybylla wanted to look away, but she discovered that she had suddenly lost control of her neck, which absolutely would not move. She heard a voice that sounded remotely like her own say, "Oh," and then add, "How awful."

"Yes, Ms. Muldoon," Greer leapt in, "how awful indeed. Imagine getting off a school bus a block from your home, and then, before you even hit the pavement, having someone fall onto you and begin to stab you. Can you imagine what that must feel like?"

Sybylla straightened up. "This was a terrible tragedy, Mr. Greer. I'm certainly not disputing that. But our immediate task is to determine the best treatment for the alleged assailant, a very sick assailant. And I can't see that locking him away in a prison, with minimal medical care, is anything like the best treatment."

Greer smiled. "You know, Ms. Muldoon, I've never been one for the theory that every sick crime is committed by a sick criminal. Some people are good and some are just bad."

"It must be very comforting to be able to tell which ones are which," Sybylla said.

Her words had more of a smack than she'd intended, and Greer looked at her closely for a long moment before speaking. With one large hand, he reached forward to sweep the grisly photographs back into their envelope, which he placed directly in front of him on the desk, then folded his hands on top as if he was praying over them. "There's something I'd like you to try to remember about me and my office. I represent the people of this city, and that includes you. When I prosecute your client, and I intend to do so in as vigorous a manner as you will ever see, I have your safety as much as anyone else's in mind. I have eight million clients who deserve to be safe. You have one client, who is determined to compromise that safety. This kind of random violence is an intolerable disease, and if I seem overzealous about it, it's because I think I've discovered the cure."

"Why are you telling me this, Mr. Greer? Do I look like I need basic civics instruction? What does any of this moralizing have to do with doing our jobs?"

"I merely wish to make my position clear to you, my young friend. You're stubborn like Dermot, I can see that. But he seems to retain a greater sense of perspective. I hope you won't take my advice amiss, but if you ever have any intention of having some impact on the law or public policy, you'd better find some more worthy principles to defend. In my opinion, people like your Trent have a few too many rights in the first place."

Sybylla stood. "Is that it?" she said. "Have we covered everything?"

Slowly, Greer got to his feet. "Make no mistake," he said, his voice suddenly low. "Eventually, this matter will go to trial. There will be no deals. And your client *will* be convicted. I intend to do everything in my power to ensure that he never again has an opportunity to be a destructive force in the lives of our citizens."

"Or a *constructive* force in the life of any other politician?" she said archly.

He pursed his lips in distaste. "Good-bye, Ms. Muldoon. We'll meet soon, in court."

Sybylla gave him a deeply insincere smile. "I wish I could share your confidence about Trent's recovery. But I thank you for your concern."

She left the office wound up in irritation, then headed over to Legal Aid. Barring gas explosions and hijackings, a trial like this could put Greer at the top of the local news every night, casting him easily in his favorite role: Justice Avenger. By the time it was over, everyone in the city with a television would be bringing him frankincense and myrrh.

The minute Sybylla shouldered open the door, Rachel reached for a wad of pink message slips on her desk. "Steiner wants you."

"Is it my mind, d'you think?" she teased. "Or more of an animal thing?"

"And these. I'm ignoring that."

"Wow, I'm popular," Sybylla observed unhappily. She made her way back in the direction of Steiner's office, where she assumed he was waiting to hear about her meeting with the DA, passing the grimy laden desks that filled the room and nodding hello to her colleagues as they met her eye. When she had first joined the office, Sybylla had made an effort to know her coworkers—"the team," Legal Aid recruiting materials had stressed, no doubt meaning "the forces of good"—but as more and more of her predecessors and contemporaries moved on to private firms or even crossed the fence to join the DA's office, she found herself less motivated to befriend each new batch of recruits. She couldn't remember the last time she had socialized with colleagues. In fact, it was hard to remember the last time she had socialized at all.

Steiner waved as he watched her approach through the office door he kept permanently open. Then he turned to someone seated opposite his desk, out of Sybylla's sight, and stood up as she neared, much to her amusement.

"What gallantry!" Sybylla laughed. "Did I miss the Emily Post corporate seminar?"

"Highly amusing," Steiner said. "Look, Syb, I want you to meet my coup from uptown. This is Sam Larkin. He's starting today."

"Oh," she heard her own stupid voice. "It's you."

"I'm sorry?" He seemed perplexed. "We've met?"

"You've met?" Steiner said.

Sybylla reddened. "I almost wound up on your jury. The Old Spice Rapist."

"Y . . . es," he said slowly. "I remember you."

She turned to Steiner. "Jury duty?" Sybylla prompted. "Remember? I was in voir dire on his case." When she looked at Larkin again, she had a sudden overpowering urge to let her fingers do the walking through those little black curls, but she chided herself instantly. Certainly, he was cute. Empirically cute, even, but when was the last time she fell for a guy in a Brooks Brothers suit? From his probable Rolex to the flushed, athletic complexion that people tended to acquire in prep school, Sam Larkin looked suspiciously like somebody who'd wandered through the wrong door, misreading CAPITAL CRIMES as CAPITAL GAINS. He might be attractive, but what would they have to talk about? Which of them would be taking the g and t's to the head of the Charles regatta?

"Sorry about the verdict," she managed finally.

"It wasn't unexpected," Larkin said. "The police let the victims wait in a room together while they did the lineups, and after each one finished, she'd go back into the room with the others. Who knows what they talked about? It's no wonder they all picked him out. Besides, the clearest thing most of them remembered about him was the Old Spice. None of them really got a good look at his face."

"I read you're going to appeal."

"Sure." He nodded at Steiner. "I've just been talking that over with David." *David?* Sybylla thought. Who's David? "I'll be doing mainly appeal work here. That's my primary interest." He gave a curiously elated sigh. "It's just so great to be working with actual people for a change. I was so buried in contracts at Chase, Twichell and Banks, I'm not sure I ever laid eyes on a flesh-and-blood client the whole time I was there."

Sybylla sat up in her chair. Young Mr. Larkin was slipping from unlikely to downright dubious. "You left Chase, Twichell and Banks? To come *here?*"

Larkin chuckled. "You sound like my dad."

Steiner took a gulp of his coffee. "No, she sounds like her own dad."

"Yeah." Larkin turned to her. "I'd had enough. I'd been asking for a pro bono case for years. I kept having to explain to the powers that be what pro bono *meant*. They'd never had an associate who wanted to do such a thing. Besides"—he shrugged—"what's a seventy percent pay cut compared to a clear conscience?"

"Well, we do have to work to keep them clear, you know," Sybylla warned. "Just wait till you defend your first child molester."

Steiner threw back his head and laughed. "We can always count on Sybylla for the wider perspective. She was raised to argue both sides of anything. Besides, she's our poster girl these days. Her client—"

"I know," Larkin said, turning to her with enthusiasm. "I hope you'll let me help you," he said eagerly. Then he added quickly, "Not that you'll need help, of course. But if it should go to appeal . . . Not," he stammered, "that I'm assuming he won't be acquitted, but . . ."

"Much obliged for the offer," she told him, oddly put out by his eagerness to assist, "but I'm sure you'll have plenty of your own cases to sweat over. Our boy David is a tough taskmaster." Sybylla got to her feet. "I've got to be in court."

"We'd hoped you could join us for lunch," Larkin said, standing up.

"We did?" Steiner said under his breath. He raised an eyebrow.

Sybylla turned to Larkin. "Listen," she said. "About your client, quite apart from whether he committed the crimes or not, I personally feel that *any* man who wears Old Spice deserves incarceration."

"That's a couple hundred thousand in this city alone." Larkin grinned.

Out of the corner of her eye, Sybylla saw Steiner watching them.

"What about you?" she said. "Do you wear that stuff?"

In a kind of slow motion, Larkin leaned forward, closing the space between them until they were on the cusp of an intimate posture. Then he gave her a grin that, despite every ounce of good sense in her body, shot straight to the palms of her hands. "Not anymore," he said.

CHAPTER

EIGHT

The Hyperion Club was an establishment so successfully hidden that one might have lived next door to it and still been unaware of its existence. The club's members were indeed lofty, but theirs was not the limousines and paparazzi brand of celebrity. There was no canopy, no doorman, not even a sign announcing the club's existence to the wider world. There was merely a small brass square with the number 25 etched deeply into it, and the square was not even highly polished, as if to shun even that degree of self-advertisement.

The building, a handsome limestone mansion half a block from the eastern edge of Central Park, had once belonged to a coal baron who sold his business early and moved on to less messy—if not less dirty— fields of endeavor. He had died at an advanced age early in this century, estranged from his children and grandchildren, and had left the house, along with an endowment sufficient to keep it in the manner to which it was accustomed, to the club he'd founded with his friends, a club dedicated to the idea that business and power thrive in an environment free of failure. Members of the club had attained the absolute heights in their fields; in the cool marble rooms of the Hyperion, they met as equals.

Dermot Muldoon, nursing his heavy tumbler of seltzer by the mansion's front study window, was content to let the buzzings and murmurings around him recede into gibberish. He had been in Washington all morning defending virtually every significant legal stance he had ever assumed while a mock panel of the President's advisers frowned and wrote notes to one another, then enduring a congressional walkabout bizarrely termed "informal" by the minder assigned to him. He had done well, he knew—not from the approbation of those who were vetting him, nor even from the encouragement of those associates well enough connected to know what was happening, but from the fact that he had detected in himself a strange detachment from the entire process, and that detachment was keeping him sharp. It would not do to be seen to want this too badly, he thought.

But Dermot did want it. He longed for it. Though his supporters would carefully cast his longing as that of a devoted public servant, merely seeking a higher level of servitude, and though his inevitable detractors would happily cast it as a reach for personal glory, Dermot himself understood his desire with far greater clarity. He understood, for example, that reaching this goal would mean there were no further goals to reach, which meant, accordingly, that he could dismiss from his life the ambition that had caused him such agony and brought him such terrible grief. What would it be like to live without that? he mused, rotating the tumbler slightly and watching the small bubbles break against its inner surface. What would it be like to wake in the morning without that burden, and to sleep without it? He conceived, first, a giddiness—the kind of elation he had known only once, years ago, during the first months of his marriage, before things had turned so unbearably sour—then, when the elation had passed, he imagined a kind of clear-sighted calm, filling him and steadying him and letting him focus utterly on the law.

He sighed and turned to the window, idly watching the bundled and faceless pedestrians making their way along the dark street. He was exhausted, and he thought with intense yearning of the small room upstairs where the club's valet had already unpacked his suitcase, but the day's most difficult task had not taken place in that nondescript meeting room at the White House, nor in some senator's inner sanctum; it lay directly before him and in the unsuspecting approach of his most formidable critic.

Looking further into the evening gloom, Dermot found that he was able to pick his daughter out of a small cluster of approaching pedestrians—not by her height, which she had inherited from her mother, nor by the deep red of her hair, which she had inherited from him, but by the impatient bounce in her stride, a thoughtless rhythm that nonetheless signaled to those beside and even before her that it made more sense to avoid the person it belonged to than to challenge her aggression; before his eyes, the little group did indeed make way for her to move ahead of them, and as she passed below the lit awning of the restaurant opposite the mansion, he saw and could not help but smile at the grim and oblivious set to her jaw. He also saw the bandaged right hand that swung like a white flag at her hip, and he felt his smile fade.

If only it *was* a white flag, he thought. If only she would finally surrender the nonsensical idea that her brilliance and legal talents could find no better outlet than this dubious one in the public defender's office. If only the injured hand—Dermot did not have to be told that it had been acquired in the line of duty—could prove the final straw to break her resolve. She would have no trouble finding a place to practice, even without Dermot's help, and with a few phone calls from him, he could easily set her up in some of the best law firms in the city. It would be so easy, he thought, feeling the fantasy slip its bonds and take flight; she would have a clean, spacious office, a solicitous support staff, a salary commensurate with her considerable abilities, and, most important, the kind of professional visibility Dermot knew she would thrive in. And if she wanted to hang out a shingle of her own, which was hardly Dermot's ideal, although still immeasurably preferable to her current setup, he was ready, able, and more than willing to write her a check and get her started. If only she would *listen* to him.

He shook his head. Even in his worst moments, when he was so fed up with her that he forgot how relentlessly he had urged her to study law in the first place and wished she had chosen just about any other trade to ply, Dermot had to admit that he need look no further than himself to find the source of his daughter's stubbornness. She got it from him, plain and simple, part of a package deal with that hair, the pale skin, the tendency to fidget, the love of a good fight. He remembered, clear as a bell, the day he had coaxed her down from Yale for what he had anticipated as a celebratory and noncombative lunch at Arcadia, over which they could consider the lengthy list of blue-chip firms he had sent her as a guide. Instead, she had waited only until the maître d' withdrew to announce that she wouldn't be needing his list. She had sent out one resumé and one resumé only, to the Legal Aid Society of New York, and guess what? They'd offered her a job.

He had looked past her then, a little light-headed, a little lost, and his eye traveled down the long line of lunching ladies, artfully arranged along the banquette in the narrow dining room of the restaurant. She was beautiful, too, his daughter—even at that moment, her head cocked a little and her jaw braced against the outraged response she anticipated. He felt the outrage, certainly, but just then its expression eluded him, and all he could give her was disappointment and fatigue. He had been overwhelmed by a vision of her as a brilliant attorney who might become a judge or a senator or even more; now he saw her meeting in grubby rooms with grubby, dangerous clients who were barely articulate enough to whine about their fraudulent innocence—frightening, worthless people on whose behalf his daughter's intellectual gifts would be wielded. He knew that she would be good at it, too. And he knew something else. Sybylla, flushed with the importance of standing between a crime and its punishment, and able sometimes to avert that punishment, would be seduced by the power it implied. She wouldn't try the job for a year, then burn out and move on as public defenders frequently did. She would love it. She would stay forever. He shook his head, feeling the physical wound her announcement had inflicted. He couldn't shout. Later, they would scream and row, but on that winter day, he could only shake his head at her and mutter, "What a waste."

And it all happened as he had predicted in that instant. She had declined his offer of a nice apartment in a doorman building and moved into her little hole-in-the-wall on the Upper West Side. She rode the subway to work, dressed well enough for court, but not well by any real standards, and worked herself to shreds for rapists, muggers, and crackheads. She was on a treadmill in that miserable, depressing office downtown, racking up the miles but getting nowhere, and it made him sick to think of the pride she took in her work.

Not now, he told himself, watching her make her way up the street, stopping to peer at the number over each brownstone door. Even with the rage she inspired in him, Dermot could not look at his daughter without feeling the surge of love in his chest. He had once read that humans were tied to their bodies by a kind of silver cord that severs only in death, but Dermot could not help but feel that he was tied to Sybylla's body, not his own; she was his, and he was tied to her. Like one of those undeserving losers she got out of trouble, who then took their first opportunity to get back in, he was caught in a recidivism of paternal love. Parenthood, he reflected now, getting to his feet and preparing himself to meet her in the entryway, was the ultimate revolving door.

He waved away the servant who had left his post to respond to the doorbell and let her in himself, enjoying the brief moment of surprise that crossed her features when she first saw him. Dermot looked her up and down, taking in her rumpled clothing and haggard complexion with something akin to disapproval and just short of disbelief. "You look dreadful," he told her.

Sybylla kissed him. "Thank you, Daddy." Then she stepped around her father and moved into the central hallway, looking around with wide eyes. Sybylla had known for years that Dermot belonged to a private club where he stayed whenever he was in town (shockingly preferring this to the offer of her own foldout couch), but her father had told her little about the place. Her impression of such an establishment, accordingly, owed more to Arthur Conan Doyle and P. G. Wodehouse than to any actual experience.

It was undeniably chilly here, though whether that was due to the bare marble floor, to the hall's absence of any seating, or to the indistinct creepiness that seemed to surround her, she couldn't have said. To her right, a vast circular stairway began its coil upward past portraits of vaguely Edwardian-looking men and into the dimly lit heights of the second story. Such was this feature's dominance of the hall that it left only one of the walls—the one behind Sybylla—unclaimed, and that wall was lit by two beams, a warm light of illumination and a cool blue laser of warning. Instinctively, she turned in the direction she had come, expecting some extraordinary jewel or masterpiece, but, to her disappointment, she saw that the painting so honored by this protective glare was not one she recognized. It was perhaps five feet in length, a darkly romantic portrait of a stormy evening in a country field, with a group of figures clustered together. She stepped closer, frowning.

The figure at the painting's center lay dead, with one arm flung to his side and the other resting on his chest, his head thrown back against the cold ground. The cause of his woes was not mysterious; over him, the murderer still crouched, looking solemn but satisfied with his work and holding a long stiletto in his right fist. Nearby stood three strange ladies with expressions ranging from grim stoicism to bald horror. They were variously dressed in gowns or diaphanous slips, and while one had a kind of Pre-Raphaelite beauty, another wore a twisted expression and seemed to have coiling live snakes for hair. The ladies stood tightly together, and though their mouths were closed in silence, one sensed the shrieks of outrage that lurked in their throats. The more she looked, the more Sybylla became aware that her own throat was closed in distaste, and her face locked into a grimace.

"What?" she heard her father say.

"It's so . . ." Her thought petered out. Unpleasant? Distasteful? "It's kind of awful, isn't it?" She leaned close to peer at the bronze plate that presumably bore the artist's name: A. Böcklin, DIE FURIEN.

"His crime?" Dermot said, stepping beside her.

"Hm?" Her eyes returned to the murder victim, the man leaning over him. She hadn't meant that. "No, the ladies—are they sisters or something?"

"Something like that. I'm not as up on my Greek mythology as I ought to be. They're Furies."

"Fairies?" She wasn't sure she'd heard him correctly.

Dermot shook his head. "No, Furies. They pursue the criminal, or something of that nature. They're waiting for him to finish, you see?"

Sybylla looked again. He was right. The ladies were holding themselves in check, waiting until the murderer had finished. "What will they do to him when he's done? Kill him?"

"Hound him, I believe," he said distractedly. "Shall we go into the dining room?"

"It's really pretty dreadful, isn't it?" She somehow couldn't take her eyes off the thing: the storm-whipped trees, the blowing high grass, the emaciated lady's snake-filled hair.

"I've never given it much thought." He reached for her arm. "Come on. I've ordered dinner for us." Then, without warning, he looked down and took her bandaged hand gingerly in his own. "Do I want to know about this?"

"Oh, I really don't think so." Sybylla smiled.

"What about the other one?" He was eyeing the smeared ink on her good hand. "You might want to wash this one."

Sybylla shrugged. "No point. It's indelible. Hey," she said, taking in his sour expression. "Don't give me that. I've been working my tail off. It's a busy season for us."

Her father sighed. "They all seem to be busy seasons for your clientele." He set his jaw. "All right. You look like someone from the street, anyway. You might as well be filthy."

"Gee," she said. "You're in a good mood."

"I want to talk to you. Come on."

He led her to the far end of the hall and pushed back one of the heavy mahogany doors for her. This opened onto a grand salon with high windows overlooking an immaculate private garden. The room was carpeted with an important-looking rug and crowded with ancient sofas and armchairs, most of them filled with men talking in small hushed groups. The formidable stone fireplace housed an impressive fire, beside which a servant stood with a long poker, gently prodding a log into place.

As she entered the room and began the long journey along its length toward an adjacent dining area, Sybylla heard the unmistakable sound of conversations being abruptly suspended. Heads slowly turned to follow her progress, and the tinkle of ice in crystal filled the silences. Dermot, walking behind her, muttered and nodded curt hellos, but she was not introduced to any of the men who watched her. As she walked, she grew uncomfortably aware of the wrinkles in her clothing, the grimy aftermath that her day in the trenches had left on her skin, the wisps of her red hair out of place. Back at the door they had entered, conversation began again, following slowly in her wake like a wave, until it lapped at her heels. Sybylla and Dermot entered the dining room, nearly equal in size to the salon, but even gloomier in decor. The only visible waiter gestured at the corner table and arrived there quickly enough to pull back Sybylla's chair with the unmistakable awkwardness of someone unused to seating women. There were no menus.

"Jesus," Sybylla said. "They act like they've never seen a woman before. Don't people bring their wives at least?"

He shrugged. "Occasionally. I suppose."

"All those white men," she mused. "I didn't think places like this existed anymore."

"Why do you say that? This city is full of clubs. There are two or three within a block of here."

"Yeah, but . . . just look at them." She gave him a sour grin. "No coons, no spics, no yids, no chinks. No broads, of course. Though obviously they've let in a mick or two."

He looked absently past her. "I wouldn't know about that sort of thing."

"Why wouldn't you?" she said seriously. "Don't you have a membership list?"

"Sybylla," he said curtly, "this is a private club, protected by the Constitution under the right to free assembly. It does not have to answer to you or to anyone else who is not a member. Criteria for membership is a private matter and does not concern you."

"Hey!" She sat back. "I was only making an observation. A good attorney is always observant. Didn't you teach me that?"

"A good attorney also knows when to shut her mouth and listen," he snapped.

Sybylla stared at him. Somewhere in the short space of time since her arrival, this corner had been turned, but she had missed it. She had not thought to anticipate anything more than the pleasure of a rare evening with him, and perhaps an illicit foray into the kind of legal debate she allowed herself only in his company. It was a relief, after all, to argue the law Dermot's way, with issues removed and elevated from their human faces and thus somehow relieved of the pain they symbolized. She and her colleagues seldom had time to discourse on such lofty levels of jurisprudence—they were too busy trying to get someone out of jail in time to collect her kids from the welfare office before foster care got hold of them—and Sybylla, almost despite herself, always found the cadence of intellectual argument to be insidiously enjoyable. Trouble was, with her father at least, such debates had a way of segueing into loud condemnations of the choice she had made, and woeful declarations that her so-called brilliant legal mind should be breathing such rarefied air on a regular basis.

The waiter came and deposited two plates of pâté before them. Dermot, his eyes locked on his daughter's face, waited until he retreated before speaking again.

"In all these years you've been wasting your life down at Legal Aid, I've never hidden my disapproval from you. But—and I hope you'll agree that this is to my credit—I've never asked you outright to leave."

"So that's what this is all about." She smiled, almost relieved. "You're finally coming out with it."

He shook his head, impatient. "Don't talk. *Listen.* I am not asking you to leave Legal Aid. I am asking you to remove yourself from one particular case. I am asking you to let another Legal Aid lawyer represent one particular client. I am asking you, for once, just to let somebody else handle it. You've got an endless number of criminals and psychos; you can nurture them to your heart's content. Just not this one, anymore."

"You're talking about Trent," she said, getting it at last.

"I am. Just one out of the whole city. Let it go."

Sybylla tasted her pâté, an undistinguished concoction.

"But why? I don't understand."

"Do you need to understand everything? Do you have to know everything?"

"Listen, Daddy"—she shook her head—"I don't know who's been talking to you, but it can't have been Trent's doctor. They're calling him a textbook schizophrenic. He's not going to trial, so I'm not going to be doing any of the pontificating you're worried about. This case is going the way of the saber-toothed tiger, believe me."

"You don't know that," he said tightly. "They might . . . I don't know, fix him up enough to stand trial. I don't want you mixed up in it."

"Well, if that did happen," Sybylla told him, furious, "then of course I'd do my very best to ensure Trent received a fair trial. Hey"—she stabbed a bit viciously at her pâté—"I don't particularly want him back on the street myself."

"Well, let someone else get him a fair trial. You're a very capable attorney, Sybylla, but you're not the only one in the world who can accomplish that particular task."

"No," she said simply. The waiter was hovering. Sybylla handed him her plate without taking her eyes from her father's face.

"*Why?*"

"He's my client. It's my job to defend him. And you haven't given me a good enough reason to abdicate that responsibility."

Dermot leaned forward, his hands folded in the space before him. "Sybylla," he said. His voice was so suddenly soft and almost tearful that she felt unaccountably chastised. "Sybylla, will you trust me?"

Would she trust him? Of course, why wouldn't she? But trust him with what? Her life, certainly, but not her career. That, he had shown himself far from protective of.

"Daddy." She sighed. "I just want to understand. What is this all about?"

A hand reached before her. She sat back, instinctively expecting a plate to appear, but when it didn't, she looked up into the light. High above her, looking down with an unmistakably paternal expression, was a tall and narrow man with closely cropped silver hair and a thin mouth turned up at the corners in an odd facsimile of a smile—though there was nothing of pleasure in his manner. He was expensively maintained and expensively clothed in the kind of utterly correct suit that could be produced only on one particular street in one particular neighborhood of one particular English city, and he stood very still in a posture that only the most self-assured of privileged men can manage to bring off without seeming awkward.

Sybylla stared at him for an instant past the outer boundary of good manners, but the man never budged. She felt as if he was waiting for her to speak, as if he knew her and expected her to know him, though she felt certain she had never seen anything quite like him before. Even so, the voice that broke the silence at last belonged to her, and it said something so odd that the man's strange smile extended itself to reveal white glittering teeth. What it said was, "You must be . . ."

But whatever the name was of whoever he must have been got somehow lost between her brain and her vocal cords. He laughed shortly at her confusion, then leaned slightly forward in a parody of chivalric gentility. "I must be Robert Winston," he said.

CHAPTER

NINE

———

"**S**ybylla," her father said, somewhat redundantly, "this is Robert Winston, an old friend." She caught the discomfort in his voice as he added, "From law school."

"Ah," she said, looking up at the tall man. "Yes, of course I remember."

This only made Winston's strange smile deepen further. "Yes, of course you remember?" he said with a mocking edge. "I should infer, then, that you've been hearing of me for years?"

It was said so smugly, so secure in the knowledge of her white lie. She found herself unable to let it go.

"Why shouldn't I?" she asked him.

"Sybylla," Dermot said tersely, "for God's sake, don't cross-examine."

"Last time I saw you, I think . . . yes"—he actually appeared to consider—"I'm sure you were in diapers."

Wonderful, she thought, feeling herself begin to regress instantly. What was there left to say to an authority figure who had seen you in a precontinent state?

"Well, I've made some progress in that area," she commented, and the tall man laughed.

"I'm happy to hear it. May I join you?" He was already pulling up a chair. Sybylla, glancing at her father, saw an unmistakable flash of annoyance. No, more than annoyance, she thought. Dermot was wary, almost fearful. But he held his tongue.

The tall man settled his long body into a chair. "I'll only stay a moment," he told Dermot, though his eyes never left Sybylla's face. "It's so good to see you again, my dear. You've turned out very much like your mother, and she was also lovely."

"*Robert.*" Dermot's voice was soft but shot with steel.

Self-consciously, Sybylla picked up her fork and pressed it into her ink-stained palm. She had not met many people who had known her mother, and she wasn't sure how to act around them. "I don't remember my mother," she finally said.

"No?"

"No." She glanced at Dermot. "She died when I was born, you see."

There was a moment of silence, discernibly strained. Then, somewhat inappropriately, Robert Winston smiled. "Yes. I do see."

Sybylla frowned. "Do you practice law in New York?" she asked.

Winston looked at her. "I do not practice law. I have perfected law."

Her father turned to Sybylla. "Mr. Winston is a trial consultant. His company undertakes studies on jury selection, presentation impact, witness preparation, that sort of thing."

"Oh yes," Sybylla said. "I've heard about this. You're the people who tell the attorney what suit to wear, is that it?"

He looked at her for a long, elastic moment. She could almost see him decide to let it pass. "Yes, in a manner of speaking. But more importantly, we keep track of the trends. What's happening with juries, what they're responding to. Whether they are becoming more stringent or more lenient. What tactics are proving most effective. What modes of presentation are having the greatest impact."

Sybylla smiled. "And naturally, you provide this information to all attorneys equally, sort of as a public service."

"Naturally, not. We are an entrepreneurial endeavor, in a country that professes to value the entrepreneur. Our service is available to those attorneys who purchase it."

"Mostly defense attorneys, I take it?"

He turned his full array of shining white teeth to her. "You'd be surprised."

The waiter returned, setting down two small plates of elderly endive, speckled with shredded carrot. Whatever its claim to fame, she reflected, the Hyperion Club could not boast any culinary distinction.

"Would you like wine?" Winston asked as the waiter lingered. For someone only staying a minute, she thought, he seemed to have assumed a host's demeanor. It was bugging her father, she knew, but Sybylla *did* want wine, and she said so. The man signaled with the flick of one elongated wrist.

"Tell me about you, Sybylla," Robert Winston said when the waiter had gone.

Sybylla, looking up, met her father's gaze. "I'm sorry, what about me?"

"Tell me about your work," he said. "I understand you're a public defender."

Dermot leaned forward. "Sybylla and I have a sort of pact not to discuss her job," he said with strained humor. "It has an unfortunate effect on my blood pressure."

Winston smiled genially. "Well, my blood pressure is extremely good. And I *would* like to hear about Sybylla's work."

Dermot sat back in his chair.

"How long have you worked in the public defender's office, Sybylla?"

She glanced at her father. He stared stonily at his depressing salad. "Five years now."

"And how long do you expect to stay?"

"I have no plans to leave. I enjoy my work."

"Do you?" He shook his head. "How odd. I would think a year or two of that kind of proximity to that kind of criminal would be enough for anyone to take."

"Everyone deserves a defense." She shrugged. "It might as well be a good defense."

"Oh?" Winston cocked his head, as if genuinely curious. "Why?"

"Why what? Why does he deserve a good defense?"

"Why does he deserve a defense?"

For a moment, she was speechless.

"Well, for one thing, because our Constitution says so."

"I believe there is a mention of a right to life in the Declaration of Independence. Does that mean the government has a responsibility to provide its citizens with an alternative to mortality?"

"Don't be ridiculous."

"I am not ridiculous," Robert Winston said. "I am merely pointing out that, like anything else, the Constitution can be manipulated in inappropriate ways. It is an interpretation to say, for example, that each and every rapist or murderer deserves an advocate equal in quality to that of the state."

"You question this?" Sybylla said calmly, spearing a sad bit of tomato. "How old-fashioned of you."

"No, my dear," said Winston. "I suggest that it is you who are old-fashioned. Our society has grown weary of the trends of the last quarter century, the relentless expansion of rights for the accused. In themselves, such rights might not be so offensive, but each and every one of them has come at the expense of the rights of victims. It's a state of affairs that I and many like me find reprehensible."

She looked happily at the Chablis being poured into her glass by the waiter. "The rules have to be there for everyone or for no one at all. If you're going to throw away one person's rights, you'd better be ready to toss your own."

Winston considered his own wineglass, swirling the chilly pale liquid. "In principle, I might almost agree with you, but crime does not exist on a conceptual level. It has a human face."

"You might find this difficult to believe"—she turned in her chair to face him—"but the accused has a human face, too. And sometimes we— by which I mean, the publicly appointed counsel—turn out to be the first people in the defendants' lives who are actually willing to stand behind them and fight for them."

He smiled. "But isn't that, in itself, supremely ironic? When people contribute to our society, society only takes from them. When people take from our society, society only gives to them. A street person does not pay taxes, but we give him medical care, shelter, food, education, job training. Not to mention the benefit of your own very expensive education. Tell me, what incentive is there in a system like that?"

"Poverty's not a crime, you know." She smiled darkly. "At least not yet."

"No," Winston agreed. "But in a society that meets basic needs of housing, medical care, and education, perhaps those who live in poverty should begin to share some responsibility for their situation. At some point, people make the decision to live the way they want to live. In the meantime, we all live with the consequences."

She stared at him. It had been a long time since she'd met one of this breed.

"So when we find people who have made the decision to live violently, and to visit their violence upon innocent victims, should we not remove them from our midst? I'm not even speaking about capital punishment now. I am merely speaking of removal. I am speaking of separating these criminals from their future victims."

"Well, we can't punish someone for crimes they might commit in the future. If we did that, we'd all be in jail. We're all capable of murder, you know."

Winston smiled paternally. It was chilling. "Not you, my dear. You couldn't kill. Not if your life depended on it."

It sounded like the worst insult imaginable.

"You know, I'm just as much for a safe, nonviolent society as the next guy." A nasty edge had crept into Sybylla's voice. "But there's the little matter of the Bill of Rights. It's a shame our founding fathers had to get so righteous about protecting us from malicious or irresponsible prosecution."

"It is, actually, a shame, you know. Not in principle, of course. But somewhere over the past two hundred years, some of those shining proclamations have undergone a bit of a sea change. They're like one long game of telephone down through the years, where the first person in the line whispers something admirable like 'The police can't just bust into your home because they feel like it,' and two centuries later it comes out as 'Even if the police know you did the crime, even if you run away from them with blood dripping from the knife in your hand, even if the smell of a cellarful of decaying bodies assails their nostrils as they stand on your front step, they can't go in without a proper warrant to search for a specific item.' It's the law, of course. It's the distant descendant of what the Constitution intended. But is it right?" He considered his wine. "It isn't even *about* justice anymore, you know. It's only about what a jury can be made to accept."

Despite herself, Sybylla spoke up. "But that's as it should be. Any other standard lends itself too readily to false accusation and false imprisonment."

"Yes." Winston was thoughtful. "That's your nightmare, isn't it? The innocent man?"

Sybylla tried for levity. "We're all innocent when we're born."

"Tell me. Your client of the moment, this man who stabbed the child—is *he* innocent?"

Sybylla looked at him squarely. "It's not for me to say," she told him. "I do know that this man was never violent in the past. His friend says he disappeared a few months ago, and this is how he has surfaced again. No one understands it."

"What has he said to you?" Winston asked.

Instinctively, she covered her injured hand. "You know I can't talk about that, Mr. Winston. Surely you concede the importance of attorney-client privilege."

He reached for the bottle and refilled her glass. "You'll try for insanity, I take it?"

"Frankly, I doubt the case will ever come to trial," she said shortly, wanting to terminate the subject.

"But if it did come to trial," Winston pressed, brushing off the detail of Trent's utter madness, "would you plead insanity then?"

"It's a possibility." Her curtness was unmistakable.

Winston was looking at her with a queer kind of approbation. His benevolence, she couldn't help thinking, was almost as disturbing as his disapproval. "She's a tough one, Dermot," he observed, narrowing his eyes as if he were evaluating horseflesh. "She's yours, all right."

Sybylla, who had almost forgotten her father entirely in the heat of her exchange with his friend, now turned to look at him. Dermot was staring at his untouched salad. Presently, an arm appeared to take the rejected endive away.

"And how are you holding up, my friend? How are you weathering all this excitement?"

Sybylla pricked up her ears. "Excitement?"

Winston grinned. "But surely you're celebrating."

"No." Dermot was abrupt.

"No," Sybylla agreed. "But should we be?"

"You mean he hasn't told you?" Winston had found his rhythm. "No need for such modesty, my friend. It's a done deal, you know."

She looked at her father. "Daddy, what's happened?"

Dermot shrugged, uncomfortable but ultimately willing. "I had a call last week. This is confidential."

Sybylla nodded, tense.

"Byron Jennings Wofford is going to step down at the end of the current term."

It hit her like a truck. Wofford, long known to be in failing health, had always told the press that he would never retire. As a Supreme Court justice, that was his privilege, of course, but the past two years had seen a notable lapse in his effectiveness as a jurist. This information pointed in one direction only, but she still wanted to hear it from him.

"Well, well. Tell me more."

"I was merely asked if I would like to be considered for the job. I thought about it overnight and told them yes, I would. It will be announced in due course."

"Daddy." Sybylla shook her head, awestruck, still struggling to process the information and its tangled implications for her personal and professional lives. On one hand, Dermot's ascension to the Supreme Court would quite possibly result in major new hardships for her work. As the Court slithered to the right, there was a greater move toward widening the rules of evidence, since the public was frustrated when crimes weren't prosecuted because of procedural missteps—a badly worded search warrant or an irregular arrest—or were reversed on appeal for the same reasons. Such legal loopholes were a vital weapon in the arsenal of every public defender in the United States, and without them, Sybylla's acquittal rate was likely to drop significantly.

But then again, her father was going to be a Supreme Court justice. The thought of Dermot taking his place on the Court and assuming the role in legal history that he had devoted his life to seeking was an undeniable thrill. Despite their political disagreements, she knew that his allegiance to the law was no less fierce than her own: he was its scholar and its critic and its acolyte, all. Now he would shape law for the nation and the future.

She shook her head at him. "It's wonderful, Daddy. I'm happy for you."

Dermot swallowed his pleasure. "Well, let's not jump the gun. I still have to be confirmed, you know. The Senate being what it is, that's no mean feat."

"You'll do great." Sybylla grinned. "Oh, this is fantastic. You *were* going to tell me, weren't you?"

"I was." He glanced at Winston, who was getting to his feet, finally prepared to leave them. "Just not necessarily tonight."

"Well," his friend said, stepping behind his chair, "I'd better move along. I don't want to intrude upon the celebration, after all, and I see my dinner guest is here. My dear"—he leaned down to Sybylla—"I cannot tell you how pleased this has made me. Good luck with your very challenging case." He reached into his suit and extracted a blood-red lizard wallet. "Here is my card. Come out and visit us. I'll have one of the staff give you a tour, and he can answer all your questions."

"Robert," Dermot hissed.

Sybylla looked at him. His face was pink with anger.

"Why shouldn't I?" Winston smiled. "You never know, she might even decide we're not so bad in the private sector, and I'm always looking for bright people. Now I must go." He turned again to Sybylla. "My dear, a pleasure to meet you properly."

"By which you mean, not in diapers," she observed.

"And looking so like your beautiful mother." His eyes lingered, a little disconcertingly, on her face. "Your Wild Man is fortunate indeed to have such a capable and devoted advocate. I certainly hope he appreciates you. I hope, to put it another way, that he is not so ungrateful as to, for example, bite the hand that assists him." Numbly, from the corner of her eye, Sybylla watched her father turn his head to stare at her. The bandaged hand was in her lap. Pointlessly, she covered it with her napkin, then swallowed. "Good-bye, then. Dermot." He nodded. Then he turned and moved swiftly away.

Intent on avoiding her father's gaze, Sybylla found herself studying Winston's card as if it were the Rosetta stone itself. In fact, it was very nearly as interesting.

"Daddy," she said, taken aback. "This is right in our neighborhood."

Silence from across the table.

"Look at this." She extended the card, as if its wonders could deflect what was coming. "Legal Research Associates. It's on Seneca Road in Great Falls. It can't be more than a mile from our house."

Sybylla filled the ensuing silence with a large gulp of wine, then tried another parry.

"What a creepy guy!" Her stage whisper had an edge of forced joviality. "Sometimes I forget you have such unlikable friends."

Across the tundra of their table, Dermot exhaled. "Not a friend."

"Oh no? You called him a friend."

"Not a friend. He . . . A long time ago, he did something for me. I haven't forgotten. That's all."

"That's *all?*" She pressed her advantage. "What do you mean? What kind of something? Like an 'I know just the guy for your vacant seat on the bench' kind of something?"

Vehemently, Dermot shook his head. "I will not do this, Sybylla. We're not here to talk about my career."

"Oh." She nodded with exaggerated comprehension. "That's right. I remember now. We're here to talk about *my* career. Well, how nice, for a change of pace. But why tonight, if you don't mind my asking?"

"Why *tonight?*" Dermot reached across the table and grabbed her bandaged hand. "Look at this!" he hissed, turning the wrist, showing her the gauze she had put there herself. "Look what that bastard did to you! And you knock yourself out for him. You can't find another way to be compassionate? You're willing to sacrifice your whole career for the monster who gave you this to remember him by?"

"What do you mean, 'sacrifice my career'? Daddy, I hate to break it to you, but this *is* my career. I *am* a Legal Aid lawyer. This is what I *do.*" She sat up in her chair. "Look, I accept that you're never going to be happy about it, but I'd just be really grateful if you could stop being so angry. It won't change anything, you know. It'll just make you more miserable."

"Not angry."

He spoke so suddenly softly that she couldn't make it out.

"What?"

"Not angry. I'm not angry." He let go of her hand. "I'm afraid."

It was unprecedented, and slowly it sank in. He had never, in all the time she'd known him, admitted fear to anyone, least of all to her. Dermot, the most contained, confident, and capable man she had ever known. Afraid.

She shook her head. "But why?"

"Listen to me. I am going to do something that's very difficult for me, and I want you to respect that. I am going to plead with you. Please, Sybylla. You may never do anything purely for me again, but please do this. Remove yourself from the Wild Man case. Let another lawyer represent him. You're playing with something you can't possibly understand."

Intrigued, even lulled by his supplication, Sybylla snapped to attention at this last remark. "What do you mean, I can't possibly understand?"

The waiter appeared. Two plates laden with chateaubriand were placed before them. She waited until he was gone.

"What's this all about?" she demanded. "Are you going to come clean with me or not? Because if you are, I'm all ears, but if not, I can't see the point of this discussion. So let's have it."

He shook his head tersely. "No. My plea should be enough. Take yourself off the case."

Suddenly, Sybylla went cold. "It's the nomination, isn't it?" she said abruptly. Dermot was silent, his face blank. "It's the nomination. You think my association with Trent will harm you in some way. That's it, isn't it? It's a smudge on your record," she spat, warming to her theme, "to have a daughter defending a psycho like Trent." She stared at him. "I don't believe this. I know you want it, Daddy. I mean, I know you've always wanted it, but don't you see how unethical it is to ask this?"

"Perhaps," he said tightly. "But I'm still asking."

Sybylla felt the muscles of her face clench tight with fury. If Dermot was truly worried about the stink rubbing off on his confirmation process, it was a worry she herself found decidedly excessive, since even people who didn't particularly like the results of her work acknowledged the need for public defenders. *Somebody* had to do it, after all, so why not the daughter of a Supreme Court justice? She couldn't imagine anyone in the Senate or even in the public at large holding a daughter's legal leanings against her vociferously conservative father. Could Dermot really be so insecure about his prospects?

The steak actually looked good, and its unexpectedly intoxicating smell made her suddenly, ravenously hungry, but she was now too furious to stay.

"I'm sorry you feel this way, Daddy. I truly wish I could accommodate you, but I am very deeply committed to the principles of my work, and, by extension, to Trent. I can't do it, and I wish you hadn't asked."

"I wish I hadn't *had* to ask," her father said, his soft voice belying the stiff glare he gave her.

Sybylla got to her feet. Dermot reached out for her hand, but she moved it beyond his grasp. "Sybylla, please."

"Good night, Daddy."

It was hard to make an assertive exit, distraught as she was. At the door to the dining room, she had to stop and steady herself for a moment. Then, turning, she allowed herself a quick glimpse of her father, who was still sitting at the table, looking fixedly down at his rapidly cooling steak. He did not meet her gaze, but past him, deep in a dim corner of the room, Sybylla found herself looking squarely into the eyes of Robert Winston and his dinner guest, the honorable district attorney for the County of New York, Mr. Andrew Greer.

CHAPTER

TEN

———∿∿———

Bellevue Hospital Center's phone system appeared to have evolved very little past cans and string. A few days after her disastrous encounter with Dermot, Sybylla sat in her office fossilizing into her uncomfortable chair as the incomprehensible network bounced her all over the hospital, occasionally dead-ending with a variety of faint, bored, or even disoriented voices—as if the patients themselves had seized control of the switchboard. "Bellevue Hospital, extension please?" the same tired woman said every now and then, and once there was a chirpy "Someone helping you?" and once a vaguely threatening "Yuh, Maintenance."

"Bellevue Hospital. Extension, please."

"Waiting for Dr. Turturro." She sighed. "*Been* waiting for some time."

"Dr. Turturro? Wait a minute."

Whyever not? she thought.

"You waiting for Turturro?" A different voice came on. "What's your name?"

Sybylla told her.

"Yeah, there's a message here. 'Please come this afternoon. Patient is asking for you.'"

"You're kidding. He's talking?"

"That's what it says." She sounded bored.

"Can I come now?" Sybylla asked.

The woman chuckled. "I don't care what you do." She hung up.

Sybylla put down the phone and gathered her things. "Patient is asking for you" implied something like organized thought, and Sybylla had rarely seen anyone as unlikely to experience organized thought as Trent in his current incarnation. The droning, raving man who had calmly bitten into her flesh seemed to her a consciousness irretrievably lost to some personal chaos. The truth was that she had given up hope for Trent as a person the minute she'd recognized him in the body of that madman on the nineteenth floor. Any action she had taken on his behalf since then, any statement she had made or strategy she had considered, was in aid of the principles his case represented—that he was someone to be helped, not blamed; that his ills were society's infection of the individual spirit; that his struggle signified a wider and more profound struggle. She had not believed the Trent she'd known in the past would ever return.

But now he was asking for her, whatever that meant. She left a note for Steiner and took the subway uptown.

Turturro was at the ward desk when she arrived, arguing heatedly with a Mr. Clean look-alike wearing a sagging Mets jacket. The man raised and lowered his fist for emphasis in a gesture that resembled a fishing rod being cast.

Sybylla elbowed in. "Um, got your message."

Turturro looked up. "Oh good, you're here."

"He's talking?"

"Oh yeah." He chuckled. "You could say so. C'mon."

Mr. Clean grabbed his arm. "Hey. I ain't leaving without her."

"Sir," Turturro said carefully, "I wish I could help you, but I can't. Your wife is here for observation and cannot be released without a court order."

"I ain't leaving." The man cast his fishing rod.

Turturro sighed. "That's fine." His voice was long-suffering. "Come on, Ms. Muldoon."

He slid his card into the security lock and the door clicked open. "Damnedest thing." Turturro shook his head as he walked. "Night orderly goes in to check on him about three this morning, Trent says to him, 'Would you call my lawyer please?' So polite. When I got in a few hours ago, he was sitting by the window in his room, looking a little woozy. He said he was feeling nauseated. *Nauseated* was the word he used."

Sybylla looked at him. "You're surprised."

He shook his head. "Well, a bit, to tell you the truth. Schizophrenics frequently have lucid periods, but I've personally never witnessed such a complete reversion from severe psychosis to apparent rationality in such a short time."

"So that's it? No more hallucinations? He's back to normal?"

"Well"—the tall man chuckled, guiding her to an adjacent hallway—"you know, we like to steer clear of concepts like 'normal.' Normal is a net cast pretty far and wide to a psychiatrist. But yeah, he seems pretty much on the mark. He knows who he is and he knows where he is. No more screaming, no more apparent terrors or violence."

"Does he know why he's here?"

"Not at all," Turturro said helpfully. "I thought I'd leave that to you."

Sybylla shook her head. If it was true, if Trent was suddenly capable of understanding the charges against him and helping her mount his defense, then the trial she'd so cavalierly discussed with her father and with Andrew Greer might actually take place. She had to bite her lip to keep from cursing aloud. It would be an unwinnable trial, too, since civil liberties were no match for disfigured little girls.

"I'd better get a copy of the intake report," she said, almost to herself.

"What's that?" He had stopped before one of the doors.

"Your intake report. I'd better have a look at it." She looked at him. "Might be a trial after all, you know."

"Oh. Sure." He slipped his card into the lock. "I'll leave a copy at the ward desk."

"I'll need to speak to him alone," Sybylla said.

He turned to glare at her. "You're kidding, right? After last time?" He glanced down at her hand; the gauze had given way to a Band-Aid.

"Attorney-client." She shrugged.

He shook his head and opened the door.

Sybylla squinted into the gloom and saw Trent, emaciated, seated cross-legged on his bed. Slowly, he turned his face to the doorway.

"Hey," he said. Then, forming the words, as if they belonged to a newly learned language: "Your hair's different."

Her hair? Automatically, she reached up to her shoulder and took a lock between two fingers. He was right. She'd clipped six inches since last summer.

"I cut it," she said, her head reeling.

"Looks nice," said Trent.

The pleasantries felt absurd. Trent was straitjacketed. "I got out," he said suddenly. "I don't know how I did, but I did. I got out of there."

"Out of where, Trent?" Automatically, she took a step toward him. Turturro's arm shot out to stop her.

"The place."

"What place?" Her heart was sinking a little. He might be calmer, but "the place" still sounded plenty paranoid.

"They took me to a place. *You men at ease.*"

"I . . . what?" She glanced at Turturro for help. He was watching Trent carefully.

"*You men at ease.* Everybody kept saying that. Then I got out, and I got on the train."

She shook her head, as if to dislodge her confusion. "You know who I am, right?"

"Sure." He nodded affably. "You're Sybylla. You're gonna get me out of here."

She turned to Turturro. "I don't think I'm in any danger here. And at this point, I think I really should be speaking to my client in private."

The tall man sighed, then shrugged his compliance.

"I'm fine," Sybylla told him, willing it to be true. "Look at him. He doesn't look strong enough to lift a finger, let alone throw off a straitjacket."

"I shouldn't be doing this." Turturro shook his head as he left.

Sybylla turned to her client, who watched her intently. Despite the fear Turturro had succeeded in instilling in her, despite her real interest in learning what Trent had to say, a baser element in Sybylla's character felt an undeniable thrill. She was alone with the Wild Man, perhaps the single-most-hated person in the greater New York area at the moment. She wanted to sit, to get her head down to his level, but the only seating the bare room offered was the other end of Trent's thin bed. She decided to remain on her feet.

"Dr. Turturro says you know where you are. Is that right?"

"Sure." He shrugged his thin shoulders under the heavy canvas. "I know where Bellevue is. I come to see Bennis here when his stomach got bad last year." He frowned at Sybylla. "They didn't keep him in no locked room, though. They didn't make him wear . . ." He gestured in mute frustration with his bound arms.

"Do you know why you're here?"

"I blacked out or something?"

"Maybe," she said carefully, turning over the idea in her head. "Maybe it was something like that. Do you remember meeting with me a couple weeks ago? Here at Bellevue?" And you made a meal of my hand, she silently added. Trent looked blank.

"Yeah?" He pursed his lips. "You sure?"

Sybylla's thoughts were racing on ahead. An insanity defense, based on the defendant's claim of memory lapse. Maybe she could find a shrink to diagnose multiple personality disorder—somebody famous, who'd written a few books. She'd put in a call to Dreyfus as soon as she got back to the office. The man was a thorough publicity hound and a bit of a quack, but he came across as sage and dignified on the stand and he delivered results; the year before, he'd helped her pull off an insanity defense for a woman who'd suffocated her newborn twins, by testifying that postpartum hormones had aggravated her latent schizophrenia. "Dreyfus," she wrote on her legal pad. "Be sure to tell him it's Wild Man." The good doctor could be counted on to provide the appropriate expertise.

"Trent," she said squarely, "as your attorney, I need to advise you that you've been indicted on a charge of first-degree assault. You're accused of attacking a little girl with a surgical knife."

He was staring at her, his dark eyes huge. "No," he said finally. "I didn't."

Sybylla nodded. In her line of work, denials were the norm. "All right. But you should know, four people told the police they witnessed this attack and identified you as the assailant. Also, a surgical knife with your fingerprints on it was found in your hand. And the clothing you were wearing had blood on it, which appears to have been the victim's."

"No." Trent shook his head. He seemed put out, offended that she would even suggest such a thing. "I didn't do that."

"Okay," Sybylla said. "We're going to enter a plea of not guilty. Do you understand?"

"Sure. That's right." He seemed dazed, but following. "I'm not guilty."

"So you don't remember anything at all about the attack?"

"I *told* you." He was frowning now, impatience in his voice.

"Well, what *do* you remember? What's the last thing you remember before you were here at Bellevue?"

Trent closed his eyes. He had the grim, gray complexion of a person who had never known entirely good health. Aged by life, acquainted with the night.

A spasm shook his thin shoulders. "Fucking cold," Trent said. "Fucking *freezing.*"

Sybylla, who felt very warm, shook her head. "You okay? Should I get you a blanket or something?"

"Not here!" he hissed. "Not here! Freezing, like the floor's ice or something. I told them. I said, 'You can't keep me here. I know my rights and you gotta take me back!'"

She sighed. All this paranoid raving would serve them well when Dreyfus came to interview Trent, but it wasn't getting them anywhere right now.

She decided to switch gears. "Something I want to ask you about," Sybylla said. "There was an incision under your arm." She lifted her own left elbow and pointed. "About here. They removed a little thing—little white disk. Any idea what it was?"

He shrugged, uninterested.

"Trent, have you been involved in any medical studies? You know, for a new drug or something?"

No response.

"Did anyone tell you they were going to put something under your skin? To make you feel better? For some medical problem you have?"

"Blood pressure," he said mildly, distracted. "I have high blood pressure. Nobody gave me anything, though. It wasn't that kind of hospital, you ask me."

"So you have no idea how you came to have this little disk under your arm?" Sybylla was disappointed. They seemed to have made no forward motion whatsoever, and she still had no real idea what had happened to him. "You're going to have to give me a little more help, Trent. You were missing for nearly three months, and then you come back with a scalpel in your hand. What happened to you? You can tell me, you know. I'm your lawyer. It's against the law for me to tell anybody what you say."

He was shaking his head violently. "Better if I don't tell you nothing."

"Better for whom?" she said, exasperated. "I don't know how you can expect me to defend you at trial if you won't tell me what happened."

He sat up, suddenly ramrod-straight inside the canvas restraints. "Trial?"

"Sure. I don't think the DA's interested in offering a plea." Not with a gubernatorial campaign to be launched, she thought.

"I get a trial?" He was entranced. He leaned toward her. "Sybylla," he said, his voice barely a whisper.

"Yes?"

"I'm going to tell. I'm going to say what happened."

"About the little girl?"

Trent's eyes widened. "I don't know about any little girl. I can't say anything about that. But I'm going to tell about the people. They put me in a van. I didn't want to go. I said I didn't want to go to the shelter. I like my squat. I like the bridge, but they didn't listen. They threw me in."

"You mean you've been in a shelter?" Her head swam. "All this time? What shelter?"

"I had my own room." He nodded up at his ceiling. "Like this."

"A room like this? A hospital room?"

"You men at ease," he said simply.

"I . . ." She was lost. "Trent? Was it an army hospital?"

"All these people screaming," he went on, oblivious.

"Listen to me, Trent." Sybylla snapped open her briefcase and shoved in her woefully sparse notes. "I don't know what you think you're going to say at your trial, but I can tell you right now that if it doesn't have to do with the crime you're accused of committing, it'll do you more harm than good. And we're talking major harm here, Trent. Like many years of hard-time harm. So if you have something to say, you'd better say it to me right now."

The gaze lifted to meet her own: sunken eyes with dark folds beneath them, a small mouth with inelegant teeth barely visible. Sybylla saw the conviction in his expression. He knew something. He had something to say.

"Will you at least tell me what your testimony will be? So I can prepare my questions and give us the best-possible chance of a good outcome?"

He shook his head, heavy with solemnity. "I can't do that. If they thought you knew about them . . ."

"What? If they thought I knew *what?*" The paranoia was beginning to piss her off.

"You just fix it so I can talk on the stand. If you say it under oath, they have to believe you, don't they?"

She almost smiled. If only that were true.

"I want to leave," Trent snapped, changing tack abruptly.

Sybylla shook her head. "No. I don't think it's reasonable to expect that."

"I want to leave!" he shouted. "You get me out."

You get me out. How many times since becoming a public defender had that phrase assailed her ears? As a plea or as a warning; it was hard to say which she liked less or which troubled her more. Clients who couldn't make bail, calling collect from Rikers, inmates from upstate, using their spare time to let her know they were still incarcerated and considered her solely responsible for that fact. *You get me out.* As if she could. As if she, their advocate, had metamorphosed into their jailer.

"Trent, I can't. But I can work with you so that we can make the most of our chances at trial. I wish you would let me advise you. That's what I'm here for."

"I want to get out of here!" he screamed, and instinctively Sybylla stepped back.

"Listen to me, Trent," she said, her voice firm. "I'm not going to lie to you. We're in some serious trouble here. I'm going to do what I can, but you have to work with me and you have to trust me. Can you do that?"

After a moment, he nodded.

"Now I'm going to send another doctor to see you. I want you to co-operate with him whatever he tells you to do." She got to her feet. "You should have a court appearance soon, to set a trial date. They'll take you downtown and we'll have a chance to talk then."

Silence. She turned to leave. As she reached the door, he suddenly spoke her name, and Sybylla stopped. He looked pitiful, abandoned and hopeless on the bed, his small body awash in the straitjacket, as if someone had vastly overestimated his power, and she had to listen intently to make sense of what he was saying, his queer but oddly mesmerizing chant of dejection: *You men at ease, you men at ease.*

CHAPTER

ELEVEN

T rent's performance on his second 730 exam a few days later showed a considerable improvement over his first. This time, he not only correctly identified the President of the country but also the mayor of the city. He had even met the mayor once, Trent explained soberly to the two shrinks who questioned him. Back a few years, when the man had hoped to launch a new shelter program and had taken a TV crew on a photo-op tour of the shantytowns. No extra points were given.

By the time the shrinks got around to the legal stuff, Trent's confidence was soaring.

What did the judge do? Made sure everybody in the courtroom did his job. Her job. He glanced at Sybylla.

What did the DA do? Tried to make a case against him.

What did his lawyer do? Saw that people got to hear the truth.

That was good enough for the shrinks. Trent received his newly declared competency as an utter vindication, as if the issue of his guilt or innocence on the indictment were moot.

His case was due to be called in Part 20, the central arraignment court, on the Tuesday following Trent's exam. Ordinarily, such a straightforward proceeding as an arraignment might have preoccupied barely a minyan of Sybylla's brain cells, but *New York* v. *Trent* was starting to cut into her sleep and boost her already-considerable coffee habit to five cups a day. Number one, a large-sized Kenya from Au Bon Pain, was going down nicely on the morning of the arraignment, when Sybylla looked up and saw that the object blocking her doorway was Sam Larkin.

"Oh," she said wittily.

"How's it going?"

"Which 'it' would that be, now?" She crossed her legs and swung her chair, not violently but nonetheless noticeably, away from him. It was perhaps a more dismissive gesture than she might have meant, but even now, she could not entirely escape her discomfort with Sam. He was affable and pleasant, eagerly interested in her without being overbearing, and endlessly rewarding to look at, but he remained an incongruity to her, and that was irritating. Like an officer among the grunts, he stood out among his new compatriots with his extremely well-made clothes and his extremely well-bred manners. Indeed, he seemed barely to notice the grubbiness of his physical surroundings, and he dealt with the clients Steiner sent him with such correct deference that they might have been millionaires who had arrived to refine some obscure point in their wills. Sam had transported his belongings from Chase, Twichell and Banks into the small office next to Sybylla's, and whenever she passed his open door, the sight of his framed Klee reproduction, Harvard Law School diploma, and leather desk set made her smile at the absurd juxtaposition they created. Maddeningly, however, he seemed not to notice.

This wasn't the first time he had appeared in her doorway, ostensibly on some neighborly errand or query, but ultimately to chat about Trent and whatever developments might be at hand on his case. Sybylla, circumspect by nature, found his questions simple to evade and his offers of help equally simple to parry, but the exchanges left her vaguely uncomfortable. She supposed he meant well, and he was hardly the only one of her colleagues to be attracted to her high-profile case, but he hadn't learned the office protocol regarding territoriality, and she had neither the time nor the patience to instruct him. When he had left her, retreating to the curious finery of his office next door, she found herself flushed, both with anger and with something else that made her even more uncomfortable. It wasn't as if she had leisure for this sort of thing. And anyway, it pissed her off to discover herself attracted to someone who so clearly wasn't her type.

"*You* know," he insisted, as of course she did. "The Trent thing."

"Ah." Sybylla nodded. "The Trent thing. Arraignment today."

Funny. It hadn't sounded as if she'd said, Why don't you come in and have a seat? But that's what Sam did. She watched him pull up her ratty client chair and settle into it.

"I want to help." Sam smiled. "With Trent."

"So you've said."

"C'mon, Syb." Somewhere in the past weeks, he had adopted Steiner's nickname for her, though in his voice it sounded vastly different. "There must be something I can do."

Sybylla looked at him evenly. "I appreciate it, Sam. I do. But you must have tons of work of your own, and an arraignment is pretty much by the numbers. There's even a sign on the floor that says Stand Here. You just hit your mark and say your line."

He looked fleetingly disappointed, but he rallied. "What about trial preparation, though? There must be something you can shift to me."

She threw up her hands. "It's under control. Really."

"You're doing insanity, right?" She hesitated. Then, scolding herself, she nodded. "Well, I did a lot of psych in college. Can I at least look at his shrink's report?"

Sybylla sighed. She wanted to say no, but none of the excuses that came to mind sounded viable, and she didn't dislike him enough to be purely nasty. And as the file was a scant half inch from her elbow, clearly marked in fat red letters: NY V TRENT, she could hardly tell him she didn't have it at hand. With a nod, she flipped back the manila cover and gave Turturro's report to Sam.

"His doctor said there were no red flags," she told him as he began to scan it greedily.

"Paranoid schizophrenic," he muttered.

"Yes. So it appears."

"Did your own shrink agree?"

"Appointment's set up. It hasn't happened yet. I got this great doctor, though. If anyone can pull this off—"

"What's this about the arm?" Sam cut her off. "This thing under the arm?"

Shit, Sybylla thought. She had forgotten that the disk was referred to in the intake report. Until there was a definitive analysis from Susu,

Sybylla didn't want anyone to know about the thing. If Sam mentioned it to Steiner, she knew, her boss would be furious about her unorthodox step.

"Oh . . ." she managed to say, "it's nothing. I looked into it."

He caught her eye. "What kind of nothing?"

"Oh, some blood pressure thing or something. Perfectly safe."

"Are you sure?" he pressed, infuriating her. "I mean, could it be some weird drug reaction causing his schizophrenia?"

She waved a hand. "Dead end. You see anything else?"

He returned to the paper in his hand. The horrible fluorescent lighting on her office ceiling turned his black curls greenish, and she couldn't help indulging her habitual fantasy of touching them. Surely he wouldn't mind, she thought, leaning imperceptibly forward to get a better view of his forearms—the crisp cuffs of his pinstriped shirt rolled neatly back, the emerging black hair, the movement of sinew beneath skin announcing, Body. Real body, clothed to conform with societal convention, but otherwise fully functional, thank you. "So, you majored in psych," she heard herself say in an evident attempt at self-distraction.

"Minored," he said shortly, continuing to read. "Majored in women's studies."

He looked up abruptly, into her silence.

"What, you think you need a uterus to take women's studies?"

"I . . . no," she managed. He went back to reading.

"Whoa," Sam said.

Sybylla started. "Excuse me?"

"You see this? On the urine analysis?"

"See what?" She leaned forward over the desk.

He held it up. "Here. 'Trace amount of lysergic acid diethylamide detected in urine specimen taken on admission.' "

She frowned. "Lysergic . . . what?" It sounded like *detergent.*

Sam gave her a slightly doubtful look. "Lysergic acid diethylamide. That's LSD."

For a long moment, Sybylla sat in stunned muteness. "What the hell does that mean?" she finally managed to say.

"Means instant insanity." He folded his hands behind his head and leaned back in the chair. "That's what we called it in high school. Didn't I ever tell you about my teenage-wasteland phase?"

"Your . . . what?" she said, still dazed and now irresistibly sidetracked.

"You might not believe this, but during my sophomore year, I was known to one and all as 'Zombie' Larkin, though it was mostly show, I have to admit. I was even in a band called the Dead Monkeys."

"Oh yeah? What instrument?"

"Well, you see"—he was grinning—"it was that whole idea of instruments, *musical* instruments, that we were trying to get away from. I was a backup screamer. But more to the point, I also did acid. Twice."

"And what was it like?" She shrugged, embarrassed. "I mean, I'm only a Catholic girl from a nice Republican suburb."

Sam smiled benevolently. "First time, I put on a Grateful Dead record, since I figured that's what you were supposed to listen to while tripping. I'm telling you, I *saw* the music. It floated around my head. The colors were amazing. It was like all your senses get put into the blender and you come out able to hear smells and touch sounds and see tastes. It was unbelievably intense."

Intense, she silently agreed, remembering the focus with which Trent had first studied her hand, then brought it to his lips, and then to his teeth. "What about the second time?"

"Oh." He gave a little shudder. "I got this feeling—it hit me about an hour after I took the drug—like all the awfulness in the world was running through my veins. I just sat down in the middle of Main Street in Cos Cob and started howling. I know"—he laughed, taking in her look—"but it was a ten-hour tour of the Inferno, I'm telling you."

Her eye fell on the page in his hand. "Jesus," she heard herself say.

"So maybe he was on acid when he attacked her."

"But it can't be that simple. There's got to be more."

"Why?" He was serious. "Why does there have to be more?"

"There just has to." She looked up. "Sam, I really appreciate your help, but I need to make a call now. Do you mind?"

There was a beat, and then he jumped to his feet. "Sure thing. See you later, okay?"

"Okay." She was already reaching for the phone, her mind racing.

By some miraculous turn, the Bellevue operator managed to connect her to the right extension on the very first try. By some further miraculous turn, Turturro himself picked up the phone. He was silent as she screamed her discovery at him and silent as she railed at him for not telling her sooner. She was stridently delineating the ways in which his failure to point this LSD result out to her had very nearly subverted the basic principles of justice itself, when she ran out of breath.

"Why don't you ask me what it means?" Turturro said shortly, cutting in.

"*What?*" she yelled.

"Why don't you ask me what it means to your case?"

"All right, what does it mean?" Sybylla said, glaring at the report.

"Not a damned thing."

"But you . . . your report says that Trent was on LSD when he st— when the little girl was stabbed!"

"It certainly does not," Turturro huffed. "And don't ask me to testify to any such thing, either. Now listen to me, Ms. Muldoon. There is a well-established period of influence for a conventional dose of LSD, and that's eight to twelve hours. It's a very limited window, and from what I understand, it doesn't fit your situation even remotely. Over twenty-four hours had passed from the time of the attack to the time that sample was taken for analysis. It simply isn't possible. And please remember that he continued to act out violent schizophrenic episodes for many days after he arrived at Bellevue."

"But he isn't acting out any longer, right? His schizophrenia seems to be over, right?"

"By no means," Turturro said in measured tones. "The ability to pass a competency exam has nothing to do with remission of mental illness. Trent is still exhibiting severe paranoid delusions. He talks constantly of 'the people,' and 'the room.' Now I'm just as happy as you are that he no longer seems to be violent. But over? Not at all."

"Look," she tried again, "it's just so weird. What was he doing on acid if he was crazy? I mean, if he was as crazy as you say he is, how would he even be able to score it?"

Turturro groaned. "Don't ask me. Crazy people can do crazy things." He spoke deliberately. "Maybe that's why they call them crazy."

Sybylla stifled her irritation. "Dr. Turturro, is there any possibility at all that LSD could have contributed to the attack? I mean, that it was this drug and not schizophrenia at all?"

"No way," the doctor said shortly. "I told you. No acid trip can last more than ten or twelve hours. The LSD could not have been responsible for his behavior both at the time of the attack and during the period following his admission to Bellevue, let alone since. It's impossible."

"Could he have gotten his hands on a subsequent dose somewhere along the line?" She was grasping at straws, she knew.

"Absolutely not," Turturro said shortly. "At least not here. We may not be the most secure institution in the city, but he hasn't seen anyone but doctors, orderlies, and you. Besides, he was in no state to set up a drug buy, believe me. No," he said sagely, "I'm still going with schizophrenia. My own best guess is that his mental illness directed this violent acting out, and that somebody gave him the LSD at a later time. While he was being held overnight, probably."

"You're kidding. Somebody gave him the drug while he was in jail? Why?"

"Who knows. A joke, maybe. Somebody with a long night in jail ahead of him, maybe he wanted some entertainment. Slip a little acid to the crazy guy. It's a pretty easy drug to transport, after all. All you need is a bit of paper. That timetable would explain our finding the trace in his urine twelve or so hours later."

Sybylla shook her head. She could think of no other avenues to follow.

"Funny thing is," she heard him say, "you give LSD to schizophrenics and it's not supposed to come out that way."

She frowned. "Excuse me, what did you say?"

"I'm trying to remember," Turturro mused. "It's been ages since I read about this. I think there's research that suggests LSD has a more or less opposite effect on psychotics. Way back in the dark ages, when the CIA was trying to figure out how to use acid to subvert the Russkies, they underwrote LSD research in mental wards and found out it had a calming effect on schizophrenics."

"You mean it doesn't just make them crazier?"

"No, apparently not. The patients in the study became almost functional, more like normal people. It was a primitive study, though." He shook his head. "Wasn't followed up or anything."

"So . . . what you're saying is, this LSD thing is sort of a red herring, right?"

She heard his chortle. "That's about it, Ms. Muldoon. In any case, I wouldn't rest a defense on it if I were you. No offense."

"None taken," she said sourly, having taken plenty.

After they had hung up, Sybylla sat glaring at the lab report, furious at it for first raising and then dashing her hopes. At the end of the day, Trent's only real shot was a shrink's compelling argument that a schizophrenic hallucination had compelled him beyond reason to take a scalpel and attack Amanda Barrett. With luck, he would receive decent therapy and would eventually improve sufficiently to be released. No magic wands, after all; just the tried-and-true American-as-apple-pie insanity defense.

The phone rang. She glared at that, too.

At ten rings, she heard the wall behind her head get pounded.

"Why don't you pick it up?" hollered Sam from his office next door.

"Because I'm not here," she yelled back.

"Sure you are."

"Whoever it is," Sybylla shouted, "I *know* it's no one I want to talk to."

"Well it's driving me crazy," he said. "Pick it up."

She sighed. "Okay." With regret, she put down the lab report and picked up the phone.

"Sybylla Muldoon."

"Hello," he said.

"Who is this?"

"This is Sam Larkin, your neighbor."

Sybylla put her feet up on the desk. Somewhat disconcertingly, she noted that she was smiling. "Mind if I ask why you're calling me when you can just shout?"

"Why should I shout when I can call you and talk like a normal person? Listen, will you have dinner with me sometime?"

She was glad he was on the other side of the wall. She wouldn't have wanted him to see her this incapable of a comeback. "Sam," she said finally, "it's not that I don't want to. Really. I'm just not sure it's a good idea."

"Why isn't it a good idea?" he asked, sounding genuinely confused.

"Well, for one thing, you see me every day. What if you find out I have garlic breath, or I voted for Bush?"

"Syb," he said wearily, "I love garlic. And I know you didn't vote for Bush."

"My dad did," she said, apologetic.

"So? Are you your father's keeper?"

There was a moment of silence. "An office romance," Sybylla mused. "How déclassé."

"No romance with you would be déclassé, Syb."

The way to a girl's heart, she thought, was through her heart. This insight made her grin so stupidly that she was rendered temporarily mute.

"So," Sam said affably, "what about that dinner?"

Well, she had to eat, after all, and even she had a saturation point for salad-bar pickings and ice cream. Maybe it wouldn't be the worst-possible thing. He was nice enough. He couldn't help it if he'd sprung fully formed from the mind of Brooks Brothers.

"Surely you're confusing me with somebody who has a social life," she heard herself mutter, giving it one last try.

"I'd never do that."

"Well," she heard herself say, "as long as that's clear. I guess." He was waiting. She heard his breathing from miles away on the other side of the wall. "Okay, then."

"Okay," said Sam.

She made an excuse to hang up, which she did with a perceptibly shaking hand. Sybylla groaned. Already, paranoia had begun to set in. With paranoia at 9:00 A.M., the day was looking decidedly unpromising.

CHAPTER

TWELVE

She was late for the arraignment—confidently late, since she knew that Judge Harrald, who had presided over arraignments since Hammurabi was the law of the land, would also be late (he liked to linger over coffee and the *New York Times* crossword in his chambers, and he wouldn't enter the courtroom until he'd finished both). There was also an irksome piece of old business she had to see to first in another part of the building, an assault case that had dragged on for months and was due to have gone to trial today.

Sybylla's client, an especially unsavory man with a pumping-iron chest and gold chains adorning it, had been indicted with the beating of his girlfriend. Despite the woman's statement and a very lurid series of photographs depicting her injuries, the creep had insisted on a plea of not guilty because he was convinced that the victim would never testify against him. To Sybylla's disgust, the client had been right; his girlfriend—ex-girlfriend, Sybylla hoped—had phoned the ADA the night before from Florida, in hysterics, and now they all had to gather one more time—the prosecutor, Sybylla, the bodybuilder and his band of boisterous supporters—to watch her move that the charges be dropped for lack of interest. When the gavel fell—"So moved"—she shook her head to the man's offer of a celebratory drink and sped upstairs.

As anticipated, Harrald had not yet appeared, but the room was already busy as an ant farm, with attorneys forging pacts and cutting deals. It was an efficient system, efficient certainly in comparison with how things were generally accomplished at 100 Centre Street. The attorneys did their dance together and made their arrangements, huddled in the front rows or leaning against the walls of the large room. Then the defendants waived their rights to trial and blandly recited the narratives of their guilt and the court officers collected them and escorted them back to the pens, their first stop as the convicted felons they now were. And after the buses took them to Rikers or Fishkill, a new group appeared and it began again. But every so often, the ritual failed to achieve a deal, or the defendant stubbornly insisted on his innocence or was savvy enough to want to take his chances with a jury. Then Harrald took off his bifocals and glared at everyone, defense attorney and prosecutor alike, as if their ornery lack of cooperation, of willingness to dance, were responsible for clogging the court calendar and causing the inexcusable delays the system was plagued by. Only when his outburst was over did the case get spun out, a courtroom and a judge extracted from the court officer's big drum, and the next case called.

Sybylla headed to the front of the room, hoping to grab a brief conference with Trent before they had to appear. Most people recognized a purposeful walk when they saw one and were considerate enough to get out of the way without comment.

Most people.

"Well," said a familiarly slimy voice in her ear, "if it isn't my prospective juror."

Burkowitz. Oozing his own dubious version of charm.

"Thanks a lot. I really enjoyed the civics lesson. So kind of you to take up my time."

"My pleasure." He perched on the back of one of the benches, one ample buttock hanging off the seat. "You shoulda seen your face."

"Listen, Wendell, I only hope I'll get the chance to return the favor someday."

He chuckled, enormously pleased with himself. "I suppose you'll be wanting some kind of a plea on Trent."

"And why would you suppose such a thing?"

" 'Cause not even you are nuts enough to try and make a go of this one. You can't win it. You'll come up smelling like a dead fish."

"Sweet of you to show such concern about my professional future. Not to mention my body odor. But then again, it isn't the first time you've come sniffing around, is it?"

He blushed to his pudgy earlobes. "It's just as well. Greer won't give you an inch on this one, now or ever. He's gonna ram your guy to the wall."

"What a quaint notion," she said sourly. "Sounds like something you'd read about in an Amnesty International brochure."

Bidding a happy farewell to Burkowitz, Sybylla made her way up to the front of the room. On the low table before the judge's bench were four thick indictment jackets, one each for the defendants seated in the corner of the room, like dunces in a one-room elementary school. Unlike dunce caps, however, these men wore masks over their mouths and noses. TB, Sybylla thought. The new drug-resistant strains ran rampant through the penal system. She nodded to an acquaintance seated in the front row of the courtroom and headed for the door behind the clerk's desk. When she flashed her ID at the officer, the heavy door was unlocked for her and she was admitted to the pens. Trent, like the celebrity prisoner he was, had a cell to himself. Sybylla took a seat on the corridor side of the wire mesh and fished out her file. "How you feeling?" she asked him.

He nodded.

"You clear on what happens today?"

"No," he said, his voice hushed. "You tell me."

"It's pretty straightforward. They'll bring you out. You'll stand next to me. Don't look at anyone but me or the judge. The press will be there, and someone might try to catch your eye, get some kind of a reaction out of you. Don't do it. Just be calm. The clerk will read the charge and then, when the judge asks how you're pleading, you say, 'Not guilty.' That's it. Then they'll assign us a courtroom and we can get a date for trial."

"Good," Trent said. "I wish we could go to trial today."

Sybylla rolled her eyes. It was bad enough, Greer pushing on this thing as if it was his personal ticket to the cover of *New York* magazine, without Trent rushing her, too.

She leaned forward and dropped her voice. "Listen, Trent. There are some things I need to ask you about. You told me last summer you didn't do drugs."

His expression was blank.

"Didn't you tell me that?"

"I don't do drugs." The voice was cold, even accusatory.

"So why did you have LSD in your system when you arrived at Bellevue?" He glared at her. "You know," she said helpfully, "acid."

"It's not true."

She shrugged. "I'm sorry, Trent. It's true. I've seen the lab report."

There was a long moment. Slowly, he began to shake his head.

"What, Trent?"

"Fuckers," he said. "They must have made me."

"Who? Someone downtown, in the holding cells? Was that when it happened?"

He didn't answer. He seemed fixated, staring at some unremarkable spot on the wire mesh between them. Evidently, the subject had been unilaterally closed.

Sybylla sighed and tried a different tack. "Listen, Trent. There's something I need to discuss with you. I'm pretty sure what your answer's going to be, but this is part of my job, so don't kill the messenger, okay?"

He looked at her vaguely. "Okay."

"The DA has told me himself that he won't be offering a plea in your case, and frankly, I doubt he will. But sometimes they do say that, you know, when they're really willing to consider some reduction in charge for a guilty plea. The point is, are you in any way agreeable to that? We could ask for—"

"No," he hissed at her. "No way."

"All right." She doodled a large *X* on the cover of her file. So much for a plea. She took a breath. "I've been making some headway on our defense, Trent. I've talked to a lot of doctors since I last saw you, and a couple of them are really interested in your case. I've made appointments for you with two of them next week, one of whom is a guy I've worked with before—very effective on the stand. Very persuasive to jurors. The other guy I don't know personally, but he testified in a case in Boston a few years ago and his professional opinion was a very decisive factor in the jury's deliberations. I think we're really lucky to have these people interested in working with us, so please do just what they say, all right?"

Silence. She looked up. Trent was staring at her.

"All right, Trent?"

"What *doctors?*" he hissed.

She was blank for a minute. "What do you mean? For your defense."

"What defense would I need some *doctor* for?"

She paused. Had she never actually mentioned this? It had all seemed so obvious to her. Surely Trent had understood what it meant when she asked him to cooperate with the psychiatrists she would be sending. Surely it was obvious that this was their only chance.

She took a breath. "An insanity defense, Trent. Naturally."

He exploded. From beneath the desk, she heard the clank of his leg chains. His shoulders raised in outrage. "Fuck no." His voice was shot through with steel. "No fucking way. I'm not crazy. Who said I was crazy?"

"Obviously you're not crazy *now*, Trent," Sybylla said, trying to soothe him. "You're perfectly fine. I can see that. But you said yourself there are some things you're not remembering clearly. Now it's possible you did black out, as you put it, and it's also possible that during that time you may have done something you find unthinkable now. I've seen it before, Trent. Sometimes people just snap, you know?"

"You can't make me say I'm crazy," he warned, dashing her hopes.

"Of course not. I'd never advise you not to tell the truth. In any case, it isn't for you to say, really. You wouldn't even have to testify. We'd call experts to attest to your mental state. And if the plea is successful, then your case would be reviewed every six months, and if there was nothing wrong with you any longer, then you'd be released." His mouth was tight. "Listen, Trent," Sybylla said, dropping all pretense. "In prison, they don't give you a chance to walk free six months after incarceration. I only want to do whatever I can to help you, and frankly, I think insanity is the way to go."

"No," he spat, his eyes fierce. "I'm not insane. Whatever was wrong with me, *they* did it. I'm not taking the rap for that. No insanity defense, Sybylla. You send me some court shrink and I get another lawyer."

That was it, then. All her preparation out the window, and in its place a notable dearth of brilliant ideas. She hadn't the faintest notion of how she would defend him now. She put her head down. "I won't lie to you, Trent. I'm a pretty good attorney, but your case is going to be hard to win. It's just . . . we'll do our best, but I wouldn't want you to base your decision on some assumption that you're going to sail through this process. They've got witnesses, forensics, and a very sympathetic victim."

"I'm gonna tell," he informed her tightly. "I'm gonna go to the trial and tell what happened to me."

Sybylla sighed with irritation. "Well, you can't just get up there and rave about the goddamn people. I hope you realize that. And don't think I'm going to let you testify without any idea of what you're going to say. You'll have to give me a little preview of this testimony sometime."

"I can't," he said matter-of-factly.

"Right." She gathered up her things. "Then I'm in danger, is that it?" He said nothing. His dark eyes were huge. Sybylla got to her feet. "See you out there."

Greer had arrived when she returned to the more civilized side of the heavy door. He stood, taking up a good deal of space in the center aisle of the courtroom, two of his assistants around him. Ignoring them, she let the clerk know she was ready to proceed and took a demure seat in the front row. She didn't wait long.

Harrald seemed determined not to keep the great man waiting a moment longer than necessary. With a nod to his clerk and a brief direction, "Let's do Trent," the room shot to life. Waiting attorneys, press, courtroom artists, and scattered family members and voyeurs looked expectantly at the door that led to the pens, eager for the first public sighting of the Wild Man since the day after his arrest, but Trent, when he emerged between two officers, must have looked disappointingly placid. He trudged in the small shuffling steps his chains allowed, with his wrists fastened before him and his head down. The muscles of his pale face were slack and he did not look, defiantly or otherwise, at a soul. Sybylla patted his shoulder when he got to the table. She wanted the press to see that she wasn't afraid of him.

"'People of the State of New York v. Trent,'" the clerk read. "'Defendant has been indicted by the grand jury of the county of New York for the crime of assault in the first degree.' How do you plead—guilty or not guilty?"

Sybylla heard the rasp of her client's breath.

"Not guilty."

Harrald shuffled through the file. "Oh-kay." He pursed his lips. "What are we doing with this, folks? There an offer, or what?"

"No offer, Your Honor," Greer nearly shouted, his demeanor grave.

"We're not taking a plea," Sybylla tried to outshout the DA.

"Okay, okay." The judge held up his hands in surrender. "I get the message. No deal." He looked at Sybylla. "Bail status to be continued. Any problem with that, Ms. Muldoon?"

"None, Your Honor. I'm sure the DA will agree that my client should remain hospitalized, where he can receive appropriate psychiatric care."

From the other table, she heard Greer's low snort.

"So entered," the judge commented, making a note on the file. "Okay, let's get an assignment. Clerk will spin it out."

The drum whirred, and a name was pulled. Sybylla breathed a sigh of relief. Judge Jonathan Coffin was one of the more compassionate residents of the New York Supreme Court bench. She had tried several cases before him in the past, twice succeeding in getting him to throw out dubious police interrogations. Across the aisle, Greer took it like a man.

"Defendant will be returned to the psychiatric ward at Bellevue Hospital Center. Take him away, boys." Harrald nodded at the officers. Sybylla watched Trent shuffle out.

"Well," Burkowitz cooed, slithering up to her as she wedged the file back into her bag, "this oughta be fun. You and the big guy."

"He *is* big," Sybylla conceded. "If he's really going to run for governor, he should consider shedding a few pounds."

"Sure." Burkowitz laughed, walking after her. "You wanna be the one to tell him? They don't pay me enough."

She reached for the swinging door, but the ADA was on her tail.

"How're you going to defend him? Insanity?"

She hoped he couldn't see—or at any rate couldn't interpret—the shadow that crossed her face. How the hell *was* she going to defend him? Consumed with displaced bitterness, she turned to Burkowitz. "You don't really think I'm going to tell you, do you?" Sybylla snapped. "I'm curious. Why would I do that?"

His chin glinted with nervous sweat. "Because you're mad about me."

"Good-bye, Wendell. It's been real."

Fleetingly, she heard him laugh, but out in the corridor, that tiny sound was swallowed in a roar of chatter. Pressed tightly together like a rugby scrum, a single mass of flesh heaved with adrenaline, filling the hall—media types, this time with cameras. Sybylla gritted her teeth. As she approached, the swarm gave ground to embrace her. "Do you have a comment about the arraignment?" somebody shouted.

But even as she stumbled through her automatic offering—the plea of not guilty, the "No comment"—Sybylla saw plainly that she was not the main attraction. Greer stood a few yards down the hall, surrounded by serious, listening faces and doing his most effective portrayal of an angry (but eminently civilized) middle-aged man. His forehead was misted under the white lights of the camera. "This isn't just my job," he announced to the rapt heads around him. "It's my crusade."

Sybylla slipped past the throng and made her way outside, desperate for air and time to think. Insanity had been easy for her client to dismiss, but it was the only arrow in her quiver; without it, she had little more to offer than a claim that Trent simply denied the accusation, and she had a pretty good idea how *that* would go over. Most Legal Aid clients, whatever their other failings, were content enough to let their attorneys follow whatever course seemed most likely to result in an acquittal. She had never encountered anything like this before.

They were short on time, too, Sybylla thought, punching the cracked gray plastic elevator button in her office lobby. The box began its weary ascent. She had allowed Greer to push for an accelerated trial date because she had been confident of her defense plan and because Trent himself so obviously wanted to get the thing under way. To ask for a continuance now was to broadcast that her strategy was in disarray. She would just have to find another way forward, and soon, she thought, opening the door to her office.

Just past the reception desk, a small toy-strewn room boasted an ancient Zenith on which Barney videos were often played to sedate the more boisterous children of Legal Aid clients. Today it was turned to NY 1, and Sybylla had no sooner made her appearance than she was greeted by the approbation of her comrades in arms.

"Way to go." Somebody clapped her on the back.

"Yeah?" She grinned. "What'd I do?"

A glance at the screen revealed the moon face of Andrew Greer smiling reassuringly at her. The word *Live* flashed in the lower-right corner.

"Jesus." She shook her head. "Is he still at it?"

He was, but not for much longer. A moment later, Greer had lost the camera to a generic blond newscaster who solemnly announced that Amanda Barrett, "the brave little girl at the center of this terrible case," had today been released from the hospital and taken home. Sybylla stepped closer to the television, bracing herself.

With her abdominal injuries sufficiently healed at last, Amanda Barrett had been discharged from Mount Sinai quietly, but not so quietly that the word didn't seep out. By the time the limousine left the Klingenstein Pavilion, a mob of reporters was trawling the sidewalk in front of the Barrett brownstone in the East Eighties. The sleek gray vehicle was quickly covered with bodies, like flies on a carcass.

Sybylla watched Brian Barrett, the girl's father, step out first and utter a vain plea for mercy, or, failing mercy, a temporary reprieve that would allow his daughter to reach her own front door. "Have some heart," he pleaded, looking very much like a man who wasn't used to pleading. "She's only nine."

When the crowd failed to respond, he leaned back into the limo and opened his dark overcoat, using it to shield the small girl who huddled beneath it. But she could not resist looking fearfully into the light. In this case, the light came from a sputter of camera flashes.

The girl looked like a Picasso.

Sybylla watched in horror as, shamelessly and heartlessly, the network then saw fit to flash the girl's fourth-grade photograph from the Brearley School yearbook side by side with this image of her mutilated features. Next to the laughing, confident child in the yearbook, the new Amanda appeared almost obscene, with dark puckered lines emanating from a nostril, an eyebrow, what had once been the dimple beside a grinning mouth. Her stomach clenching in pity, Sybylla turned and walked back to her office.

She had barely collapsed in her chair when Sam appeared in the doorway, grinning as if nothing whatever were wrong with the world. "That," he said merrily, "was a truly masterful 'No comment.' You think when I've been here a little longer I'll be able to say 'No comment' like that?"

"Sorry," she told him. "Takes a long time to get just the right blend of nonchalance and benevolent preoccupation. You can't get it from special training alone; you need the God-given talent."

"Ow!" He put his hand over his heart. "I'm wounded."

Despite her best effort, she felt herself smile at him.

"So it went okay?"

"What, the arraignment? Sure. It's just routine." She picked up her briefcase and flung it on the desktop, a gesture she hoped would discourage further discussion on the subject.

"Anything for me to do?" Sam said, declining the hint. "Any way I can help?"

Sybylla came up with a polite smile. "Thanks, but no."

"I'm happy to do it," he insisted, "I mean, if you—"

She cut him off. "What else was on the news? I haven't seen a paper in days."

"What? Oh, I don't know." He sighed. "Usual mayhem, I guess." He was perched in the doorway, looking downcast and undeniably fetching.

She stifled her own guilt. "Such as?"

"Oh . . . let's see, they're still fighting about the Saint Patrick's Day parade. There was a water-main break on Long Island. Somebody got killed at NYU."

"Hm?" Sybylla said absently. Then she sat up. "What about NYU?"

.."There was a break-in. A professor got killed, I think." He sighed deeply. "Well, if you're sure you don't have anything for me, I'll get back to work." His smile was sad. "See you." He was gone.

Sybylla sat motionless, suspended in optimistic denial. *Don't be ridiculous. There are thousands of professors at NYU.* "Sam?" she called.

He was back in an instant. "Change your mind?"

"Professor of what? Did they say?"

"Oh . . ." He seemed disappointed. "Biology? Chemistry. Yes, I think it was chemistry. They said it was probably a drug thing."

Her whole face had gone numb. She could barely make the muscles work.

"Did they give a name?"

He frowned. "What? Whose name?"

"Sam." She got to her feet. *"A name—did they give a name?"* He was staring at her, dumbstruck. *"Answer me."*

All at once, she reestablished contact with her nervous system, bolting to her feet and tearing past him through the doorway. The large room was full of people who seemed to have stopped what they were doing in order to stare at her. She flew past the desks, leaving them in a hysterical blur behind her, and whipped around the corner, back to the waiting room, landing before the television set and fumbling with the dial in search of the noon newscasts. Channel 2: a rabid dog in Harlem. Channel 4: no, they were talking about basketball; she'd already missed it on 4. Channel 7: the tail end of a vehicular homicide in Queens. Then, in the upper-right-hand corner of the screen, an outline of an academic spire with the words splashed in red: MURDER AT NYU.

"An NYU undergraduate made a grisly discovery yesterday afternoon when he arrived for a chemistry class: the body of his professor, apparently shot to death in her own laboratory, in what police are calling a drug-related incident. The victim, associate professor of chemistry Sushila Patel—"

"No," Sybylla heard herself say.

"—was alone in the lab at the time of the apparent break-in. No one appears to have heard any sounds of a struggle or seen any suspicious persons inside what the university claims is a secure building. Police have no suspects at this time, but one of the detectives on the scene had this to say."

The visual cut to a grizzled man, his expression regretful. "Yeah, what it looks like, they were probably after drugs of some kind. Lotta these guys, they think laboratory equals crack, you know? Somebody probably got into the building, looking around, and they surprised her. Tried to make a robbery of it, maybe. Her wallet's gone." The man shrugged. "Real tragedy," he said offhandedly.

The bland face of the newscaster returned. "NYU officials have expressed deep regret over the killing, but they maintain that school buildings are safe. A meeting is set for tonight to air student concerns over the incident."

"*Incident*," Sybylla said bitterly as the news turned to sports. She wiped with the back of her hand at her face, which was suddenly slick with tears.

An arm crossed her shoulders, heavy but oddly welcome. Unthinking, she leaned back against it. "Sybylla," Sam said, his voice full of sad wonder. "You know her."

"Knew her," she said, correcting him.

CHAPTER
THIRTEEN
—◆—

Given his not inconsiderable temper, it was fortunate that Philip Hofmann, who was sometimes called "Mace" behind his narrow back, had never actually been made aware of his nickname.

Its first known usage had been twenty-five years earlier, in the interns' lounge of a vast Cambridge teaching hospital. There, the underlings he supervised retreated for coffee, cigarettes, and vitriol during the dead hours late at night, and, as subordinates the world over are wont to do, the strung out and sleep-deprived men discussed their supervisor with undisguised envy and unbridled hostility. Note was taken of his fairly indifferent hygiene, his already endangered hairline, and his tiny hands—which in punchier moments were held to imply an abbreviated manhood. In fact, he was small all over, wiry and short, but out of that undersized form, his temper howled like a hurricane, frequently leaving his victims in tears. Hence the nickname. The man might look harmless enough. But he stung.

Even in slow periods, Hofmann and his business partner of over a quarter century tended not to cross paths. The complex in which they each worked separately toward a hybrid goal had been designed with the security of their work in mind; hence, there was little in the way of chance meetings by the water cooler or routine forays to each other's offices. Normally, the lengthy absences would not even have registered with Hofmann, but occasionally, the niggling memory of his team's rather spectacular security breach would return to him as he leaned over the blank or frightened face of a subject undergoing treatment. And then he would be reminded that the person was still out there.

Whatever fate this troublesome subject had met, the implant would ensure that it involved some degree of acute schizophrenia, a psychic state not altogether undesirable under the circumstances, and one that Hofmann, in his foresight, had correctly seen as a valuable mechanism to diminish the danger of just such a security breach. At best, the subject would have walked in front of a car before he'd spent twenty-four hours outside the lower level, and at worst, even if he had managed to refrain from some violent act and was bursting to broadcast the news of his detention to the global village, he would have little in the way of rational information to impart to anybody. Just another wacko on the streets. And didn't the chairman himself rely on the invisibility of such creatures?

Only hours after the subject had disappeared, leaving one of the newer depatterning technicians gushing blood onto the frigid stone floor, the chairman himself had stepped in to assure Hofmann that he would be handling the situation. He did not doubt how seriously his partner took what had happened, but Hofmann found it difficult to accept that something decisive had not taken place by now, and the lack of news from upstairs was beginning to irk him. By far the likeliest scenario he imagined for the subject was suicide, in which case the local or possibly the D.C. police would certainly have taken possession of a deceased John Doe meeting the description of their absent friend, and had that, in fact, happened, it was entirely possible that Kolb had not yet managed to locate and confirm the corpse. Kolb, in Hofmann's opinion, was the very picture of a man born on a day the three Graces took their annual holiday to the seaside, but for reasons he himself could not fathom, the chairman had gradually come to rely upon this person for an array of services. Collections, deliveries, surveillance, investigation—activities that, arguably, required more than the modest amount of gray matter Kolb boasted—were all currently under his aegis. With so much on his plate, Hofmann thought, it was likely that he hadn't gotten around to combing the local morgues for Mr. Right.

Beyond the suicide scenario, however, there was another version of events that Hofmann had considered, with significantly less satisfaction. If the police were to apprehend an apparent psychotic who had harmed someone, for example, then it was entirely possible that the implant would ultimately be discovered and, if discovered, removed. This was a distinctly unpromising scenario, and he could only imagine the speculation that would arise among so-called legitimate scientists when they got a good look at his work. After all, even a cursory search for related research would turn up his name on some list, liberated from a grimy basement of a CIA storage facility by the Freedom of Information Act. Then they would come looking for him and try to stop him—again.

When a month had passed since the subject's escape, Hofmann sent the first of a series of notes upstairs, asking to be updated on the situation. When he still had heard nothing a week later, he wrote a second note, a little briefer and a little more direct. It, too, went unanswered. After that, he began calling, catching up to the chairman's beeper in Texas, Mississippi, Indiana, New Hampshire, interrupting him on yachts and golf courses and in the dark-paneled offices of clients. The telephoned responses, short and even-tempered, consisted of jovial reassurances that the situation was under control but that the chairman was now in conference and couldn't speak further on this or any other subject. A meeting would be set up immediately on the chairman's return, but for now, good-bye. Naturally, no meeting ensued.

And so things remained until late one Friday afternoon when a figure presented himself at Hofmann's office with a folded copy of the *New York Post* in his hand. This luckless person was a psychotropic drug specialist named Reynolds, the duly appointed emissary of his peers. He cleared his throat. "I'm sure this matter is well in hand," Reynolds began, "but I wonder if you could just reassure the team that appropriate action's being taken. We'd all feel better." He held out the paper.

"And what might 'this matter' be?" Hofmann merely nodded at the tabloid. He seemed to have no wish to touch it.

Reynolds shrugged nervously. "The Wild Man. You know, our lost boy. Trial is starting next month, it says."

Hofmann stared at him for a long moment, his jaw set, vibrating with fury. Then he snatched up the paper and stared into Trent's vacant face.

"Are you sure?" he said finally, his voice tight. "Absolutely sure?"

"No question," Reynolds said. "I'm sorry, I thought you knew. It's been in all the New York papers. *Newsweek,* too."

"On trial for what?" Hofmann ignored the groveling.

"He stabbed a little girl. The DA's prosecuting the case himself."

The DA himself? Venom surged through the small man. A recognizable hand was now evident here. Quickly, Hofmann scanned the article. The assault had occurred only three days after the subject's escape. Who knew how long the chairman must have known about this?

Hofmann simply said, "Leave." Reynolds briefly considered asking for more information, but a glance at his boss proved persuasive. He left.

With a studied calm, Hofmann picked up his telephone and pressed the chairman's priority-access extension. The call was immediately answered by his partner's distinctive low voice.

"I would like to see you," Hofmann said tersely. "Now."

"In a meeting." The reply was cheery, as if to say, But thanks for asking!

Hofmann smiled. "If you do not come downstairs, now, I will go upstairs. *Now.*" He screamed, reaching forward to pound his fist on Trent's face.

There was a pause. "Five minutes." The chairman sighed, cutting off the line.

Hofmann was amazed that this situation had been allowed to evolve to the point of a trial. Raving lunatics were not subjected to trials in the modern world. They were shunted out of the court system and kept in mental hospitals. Trial meant competency to stand trial, which meant communication skills, which were incompatible with severe schizophrenia, artificially induced or otherwise—all of which might possibly be very, very bad news.

"Well?"

Hofmann looked up, breaking Trent's gaze from the newspaper's front page. The chairman was taking in the scene.

"Ah. I wondered how long it would take." He closed the door behind him and calmly took the seat across the desk from his partner. "The Wild Man." He nodded at the paper. "He has another name, too. Trent, they call him. Trent what? Don't ask. He seems to have gotten by in life with just Trent. Do you know that the title of a legal case remains unchanged even if the defendant can be shown to have given an alias to the police? In other words, if I'm arrested in New York and I tell the police that my name is John Brown, my case will be known as *New York* v. *John Brown* even after my true identity is discovered. All the way up to the Supreme Court, under an alias. It's ironic, don't you think, our legal system, ostensibly based upon a principle of seeking truth, allowing such falsehood to persist?"

Hofmann was glaring at him. "Are you insane? How long have you known about this?"

"For some time," he said, amiably enough. "A day or so after the arrest, we put things together, though God only knows how he got himself up to New York in the state he would have been in. He also assaulted his attorney." The chairman held up his hand as if waiting to be called on. "Bit her." He spread the fingers. "Here."

"Have they found it?" Hofmann said tightly.

"Oh yes. Took it out, too."

"Jesus."

The chairman was studying his hands. "Would you believe me if I told you everything was under control?"

"No," the small man spat.

His partner smiled at him. "That is precisely why I did not tell you, then. I did not want to distract you."

"Well, I am distracted now. So you can start by telling me why that man is still alive. Or is your kraut too stupid to get inside a sieve like Bellevue?"

The chairman shook his head. "It was never an issue of getting to the man, but you must understand that his case attracted intense media attention almost immediately. For us to have gone in and eliminated him would only have encouraged a very unwelcome kind of speculation.

From our perspective, it looked far more desirable for Trent to remain a run-of-the-mill New York psychotic. We also felt it highly unlikely that the subject would have anything cogent to say, or, frankly, that anyone would be listening very carefully. So at the time, we judged it wiser to leave him where he was."

"What about now?" Hofmann prompted. "I want this thing to go away as soon as possible, you hear me?"

"Of course, my friend," the tall man said easily. "But now there are other reasons, and compelling ones, to let the trial take place."

"And what might they be?" He was only just managing to contain his fury.

The chairman smiled. "As it happens, this case has created an extremely advantageous opportunity for one of our most important clients. He's trying it himself, you see, and the poll results have been very encouraging—up a full fifteen percent for favorable opinion in his city, and a five percent increase in name recognition in the state as a whole. And that's before the trial even begins. Once it does, it's very likely to dominate local news and even make the national media."

Hofmann was shaking his head in disbelief. "I don't believe what I'm hearing. You're actually going to stand by while one of our subjects gets up on the stand and *testifies*?"

"Please." The chairman was maddeningly calm. "This defendant will never testify."

Hofmann shook his head. "Says you. What's to stop him?"

"His lawyer will stop him. She's filed notice with Andrew Greer's office that she's pursuing an insanity defense. Doctors will testify on his behalf. She won't put him on the stand. With Greer prosecuting, there's every likelihood that the jury will find him guilty, and then, after a cooling-off period, we'll simply terminate the man in prison. No loose ends."

"Well, one," Hofmann hissed at him. "There's the little matter of the *implant*, you know."

For the first time, the chairman looked discernibly uncomfortable. "It's taken us a bit of time to determine precisely where it is. Our first assumptions were mistaken, but we're fairly sure we now know where it is." He fixed Hofmann squarely in his gaze. "Don't worry. I expect to have it back soon. Perhaps even later on tonight."

"Don't *worry*?" the little man mocked. "Listen, if somebody analyzes that implant, the trail leads right to me. And be not in doubt. From me, the trail leads to you."

"The trail, as you put it, will lead to neither of us. We are as secure to-day as when we began."

Hofmann sneered at him. "And what if his lawyer gets him off?"

"Won't happen." The tall man shook his head curtly.

He couldn't help but smile. "How ironic you should say that. Aren't you always going on about juries and their 'go figure' verdicts? Isn't that the line you give your clients? Isn't that why we're in *business*?"

"Calm yourself," the chairman said shortly. "I was merely referring to a point of law. An insanity defense, despite public misperception, does not get the defendant off, as you put it; it merely shifts the site of incar-ceration from prison to a secure mental hospital. True, the defendant is then regularly reviewed for possible release, but for our purposes, that apprehension needn't apply. Once this Trent is incarcerated, we will sim-ply arrange the termination. And don't worry, it will be just as simple to have it done in a mental hospital as in a prison. Attica or Wards Island, it makes no difference to us. Either way, the man will never tell what he knows—whatever he may know."

"Aren't you forgetting something?" Hofmann sneered. "I'm sure he's already blabbed to his lawyer. You'd better make sure she's taken care of, too."

"Ah," the chairman said. He had leaned back against his chair and was studying the ceiling. "I'm afraid that's a bit more complicated."

Hofmann, sensing a nerve, leaned forward and eyed his partner keenly. "What's complicated about it? Can't bring yourself to raise a hand against the brethren? Didn't Shakespeare himself say to kill all the lawyers?"

"This one isn't exactly unknown to us, you see. She is the daughter of a friend."

"Whose friend?" he spat. "I wasn't aware you had any."

The chairman looked him in the eye. "Our friend, actually."

It was pleasant to watch the color drain from his partner's face.

For a long moment, they were silent together. The small man's hands drummed nervously on his knee, but his expression was remote and still, and the chairman felt his own thoughts begin to drift. It was all so dif-ferent from what he had once anticipated for himself, back when he and his partner had first met. Then, he might have projected a more straight-forward ascension: attorney to judge, an academic interlude, perhaps, for the prestige of it, then politics and the specific privileges and power his father had always coveted for him. But a politician's life, he had long ago discovered, was lived at the mercy of an electorate that was barely literate, and a politician's impact must be subject both to the whims of sound-bite editors and to that elusive thing called national "mood." The chairman's own power, on the other hand, was immune to the disease of political change, resistant to harm from shifts in the guard; indeed, it thrived on those shifts. He felt himself smile. For the pasty twenty years, he had been the repository of some of the most explosive confidences in American politics, a stockpile of pure domination, more precious by far than money.

"Sometimes I think you tend to forget what this is all about," Hofmann said suddenly, dispersing his partner's reverie and somewhat diminishing its pleasure. "It's not about controlling the world—at least not to me. It's not about exerting one's moral code. It's not even about justice. All of this"—he gestured at the room and, by implication, what lay beyond it—"is merely about curiosity and the natural world. I am a scientist. I pursue truth."

"That suits me," the chairman said, rising slowly. "Your pursuit of truth has been most effective to those of us striving for the public good."

Hofmann gave him a humorless smile. "Whatever you say." He folded his hands across his torso. "I want you to know that I'm not un-sympathetic to your plight. I fully acknowledge that your situation is dif-ficult. But I also want you to know that where this work is concerned, there is no person I would allow to compromise my research. I am counting on you to see to that, old friend or not."

"It goes without saying." The chairman stood up. "Now. I must leave you."

"And you will keep me informed from this point on."

The chairman sighed. "From this point on, you will be as well in-formed by the *New York Times* as by me. But if anything of a covert na-ture occurs, yes, you will be informed. Get rid of that." He nodded at the tabloid. "And try not to worry so much. Believe me, Kolb is in command of the situation, and Kolb can be extremely commanding. The implant will be retrieved very soon."

114

"I won't be stopped again," the little man said.

His partner smiled. "Perish the thought."

After the chairman had left, Hofmann sat for nearly an hour in the silence of his office, his computer dormant and dark. He was not unhappy with the path his life's work had taken—not when he allowed himself to recall its near-disastrous beginnings. Then, as now, he had striven for a goal he felt to be pure, and indeed he had achieved that goal as a relatively young man. It was part of the deal he had made all those years ago, however, that his work would never be known to the readers of the science section of the *Times*, nor even to the scientific community, and this was the thorn that had never quite ceased to torment him. Very occasionally, when some luminary in his field would visit one of the local universities, Hofmann would attend the lecture, lurking in frustrated silence near the back of the room and talking to no one, furious that his own work would never receive such a fawning public airing. As far as his long-ago colleagues knew, he had dropped from the face of the earth when the powers that be had suddenly reversed their policy on his research. Disgruntled! they probably thought. Unable to bear the whimsical shifts of the government! It burned him to contemplate their dismissal, when the reality was that he had only gone underground.

Somewhat uncharacteristically, he felt himself begin to smile.

Like so many other refugees from the 1960s, for so many other reasons, though perhaps more literally than most—he had indeed gone underground.

CHAPTER

FOURTEEN

She spotted him hunched over a menu through the restaurant window and tapped the glass as she went by, heading for the door. The instant of fright that passed over his face as he looked up gave way to a grin that went straight to the pit of Sybylla's stomach, oozing a queasy warmth. She nodded at the maître d' and made her own way to the table, where he stood like the gentleman he was to receive her.

"You mentioned the sangria this morning," Sam said, sitting down again and pouring her a glass from the pitcher beside his plate. "I took the liberty."

"Thanks," she said, eyeing it thirstily.

Sam raised his glass. "To the Old Spice Rapist, an unlikely cupid."

"What a revolting thought," Sybylla said.

He shrugged, smiling. "You missed a great trial, you know."

"Oh yeah?" She sipped her sangria. "You lost, didn't you?"

"Why do you have to be so result-oriented? Obviously, I lost. But it was very dramatic. I tried like hell to have those lineups tossed. Might have more luck on appeal."

"Hm," Sybylla commented. "Was he guilty?"

"Even if he was, it wouldn't make the lineups any less dicey, would it?"

"Man after my own heart," she said approvingly.

"In a big way," he told her.

Something of a conversation stopper. He was still grinning at her, his long forefinger tapping the stem of his glass.

"I should have warned you," Sybylla heard herself say, "I really only date boys who are card-carrying members of the ACLU."

To her surprise, he didn't miss a beat.

"Wanna see the card?" Sam reached into his blazer and withdrew a lizard-skin wallet.

She watched him, wide-eyed in surprise. "What else have you got?" she wanted to know, still suspicious. Sam flipped the little plastic sleeves.

"PETA, Planned Parenthood, Amnesty. What about you?"

Sybylla, chastened, extracted her own wallet and searched. "NARAL, NOW, Amnesty, GMHC."

"Well!" he said emphatically. "I'm glad your credentials check out."

"Were they in doubt?" She was arch.

Sam gave her a smile so sweet, it was downright unsettling. "Never. I knew you were the genuine article."

Fortuitously, the waiter arrived at this juncture. Sybylla, whose fondness for animals was always bested by her own carnivorousness, ordered roast pig and plantains.

"I'm so glad you're not a leaf eater," Sam said when the waiter left.

"Tried it in college," she admitted. "Gave it up. I missed roast beef sandwiches too much."

"I tried it for about a week. I ended up at a Burger King at three in the morning, shoving Whoppers in my mouth."

"Hopeless," she told him.

"Hopeless," Sam concurred. "Nothing worse than an animal lover who eats meat. Except maybe a pro-lifer who favors the death penalty."

"Right! Bane of my existence."

"Or a victim's rights advocate with no compassion for the abuser who was a victim himself."

"Yes!" Sybylla nodded.

"Or the people who think homosexuals go out and recruit kids who would otherwise grow up to be Barbie and Ken."

Sybylla tried to get her face under control. All of a sudden, she felt as if she were thirteen years old and in the front row of a David Cassidy concert. Even his fingernails were suddenly sexy. Why had she never noticed them before?

Their dinner, formerly a living and breathing porcine creature of undoubtedly superior intelligence and strong family values, arrived glistening in crisp roast fat. Sybylla, famished, dug right in.

"So tell me," she said, savoring the first extraordinary mouthful. "What's a nice boy from Greenwich like you doing defending murderers and rapists?"

"Not Greenwich." He looked scandalized. "Cos Cob. Next stop along the line. We're very particular about those distinctions in the suburbs, you know."

"Sorry."

"Well, it's not precisely the way I looked at it, defending murderers and rapists. I mean, I wanted to defend *somebody*, some flesh-and-blood person, and it seemed to me that it might as well be somebody whose life I could really have some positive impact on."

"But that would be true of any criminal defense. Why Legal Aid?"

He shrugged. "I suppose because I could afford to do it."

"What, you mean financially?"

"Well, that was part of it. I mean, I'm fortunate that way. I have some money of my own. But also, I felt secure enough about myself not to have to work with people who are just like me. Look"—he took in her perplexed expression—"I could have stayed at Chase, Twichell doing mergers as long as I wanted, maybe representing a client's kid if he mowed somebody down while driving stoned or something, but it just didn't feel . . . I don't know, *real* to me. It was too safe. Too much the kind of stuff I'd grown up with. And you pick up the paper every day and there are real defendants facing real trials. I just thought, These are the people I should be serving."

Sybylla frowned down at her plantains.

"The way I saw it, I have my private life to have drinks at the country club, if that's what I want to do with it. You understand? But your work life is something different. It's about . . . I guess, *engaging* with the world. And that's what I wanted to do. So that's why I'm . . . How'd you put it? Defending rapists and murderers."

Thoughtful, she nodded.

"Besides, I could ask you the same question. Great Falls, Virginia, and Cos Cob, Connecticut, probably aren't so different. How'd you end up at Eighty Lafayette?"

It wasn't the first time she'd been asked, but she had never worked out a response suitable for anecdotal retelling.

"I don't know, really. I mean, it wasn't a bolt of lightning or anything."

He eyed her. "I don't mean to be blunt, but your dad's not exactly known as the most liberal of jurists. How'd you grow up with him and end up the way you are?"

"What do you mean? How am I?"

"Well"—he ladled some red beans onto his plate—"a card-carrying member of the ACLU. Did you have a really liberal mom or something?"

Sybylla shook her head. "No. I mean, I might have. She could have been Marlo Thomas, for all I know. I just never got a chance to ask her, and my dad doesn't really like to talk about her."

She took in his confusion, and blushed, ashamed of herself. "My mom died when I was born," she told Sam.

"Oh." He put down his fork. "I'm sorry."

"It's okay. I mean, I never knew her, so . . ." She glanced up at him. He was still looking at her. "It was an emergency cesarean," she said, answering his unspoken question. "She hemorrhaged."

"I see." He smiled kindly. "So. We eliminate the liberal mother diagnosis. We must look elsewhere to identify the source of this liberal contamination."

"We must." She smiled at him. "All right. It was seventh grade. I fell in love."

"With whom?" He looked affronted.

"Atticus Finch. I loved Atticus Finch. I loved his passion. I loved him standing between Tom Robinson and the lynch mob. I loved how he called Boo Radley Mr. Arthur. I wanted to have two kids named Jem and Scout and be the only voice of justice in my small, backward Alabama town. But unfortunately, I was a girl, and I lived in Great Falls, Virginia. So I became a public defender. It seemed a reasonable variation on the theme."

He lifted his glass. "Atticus Finch would be proud of you."

She shrugged, embarrassed.

"Tell me about your dad," Sam said.

"You mean my dad the dad or my dad the judge?"

"Whichever. Aren't they the same?"

"Yes and no." Sybylla shrugged. "Let's say his *very* righter-than-right views did carry over into his professional expectations for me, but on the other hand, he did *have* professional expectations for me, so he gets a few points for that. I mean, he never ever led me to believe that I was supposed to grow up and get married and that would be the whole thing. It was always law school, money, partnership. There was a pretty specific timetable, too. I was more or less supposed to be a partner by now, with a corner office. He had this whole list of firms I was supposed to apply to after law school. He took it pretty hard when I told him my plans."

"Very effective rebellion, you have to admit."

After a moment, Sybylla nodded. "I accept that, I suppose."

"And your father's made peace with all this now, right?"

She shook her head. "I had hopes, for the first couple of years. Then I realized that what I'd read as acceptance was only a kind of suspension. Like he figured it was only temporary, so he could wait out my youthful indiscretion. But I'm a public defender for good. It's what I want. The world doesn't need another corporate lawyer, but my clients need me." She put up her hands. "I like to feel needed, all right?"

"I know the feeling." Sam sighed. "Larry Jackson wrote me from prison a few days ago. He said I was the only person he'd ever met who referred to him as Mr. Jackson, and he wanted me to know how much that meant to him. It's so desperate. A little more respect, a little more pride, and so much of this mess could be avoided. Not an element of your father's philosophy, I suppose."

She shook her head. "Though we're actually pretty close, in our way. I talk to him fairly often, though I see him only when I go down to Washington, or occasionally when he's in New York. He doesn't stay with me. He has this terrible men's club where they all sit around and plan world domination or something, and he stays there." Sybylla paused, remembering her last disastrous meeting with Dermot over uneaten chateaubriand. "It's the kind of place where the wastebaskets are made of elephant feet."

"What's the club?" Sam asked, helping himself to another plantain.

"Oh . . . something Greek. Hyperion," she said. "You know it?"

"Heard of it," he said vaguely. "Old-world types. Very conservative."

"You're not kidding." She winced. "But my dad and I sort of have this conditional truce, that peace will prevail as long as I don't tell him anything about my work, or talk about the cases and the clients. In exchange, he doesn't rend his garments in my presence."

Sam refilled their glasses from the sangria pitcher. "I'm familiar with a number of your father's decisions. In fact"—he glanced up at her— "I've sort of been following his paper trail since law school. I hope this won't embarrass you, but the fact is that I find him rather brilliant." He paused, noting her silence. "I mean, ideologically unappealing, of course, but brilliant nonetheless. He's fascinating."

"Well," Sybylla said after a moment, "I can hardly disagree with that." She glanced up, a little sheepish. "Sometimes he'll use me, if he's trying out an argument or something like that, and . . . it sounds really awful, but I sometimes feel this sense of privilege, just being able to piggyback on his train of logic. He has an incredible mind. It's quite a ride."

Sam nodded. "Did he always want to be a judge, do you think?"

"Probably, yes. But things were looking a little hairy for a while. It wasn't an altogether-steady career path. He went through a bad patch around the time my mom died. He was drinking." Sybylla pushed a last plantain around her plate. "He lost about five years, I think."

"But he put himself together, it sounds like."

"Yes. I'm a little dim on the details. I know he got fired from the DA's Office in Manhattan. Then somehow he got himself hired by the U.S. Attorney for the District of Columbia, and he ended up with this big mob case. Remember Fentano? The guy who loved poetry and had two undercover cops killed?"

"I remember," Sam said. "One of the first successful Mafia prosecutions, wasn't it?"

"I think." She shrugged. She let a not-uncomfortable silence settle between them.

Sam leaned forward, his elbow planted on the table. "How're you holding up?"

"Oh, fine." She smiled. "It isn't my bedtime just yet."

"I meant in general. All the pressure from this case. And then your friend."

She shook her head quickly. The past week had been terrible, her own sadness only exacerbated by the cumulative grief at Sushila's funeral, where the devastation of her friend's family had been crushingly evident. She didn't want to talk about it now. "Sorry. I'd rather not."

"Okay. Want to talk about Trent?"

"Oh God," she moaned, shaking her head. "Did you get a look at that girl? It'll all be over the minute she takes the stand."

Sam shrugged uncomfortably. "Well, she *is* an innocent victim who's suffered a permanent disfigurement for no readily apparent reason."

"I know. That only makes it worse."

"You know what I think?" he began to say. Then he stopped and smiled a little sadly. "I mean, would you like to hear what I think?"

"Sure," Sybylla told him. "Why not?"

"Well, I think you should just be really kind with Amanda Barrett. I mean, not remotely patronizing. And you shouldn't question her experience of the attack. But her natural confusion about what happened— why me? why him?—*that's* where you should push. You know. That something was so terribly wrong with this strange guy. That he behaved so crazily. Like, why would this person she'd never set eyes on before want to do this to her? You want the jury to say to themselves, Even the victim says the defendant is crazy."

Sybylla shook her head. "I *can't.* Look, it isn't that I don't want to.

Believe me, I'm dying to use an insanity defense, but Trent says no way. He absolutely refused."

Sam's mouth opened in surprise. "You're kidding. Since when?"

"Since the arraignment. When I went to see him in the hospital I just assumed he'd want me to do whatever would be most effective in getting him out, since that was all he seemed to care about. So I started to get an insanity defense together and then, at the arraignment, I gave him a progress report on how we were doing. All of a sudden, he just went ballistic. No insanity defense! Nothing that smacks of an insanity defense! He said if I tried to send a shrink to see him, he'd just get a new lawyer." She shook her head. "I went from thinking we might have a shot at acquittal to having no defense strategy at all. Boom."

Sam frowned down at his empty plate. "Well, I don't think mistaken identity is one of your options—not with four witnesses and a cop practically on the scene, not to mention the blood and the scalpel. I don't think you can let Trent get up in court and say, 'Not me.' "

"Which of course is precisely what he wants to do." She sighed. "He doesn't seem to think he's on trial here at all. This is just his opportunity to tell the world about what he thinks happened to *him.*"

"Oh? And what does he think happened to him?"

"Just your basic paranoid hallucinatory scenario. Some bad people kidnapped him and put him in a room and they're responsible for anything he might have done, though naturally, he doesn't think he might have done anything. He has this fantasy that if he tells this story in a court of law, everyone will believe him because he'll be testifying under oath." Sam smiled and shook his head. "But at the same time, he won't tell me, his own lawyer, what he plans to say on the stand, because if he does, then I'll be in some terrible danger, too." She rolled her eyes. "He thinks these mythical people and their mythical crimes against *him* are what's on trial."

"Are they mythical?" Sam said quietly.

"What? Of course. The shrink at Bellevue says he's a textbook schizophrenic."

"Except he seems lucid to you."

She smiled. "Yeah. But that's just because I'm not a shrink. His doctor says the diagnosis is still the same. He's an obvious candidate for an insanity defense, but unfortunately, that's no longer an option."

"What about the LSD thing?" Sam asked. "That turn out to be anything?"

She stretched her legs under the table. "Well, I thought it would. But Trent only said it was given to him by the 'people.' He's made it part of his delusional fiction, which I now can't exploit for an insanity defense. And also the shrink's completely ruled it out as a motivating factor in the attack."

"Oh really?" He frowned. "Why's that?"

"Because Turturro said that however Trent may have come to ingest the drug, he had to have taken it *after* the crime was committed. Otherwise, it would've been the longest trip on record, over twenty-four hours between the crime and the time of his intake exam at Bellevue. Way out of the ballpark."

For a moment, he was quiet. Sybylla watched him bite his lower lip as he thought, and she felt herself smile at that, a little stupidly. He was too intent to notice.

"Well, that's that, I suppose." He sighed, looking at her again. "Unless you've got some magic bullet I don't know about."

Sybylla shook her head uneasily. She was thinking about the disk, of course, that tiny sliver of mystery that she'd so unreasonably hoped might somehow be germane. It had been the morning after the murder at NYU when her eye had fallen on a worn-down slip of soap at the rim of her bathroom sink and her thoughts had settled on the thing; then she had paused in brushing her teeth to curse aloud. With all that had happened, with the confusion and sorrow that had overwhelmed her after learning the news, the implant had been far from the forefront of her mind, and she now had no idea where the object was or how, if it did turn up, she might possibly reclaim it. Later that day, a recitation of her dual status as public defender and friend of the victim had gotten Sybylla past a secretary to the investigating officer, but the man, when he finally came on the line, did little to enlighten her. Professor Patel had undertaken a small research project for her, she told him, the subject of which might conceivably still be in her laboratory. She gritted her teeth against the interrogation she feared would follow, but the officer responded with the blandest of false sympathy. The police investigation, while naturally ongoing, had no continuing control over the crime scene; indeed, after the lab had been searched for evidence and drugs—the apparent motive—it

123

had been promptly returned to the control of the university, which was understandably anxious to clear it out. No, he said, sounding bored, as far as he knew, no disk-shaped object had been discovered. She might try NYU, but to tell the truth, they'd had a posse of maintenance guys waiting outside for the cops to finish, mops and disinfectant and garbage bags in hand. Place was a mess, he said apologetically. Hardly blame them.

Sybylla had hung up the phone with a sinking heart. Whatever it might have proved, then, whatever light it might have shone on the conundrum Trent represented, was undeniably moot. By now, the disk itself was certainly sitting in the vast, moldering landfill at Fresh Kills, Staten Island, a hunting ground where Sybylla, for one, was not going to go looking for it. In its absence, there remained only the irksome business of having to explain the stupid thing's disappearance to Turturro— or not, she thought, preemptively guilty. She'd hardly be the first attorney to misplace potential evidence, after all, and if she was very lucky, he'd already have forgotten all about it. No one else—not Steiner, not Andrew Greer, and certainly not Sam Larkin—need ever know.

She looked up at Sam. "Nope. Sorry, no more magic bullets. The truth is, I don't think I'm going to be able to get him off."

He looked down at his comely hands, smiling vaguely. "Then maybe you shouldn't get him off, Sybylla. Now don't look at me like that." He laughed, noting her horrified expression. "I mean, let's face it. If he did do what he's charged with, he shouldn't be on the street. We don't need any more little girls like that."

"Well, of course, but . . . I don't know, Sam. There's something weird about this case. I mean, I do think he did it. I'm not predisposed to conspiracy theories, and I don't think all these witnesses who saw him are in cahoots. But at the same time, I don't think it was *him*, you know? I don't see Trent doing that to that little girl. I think he must have been very sick to have done that, but since part of his sickness is that he doesn't understand he's sick, I've got to come up with some other way to help him."

She watched him nod slowly; then he looked up at her with an expression of such discernible tenderness that she felt herself redden. "You'll find something," he told her. "If that's really how you feel, I know you'll be able to do it." His eyes were so blue, and Sybylla was staring into them so deeply, it took her a minute to realize one of her hands had gone numb. She looked down. He was holding it, serenely, but without any proprietary claim. The sight of it was oddly mesmerizing.

A waiter, materializing beside their table, eyed their half-full plates with disapproval. "That's all you eat?" he demanded.

Sybylla, who felt almost obscenely full, nodded.

"I wrap it up for you."

"No, thanks," Sam said, but Sybylla cut in.

"Yes. Please."

"Aha," he said, leaning forward when the waiter had left. "Now I get it. You're one of *those* people. Chinese cartons in the fridge. Half-eaten slices of pizza with that green stuff growing on the mushrooms. You eat last night's salad for breakfast."

She shook her head. "Sorry to disappoint you, but it isn't for me. There's this woman in the alley next to my house. I take her food sometimes."

He looked mortified. "I'm sorry. I should have known it was something like that."

"It's okay." She shrugged. She felt a little mortified herself, as if there were something shameful about an act of charity in the modern world. She found herself avoiding his eyes. The meal was ending, and the inevitable awkwardness of their saying good night loomed ahead of them like a sheer face of rock.

Outside, Sybylla let the cool air wash over her cheeks. She held the foil-wrapped meat and rice in one hand and, with a remarkable lack of anxiety, found herself letting Sam take the other. They blended effortlessly into the Friday-night parade of couples meandering up the avenue. She felt as if a long-forgotten letter containing an ancient but still-valid winning lottery ticket, rerouted through all four corners of the globe, had just arrived in her mailbox. At the entrance to the alley, he waited for her nod before walking with her into the shadows at the far end. Annie was asleep under her heavy blanket, with only the white fuzz of her hair visible, but the food immediately attracted the interest of the cat, so Sybylla carefully unwrapped an edge and extracted a chunk of pork. The woman stirred but didn't wake.

"Do you know her?" Sam asked when they reached the entrance to Sybylla's building. "Do you know her name?"

She nodded. "It's Annie. Well, Annie Oakley, according to her."

"Doesn't sound like a name she might have been born with."

"No," agreed Sybylla.

Sam sighed. "Crazy?"

"I guess. Sometimes, anyway. She talks to herself a fair amount, but then again, she sometimes recognizes me and says hello. Anyway, she's not crazy enough to go into the shelters. I was walking by once—it was pouring—and I heard her screaming at this poor kid from the Department of Health and Social Services. He was trying to convince her to wait out the rain at a women's shelter. She wasn't having any of it. Can't blame her. Those places are so terrible." Sybylla hugged her arms. "I'll feel better about her when it warms up, but she's out of the wind back there at least. What is it?" she said, hearing him sigh.

Sam gave her a weak smile. "So much misery, huh? Like Dickens's London. Feast and famine side by side."

"Cheer up." She punched him softly in the ribs. "We're the good guys. We bring joy and happiness to the people. Didn't you read your orientation packet at work?"

"Musta missed that part. Too busy scanning for my company health club membership and the parking space for my Beemer."

She smiled, a little guilty. Only a few hours before, she might have thought something similar of him. She was glad she had never let him see her own superficiality.

Sybylla nodded at her own front door. "I live here."

"All right."

"This was fun." It had a strange ring, the way she said it, as if it was a put-down.

"It was." He was looking over her shoulder, but not in a focused way.

There was a faraway and faint drumroll at the base of Sybylla's spine. It seemed to beat a queer syncopated rhythm, rising steadily with a breathless pause between vertebrae. By the time it landed in her mouth, the words felt preformed, and all she had to do was breathe out to produce them. Even so, they sounded shocking to her, as if they came from some fabulously gifted ventriloquist who used living dummies and took them unawares. "I believe I'd like to kiss you" is what she said.

"I believe that could be arranged," said Sam.

His mouth was open and warm without being mushy. She felt the not-unwelcome ridge of his teeth nudging her flesh, and then the comforting slide of his tongue, touching an affectionate hello to her own. It was a sweet kiss and a fond kiss. It was a kiss that announced happiness now and passion to come, and it charmed her so much that she felt quite content to let it continue for a good long time.

Afterward, he didn't press an advantage obvious to them both. She walked him to the corner and put him in a cab, then headed upstairs to home, hearth, and feline. What she really wanted was some quiet in which to consider this rather remarkable new development, but Gideon could be heard emitting his uniquely unmelodic uproar as far away as the second-floor landing. Sybylla groaned and dug for her key, already agitated.

The lock spun, liquid, in its cylinder, catching nothing at all.

The wrongness of it washed over her. She pushed at the door and it swung open easily, without impediment.

It was as if one of those peculiarly gothic disasters had come to call— a tiny but fierce tornado descending on one particular Kansas cornfield or a bitter storm decimating one tiny patch of coastline before sneaking back off to sea. The unnatural force that had moved briskly through her little apartment had whirled her belongings into disarray and then moved on, most probably through her bedroom window and down the fire escape. Sybylla leaned heavily against the door frame. The pictures on the wall were crooked. The chairs had been tumbled, their cushions slashed. Every drawer had been yanked out and upended, leaving a layer of detritus on the floor. In the kitchen, broken glass covered the tiles, and the cupboards had been emptied of pots. She gulped some air. This isn't too bad, she told herself. Not so terrible. A big mess, that's all. She wanted to see the rest, so she could start to feel better as soon as possible.

The bedroom was worse, naturally: slashed pillows, clothes from the closet thrown onto the floor, and her VCR gone, though the thief had evidently not considered her ancient television worth moving. A few hundred dollars in traveler's checks were missing from the bedside table's drawer. She swallowed when she opened the bathroom door. Her medicine cabinet had been opened and its contents thrown onto the floor. The tiles were greasy with face cream and speckled with antibiotic capsules from a long-ago illness, and an entire packet of Alka Seltzers had been crushed over the glop, like powdered sugar atop a cake. She shook her head at the surreal humor in this, then yelped.

The laundry hamper was moving.

It's a bomb, she thought, somewhat illogically. Then, reaching out with one terrified foot, she flipped up the lid. With a shriek of outrage, Gideon sprang out and tore past her into the chaos of the bedroom.

Sybylla smiled. Cat bomb.

She turned back to the bedroom. Now that she had seen it all, it felt surprisingly manageable. Only a VCR and a little money and a major cleanup job, after all. She stepped into the room. In the inert jumble, she could begin to pick out the vestiges of her daily life: a lamb's wool sweater, the book she'd begun reading last week and hadn't particularly liked, a Bloomingdale's catalog. Suddenly, none of it seemed terribly important. She could just walk off, it occurred to her. Leave it all lying there for somebody else to clean up. Sybylla shrugged her shoulders, as if to dislodge the thought. That kind of thinking was dangerous, she told herself. She had a court appearance in the morning, and that meant something decent to wear, and shoes, and stockings, and her hairbrush, and a million other little pieces she would have to hunt and gather if she was going to appear pulled together. And she had to call a locksmith, of course, before she did anything else. And the police, to file the report of yet another New York burglary. Weariness descended on her. It seemed an imponderable amount of time since she had sent Sam home to his apartment.

Sybylla set her jaw at the tangle of clothing across the room, but her eye was drawn closer, to the much subtler color of inlaid wood at her feet, the corner of a frame. Reassured, she reached down and picked it up, turning it over to see the faces of her parents, their moment of happiness pressed under unbroken glass. Sybylla smiled and hugged it tightly to her chest, then went in search of the phone.

HELPING

HANDS

Sybylla remembered her first trial through a scrim of embarrassment, disappointment, and severe self-castigation. The embarrassment arose from being thoroughly reamed by the judge, who took Sybylla to task for everything from her questioning technique to her eager objections to what the judge theorized was Sybylla's failure to advise her client that whatever the DA had offered, it was better than he could reasonably have expected from a trial.

The disappointment was over her loss, and it was very much *her* loss. The client, no stranger to the courtrooms of 100 Centre Street, nor to Rikers Island, accepted the verdict with a shrug as the way of the world—his world—thanked Sybylla for doing what she could, and offered his wrists to the court officer without further comment. His case was transferred to someone in appeals and she never heard a word from him again. Not the most auspicious beginning for what she had hoped would be an exemplary career, right beating might, underdog against the system, that sort of thing. She'd slunk back to her little desk, received a perfunctory "too bad, but there'll be others" lecture from Steiner, and tried to put it behind her.

That was where the self-castigation came in. When the trial transcript finally materialized, she pored over it obsessively, marking her errors—so obvious to her in retrospect—with an angry red pen. She didn't doubt that whoever caught the case in appeals would find ample material to work with here.

So low was her mood, in fact, that she had actually called her father, fishing wordlessly for his approval, trying to goad him into telling her how bright she was, how suited for a career at the bar. Unfortunately, Dermot was well into his winter of discontent on the subject and given to indulging in very articulate tirades about how she was wasting her life. Clutching her phone, she listened to his utterly authoritative voice inform her that she had absolutely made the wrong decision, that the repercussions were significant but not altogether reversible, that with a few calls she could still find herself staring at her brightly polished nameplate on a mahogany-veneered door in a tall, sleek building, somewhere in midtown, if she but said the word. Sybylla, in torment, had pleaded a nonexistent dinner date and hung up the phone.

Thankfully, her wobble was short-lived. At her second trial, the client was a mother of five children age five and under, accused of assaulting the Con Edison clerk when the woman refused to turn the power back on. The kids were in court, lined up on the front bench in their good clothes, hems ragged, shoes badly made and coming apart. Sybylla's eyes filled, looking at them, worrying what would happen to them when she fumbled the ball, as she had convinced herself she would, already beating herself up about it.

But this time it was the prosecution's turn to make a mess of things. The ADA, who looked as terrified as Sybylla was herself, read her questions from the legal pad on which she'd scribbled them, and was too focused on simply getting the words out to react when her case began to slip away. The complaining witness seemed to have lost her enthusiasm for revenge, and she gave her responses in a lackluster voice, failing to supply any information not expressly requested. Sybylla's client, on the other hand, spoke poignantly about the sick baby, the dark and cold apartment, the three little girls and their brother sleeping together on one mattress. The jury acquitted in exactly eight minutes, the children hugged Sybylla, and her faith in herself, in what she had chosen to make of herself and do with herself, was restored in a blissful rush.

In the years since, she'd become a better trial lawyer—better at getting what she needed out of witnesses, better at putting her foot down when the prosecution tried to steal a base, better at making herself appealing to juries without patronizing them. To ask for more, in an era when jurors tended merely to pay lip service to the concept of presumption of innocence and when virtually every prospective juror stated in voir dire that they knew or had been a crime victim, was simply counterproductive.

In the fullness of time, Sybylla's levelheadedness had merged with her naturally superstitious tendencies to create a distinct ritual for trial mornings, which was how she found herself at Au Bon Pain an hour before Trent's case was due to be called for voir dire, working on her third cappuccino, her second chocolate croissant, and her first complete transcription of her notes. By the second pass, the material was ingrained enough for Sybylla to consult her notes only occasionally during trial; by the third, she could fairly safely leave them at the defense table and appear before the jury as a poised, confident, and knowledgeable advocate.

This, to say the least, was how the jurors would have to see her if Trent was to have even the remotest chance. After weeks of feverish but fruitless brainstorming, Sybylla had lowered her sights and devised a defense plan so implausible, so downright wacky, that its excesses nearly obscured the tiny pinprick of hope it represented. Like a pregnant hostess trying to stifle nausea over her own dinner party, she was doing her best to pretend this trial was business as usual, a set-to between two versions of the events in question, rather than an exercise in utter futility. She looked down at her notes and sagged, preemptively exhausted by what lay ahead.

During the hours of names, addresses, and occupations to come, she and Greer would be wading through the same jury pool with different nets. It was her considerable task to scoop up a few folks who were not so knowledgeable about the case that they had already condemned Trent to the deepest circle of hell and yet whose apparent lack of familiarity with current events didn't indicate a person too stupid to think independently. She also hoped to find a few jurors whose thoughts toward the homeless were charitable. And then, as if these were not well nigh insurmountable criteria themselves, there was an extra little something on her wish list.

She was looking for jurors who had had more than a passing acquaintance with hallucinogenics, preferably LSD, a few sunny trippers from those days of yore. She was looking for men or women who, when asked to contemplate the absurdity of a long, leisurely, and megabummer acid trip, would react with something short of scoffing disbelief. Because the defense she had finally cobbled together for Trent was virtually the only one she could design that encompassed both his desire to testify and his outright rejection of insanity, it fell to her to find jurors more likely to trust the chaos of their own experiences than the airtight pronouncements of the experts, jurors—in other words—likely to accept that if they themselves had flown to the moon on acid, then someone else could conceivably have writhed in hell for longer than the prescribed period of time. That way, the trace LSD on Trent's intake report could be used to *imply* intoxication during the crime. Add to this Trent's paranoid delusion of kidnapping and incarceration and you had *involuntary intoxication*—a matter of being forced to ingest a substance that had made you violent. This was actually a legitimate defense. Not entirely credible, perhaps, but ultimately no nuttier than claiming an overabundance of Twinkies had induced a murderous rage—a defense that actually *had* worked for somebody in San Francisco. Sybylla sighed. If she could get even one veteran of a bad LSD trip onto the panel, she theorized, she had a hung jury. With two or three . . . Well, she was not even going to consider the possibility of acquittal.

But how to find them? In many of her past trials, she had used voir dire as an opportunity to preview her case for the prospective jurors and watch their reactions. If their eyes rolled at the words *mistaken identity* or *circumstantial evidence,* she tried to get them off the panel, but if they listened seriously, contemplatively, they were live ones for the defense and she did what she could to get them on. This time, however, her defense strategy would have to remain hidden beneath the veil of the ostensibly similar but ultimately quite different insanity defense, and it could not be allowed to peek out until the prosecution had rested its case. Sybylla fully intended to build as compelling a case as she could from the LSD trace and the phenomenon of Trent's disappearance—to which Bennis had readily agreed to add what substance he could—and its only hope of success depended on its ability to surprise. She could not give Greer any advance opportunity to poke holes in a very flimsy story. Accordingly, Sybylla was determined that neither the acronym LSD nor any of its colorful aliases would pass her lips until Trent was on the stand, enlightening the jury about his "people" and their "room" and looking for all the world like somebody who'd taken a major chemical trip to Erewhon.

Her subterfuge had been elaborate. In accordance with the law, Sybylla had notified the DA's office of her intention to pursue an insanity defense, a move that came as no surprise to them, though she'd had a devil of a time convincing Trent to cooperate with the prosecution's shrink. Serving the notice, however, did not expressly require her to follow the defense plan, and when Greer discovered the tables turned on him, he was very likely to start screaming, but that was his problem. Having finally devised a defense that Trent would accept, her problem was to present it as seriously and competently as she could.

She was just deciding to be noble and forgo one final croissant when a shadow fell over her table. Sybylla squinted up and smiled, despite herself.

"How'd you find me? This is my shameful little routine I don't want anybody to know about."

"David," Sam said, taking the seat opposite her. His tray, she noted with unbridled greed, held two chocolate croissants. "He said you come down here whenever you have a trial and stuff your face. It sounded so sweet, I had to see." He sprinkled sugar in his coffee and stirred. "Can I help? I mean later on. Can I tag along?"

She studied him for a minute. He was keeping his eagerness in check, but only just. Once, in the past weeks of intense preparation, he'd mentioned the possibility of sitting in on the trial—to watch, he'd put it kindly, and to learn—but she'd laughed it off and Sam hadn't mentioned it again.

"Gal Friday?" she queried.

"I could." He shrugged. "I mean, I'd be happy to do the scut work if that would be of help."

"It would," she told him. "But why would you want to spend your time on my case? If you're taking notes for the appeal, it's a bit premature."

"Now now," Sam scolded, "it isn't that at all. Yeah, if it goes to appeal, I'll be in a better position to handle it, but I'm not assuming that'll happen, Syb."

"Well, that's something." She studied him. Sam sat opposite her, his hands nervously tapping the Styrofoam cup, suspended, waiting for her to speak. It was inescapable, she thought, the edge of suspicion that nagged her whenever she looked closely at him, peering too intently at the genial, attractive, and avidly interested man he seemed so readily to be. In the weeks since their date, her caution had seemed to abate slightly, but now it was back in force. Because it's the sheer unlikeliness of him, Sybylla thought, following the crooked outline of his mouth and trying to recall its specific texture and heat. *Because I haven't the faintest idea what he's after.*

"All right." He laughed, disconcerting her by seeming to follow her thoughts. "I'll admit it. I have an inside angle."

Sybylla sighed. "Well, points to you for saying so. What's your angle?"

"My God, you're a suspicious one, aren't you?" He tipped back his coffee cup and drank. "Nothing so terrible, I assure you. I just want to learn, that's all. You know I'm a little green at trying cases. Well, you're aware of that firsthand. I want to see how somebody who knows what she's doing in a courtroom handles a case like this."

"Like this? Meaning what?"

"Meaning a case I don't have any notion of how you're going to win."

"Winning isn't everything," Sybylla said archly. "Unless you're just *result-oriented.*"

"But you have a plan," he pressed.

"I might." She looked at her watch. "But I don't have time to tell you about it now. If you want to come on board, you'll have to fly blind."

He grinned. "So it's all right? I get to attend the trial?"

"Depends." Sybylla nodded at the croissants. "Is one of those for me?"

He glanced down, confused. "Oh. Sure." He watched her take an utterly hedonistic bite. "That's it? I give you a pastry, I get to stay?"

She grinned at him. "It never hurts to walk into court with an attractive associate."

Sam winced. "You're so sexist. I'm going to have to go on a men's retreat or something if you keep up with this emasculating behavior."

Sybylla chewed her croissant, sprinkling the pastry flakes on her fingertips over the tabletop. Then she sighed, surveying the wreckage of croissant crumbs before her, consumed by self-loathing. "I can't believe I just ate three croissants."

"Three! God, you're a pig." He got to his feet and crumpled his empty coffee cup, lobbing it into a trash can. "Sybylla"—he looked serious—"look, I'll only say it once, so you don't have to worry. Thank you. I appreciate this."

"Let me hear it again after you spend the day making notes on prospective jurors' favorite TV shows," she told him, heading for the door. Leaving the café, they bucked the flood of city workers on their way in. The day was overcast and chilly and the homeless in Foley Square were clad in plastic garbage bags against the impending rain. Their stillness in the eye of the storm, the continual swirl of bodies made by workers arriving, taking possession of these buildings, leaving at night, was arresting, and Sybylla thought, not for the first time, that Trent's case brought the reality of New York's homeless into sharp relief, the suffering they endured, its painful contrast to the wealth and purposeful activity all around them.

Sam waited for her in the hall as Sybylla attempted unsuccessfully to scrub the black felt tip pen marks off her palm, then the two made their way into Judge Coffin's high-ceilinged courtroom, its grubby linoleum floor some barely discernible beige color. Straight ahead, behind the judge's wooden bench, IN GOD WE TRUST was affixed in large letters to the wall, a sentiment Sybylla had never entirely comprehended in this setting. If we truly trusted in God to judge us and punish us, she reasoned, then what are we doing *here?* Why bother with this decrepit, unwieldy, cruel, and inefficient system?

The room teemed with energy. The press, barely corralled into the rear three rows, craned their necks as she entered and, ridiculously, she thought, made notes. (What were they writing down? That she had arrived on time? What she was wearing?) Farther up: lucky voyeurs and a klatch of English suits and ladies-who-lunch Chanel, which could only be the Barretts and their friends, sans daughter. Little Amanda, it was clear, was to be kept under wraps until the moment was right. She let her heavy bag fall loudly on the sturdy defense table, then began unloading files. Beside her, Sam was unsnapping his briefcase. "Don't look now," he said quietly. "Here comes D'Artagnan."

Naturally, Sybylla looked back immediately.

He was working the room like a bride, trawling up the aisle and nodding to his fans on either side, stopping to press flesh with the reporters and chat paternally to the Barrett camp, looking very much like the man with the mission he was always claiming to be. He wore a sober brown suit, his white shirt pulling a bit around the buttons, his brown loafers shiny. When he reached the front of the room, he stepped amiably across to Sybylla and extended his hand, holding it for an ample moment in a thoughtful gesture for the courtroom sketch artists. "Ms. Muldoon," he said snugly.

Sybylla's throat tightened in distaste. Unbidden, the memory of Greer and his buddy Robert Winston leering at her from a dim corner of the Hyperion Club dining room reconstituted itself before her eyes. In her annoyance, she forgot completely to accept Greer's hand, a nonevent later inflated by the attending press into TRENT ATTY SNUBS DA. But of course, she scolded herself, that had indicated no sin greater than mere voyeurism. Sybylla had, after all, just been having a perfectly visible row with her father, the future Supreme Court justice.

Greer turned his head to look at Sam. "My cocounsel," Sybylla said shortly. "Sam Larkin."

Sam nodded.

Greer pursed his lips. "Old Spice case. Am I right?"

"You have a good memory," Sam said.

"You did well," he said thoughtfully. "For your first time out."

He's not even aware that he's condescending, Sybylla observed. Greer hadn't withdrawn his hand and it stuck out, a badge of sportsmanship, which Sybylla now dutifully shook. "Think we'll get through voir dire today?" she said. "Or are you planning to turn this into a marathon?"

"Today," Greer said. "I'm sure we can find twelve good people and true today."

Twelve knee-jerk conviction machines, you mean, Sybylla thought. She said a terse good-bye to the DA and returned to her files, fuming so hard as they emerged from her bag that she barely noticed Sam take his seat.

CHAPTER

SIXTEEN

Sybylla's initial spar with Greer seemed increasingly benign as the two began to clash over jury selection. First, in a small chamber off the courtroom, prospective jurors were quizzed on their familiarity with the case, and not surprisingly, more than a few were well-informed and not shy about stating their opinions. With those weeded out and excused, the rest were voir dired. Again and again, the jury box filled with prospects on whom the two attorneys bore down with questions, and again and again those prospects were sent out in the hall to wait like errant schoolchildren while Sybylla and Greer systematically decimated their ranks. First, Judge Coffin would turn to the DA to hear his challenges for cause, and then to Sybylla to hear hers, and that, between the social workers and liberals Greer contrived to excuse and the reactionaries and crime victims Sybylla wanted to excuse, wiped out nearly all of the prospective jurors.

Of those who remained, most fell prey to peremptory challenges from either side. Though Greer hadn't been able to make her admit it, one woman clearly had a loathing for law enforcement. Imprisoned brother? Too many speeding tickets? Didn't matter—out she went. Sybylla used one of her perempts to get rid of a man who swore up and down that he'd never heard of Trent (Coffin had agreed that use of the Wild Man label would not be allowed) but who used his time in the jury box to send reassuring looks at the girl's parents and evil glares at the defendant. Out.

She saw the rationale to Greer's strategy clearly enough. No artists or writers (they look too hard for motivation), no readers of the *Amsterdam News* (who tended to believe that every black prisoner from coast to coast had been framed by the government), no one who had ever worked with or given money to the homeless (compassion outweighs reason). He didn't like women, Sybylla saw. At least women below middle age—too open-minded? He didn't like blacks, though he was always careful to find a discernible reason to have them excused. He didn't like students, or anyone who seemed by their manner or their news sources or their pastimes to make a habit of thinking independently. Such people could not be trusted to do the right thing.

Sybylla, for her part, was just as relentless. She goaded the two or three Asian jurors who came through the jury box into admitting their disdain for the homeless, as indeed for anyone who didn't work as hard as they did. She told the several violent-crime victims that if their ordeals had happened to her, she would not be able to be an impartial juror— how could they? She told those parents of young children that while the trial would involve a young child, it wasn't *about* a child; could they really stay focused on their job—to judge the facts relating to a troubled adult—when a child was involved? Grateful for an out, most of them said no.

By lunchtime, they had worked through the sixty jurors they'd been sent, and Judge Coffin ordered up a fresh panel for after the break. The prospect of seating a fair and impartial jury before the millennium was looking increasingly unlikely, but things picked up in the afternoon. Sybylla, who had been on the lookout for potential LSD users, finally found a live one in a stockbroker who had graduated from Hampshire College.

Hampshire College. The name, she noticed, seemed to slip right past Greer, to whom it probably sounded bucolic and Anglophilic—sub-Ivy, as it were. But Hampshire had been founded in 1970, in the cradle of the counterculture. It was very, very alternative, the kind of place, she mused, where they probably gave academic credit for LSD usage. This mild-mannered, Brooks Brothered, futures-trading family man was a former Deadhead, unless she was much mistaken. She suppressed her smile when Greer let him pass. One in the hole for her side.

Sybylla and Sam wrote frantically, taking notes as Greer asked his questions: juror number three had an uncle on the force; juror number two had a daughter Amanda Barrett's age; juror number eight got her news from the *National Enquirer;* juror number ten was so enamored of the job the DA was doing that he took the opportunity to say so ("and I jus' wanna tell you that if you *do* run for governor, I fer one am gonna vote for you"), prompting Sybylla to try to have every prospective juror within earshot excused. Sam wiped his damp forehead with the cuff of his pinstriped shirt. It felt as if it would never end.

But slowly, things began to improve. By two in the afternoon, they had four agreed-upon jurors. Another wave of prospectives in the box and they had four more. Finally, impossibly, Sybylla found herself watching Greer as he strutted and sputtered before them one last time, soliloquizing about the heavy responsibility they faced, how the city would be putting its faith in them, and did they understand the gravity with which that faith was placed?

Fourteen heads nodded solemnly.

Greer, looking like a weary general, turned heavily to Coffin and said that he was satisfied.

Slowly, Sybylla got to her feet and stepped before the jury box, meeting the tired gazes of fourteen citizens prepared to sit in judgment upon Trent. They looked normal enough. Decent people, as best she could tell. No Trojan horses. In addition to the stockbroker, there were two teachers (very civic-minded, teachers; very careful about getting it right); a Con Ed worker, who said he was unmarried and whom Sybylla believed was gay (Greer had missed that completely, she thought); a nurse; a McDonald's manager; a housewife; a guard at the Museum of Natural History (not an LSD candidate, she thought, but perhaps he'd absorbed enough knowledge about the human animal to accommodate Trent's behavior); a recession-hit contractor, who, Sybylla noted, pulled out a copy of *The Nation* during the long waits; two retired ladies who looked fairly thoughtful; a truck driver; a home health-care worker; and a man who said he "dealt in African art."

She still had three of her twenty perempts left, but fatigue overwhelmed her as she regarded the faces in the box, and she doubted she had the stomach for any more individual questioning. It was time to change nets and see if any of these little fishies felt like jumping into them.

"Hello again, ladies and gentlemen. It's been a long day, hasn't it?" Grim nods. The contractor gave her a kind look.

"Anybody here read mysteries?" Sybylla said. The retired ladies nodded. A few hands went up.

"You know how, sometimes, you think you know who did it in the middle, but by the time you get to the end, it's somebody else?"

More nods, but wary this time.

"This trial may be like that. You may find yourself listening to the prosecution's case and thinking to yourself, Well, that's the way it is. It happened just like the prosecutor says it did, and that's all there is to it. But then my client has his turn. And his story may make you think again." She put both hands out and touched the railing between the jurors and her. "I need to know that you'll wait for the end of the book before making up your mind," she said slowly. "I need to know that you won't close your mind after hearing only a part of the evidence."

The men and women looked at her intently. Out of the corner of her eye, she saw a head nod.

"Let me ask you something." Sybylla pushed back and returned to her table, leaning back against it casually. "If the trial stopped now—right now—if the judge said to you, 'Okay, jury, as of this minute, how do you vote?'—what would you say?"

They were taken aback, she saw. Juries always were. She had lifted this trick from Steiner and used it faithfully in virtually all of the felony cases she'd tried.

One by one, the jurors shrugged. "I don't know," one of the teachers said.

Sybylla made eye contact with each of them. "I'm sorry to have to say this, but each of you has given the wrong answer. If you had to give a verdict right now, the only possible verdict you could give is not guilty. You have heard no evidence to convict my client, no evidence to tie him to the crime, nothing to imply that there even *was* a crime. He is innocent until he's been proved guilty, and, at this moment, no one has done so." She left the table and returned to the jury box. "Do you understand this? I'm talking about an essential element of our law, guaranteed by our Constitution." Sobered, they nodded.

She turned and walked away from them, toward the opposite end of the room, her head down as if she was lost in thought. When she had almost reached the clerk's desk, she turned, seemingly consumed by a sudden idea. "You know," Sybylla said pensively, "even though it's been a long day, and even though Mr. Greer and I have asked you a lot of questions—personal questions, I know—we still don't know very much about you. There are so many things about each of you that are hidden to us. Some of them are immaterial to this case, but others . . . who knows?" She gestured solemnly to them. "*You* know. One of you could be a member of the KKK. One of you might feel that the solution to homelessness is to incarcerate the homeless. How would I know that about you unless I happened to ask you that question directly?" She let her gaze drift above the jurors' heads, as if she was thinking aloud. "But I can't ask you those questions. I can't read your minds. I have to trust that you will tell me what I need to know, and that's a leap of faith, believe me."

She glanced at Sam. He was admiring, holding his smile in check.

"So tell me now. Please. Is there anything you've heard today, or anything in your life, your character, that would prevent you from being the open-minded jurors we need you to be?" She paused to let the silence settle. "You know," Sybylla said warmly, "it isn't such a terrible thing to be incapable of open-mindedness. All of us are swayed by our experiences, and by prejudices. If the school bully who beat you up had red hair, then maybe there's a tiny part of you that resents people with red hair, even though you may know this to be irrational. That's harmless enough. But much less harmless, ladies and gentlemen, are preconceived ideas that may touch upon this case and upon my client. Most of us avert our eyes when we walk past people who live on the street. Sometimes we give them money and sometimes we don't, but rarely do we want to engage them in conversation, bring them into our lives. Now this trial is going to take us deeply into that very world, and it's an ugly world. Are you prepared to put aside everything you think you know about homelessness?"

Behind her, Greer lumbered to his feet. "Objection, Your Honor. This is a voir dire, not a sociology lecture."

Sybylla stood her ground, ignoring the interruption. She looked from juror to juror.

"Finish up, Ms. Muldoon," Coffin said, an edge of bemusement in his voice.

She sighed and walked briskly back to her table, where she stood behind Trent, planting her hands on his shoulders. "This is my client Trent. I'm going to defend him vigorously, because that's my job. When he looks at you today, he has to see a group of people who are willing to be fair and impartial. Please think about those words—*fair* and *impartial*. Because, believe me, if it were you in this chair, or your mother, or your child, you'd be as desperate to have fair and impartial jurors as he is right now." Scattered nods. She walked slowly back to the box. "It's a difficult thing the court is asking you to do, I know that. To sit in judgment on another human being is a terrible responsibility. You must set aside your emotions, your religious convictions, and rule according to the evidence, and there's no guarantee that you're going to leave this experience with the warm glow of having done something indisputably *right*. No guarantee at all. Can you do it?"

Silence. Rapt faces.

"Now is the time to say so. There's no shame, but we need to know."

She had a rule: when the first one broke eye contact, she turned away from the rest.

A long five seconds later, Mr. McDonald's looked away.

Sybylla turned to Coffin. "This panel is acceptable to the defense, Your Honor."

"Thank you, Ms. Muldoon."

It was nearly five. After swearing in the jury, Coffin called for opening statements the following morning and sent them all out into the urban dusk: rush hour.

"Why don't you come home with me?" Sam asked suddenly. Sybylla turned to him, awkward but unaccountably wanting to say yes. "I can make you dinner and tell you how brilliant you are. You can clue me in on what you've got planned for tomorrow."

She gave him a nervous smile. "Sounds great."

He waited for it. "But?"

"But." Her mind raced. She knew there was something. "I have this awful cat. Did I ever mention my awful cat?"

"Don't think so." He frowned.

She shrugged. "He has to be fed. I'm sorry." Annie, too, she added to herself. Between her late nights of preparation and her general distraction, she hadn't been to the alley in weeks, and she was feeling a little guilty. Sam was bouncing his briefcase off of his knee and looking dejected.

"Want to come?" The voice was Sybylla's, and it took her by surprise.

He looked up. "You sure?"

"Sure I'm sure," she said, trying to sound convincing. "If you give me a minute to do the cat thing, we can go out, get a bite in the neighborhood." Going out sounded good, she thought. Genial, but not too cozy. "How about it?"

"I'd love to. Thanks."

A taxi pulled up to the curb a few feet ahead of where they stood. "Should we?" He gave her a leer.

"It'll cost a fortune," Sybylla said tentatively.

They leapt in unison, narrowly edging out a pack of hopefuls. "Columbus and Seventy-fourth," she crowed. To the urban victor go the spoils.

"But I don't understand," Sam objected, leaning heavily against Sybylla as the cab swung hard around Columbus Circle a few minutes later. "You're the one who told me the LSD thing was a dead end."

"I know." She nodded, the flicker of streetlights rattling over her face. "And factually, it is. But science can be a bit more malleable in a courtroom than in a newspaper, for example, or on television. It's subject to the same distortions jurors can feel about any expert testimony. For example, if you can show that other experts disagree with the expert on the stand, it won't matter that the guy who's testifying has the best credentials on the entire planet—to a layperson he's just one guy disagreeing with another guy, so who's to say which one's right? And then there's the purely human stuff. If the juror just plain doesn't *like* the expert, if he thinks the guy's a snob, for example, he may lend less credence to what he's saying, or even disbelieve him entirely, you know, just to sort of punish him for his arrogance. Jurors can't be depended upon to digest graphs and analyze scientific data. They'll listen to the testimony, but if it doesn't make sense to *them*, it's worthless. You see what I mean?"

Sam nodded. "I do." He paused, thinking. "But even if you do get the jury to discount the LSD time frame, then what have you really got?" He seemed even more perplexed than before. "He still took the drug, didn't he? And intoxication isn't a defense. I mean, people who commit crimes when they're high on drugs are convicted all the time."

"Yes," she agreed, "but Trent swears that he never took LSD or any drug willingly. I told you, he has his own version of what happened to him, which he is absolutely determined to recount on the stand, most of which I *still* haven't heard." She rolled her eyes.

"And you're actually going to let him get up on the stand and just ramble about all this stuff?" Sam's voice seeped with disappointment. It went through her like an arrow.

"Well, more or less. Actually, there is something in the way of corroborating evidence, I mean, we won't be entirely out there in the stratosphere. One of Trent's friends is going to testify that he saw Trent being forcibly put into a city services van just before Christmas, and city services has no record of him. I've checked. Not that that's surprising, given the state of the agency. But the point is, Trent was not heard from after that day until the day of the attack."

"Says him." Sam shook his head. They had stopped for a light. "Anything else?"

"I wish there were. Mistaken identity, as you yourself pointed out, is not an option, and he won't let me claim insanity. I have to go with what I've got, and what I've got is a confirmed disappearance, a passionate story of imprisonment and abuse—details to be provided on the stand—and evidence at the time of his reappearance of a drug that nobody he knows has ever known him to take. Now given the complete hopelessness of discrediting four witnesses, solid forensics, and a little girl who's going to point to Trent and cry, and given Trent's stand on insanity, I have no choice but to use the LSD and try to create enough doubt about when he ingested it to get at the issue of intent." She shook her head at the NO SMOKING sticker affixed to the window, its edges shredded and curling. "Look at it this way, Sam. We have testimony to support that he was missing. We also have testimony to support that he had the drug in his system when he reemerged. Two poles to hang a defense on, albeit not a terribly weatherproof one."

Sam shook his head. "I can come up with a far more likely scenario to explain those two poles than abduction and the forced ingestion of a controlled substance."

"And Greer will, I have little doubt." Sybylla shrugged. "But it doesn't really matter, you know. It's called reasonable doubt. I came up with a version of the facts that fits the facts. And this defense plan has other benefits. I don't lose face by telling the witnesses they didn't see what they saw or the forensic guys they didn't prove what they proved. I don't blame the victim. The jury will like that I'm not wasting their time by squabbling over how many feet away the witnesses were when they saw Trent attack the girl. Plus, I get mileage from the witnesses, too. At least one of them describes Trent in her statement as a crazy man."

Sam turned to her. "But how does that help if you're not using an insanity defense?"

She couldn't deny herself a little smile. "But Greer thinks I *am* using it. I told his office I was, and they've sent their own psychiatrist to interview Trent and presumably come up with an opposing diagnosis. However, filing the notice doesn't *require* me to use that defense. My point is that schizophrenic behavior and LSD-induced behavior are similar." She smirked at him in the fading light. "Didn't you yourself call it 'instant insanity'?"

Slowly, he began to grin. "It's so sneaky," he said, his voice newly admiring.

"You notice how I never raised the issue of insanity in voir dire, right? I didn't ask anyone what they thought of mental illness, or whether somebody could be temporarily insane, or any of that. And I'm not going to be bringing it up in the opening statement, either, or when I cross-examine Greer's witnesses. If I did that, then switched tacks later on, the jury would see it as scrambling for a defense. The LSD has to be a total sneak attack. It has to appear that this has *always* been our defense, that Trent was intoxicated with a dangerous hallucinogenic drug against his will, which caused him to do this terrible thing." She grinned up at him. "You know, I can't wait to see Greer's face when he realizes he's been barking up the wrong tree all along. It'll almost be worth it just for that."

"Yes," Sam said softly. "I suppose it will."

After a moment, she faced him. "I don't expect to win it, you know—in case you thought I did."

He turned to her. "I think you're wise not to be terribly optimistic," he said simply. "It's not your fault. You've done the best you could, I can see that."

She shrugged, reaching for her purse as the cab turned onto Columbus. "I've been trying like hell to find an LSD expert who'll help me widen the parameters of the affected time period, but everyone I've talked to pretty much says eight to twelve hours, and that's it. With that guideline, the only possible source for the ingestion of the drug was while Trent was down at Police Plaza. Turturro thinks someone in the cell with him gave him the drug as a joke. Some joke!" She shrugged. "'Let's see what happens when we give the crazy guy LSD. . . .'" Sybylla sighed. "Poor Trent. He is clinging for life to this extraordinary scenario of how he came to be standing over the little girl with a scalpel in his hand—without exactly admitting he hurt her, by the way." She grimaced. "It's incredible what people will do to protect themselves from guilt over what they've done."

She directed the cab to her corner Korean and threw a ten at the driver before Sam could reach his wallet. "I just need to pick up a few things," she told him, heading for the hot food. She ladled a cup of chili for Annie, a bunch of grapes, and grabbed some ice cream for herself. Then she made her way to the front and set the food in two piles. "May I have two bags?" she said to Mr. Ko.

He took her money. "Okay. But she no there," the man said.

"I'm sorry?"

He didn't even look up. "You friend. You lady. They take her away."

Sybylla swallowed. "The woman in the alley?"

"Yeah." He was shoveling her food in the bags. "I tell you. They take her to shelter. I go out last week, they screaming and racket. They van park in front of my place, for my delivery. I say, 'Move you van.' He don't move. That lady screaming and my delivery truck coming, so I go out again. I say, 'You in my place. Move you van.' He say to me he be only another minute, but he more than a minute. My delivery van has to circle the block." He shook his head, irate. "Anyway, she gone. Gone to the shelter, the man say."

"I don't believe it," Sybylla said softly. Sam reached for the bags and took her arm.

"Come on," Sam said, his voice gentle. "Let's see."

Numbly, she walked behind him out of the store and crossed her street. The alley was dark and silent, and Sybylla knew the instant she stepped inside that the grocer was right. She was gone. Annie's shopping cart, containing her worldly goods, had been rudely upended, its contents spilled onto the ground. The overhang beneath which the woman had lain was empty, with only a grubby down coat left spread on the ground. "I don't believe it," she heard herself say again.

"Syb, look, obviously she felt she wanted to go to the shelter for a few days. Maybe she wanted to see a doctor or just sleep in a bed for a little while. I don't doubt for a minute that she'll be back next week. I promise, it isn't a tragedy."

She shrugged. "You're right, I guess. I'm just surprised. She didn't seem to want to have anything to do with the shelter system."

"Well, look, Syb, this woman was probably very sweet, but you're attributing some fairly rational motivations here. Didn't you say she was mentally ill?"

"Yeah," she admitted.

"So maybe she felt an episode coming on or something and she wanted to be inside. With care, you know?"

"Care!" Sybylla snorted the word. "*Right.*"

"Sorry." He gave her shoulder a tentative pat. "I am."

"Okay." She nodded miserably. "Hey—"

"What?"

"That's . . . Here, give me that bag, all right? I want the chili."

"Now?"

"Shh." She found the Styrofoam cup and peeled off the lid. "Here, kitty. C'mon, sweets."

"Where is he?" Sam whispered, looking around.

"Shh. He's scared. C'mon, kitty."

Slowly, the cat came forward, looking terrified and ravenous in equal parts. As he approached, she spilled some of the chili onto the cup's plastic lid and let him eat in peace. Then, cooing at him, she scooped up the filthy animal.

"You're taking him?"

"Till she comes back." Sybylla nodded at the empty place.

"I'd better warn you," Sam said grimly, "I am not a cat person."

"That is a serious character flaw on your part," she told him, walking briskly toward home. The cat struggled as they climbed the stairs. "Hush, kitty. A whole bowl of milk, just for you. And then we'll talk bath."

"Groan," Sam said.

"Will you open the door? My key's in the outside compartment."

He fished it from her purse and opened the lock.

"Okay, lovey." She hustled him into the bathroom, ignoring Gideon's outraged wail.

"You already *have* a cat," Sam said, sounding equally pissed.

"Sam?" she called from the bathroom. "Will you bring me the milk from the fridge? And a bowl?"

He opened the door a crack and handed them in. Sybylla watched as the famished animal drank the entire half-pint. She sighed and hunted out an old towel for the cat to begin marking as his own. "I'll be back," she informed him. She slipped from the room.

Sam was standing in the middle of the room, engaging Gideon in a Mexican standoff. "This is Gideon," Sybylla said by way of introduction. "He's a nasty piece of work."

"So I see." Unexpectedly, he smiled. "Gideon. After Clarence Earl, no doubt."

"The same. This one was a drifter like old Clarence. I used to see him all over the neighborhood." She paused. "Sam, look, would you mind very much if we skipped the restaurant? I don't really want to leave Annie's cat alone. He's pretty scared."

Sam nodded. "Somehow I figured." He sighed and stretched, then indulged in a leisurely gaze around the room. Abruptly, belatedly, Sybylla processed the information that he was in her house. She ducked her head and tried to remember the last time she'd cleaned.

"It's nice, this place," he said, not sounding too convinced.

She smiled. "Remember that film *Wall Street*? Remember what Daryl Hannah says about the Upper West Side? 'Home of the house-plant and exposed brick wall?' " She opened her arms. "As you see."

"Can I peek?" he asked, meaning the bedroom.

"Sure." She was trying frantically to remember if she'd left anything odious around. Panties on the floor? Drool marks on the pillow?

"This your mom and dad?" he called.

Sybylla went to the doorway. "Yup. Young and in love."

"Looks that way." He smiled. "Your mother was beautiful, wasn't she?"

"I've always thought so."

"Not surprising, is it? Given you."

She stood awkwardly at the door to her own bedroom and didn't respond.

"*Well*," Sam announced emphatically, saving her. "I like your apartment."

"Thanks. I'm not much good at homemaking. In fact, if you don't mind, I'd like to direct you to my career gal drawer of take-out menus. You'd be doing me an immense favor if you chose one and did the honors."

He started for the kitchen.

"I'm going to name the cat Atticus," she announced.

"Naturally."

She fed Gideon and gave him a stern lecture about charity beginning at home; then she edged her way back into the bathroom armed with a half-full bottle of antiflea shampoo and a stack of towels. She shut the door behind her. "Okay, you," she told the petrified feline. "Here's the deal. Anything with four legs can stay, but anything with six legs has to go. We understand each other?"

The cat dove under the claw-footed tub. Sybylla turned on the water.

"Come along, now." She reached underneath and extracted the quivering mass of grungy fur. "I told you, nothing with four legs need fear my tub of death."

Atticus did not "go gentle into that good night," but after the first few minutes, he seemed to relax somewhat, submitting to the gentle but insistent motions of Sybylla's hands. The water turned gray, then black as the cat's mews softened and his true coat, white with orange markings, emerged.

"You're good with him."

Sybylla looked up. She hadn't heard him enter.

"Yeah. I have good communications skills when the other creature doesn't have an opposable thumb."

He shook his head. "Typical Sybylla. Do you know, you are one of the most awkward people I've ever met when it comes to accepting compliments?"

"Hey, I'm sure I don't deserve *that* praise."

He knelt down on the bathroom floor and helped her lift the newly struggling cat onto the bath mat. Atticus arched beneath the towel she threw over him.

"I can prove it to you, if you want."

Sybylla sat back on her heels and looked at him.

"Do you want?"

Perplexed, she eyed him. "I suppose."

"You're a fine lawyer," he intoned, his voice grave.

"Thanks!" Sybylla said brightly. "See? I took that okay."

"That was just a warm-up. We haven't really started yet."

"Oh." She nodded. "Okay."

"I've known you, what, two months? I haven't yet heard you utter a single thing that wasn't in some way witty, intriguing, even fascinating."

Sybylla peered at him. "Are you reading this off a crib sheet or something?"

"*See?*" he crowed. "Y'see? You just can't take it, can you?"

"Sure I can," Sybylla huffed, pissed at herself. "C'mon, enough with the kid stuff. Hit me with your best shot. I'll surprise you."

He seemed to be considering it. "All right." Sam nodded. "Here it is. I meet you, and I think, Here's this incredibly beautiful woman who's just spinning so fast, I'll never get a good look at her. All I can see are these sparks flying off you. I see that you're clever, and funny, and you're hard, but then you do these incredibly kind things." He sighed. "That day in the office, when your friend died, you know it was a terrible moment, but it was also the first time you sort of forgot I was there, and I could really look at you and see the whole of you." He smiled. "You know that saying about how the whole is greater than the sum of its parts?"

Speechless, she nodded.

"I think it's true. I think that's when I fell in love."

Beneath her hands, the cat bucked and wrenched itself away. Vaguely, Sybylla heard it dash out of the bathroom and tear beneath her bed.

"With me?" she managed.

He gave a long-suffering sigh. "No. Not with you. With some lady selling real estate in Dubuque." He shook his head. "I knew you couldn't take it."

She reached for him, letting her hand press the side of his face. It was oddly hot. His cheek or her hand, or both, everything was suddenly hot and the air felt thin. All these weeks, she had let her suspicion do chronic battle with the bald fact that she was drawn to him, that something in him defied his manners and his clothes and the person they seemed so intent on suggesting. Clearly, he was far more than the sum of his parts as well, and it shamed her a bit that he had been so much more willing to see her true self than she had been to see his. She was seeing it now at least, and he was watching her do it. His eyes in their deep blueness were waiting for her to do something that would either meet or dispel his expectations.

"I can take it," she heard her own voice say. Then she kissed him, so hard and so emphatically that the man from Empire Szechuan, when he arrived a few minutes later, had to ring loud and long to be heard above the din.

CHAPTER
EIGHTEEN
—⁓—

Well now. She blushed into her bathroom mirror the next morning. Sam had left for his own apartment downtown to find some clothes that had not, as he put it to her, been compromised by lust. Sybylla could not help but agree. When they finally located the shirt and jacket he'd arrived in the night before, he was shy a button and his Brooks Brothers jacket had ripped all along one of its classically cut shoulder seams. Still, he looked happy enough as he left her, giving her a kiss at the apartment door that drove all thoughts of Trent, Andrew Greer, and, indeed, the known cosmos from her mind. The minute he left, the thought of not seeing him for two hours seemed downright punitive.

"Morning," Sybylla told Gideon, ignoring the dirty look he gave her when he leapt up on her wicker clothes hamper. "Now listen. You're the host and Atticus is the guest. I expect you to behave like a gentleman and not drink his milk."

She went back to brushing her teeth. In fact, she hadn't seen Atticus since the night before, and she only hoped he was still somewhere in the apartment. The poor traumatized feline had been driven from his safe haven underneath the bed when it had turned out not to be such a peaceful location after all. Where he was now was anyone's guess. She went to the kitchen and poured several bowls of milk, on the assumption that even a glutton like Gideon couldn't consume them all, then headed for her closet to find something suitable.

Now that Sybylla had impressed the solemnity of their charge upon the jurors, it was time for them to start admiring her a little, and liking her a little. Today she would be eloquent and determined and just as amiable as she could, and accordingly she put on an old standby from her wardrobe: a floral dress cut wide around the neck, with a dropped waist and a below-the-knee hemline. It was a girlish dress, ersatz Laura Ashley, and it looked a bit young for her, which she wanted. She put on white tights and flat black shoes and a hairband, pushing her hair far enough back to keep it out of her eyes but not so far that it failed to cover the notch in her right ear. "Alice in Wonderland," she told the mirror, approving her image. When Andrew Greer walked into the courtroom, he came with some pretty imposing baggage: he was the DA, officially sanctioned by the electorate as the good guy. She, on the other hand, having no public profile to precede her, could define herself as she wished. She would never be able to match her opponent as a commanding and lordly presence in the courtroom, but this persona might help to undercut Greer's stature, and with luck, some of the jurors' parental approbation might rub off on Trent.

It was a wretched morning on the subway, with two stalled trains on the East Side and the rest of the system suffering the ripple effect. Her stomach was in knots by the time she finally made it to Foley Square at quarter past the hour and took off like a sprinter for 100 Centre Street. Sam was on his feet beside Trent, explaining to Judge Coffin that she was on her way, when Sybylla burst through the door and hustled down the aisle in a lather. So much for Alice in Wonderland.

"Sorry, Your Honor," she mumbled, willing herself to calm down. "It was unavoidable."

"Nevertheless," Coffin intoned, his head perched heavily on the palm of his left hand, "you must do your best to avoid it in the future." He nodded at the prosecution table. "Mr. Greer managed to be on time."

Not all of us have city cars to chauffeur us around, Sybylla thought.

"I apologize. I'm ready to begin whenever you are."

"Excellent." Coffin nodded to his bailiff. "Bring them in, Carl."

The door to the jury room opened and the fourteen filed in, looking alert, even avid. Overnight, they had changed, Sybylla thought, from random citizens assembled by selection and attrition into a gathering of people fired with purpose: they were a jury. All of this, everything they were going to see and hear, was for them. It all hinged on them—the system, the defendant's fate, even the principles they all purported to live by. Sybylla found it a little amusing, the transformation, but she welcomed it, too. A serious, self-important jury meant a careful jury, and that was exactly what she needed.

"Good morning, ladies and gentlemen," Coffin said. Desperately, Sybylla wished she had some coffee. "Now before we get started, I just want to reiterate what I said yesterday about your exposure to media during this trial. You've all sworn you'd avoid television and newspaper reports and conversation about the case, and I've taken you at your word on that." He poured himself a glass of water from his thermos. "Let me explain something to you about evidence, ladies and gentlemen. You know, sometimes after a trial, the jury goes home, reads something in the paper that they didn't hear in court—something that might have swayed their decision. There are reasons for this, believe me. The rules regarding admissibility of evidence are complicated, but they absolutely preserve the integrity of the evidence you do hear. What you will hear in this courtroom—on both sides of the case—weighs more than what you might read in the paper. Remember that." He took a swallow of his water. "A newspaper doesn't have time or the inclination to find out if it's true. So forget all that stuff you think the rest of the world is finding out about this case. *You're* getting the real story here." He paused, surveying them. "Don't worry, I'm not going to sequester you. It's bad for you and it makes me look bad." He smirked. A few of the jurors smiled back. "But I find out anybody's picked up the *Daily News,* you won't even get a chance to go home and get a toothbrush. Am I clear?"

Solemn nods. Sybylla rummaged through her bag to find her opening statement—three transcriptions. It was memorized.

"Okay, folks." He grinned like a football fan at the moment of kickoff. "Let's go."

The court stenographer began to clack.

"Mr. Greer? Your opening statement."

"Yes, Your Honor," Greer said humbly, rising to his feet. Sybylla looked over at him and smiled. He was doing his "lowly servant of the law" number, shambling, not too nattily dressed. The DA approached the jurors and laid his hands solemnly on the railing. "Good morning, ladies and gentlemen. I hope you're all well."

Unsure of whether they were meant to respond, they frowned at him.

"I've tried a lot of cases in my time. Murders and assaults, rapes. Abductions. White-collar crimes, too. And let me tell you, a lot of terrible things go on in this city. And usually, they seem so clear at the beginning. 'Joe took a gun and shot Dave. Dave died. Joe is guilty of murder.' But you know, so many times, you start to look a little closer, you see it's not that clear-cut at all. Maybe Joe was defending himself. Maybe he wasn't defending himself from something that was happening then, but from something he felt would happen in the future if he didn't kill Dave. Maybe Joe was just playing around, didn't know the gun was loaded. Maybe Dave was in the last painful stages of a terminal illness, and Joe was motivated by love." He peered at the jury, earnestness oozing from every pore. "There are a million stories for every action. Some of them ring true; some of them don't. Some are worthy of real consideration, and some aren't. But nearly all of them serve to take that black-and-white situation and make it some shade of gray. Ladies and gentlemen, the case before you now is not like that." He turned, his right elbow still resting on the railing, and nodded at Trent. "What we have here is that very rare thing in the criminal justice system: a truly black-and-white case. What we have is a little girl. A child, ladies and gentlemen, living a day in the life of a child. She got up in the morning and braided her hair. She put on her school uniform and ate her breakfast. Then she went to school and studied all day. Her class was doing a project on the Dutch settlement of New Amsterdam." He grinned at the two teachers. "Just about where we're sitting today, if I'm not mistaken. In math, the day's lesson was long division. At gym period, they went onto the playground and played Steal the Bacon. Remember Steal the Bacon?"

"Oh, *please,*" Sybylla muttered. Sam's eyes were locked on Greer.

"And then, at the end of the day, this little girl took the school bus to her stop on Fifth Avenue, a block from her house, just the same as she did every day. The little girls were planning a sleepover for the following weekend. One of them told the group about her new puppy. And then, as the little girl was stepping off that bus, a stranger—a man she had never laid eyes on before—came flying out of the entrance to the park and attacked her with a scalpel. This man slashed her face and ripped open her abdomen. I'm sorry to tell you that I'll be showing you photographs of his handiwork. This beautiful child never knew what hit her. One second she was laughing with her friends; the next, she was down on the ground, covered with blood."

He turned deliberately and walked back to his table. "We may never understand why he did this, but I'm not terribly bothered by that. Because on one hand, we have a little girl who suffered grievous bodily harm at the hands of this stranger and will never be the same. And on the other hand, we have a man who lives as a parasite in this city—"

"*Objection.*" Sybylla was outraged. "Completely inflammatory."

"Please tone it down, Mr. Greer," the judge said.

"Well"—the DA shook his head, as if perplexed that anyone could challenge the wisdom of his words—"let's talk about the excuses his attorney is going to throw at you in hopes of somehow muddying this painfully clear situation into that delight of defense attorneys—the 'gray area.' Now, I have reason to believe that my opponent, young Ms. Muldoon here, is going to tell you that her client 'suffers' from a particular kind of mental illness. What kind of mental illness is that? It's the kind that allows him to be out of his mind when he committed the crime, yet to be perfectly fine now and able to aid in his own defense." He shot a look at Trent. "Vigorously," he sneered. "It's a strange, elusive condition that allows him to procure a weapon, select a victim, and attack that victim with extreme force, and then, in a matter of days, be perfectly fine." He paused. "Now it's not that I don't think Trent suffered from a disease. I do. It's a disease called envy. A disease called malice. It's a disease of somebody who looked around himself one day and realized that he was living on the street; then he looked around again and saw people with homes and money. He looked at this little girl, and he saw an innocence he coveted for himself. And since he couldn't have it for himself, he decided she wasn't to have it, either, so he took it. Black and white, ladies and gentlemen."

Greer returned to his desk and took up a copy of the *Penal Code.* "Let me read you something. This is the description of statute 120.10: assault in the first degree. 'A person is guilty of assault in the first degree when:

" '1. With intent to cause serious physical injury to another person, he causes such injury to such person . . . by means of a deadly weapon or a dangerous instrument; or

" '2. With intent to disfigure another person seriously and permanently, or to destroy, amputate, or disable permanently a member or organ of his body, he causes such injury to such person.' "

He set down the book. " 'To disfigure another person seriously.' " Greer shook his head, bemused. "Now. Ms. Muldoon is going to try to confuse you with psychiatrists and their"—he waved his hand dismissively—"borderline personalities, paranoid schizophrenics. But you're going to hear from the People's own psychiatrist, who examined Mr. Trent, and guess what? He found him to be just as sane as you or I." The DA turned to the jury for his final assault. "Over the next several days, you will hear testimony from four people who witnessed the crime and who came forward on their own to aid the police. You will also hear from the two policemen who were on the scene instantly. You will hear what forensics tests on the alleged weapon have shown. You will hear from the doctors who treated the victim, and finally, you will hear from Amanda Barrett herself, and, ladies and gentlemen, a braver girl you may never see. And when my colleague is finished with all of her justifications, I hope that you will be able to reach back through all that mud and remember the face of the child you're going to meet."

He paused, hooked his fingers in his jacket pockets, and gave a philosophical sigh. "Now, I'm an old-fashioned guy," Greer mused. "With all this talk of mitigating circumstances and diminished responsibility, I still believe in that old saw justice, and that's what I'm going to ask you to provide. Justice, ladies and gentlemen. Justice for that little child. I thank you."

"Ever the candidate," Sam whispered.

Sybylla was fingering her notes. She was in a state of intense aggravation, and her prepared speech had abandoned her utterly.

"Ms. Muldoon?" Coffin said.

She got to her feet, walked around the table, and half-sat against it. "Black and white," Sybylla mused. "You know, it's a rare thing to be able to see the world in black and white. Good versus evil. Valiant cowboy against scruffy Indian. Civilized colonial over primitive native. Trouble is, this is real life, and real life sometimes resists being organized into categories for our benefit"—she glared at Greer—"or sound bites for our easy digestion."

Sybylla shook her head sadly. "Would that the truth were as simple as my opponent implies. It isn't. Mr. Greer wants you to believe that this case is about one child who has suffered great injury. It's not. It's about two damaged children, and the fact that one of them is sitting in the defendant's chair today should not lessen one iota the damage he has suffered. Amanda Barrett, whose plight is wrenching to us all, nonetheless has had much good fortune in her life—a loving, stable family; a home; food; an education; the prospect of a full, happy life. If only my client had had some of the same gifts, I am certain that none of us would be in this courtroom today." Her regretful sigh was meant to pave the way for what came next. "By the time Trent was only a little older than Amanda Barrett, he was living on the streets of New York and supporting himself with the help of a lot of friendly folks who commuted in from New Jersey to see him." Sybylla looked at them stonily. "I don't think you want to know what Trent had to do for that money."

She got up and walked over to the jurors. "Mr. Greer called my client a parasite. Try pariah. Try being a kid, alone in this city, with no money and no friends, reading at a second-grade level. What did he do? He stayed alive, ladies and gentlemen. He made a place for himself in this city, and he never hurt anybody—until a few months ago."

She watched them stir, confused. "Yes, that's right. Trent did hurt Amanda Barrett, and he hurt her badly. He did a terrible thing, one that we must take very, very seriously. But unlike my opponent in this case, I'm not interested only in the what. I'm also interested in the why. He calls this muddying up the water. I call it getting at the truth.

"So why is Mr. Greer going to trot out all these witnesses when the defense has already admitted the crime? Well, there are several reasons, really. First, he wants you to get mad—so mad at my client that by the time the defense has an opportunity to start getting at the why of this case, you simply won't care about it. Second, he wants you to feel so good about convicting my client that you're going to want to decide he's guilty without sitting down to really think about the issues the defense is going to raise. Third, this is a big case for the city, and by extension for the District Attorney's Office, and if they didn't haul up each and every one of these eyewitnesses, it would look as if they weren't doing their jobs. So for the next few days, we're all going to sit here and watch the event unfold over and over through the witnesses' eyes as Mr. Greer questions them, and unless I hear something that invites a legal challenge or brings up a point I feel needs emphasis, I'm not going to cross-examine, because it's a waste of your time for me to drag this trial out unnecessarily. I'm going to let Mr. Greer tell you *what* happened. He's not interested in anything else, but I know you are. And, when he's finished, I'm going to tell you *why* it happened. And then it will be your turn."

Sybylla left the jury box and walked back to her table. "There *is* a reason for what happened. But I must warn you, it isn't a reason that will make sense to us easily, because it's a reason that lives in the streets, with poverty and hopelessness. It's a reason from Trent's world, not Amanda Barrett's, and it's as ugly as what happened between them. But if you're really going to understand this terrible event, then you're going to have to know about it and grapple with it. And it's *not* just mud. And it's *not* just dissembling."

She let her hand fall on her own copy of the *Penal Code.* "Remember when Mr. Greer read to you from this book? He lingered over the words *serious physical injury* and *disfigure another person,* didn't he? But did you notice how he kind of slipped quickly by a couple of other words? I'm speaking of the words *with intent,* ladies and gentlemen, two words that are crucial to a conviction of my client, and two words that, in my own opinion, you are going to find very difficult to attribute to him once you've heard the defense's case." She sighed audibly. "The plain fact is that Trent couldn't have formed intent to go to the corner store that day, let alone to stalk and attack a little girl.

"The people who are going to testify in this trial will swear an oath to tell the whole truth, but no one person ever knows the whole truth. The whole truth is what you, the jury, will know after you listen to everybody, and after you go back into the jury room to talk about the black and the white. *And* the gray. My client deserves that, and I have faith that you'll fulfill your duty to him." Slowly, she turned to look at Trent, whose head was down. When she looked back, the faces were empty. Sybylla thanked them and sat.

"Mr. Greer?" Judge Coffin said. "You have strong feelings about starting right away? I could use a break. Thirty minutes?"

"Of course, Your Honor."

Coffin looked at Sybylla. "Okay, counselor?"

"Fine, Your Honor."

They stood as he exited to his chambers. Trent tugged at Sybylla's sleeve. "You told 'em I *did* it," he whined in her ear. "How come you did that?"

"Hush," Sybylla told him. "You left me exactly one option, and I'm using it."

"I still get to testify," he warned.

"Naturally," she told him. "Don't worry."

The court officer was standing nearby.

"Go on back," Sybylla said. She turned to Sam. "Hi." She blushed, suddenly shy.

"Hi." He leaned close and whispered, "Feels like ages."

"Nice jacket." It was tan linen and very slick. She brushed an invisible speck off its shoulder.

"Specifically chosen for its good solid seams. Care to try 'em out?"

She glanced around, abruptly embarrassed. "None of your lip," she told Sam. "We're in court."

"Ah." He sighed. "Time lapse between lips . . . what is it?"

"Ages and eons. Maybe three hours. Three and a half. You know"— she noted the open affection in his face—"maybe this was a pretty good idea, your assisting me on the case."

"Oh? You're thinking of my research skills? My extraordinarily speedy note-taking capabilities?" He leaned close. "Or just my pretty face?"

She grinned at him. "None of the above, actually. I'm thinking of the fact that we'll have automatic grounds for appeal. Think of it, Sam. We can make precedent with this one. Retrial requested because defense counsel was in a highly eroticized state throughout original trial, resulting in mental confusion, overwhelming desire to cut testimony short, and frantic footsie playing under the table."

"It's such a great idea." He nodded. "Why didn't I think of it myself?"

"Because you haven't been at Legal Aid long enough to stoop that low." She eyed the clock. "Now, I need coffee. Desperately."

He glanced at his watch. "I think we can make it. Let's go."

Out in the corridor, Greer was already being fawned over by the press. Sybylla and Sam ducked the crush and made for the elevator bank without much ado. Sam hit the button.

Sybylla felt rather than saw the sudden migration, as if the cool, smooth floor abruptly began to tremble under the surge of reporters in her direction. Sam hit the button again.

"Ms. Muldoon? You have a comment?"

She couldn't help it. It was a little amusing. Abandoning the DA in midbite to chase down little old her? The occasion called for an effort above and beyond her standard "No comment," she thought.

"Well, we hope the jury will be able to look past the horror of the crime and get to the more critical question of why it happened. If they do, I think they will conclude that my client was not responsible for what occurred."

Something was wrong. Heads weren't nodding. Sybylla was suddenly convinced that there was something awful on the end of her nose.

"Um," a little voice said, "I didn't mean about the trial. I meant about your father."

Sam said it for her. "Her father?"

"The Supreme Court," another reporter chimed in. "The President's named him to fill Justice Wofford's seat. Do you have a comment?"

So it had really happened, Sybylla thought numbly. She hadn't spoken to Dermot since their ill-fated dinner at the Hyperion Club, and he had not warned her that the announcement was imminent. Her clearest thought—and it didn't particularly do her credit—was: I wish I'd worn another dress.

"My father is a superb jurist," Sybylla said. "I can't think of anyone better suited to sit on the Court. He'll be a great asset to it, I know."

"Are ya proud of him?" some manipulative SOB shouted at her.

"More than I can say," Sybylla intoned. She smiled grimly for the nation.

"You haven't said a word about your dad, you know," Sam said the next morning as they waited for Coffin to appear. "I kept waiting for you to bring it up last night."

"Maybe I was a mite distracted," she teased. "A girl can't help it." He didn't smile. Sybylla shrugged. "Anyway, what's there to say? I knew it was going to happen sometime."

He turned to her. "You always knew your dad was going to be on the Supreme Court?"

"No, of course not. But I knew about this. He told me the last time I saw him. We actually had a fight about it."

Sam was silent for a moment. Finally, she heard his soft voice: "I see."

A flash of irritation crossed her. "It's not politics," she said sharply. "The two of us got past that a long time ago. It's not even the effect his probable rulings may have on our work. I mean, yours and mine. It's something else he asked me to do, something that I didn't want to do. And he asked me because of the nomination; that's all. So I got mad. But I can be mad at him and still proud of him at the same time, and I am." Out of the corner of her eye, she watched Greer land heavily in his chair. "Though I do wish it hadn't happened just now," she heard herself say. "I could do without the extra attention while I'm conducting the most preposterous defense of my illustrious career."

"What are you talking about?" He nudged her comfortingly. "You're doing great. I thought you were fantastic yesterday."

"Yeah?" Sybylla grinned. She thought she'd done pretty well herself, sticking to her word and letting three of Greer's four eyewitnesses pass without cross. They'd told the same story, in any case—the little girl, the small man who ran up to her, the bright flash of a blade, and then the surreal slow motion of blood and shock—and then they'd pointed calmly to Trent. There wasn't much to be done with that testimony, even if she hadn't made such a point of not challenging the practical account of the crime. Her refrain from cross-examining helped the prosecution case move swiftly, if redundantly, along, and every time she shrugged at the judge and plaintively said, "No questions," the effect was to remind the jury that *she* wasn't the one taking up their valuable time, bashing them over the head with the same story, again and again.

The fourth and final eyewitness, however, had not remembered her lessons on plain and unadorned testimony. A matronly silver-haired woman who had been walking her bichon frise at the time of the attack, she created an interesting opportunity when she volunteered that the defendant had come rushing at Amanda Barrett "like a madman." When Greer had finished with the woman, Sybylla asked a single question from her seat.

"Mrs. Evans, I wonder if you could elaborate on something from your testimony. In what way did my client appear 'like a madman'?"

"Objection," Greer thundered, jumping to his feet. "Mrs. Evans is not qualified to answer that."

"I'm not looking for a medical qualification, Your Honor. Mrs. Evans offered an impression under direct testimony, and I'm merely trying to clarify it a bit."

Coffin shrugged. "I'm going to allow the witness to answer, as long as we stay with what she observed and her impressions thereof. No diagnoses."

Sybylla faced the witness. "Mrs. Evans? Would you like me to repeat the question?"

"Not at all," the woman said primly. "I'm not a psychiatrist or anything, but you live in New York awhile and you get to recognize the crazies. This man was sick, sick, *sick*."

"*Objection,*" Greer howled.

"Mrs. Evans," the judge said, "let's try to stick with what you actually saw. Why did you characterize the defendant as 'a madman'? Try to be specific."

"All right. Well, he was screaming gibberish and waving his hands. It's not as if he ran straight at the little girl. For one thing, he was yelling when he ran into her, and looking around, not straight ahead. And then he stabbed her. I remember thinking at the time, If he'd run into a tree or a statue, he would've stabbed that. You don't need a Ph.D. to know when somebody's round the bend."

Thank God for that, Sybylla had thought, surrendering Mrs. Evans to the DA's furious redirect.

Even Greer, however, understood that the most brutal story got dull by the fourth retelling. As soon as Coffin arrived and the proceedings were under way, he called Amanda Barrett's surgeon to the stand and introduced those wrenching photographs of the little girl into evidence. Sybylla's de rigueur objection to the pictures' highly prejudicial nature was swept summarily aside, and she watched with a sinking heart as the men and women in the box passed the eight-by-tens among them with suppressed but still audible reactions. Invariably, as the last photographs left their hands, they looked up at Trent, bewildered and incensed and a little green. The dealer in African art, indeed, reached into the breast pocket of his jacket for a handkerchief, which he made a show of using to dab his brow, then pressed firmly over his mouth.

Sybylla couldn't blame them. Those images had never left her, though she had done her best to put them out of her mind as she prepared Trent's defense. She'd seen plenty of forensic photographs in her time, battered wives and girlfriends gazing empty-eyed into the police cameras, and bodies, gory and cut down with sudden ferocity, and wounds patched awkwardly with purple thread, looking lurid and painful. But the worst were the children—subdued with neglect, or maimed outright with marks and burns. At first, they had thoroughly sickened her, but now they simply pounded at a dull sorrow in her core, more evidence of the horrors that poverty and ignorance wrought. Amanda Barrett's pictures, however, had struck her with a fresh assault. The little girl had a head swollen up like a pumpkin. Her face, submerged beneath the pain inflicted upon it, would only reemerge as something unfamiliar and unwanted.

Having been sworn in, the surgeon was explaining why no photographs of Amanda Barrett's face had been taken on her arrival at the emergency room.

"Frankly, there wasn't time," the tall, reed-thin man said earnestly. "There was a risk of infection from the abdominal trauma, as well as general blood loss, and we were trying to save her left eye, which the scalpel had caught—on an upstroke, we think. Besides, you wouldn't have been able to see anything from a photograph at that point. She was bleeding too fast. It was all just blood."

Sybylla held her tongue. It would harm Trent too much to get overly picky.

"And what was your initial appraisal of Mandy's injuries?" Greer spoke from his chair. He had taken to calling the victim by this diminutive, to emphasize her youth.

"That an animal had mauled her."

Sybylla felt Sam look at her expectantly, waiting for her objection. She shook her head.

"Can you tell us what your impressions were once you had an opportunity to examine the wounds?"

"Certainly." The surgeon recrossed his legs and leaned forward. "By far the most serious wounds were two deep slashes to the midtorso, which punctured the stomach and completely severed the transverse colon, creating an immediate risk of peritonitis. The facial injuries were of less threat to the patient's life, but they, too, required immediate surgery because of the blood loss, and because of the wound to the left eye. In all, there were approximately eight cuts of varying length and depth covering the area of the patient's forehead and cheeks, including one cut—more of a gouge, really—that caused severe trauma to the left eyeball, and one cut that had severed the nerves in the left side of the patient's face."

"Was Mandy conscious at the time of her arrival at the hospital?"

"Yes." Steinbaum nodded his head ruefully. "I'm sorry to say that she was. She was hysterical and in considerable pain. She was screaming."

Sybylla grimaced. This was bad for Trent. The image of the child's conscious suffering could easily outweigh any consideration of the defendant's lack of responsibility, no matter how plausible she got it to sound. She might cobble together a fantastic defense of involuntary intoxication, but it would make no difference when the jurors imagined the little girl writhing in pain.

Greer rose from his seat and walked toward the witness. "Dr. Steinbaum, what care did Mandy receive for her injuries?"

The doctor was consulting his notes. "The first objective of surgery was to close the abdominal wounds and to establish a temporary ileostomy while the bowel healed. At the same time, our chief of plastic surgery was working on the patient's face, patching severed nerves and veins, sewing up the incised muscles, closing wounds. An ophthalmic surgeon was called in to treat the patient's eye. She was also treated for blood loss, and for a deep cut on her right hand."

The DA's last question was about the girl's prognosis.

"Well, as far as the abdominal injuries, it's probable that the patient's bowel will be able to function largely normally once the GI tract heals and the ileostomy is deconstructed. Regarding the facial injuries, there will almost certainly be a loss of sensation and muscle control in the part of the face that suffered nerve damage. It's possible that some of what she's lost may come back in time, but full recovery is frankly not possible. Chances are, she'll suffer some degree of facial paralysis for the rest of her life, and there's a permanent loss of peripheral vision in the left eye. As regards the scarring, we hope for considerable benefit from future operations." He shrugged. "They'll never be invisible, but we should be able to do better than what she has now."

Greer gave a pained expression and shook his head for the jury. "Thank you, Doctor," he said, as if he were thanking him not only for the testimony but for the care itself.

"You're welcome," the tall man said amiably.

Sybylla stood. "Just a few questions, Dr. Steinbaum. Have you treated other slashing victims?"

"I have." The man nodded. "Many, I'm afraid."

"Is there anything in the nature of this little girl's wounds that stood out for you?" It was a gamble, but worth it if he could come up with something suggestive of the animal he had evoked earlier.

"Well, yes. For one thing, this wasn't the kind of weapon I was used to seeing. Gang members tend to use straight razors for this kind of thing. The nicks and gouges on the patient's face indicated a different kind of weapon. And of course, we later found out that the weapon had been a surgical scalpel."

"Anything else?" Sybylla asked, a bit disappointed.

He grew thoughtful. "Well, I'd say there was something quite different in the . . . the manner of the wounds." He frowned. "Their lack of *order*, if you will."

Here we go, Sybylla thought. " 'Their lack of order,' " she mused. "Would you mind elaborating on that, Doctor?"

"Well, I would say that this wasn't the kind of . . . how shall I say? Specifically *punitive* injury we see in a lot of gang-related wounds, where one person sets out to mark another. With these wounds, there seemed to be a sense of frenzy in their making. The assailant was all over the place, both up- and downstrokes." He frowned. "I remember thinking at the time that there was an element of wildness to it."

" 'An element of wildness.' " Sybylla appeared to ponder. Not bad. Of course, it wasn't as good as if he had said, Only a clinically insane person could have done this, but it wasn't bad. "Thank you, Doctor."

Greer was already on his feet. "Dr. Steinbaum, your area of expertise is confined to the physical wounds themselves, is it not?"

"It is." He looked chastised.

"You have no direct knowledge to bring to bear on the motive for this attack, do you?"

"I do not," the doctor said.

"Nor on the character of the person who committed this attack?"

"No." He looked downright humiliated now, as if he had been caught lying about his sexual exploits to the entire fraternity.

"So the statement you made just now, about the *wildness*"—he pronounced the word caustically—"is really just complete speculation, isn't it?"

Overkill, Sybylla thought.

"I suppose so," Steinbaum mumbled. "Yes."

"Thank you, Doctor. That's all."

Greer next called the forensic weapons specialist, a dry little man who described Amanda Barrett's wounds as appropriately corresponding to the strokes of a standard surgical scalpel like the one taken from Trent's clenched hand. He was followed by a forensic serologist, another character who seemed to lack a basic joie de vivre. He blandly narrated his findings that the blood covering said scalpel was Amanda Barrett's. Sybylla didn't cross-examine either witness.

By the time she and Sam returned from their rushed lunch at the Thai place behind 100 Centre Street, rumor was rampant throughout the building that the little girl herself was about to testify. "Relax," Sam said, massaging her shoulders in the elevator they miraculously had to themselves. "You can handle this."

"But it's the worst thing, getting some little kid up there on the stand and having to ask about whether your client molested her or hurt her. You'll find out," she told him. "Just wait till you handle one of these delightful people on appeal."

"I know, but you're doing the only thing you can do with the prosecution case. What that doctor said, and that woman this morning . . . you'll be able to use that later on."

"I suppose." She sighed. "The truth is, I've been dreading this since Greer showed me his pictures. I mean, I'm not immune to how awful it is, what happened to her."

"Nor am I." Sam nodded. "But you think something happened to Trent, too."

Sybylla nodded.

"Greer is here to worry about the victim. Let him do it. You worry about Trent."

She looked him over. "You're beginning to sound just like me," Sybylla observed. "I think you've been hanging around me too long."

"Not long enough," he amended.

The door slid open to pandemonium.

"Ms. Muldoon?" somebody screamed. "What are you going to ask her?"

"Sybylla! Will you cross-examine?"

Someone's microphone bumped her chin. She held out her arms like a movie star fending off paparazzi.

"Come on." Sam took her elbow.

"How does your father feel about your defending people like the Wild Man?"

She couldn't stop herself. "My father upholds the Constitution," she shot back. "You should try it sometime."

She heard Sam mutter, "Shit."

Back at the defense table, he shook his head as he took his seat behind her.

"I'm sorry. I couldn't stop myself."

"It's just the sort of thing they twist." He sighed. "You know that."

"Yes. But it pisses me off. The media seem to think that the First Amendment and the Sixth Amendment come from different documents."

"And they always will think that," Sam scolded. "So stop trying to fix it, 'cause you can't." He paused. "You okay?"

Sybylla shook her head no, then changed her mind and nodded yes. "Just tired. Didn't exactly get a full night's sleep last night." She smiled at him. "Look, if Greer rests today, we can get to Trent first thing tomorrow." They had decided to begin with Trent, conjuring a bit of compassion for his history and his circumstances and reassuring the jury that he was rational, then gradually focusing on his abduction scenario and culminating in the LSD assertion. Then they would get Turturro on right away to lend credence to at least one part of the yarn, and afterward, Bennis would confirm Trent's disappearance. Finally, they would bring on Sam's LSD man to try to whip up sufficient smoke and mirrors on the subject of lysergic acid and its effects. "You told your guy we'd probably need him before the end of the week?"

Sam said yes. He had dug up a fifteen-year-old article in *Psychology Today;* its four pages of text essentially boiled down to an assertion that there was still a great deal that was not known about the drug. Over the phone, the author of the article had reacted to the proposal of a twenty-four-hour acid trip with something short of outright dismissal, and Sam had jumped all over him. He was a science writer, not a Ph.D., but he was the best they'd been able to find.

"We'll need to interview him first."

"Yeah, he knows. Frankly, I think he's thrilled out of his gourd about the whole thing. I mean, let's be honest. This guy is not an authority." He turned sadly to Sybylla. "You do realize that Greer will rip him to shreds."

"I do." She sighed. "Well, we'll keep looking. See if we can come up with someone better in the meantime."

Sam, who had already looked, shrugged his assent.

"Have you talked to Trent about how to act when the victim's on the stand?"

Sybylla nodded. "I don't think we'll have a problem. He's still under the impression that none of this, none of what's been said so far, has anything to do with why we're here. To him, it's all somebody else's story." Sybylla found her notes for cross on the victim and started transcribing them. "You know, I'm as ready to accept an assertion of innocence as anybody else in my line of work, but Trent's really wearing me down. His 'bad people' scenario is hard enough without his insisting on a conspiracy to frame him."

"Maybe it's true," Sam whispered, riling her.

"Oh, God," she groaned. "Not you, too."

Greer came down to his table, having wrested himself from the press. He and Sybylla exchanged nods.

"All rise." The court officer was calling the case. Coffin stomped in, frowning.

He addressed the room: "I want to say something now, before we bring in the jury. Prosecution has informed me that the victim will testify next. I'd like us all to bear in mind that this is a young child who will be giving undoubtedly traumatic testimony, and I would ask you all to behave accordingly. Members of the press"—his gaze shifted to their pews—"please be discreet. And the rest of you. No displays of emotion. Anyone cries, screams, whatever—even *breathes* wrong—they're out of here. Family, too. Understood?"

They bowed their heads like a congregation.

"Good. Bring 'em in, Carl."

Sybylla shifted her chair toward Trent and put her hand over his as the jurors entered. She liked them to see her this way, relaxed and intimate and apparently without fear. If they could infer that Trent inspired such consideration, the theory went, then they would be more apt to accord it to him themselves.

"Mr. Greer? Call your next witness," Coffin intoned.

"Your Honor," the DA said gravely, "we call Mandy Barrett."

The jurors, who had not had the benefit of Coffin's warning, were the only ones to react. They craned toward the door, almost unseating themselves as the small child, her blond head bowed, entered the room and was led forward by her mother.

The damage was wrenchingly obvious. The lavender lines played over her face like a game of Chutes and Ladders, and her left eye bore a pirate patch. The worst thing, however, was that telltale hunch, an obviously recent addition to her posture, which pleaded with the world not to look at her. Sybylla ached for that. For the first time, something in her recoiled from Trent.

The child was sworn in. She climbed slowly into the witness chair.

Coffin leaned over paternally. "Hello, Miss Barrett. My name is Judge Coffin."

Amanda nodded. "I know." Her voice was tiny.

"Part of my job is to make what happens in this courtroom as painless for you as possible, and I want you to know that I take that very seriously. So you just let me know if anything upsets you or if you need to take a rest for a while. Will you tell me?"

"Okay," she said.

"Okay, then. Mr. Greer?"

He got to his feet. "Hi, Mandy!" the DA chirped. "How are you feeling today?"

Asshole, Sybylla thought.

"I'm fine," the girl said sadly.

"Now, you remember how we talked about what it would be like for you to testify here?"

"Yuh." She glanced at her mother in the pew behind Greer, then straightened up a little. "I mean yes. I do."

"And what was it we agreed about your testimony?"

"We said I would pretend we were sitting in my room at home. And you would ask me the questions and I would answer them and tell the truth."

"And can you do that? Can you pretend that?"

She's nine, you jerk, Sybylla thought. Not three.

"Yeah. Yes." Amanda sighed. For the first time, she turned her face up and looked at the spectators squarely, sending a rush of burning pity down Sybylla's spine. Remembering herself, the girl ducked her head.

"Now, Mandy, I want you to tell me what happened to you on the afternoon of March fourteenth."

"On . . . March fourteenth?"

"On the day you were hurt."

Tentatively, her eyes stole to the defense table, then looked rapidly away. She'd been told not to look.

"I was on the bus. Sabrina and I were talking about her skating party. It was her birthday."

"You got on the bus at your school?"

"Yes. At the side door. The bus goes across Eighty-sixth Street. To the park. It stops near my house."

"Where do you get off the bus?"

"Eighty-fifth and Fifth. Sabrina was coming to my house, so she came with me. She was right behind me getting off the bus."

Greer walked slowly up to the witness and braced his elbow on the railing between her and himself. "What happened when you got off the bus, Mandy?"

She swiped at her face with the back of one hand, but Sybylla didn't see any tears. "I . . . don't remember very much. I remember someone running up to me. Then I was on the ground and my face felt hot."

"Did you see this person who ran up to you?"

The girl half-nodded, half-shrugged.

"Mandy," Greer nudged, "we need you to say yes or no. Did you see the man?"

"I kinda did. I mean, I saw his, like, chest, and his hair. He had sorta blond hair, and he was . . . he had on a white T-shirt. That's all I saw."

"Did the man say anything to you?"

"Well, kinda. I mean, he was saying a lot of stuff, but it didn't make any sense. I remember he said, 'Don't hurt me' over and over, and I thought, What's he talking about? He's hurting *me*."

Greer's face was bursting with energetic compassion. "What happened then, Mandy?"

The child shook her head. "I don't know. I was in the hospital after that."

"Do you remember the ambulance?"

"No."

"Do you remember driving to the hospital?"

"No."

"Do you remember being taken into the emergency room?"

He's going to go through every step of the procedure, Sybylla thought grimly. An hour from now, he'll be asking her, "Do you remember the sixteenth stitch in your left eyeball?"

Fortunately, Amanda Barrett herself put a stop to it.

"No. I *told* you. I don't remember. When I woke up, it was, like, three days later."

Taking the cue, Greer shifted seamlessly. "And what was it like to wake up in the hospital?"

"My stomach hurt. There were bandages on my face. My mom was crying."

He knew when to wrap things up, too. "Mandy, what's it like for you now?"

She frowned. "What do you mean?"

"I mean . . . well, tell me, does your tummy still hurt?"

She sank even deeper into her hunch. "It's okay," her little voice said.

"Well, how is it different than it was before?"

The creep. Sybylla curled her lip. He was trying to get the child to talk about her ileostomy. That was probably even more distressing to her than her facial wounds.

"I have to . . . *you* know. I have to wear my thing. But it's only temporary, the doctor says. He says I can wear a bathing suit. I mean, not this summer, but maybe next summer." She said it as if next summer were an immeasurable amount of time away.

"Mandy, what 'thing' do you mean?"

Outraged, Sybylla was about to call for a sidebar, but Coffin came to the rescue.

"I believe the witness is referring to her temporary ileostomy. Please proceed, Mr. Greer."

"Thank you, Your Honor. Mandy, when you look in the mirror now, what do you see?"

There was an audible gasp from the jury box, and Sybylla shot to her feet, demanding a sidebar over the uproar. The girl in the witness box was crying, but Greer was strangely content with the devastation his question had wrought. The jury would never forget this sight: the little girl with her ruined face and broken heart, wiping pointlessly at her cheeks with the back of her hand.

"I withdraw the question. Thank you, Mandy. You're a wonderful little girl."

"Slimewad," Sam hissed between clenched teeth.

Judge Coffin leaned over the witness box. "Amanda? Would you like to stop for a while? Or should we just go on now and finish up?"

Impressively, the girl pulled herself together. "I want to finish," she told the judge.

He nodded. "There'll be a few questions from Ms. Muldoon, and then you can go home. All right?"

"All right." She looked up as Sybylla rose from her seat.

"Hi, Amanda. My name is Sybylla."

The corners of her mouth flickered upward and dropped again. "That's a pretty name."

"Thanks. So's Amanda."

She shrugged. "It's okay."

"What do you like to be called? Do you like to be called Mandy?"

The child wrinkled her nose. "Nuh-uh." Sybylla suppressed her own smile.

"All right, Amanda. I'm a lawyer, like Mr. Greer. And I'm going to ask you some questions that he didn't ask you. Now, you're a native New Yorker, aren't you?"

Amanda nodded. "Yes."

"And you've lived in the city all your life?"

"Yes."

Sybylla walked around the table and leaned back against it, casual but not close enough to crowd the girl.

"What do you like about living in the city, Amanda?"

She bit her lip. "I like *The Nutcracker.* I like my school and my friends, and skating at Sky Rink. I like Bloomingdale's and going to Serendipity after. I liiiike . . ." She pondered, looking like a real nine-year-old for the first time since she'd entered the room. "I like my riding lessons. I ride horses at Claremont. Sometimes we go into Central Park and people watch us. One time, my friend— her horse ran away with her and the instructor had to run after her and catch it."

"Do you stay in New York in the summertime?"

"Oh no," Amanda said disapprovingly, as if she knew no one who did. "We go to Amagansett. We have a house."

"That sounds nice. Is it at the beach?"

"Uh-huh." The girl nodded. "There's this, um, like, staircase going down to the beach from our house. One time, the tide came in so far, it washed the bottom step away."

"Wow." Sybylla smiled. Then: "Amanda, do you ever see people on the street in the city who seem, well, a little funny?"

The girl considered. "You mean weird?"

"Yes, weird."

"Oh sure," the native New Yorker said. "Like, there's this guy near the pizza parlor on Lexington who's always pulling at his pants. He lives in the alley next to the pizza parlor."

"Right," Sybylla agreed, as if the Lexington Avenue pizza parlor man was the very one she'd been thinking of. "Any others?"

"Well, I see this lady on the Madison Avenue bus sometimes. She talks to herself, and she goes up and down the aisle yelling at people. One time, she yelled at me. It was awful."

"I'll bet." Sybylla nodded. "Let me ask you something, Amanda. Do you ever talk to weird people like that?"

The girl shook her head emphatically, anxious to pass on her wisdom to those ignorant on this very urban subject. "No. That's wrong. You should never talk to them, because they're not like us. I mean, you don't know what they'll do. My mom says they're cr—"

Greer was howling, "Objection" so loudly that the child winced. "Hearsay, Your Honor."

"I'll sustain that. Ask your next question, Ms. Muldoon."

Sybylla couldn't help but grin through this brief exchange. Amanda's parents had obviously schooled her in the fine art of discerning and evading the New York schizophrenic.

"Just one more question, Amanda. It's a hard question, and I want you to think about it very carefully before you answer. All right?"

Almost imperceptibly, the girl nodded.

"I know you must be very sad about what happened, and I know you must be very angry, too. But when you think about it today, do you ever wonder *why* it happened? Why this person you'd never seen before did this thing to you?"

She had a real moral weight, this Amanda Barrett. She wasn't just a blond slip of an Upper East Sider, winging between her riding lessons and her Amagansett beach house. Sybylla watched her submerge herself into her conscience and wrestle with the question she'd been given, and when she spoke, finally, it was to lend the proceedings an unanticipated touch of grace.

"Maybe he thought I was talking to him," the little girl said.

With the prosecution case rested and largely complete (the DA's shrink, naturally, would be held back for rebuttal, but Sybylla doubted his services would be required once she played her acid card), she breathed a tentative sigh of relief. From here on in, she told herself, all of the surprises would be hers, and all of the scrambling for appropriate responses on cross would be Greer's. It was a heady feeling. Her handling of the State's case had been fairly strong, she told herself, and while things as they stood still looked very much like a losing proposition for Trent, Sybylla knew that without the option of an insanity defense, they wouldn't have stood a chance with any other strategy.

If only Trent would change his mind, she thought, sighing, as she made her way down Broadway with her gym bag swinging at her hip. There was still time to score a touchdown with insanity, and the beauty of her subterfuge was that the defense would retain this option up until the very moment somebody uttered the acronym LSD. As it was, she'd already gotten one of the witnesses to call Trent "sick," the doctor to discern in him "an element of wildness," and the victim herself to compare him to the crazy lady on the Madison Avenue bus. Not bad for an insanity defense that hadn't even properly begun. She would have a word with her client before the case was called tomorrow morning. Make a last-ditch effort to warn him plainly that his prospects for prison looked excellent as things stood. She could only do what she could do for him, and what she could do was limited. She wasn't a magician, after all.

The cool evening air felt sweet. Sybylla had not been to the gym in over a month now, between trial preparations and, more recently, the advent of Sam. Then, too, she had been reluctant to return to the place where she had last seen Susu, as if nothing had happened. But tonight she had energy to spare, and it seemed like the right time to reclaim some sense of normalcy in her routine. Sam, meanwhile, had opted to press his nose even closer to the grindstone and was spending the evening at the public library, trying to learn something—anything—about LSD that might help them, or at least bolster their argument enough that they wouldn't get laughed at openly.

The gym windows were steamy and crowded with body parts packed in Lycra. She shouldered the door open and closed her nose against the pungent smell of sweat, then made her way through the StairMasters to the front desk, where one of the receptionists was chatting amiably with the Iron Maiden. Sybylla set down her bag and fished out her card to be stamped. "Hiya," she told the Maiden. "There still a six o'clock step?"

"Sure thing," the tall woman said, peering at her intently. "You're, um . . ."

Sybylla looked up at her and frowned. She was, um, what?

"You're . . . what's your name again?"

"Sybylla?" Sybylla said hesitantly, as if she weren't at all sure.

"Yuh, I thought. Christ, you'd think I wouldn't forget a name like that. Hey, I'm real sorry about your friend."

Sybylla swallowed. "You saw it on the news?"

The Maiden nodded. "She'd just been in here, like, the day before or something. It was so weird." She shook her head. "Few nights later, I'm watching TV, and there's her picture. I said to my husband, 'I know that girl! That girl's in my class!' I was just talking to her, like, two days before! It was so weird. She was telling me your name. I can't believe I forgot it."

"She . . ." Sybylla cocked her head. "I'm sorry, why was she telling you my name?"

"Oh . . ." The woman turned to her, as if this was the least relevant aspect of the exchange. "She was asking me to give you something when you turned up for class. I wouldn't have bothered, but, you know, she was telling me it was real important, and she brought it along 'cause she was supposed to be seeing you on Saturday morning, but she couldn't make it that Saturday or something. And it was important, so she didn't want to put it through the mail, and Christ, she was right about that. You know, I once sent a letter across town, and it took over a *month*. Anyways, she said she was gonna call you and just let you know it was here, you know, but I guess she never got around to it, did she?"

Sybylla's head was still drifting. The Maiden was now going on about crime in the city and how as soon as she had enough saved she was moving to Boulder, where people were too busy keeping fit and eating healthy foods to have time to knock each other off for drugs. "I'm sure it was drugs," she told Sybylla, her voice intimate, as if they were old friends. "You break into a lab, you're looking for drugs. They're such morons, these people. Like, they think that's what people do in universities, sit around making drugs. You know?"

"Yeah," Sybylla said dimly. "You said . . . something? She left something? For me?"

"Oh." The woman grinned. "I'm so spaced. Yeah, she said to give this to Sybylla, the one she was always palling with before class. I knew you. I just didn't know your name."

"May I have it, please?" she asked, more perplexed than eager.

The Iron Maiden reached around the receptionist's desk with one of her long, sculptured arms and retrieved a plain white envelope, sealed, with SYBYLLA MULDOON in heavy black ink.

"Here y'go." She handed it over with a little shudder. "Gives you the willies a bit, doesn't it?"

Sybylla nodded, steadying herself against the desk. The envelope had a standard preprinted return address: New York University. Then, in smaller italics, *Department of Chemistry*. Below this, the initials SP had been noted in pencil. Tenderly, she pressed the paper with the tips of her fingers. The flat, round substance of the implant pressed back.

Sybylla felt cold—unaccountably cold, given the nearly oppressive heat being generated by the bodies around her. Nearly thirty bodies, she thought frantically, and that was a conservative count. Thirty bodies, she fixated. Who knew the people they belonged to? The people who could, if they chose, devote their entire lives to following somebody else, watching them, noting their movements, and listening to their conversations . . . and you'd never know about it unless you spent *your* whole life watching them to see if they were watching you.

As she was now, stunningly, convinced that somebody was.

Sushila, shot dead in her lab. Sybylla's own apartment, churned in a frenzy.

But not entirely, she now understood. The traveler's checks—they'd have been easy enough to remove. And the VCR, a standard item, practically a calling card proclaiming, Attention! This has been a burglary! They hadn't been looking for anything of value—at least of conventional value.

They'd been looking for this. She knew it now, with a conviction that invaded every cell of her body. For this . . . *nothing* object, this little sliver of compressed matter that someone had removed from the body of an accused criminal, and that someone else, she now realized, had put there in the first place. It wasn't an innocent double-blind study, as Turturro had suggested, a new smoking cure or a heart medication. It wasn't one of the humanitarian medications in development for implant technology that Susu had alluded to—tuberculosis or heart disease or diabetes. This thing, whatever it was, had gotten somebody killed, and it was burning a hole in Sybylla's hand.

Thirty bodies, she thought dreamily, giving in to outright fear. One of them watching her. He *must* be. He'd gone looking for the implant at Susu's lab, then at Sybylla's apartment. Now he was dogging her heels, waiting for her path to cross that of his precious grail. And here she was, practically holding it up like a trophy for him.

Her breath filled her ears. She couldn't stop herself from looking around. The skinny guy hunched over his exercise bike, a magazine spread across the handlebars. He was flipping the pages but not really reading. Every now and then, he looked up at the door. . . .

The muscle-bound man on the StairMaster by the window. He had earphones on and was looking intently at the TV suspended in the corner. . . .

The bald man spotting another man as he bench-pressed a bar laden with weights. But he wasn't being very attentive about it. . . .

She frowned. That StairMaster was set too easy, and the man's legs pumped pointlessly, without really engaging the machine. His thick neck protruded from a Redskins T-shirt. He frowned up at Oprah, looking captivated. Something about him . . . Sybylla thought, reaching. The wide torso and the brutish neck, barely a neck at all. Barely a discernible neck, Susu had said when Sybylla had teased her about her admirer with the muscle magazine.

So he comes here often. She tried to calm herself. Most people do, don't they? Work out a few times a week?

He had been looking at Susu that day. Her eyes, irresistibly, strayed back to him.

Now he was looking at her.

Even without thinking she turned to the Iron Maiden, who was once again deeply in gossip mode with the receptionist. "So!" Sybylla said brightly, loud enough for the room to hear, if the room had been listening. "Class starts in five minutes?"

The Maiden looked at her queerly. "Sure."

"And lasts an hour?"

"Yes." She suppressed a smile. "As always."

An hour, Sybylla thought frantically. If she did this right, if she was in describably lucky, he would let her go downstairs for her class, confident that she would emerge again in an hour, plus ten minutes tacked on to each end for changing clothes. Eighty minutes, but only if she was lucky. An eighty-minute head start in the race for her life.

Discreetly, she hoped, she stuck the envelope in her workout bag. "Okay," she said enthusiastically, "I'll just go downstairs to change, then!"

The Iron Maiden gave a little wave. "Okay!" She imitated Sybylla's cheer.

Not too fast, not too fast, she told herself as she headed for the stairway and walked carefully down, looking frantically for the exit sign her memory told her was there, though she could not have said exactly where. She stepped aside to let a wave of aerobicized bodies pass her on their way out, then descended to the familiar beige foyer that led to the women's locker room. A glance behind her yielded the optimistic news that the StairMaster man had not followed her downstairs. She opened the door to the locker room.

Back past the sinks and toilets, the corridor led off at a right angle to the showers, a steam bath, and a massage room. A woman was leaning against the emergency exit as she struggled to put on her thigh-high boot. Sybylla retreated to the sink, splashing water on her face and forcing herself to wait, though adrenaline was screaming through every extremity. Only after the woman had grunted success and departed did she approach the exit, her heart sinking as she drew close.

EMERGENCY ONLY, its sign warned. ALARM WILL SOUND.

Alarm will sound. She bit her lip, increasingly frantic. An alarm would send the staff running and alert whoever was watching her not only to her attempted escape, but to the fact that she apparently knew she was being followed. Neither thought pleased Sybylla particularly, but the alternative—to saunter upstairs and leave by the front door— was infinitely less appetizing even than this. Desperate times call for desperate measures, she told herself, setting her jaw. She took a deep breath.

Like a sky diver making the irrevocable leap, she pushed the bar down and lurched forward, the shrill howl of the alarm magnified a hundredfold by her panic. A metal staircase led steeply up to ground level, and she hurried, barely hearing the slap of her shoes against steel. In the alley behind the gym, she took off past the kitchens of restaurants and onto Seventy-fourth Street, tree-lined and nearly abandoned. Broadway, with its bustle and noise, felt like the best bet; she walked briskly to the corner, forded the cross street, and crossed the avenue. She wanted a bar or a restaurant with a window where she could get a shot of something to settle her nerves and keep an eye on the front door of the gym to make sure she was safe. O'Ryan's looked right. It was dark save for the Celtics game blaring from the TV over the bar, and its crush of sports fans was too absorbed to do more than look Sybylla over as she ordered her drink. They turned back to their brews and their banter.

She carried her glass to a window table hidden in shadow and downed half of its contents in a protracted gulp, willing her pulse to settle. Across the street, the gym looked normal enough: pumping legs, bodies on parade. If the alarm was still sounding, it was too far away for Sybylla to hear, but her guess was that somebody had figured out how to turn it off, then reassured the patrons that nothing was wrong and that nobody had to interrupt their workout to accommodate an emergency. More malfunctioning technology. People knew all about that.

For ten excruciating minutes, she watched, uncertain what she was watching for, and as those minutes passed, Sybylla's sense that she had somehow erred in her judgment grew. What evidence had she, really, that the man who had eyed Susu that day was now following her, wanting to kill her? What evidence had she that the lab report in her handbag revealed anything more noteworthy than a petroleum base or an unusual pH balance? Or that Susu's murder and the burglary of her own apartment were not, after all, exactly what they appeared, more of the distaff side of urban life in a crime-ridden age? Somehow she had spun this fantasy from a few ingredients and an overactive imagination, and in doing so had inconvenienced her gym, maligned the probably perfectly normal man on the StairMaster (Somebody's accountant! she wailed to herself. Somebody's uncle!), and taken a few years off her own life with this onslaught of acute terror. She was a terrible person, really. She should not be trusted with her own life, let alone the legal fates of her clients. She was histrionic and infantile, and it was only a wonder that she hadn't done something stupid like this before.

Across the street, movement made her focus. The man from the StairMaster was standing in the gym's doorway, still in his gym clothes, looking around frantically. Riveted, she watched him bound to the phone stand on the corner and, without a moment's hesitation, yank the woman talking there away. The woman didn't argue. She ran. The man punched numbers, then pounded the Plexiglas with his fist. Sybylla took in the strange comedy of his mute fury, like a fight in a silent film. Then, his call completed, he began to run up the avenue, turning east, toward her apartment, Sybylla knew. She gripped her drink, still and numb.

" 'Nother one?"

Sybylla jumped and looked up. A waitress. Irish voice.

"Would'ja want another?"

"Yes," Sybylla managed. "Yes, I would."

"Gin an' tonic, was it?"

"Yes. Thanks."

She watched her leave. It would be hours before Sam was home from the library. Should she go there? Or would someone be watching him, too? Was his apartment safe? Was his phone safe? Sybylla shuddered. Would she ever leave this bar?

The waitress brought her refill, and she reached into her purse for money, brushing her hand against the envelope with its lethal bulge. When she was alone again, Sybylla drew it out and carefully opened the flap. The implant in its plastic sleeve was clipped to the lab analysis and to a note in Susu's spiky script: "Pretty wild, huh?"

Sybylla swallowed and turned to the second page, idly reaching for the sugar bowl on her table, picking up one of the cubes, and rolling it between her fingers. Without thinking, she popped the white block into her mouth, letting the sweetness clamor over her taste buds and slither down her throat to her stomach. Then, without warning, it exploded in sourness as her guts clenched around it and the words on the page made abrupt and terrible sense. She spat the sugar cube into her hand, choking for air.

Sybylla was tucked far back against the banquette, gazing bleakly at an outsize bottle of Kirin Dry. She gasped when she saw him, and jumped as if someone had just electrified her seat. Her long hair hung forward over her face and her normally pale skin was a stark chalk-white.

"Jesus." Sam was staring.

She shuddered. "C'mon. Sit down. I may not show it, but I'm glad to see you."

"I believe you're smashed." He slid his weighty briefcase under the table and took the opposite pew.

"Should hope so. I've been working on it for hours."

He shook his head at her. "Why do I get the feeling this isn't your usual urban erotic fantasy? When I listened to your message, I thought, Couple on the lam! Lawyers in love! It was a terribly sweet gesture, but to be frank with you, I'm not in top form just at the moment. If you'll recall, I went straight from court up to the Donnell Library, where I've been stuck in a carrel all night, reading about people giving acid to tarantulas. All I wanted to do when I got home was change out of my clothes, climb into a bath, and get something to eat. Instead, I get this cryptic message about how I'm in serious shit and my life is in danger, and I'm supposed to pack for a trip of unknown duration with all these unidentified nefarious people supposedly following me. And where to? To this crummy place where we already ate one mediocre meal last week? Why didn't you tell me to meet you at Le Cirque? At least we'd have had a good dinner."

She was picking at the wrapper on her beer. "I didn't want to name a restaurant on your answering machine. I didn't know who might be listening. So it had to be someplace only you would know how to find. Besides," she said sadly, "I'm not dressed for Le Cirque."

"So I see." He sighed deeply. "All right. Let's have it, then."

Sybylla looked at him. "Well, it's nothing too terribly interesting. I just happened to find out why my friend Susu was murdered, and it kind of threw a wrench in my plans. Especially since it looks like the same folks might want to have a chat with me."

"But that was about drugs. Why would some junkie be interested in you?"

"Not drugs," she said dryly. "Drug. One drug." She reached into her bag and flipped the little plastic sleeve onto the table. "This drug."

He stared at it, then shook his head. "Sybylla. Look, do you mind if I order something to eat while we discuss this? I'm starving, and I've been reading up on LSD all night."

She snorted.

The waiter was pushing the shrimp tempura with such fervor that Sybylla could only visualize a crate of elderly shrimp waiting hopefully in the kitchen. Sam ordered the steak teriyaki, aggressively well done, and though Sybylla declined, he ordered the same for her.

"Gee. Never realized you were such a macho guy."

"You look like you need to eat," he said unapologetically.

"I'd like another Kirin Dry," she told the waiter.

With a glance at Sam—For permission? Sybylla thought meanly—the waiter left.

Sam leaned forward, his elbows braced on either side of the Sapporo place mat. "You want to start at the beginning?"

"Not particularly," she said, sulking. "But I think I should, don't you?" With a sigh and a preemptive apology for not having told him sooner, she filled Sam in on her first interview with Dr. Turturro and the implant he had removed from Trent and nonchalantly dismissed as irrelevant to his patient's "textbook schizophrenia." She told him how she had willfully kept the thing out of proper channels and instead passed it to Susu, whose interest in mysteries she had tapped to pique her enthusiasm for its analysis.

"I had no idea it was such a hot item. I had no idea it was *anything*. Turturro was totally uninterested. He thought it was from a medical study or something. Like a new stop-smoking device. I remember that I asked him whether this could have had something to do with Trent's mental state. And he was so fucking patronizing. No, he said, they don't test dangerous drugs like that on people. Even *homeless* people."

He was staring at her with a certain disapproval. "I hope you realize, I still don't have the first idea what you're talking about."

Having decimated the wrapper, she began to shred the edge of her place mat. "When she died, I thought that was the end of it with the implant. I thought it'd get tossed out when they cleaned up the lab. But it wasn't *at* the lab—that's the point. She'd already finished with it there, and when they broke in, she didn't have it to give them, so they did the next logical thing. They went to my apartment, but it wasn't there, either. You should've seen the mess in my bathroom. They were *very* interested in my bathroom. They were looking for *this*." She shook it in his face. "And all the time, it was sitting in a drawer at my gym, waiting for me to show up and claim it. And when I did, this evening, this big beefy guy without a neck came hotfooting it after me."

"You're kidding," he said, getting alarmed for the first time. "Some guy chased you?"

She shook her head. "Not exactly. Sort of. I went out by an emergency exit, and a few minutes later, he came busting out the front door. I was watching from across the street. Then he ripped some poor lady out of a phone booth and made a call, and then he took off in the direction of my apartment."

Sam looked at her very seriously. "You do know how this sounds, don't you?"

"No. I don't. I only know what happened, and I'm sorry you appear not to believe me."

"Oh no," he told her, "it isn't that. It's just that what you're describing has lots of other explanations than the one you seem to be embracing. For example, what specifically links this neckless guy with you? I mean, couldn't he have suddenly remembered it's his mother's birthday or something and gone to phone her?"

"After first looking frantically up and down Broadway for his mother? No, I don't think so. Besides, I'd seen him before. He was staring at Susu. I remember, I told her she had an admirer. The bastard."

Sam sighed. "So what do we have, anyway? What's it add up to?"

"Legally, nothing. Don't worry, I'm well aware of that. But something's happening here, and it's all about this." She picked up the implant. "Look, if I'm wrong, we've got a lot of isolated and unexplained weirdnesses, okay? But if I'm right, suddenly everything makes sense. Except"—she sighed—"for the fact that I don't understand any of it."

"Okay." Sam nodded. "Let's accept the hypothesis that you're right." He eyed her. "For the moment. What are you right about? What *is* this?" He tapped the little plastic pouch. "What insidious substance is causing all this upset?"

Sybylla sighed and leaned back as the waiter set down a plate of meat crusted with pungent teriyaki sauce. "You probably know more about it than I do," she told Sam as he speared a first bite of steak. "It's LSD."

Inches from his mouth, the fork stopped. Finally, he looked interested. "Wait a minute."

"It is. I mean, a few other things, too, that I don't know anything about. But look." She found Susu's much-inspected report in her purse and pushed it across the table to him.

Quantitative & Qualitative Analytic Report
Specimen Number: NA
Requestor: Sybylla Muldoon

DESCRIPTION
Object is disk-shaped, flat, and waxy white. Does not conform to any commercially available pharmaceutical delivery system.

PHYSICAL CHARACTERISTICS

Weight:	29.7 grams
Absolute Density:	2,973
Diameter:	1.48
Melting Point:	42 degrees Celsius

CHEMICAL ANALYSIS
(Gravimetric assay determination)

Lysergic acid diethylamide:	7.3 grams
Scopolamine:	1.8 grams

| Polyglycolic acid: | 11 grams |
| Polylactic acid: | 9 grams |

Prepared by: S. Patel

"Lysergic acid," she pointed, accentuating the obvious. "This thing's a communion wafer from hell. It's a time-release device, you see? Once it's inside the body, it introduces a constant level of the drug, until it runs out or until it's removed. I got a whole lecture from Susu about implant technology and all the astonishing medical breakthroughs it's going to provide for people who can't be trusted to take their medication regularly. Tuberculosis, diabetes, hormone therapy for cancer . . . It's the coming thing, you see. But this little item"—she picked it up between thumb and forefinger—"where this fits in, only the people who made it can say. Whoever they may be." Sybylla's eyes locked on Sam's. "And it came out of Trent's upper arm. Now what do you suppose it was doing there?"

Sam was staring. "Haven't the faintest," he said finally.

"Remember all that delusional stuff Trent's been spouting since his arrest? I say it's starting to look like he's been telling the truth."

Sam gazed down blankly at his plate. He seemed to have forgotten how hungry he was. "Jesus Christ. Why would *anyone?*" He shook his head. Then, after a minute, he said, "The time frame."

"Yup." Sybylla was right there with him. "So much for the eight- to ten-hour acid trip. As long as that thing was inside Trent, he was definitely not compos mentis."

"He was tripping when he stabbed her."

Sybylla rolled her Kirin bottle between her palms. "I knew Trent wouldn't do this. I knew it."

"Then . . . when did you say they took it out?"

"The morning he was admitted to Bellevue. And a couple weeks later I got the message he was asking for me. When I went to see him later that day, he was a bit woozy, but essentially fine. Memory lapses, of course. Intense paranoia"—she shook her head—"or so I thought. But fairly together. As I'd remembered him, more or less."

Sam pushed his plate away and signaled for a beer of his own. "We don't know anything, Syb. Not really. This is all speculation."

"Listen," she hissed, "I know one thing for sure. As long as this is a secret, I'm in danger, and you, too, and anyone else who knows about this thing. We've *got* to get Turturro up there first thing tomorrow to testify about the implant. Then I have to get this report into evidence, or somehow make it public. That's our protection, don't you see? While it's a secret, we're vulnerable. It's not only about Trent anymore. It's about us, and I don't mind telling you, I'm scared to death."

For the first time all evening, he agreed with her.

CHAPTER

TWENTY-TWO

Amazingly enough, Turturro wasn't thrilled to be called at six in the morning, nor to be told that he would testify first when Trent's defense got under way a few hours later—a change in plan that would necessitate his rescheduling half a dozen appointments and a standing responsibility to head teaching rounds. By the time she got around to mentioning the fact that her questions on the stand would focus not on Trent's mental health but on the LSD trace and the implant recovered from his arm, the psychiatrist was livid.

"You're not going to get me to testify that that little bit of LSD in his bloodstream had anything to do with a psychotic episode over twenty-four hours earlier, you hear?" he was howling into the phone. "If he was testing positive for lysergic acid at Bellevue, the earliest point of ingestion for the drug is twelve hours earlier, and that's it. Am I making myself clear?"

"Absolutely," Sybylla said hastily. It would be far more effective to elicit his surprise on the witness stand than to tell him now.

"And as for that implant, I don't know what you think you've found out about it, but I doubt very much that it's anything a scientific analysis could point to for culpability in these circumstances."

"Dr. Turturro," Sybylla said firmly, "you are a scientist and I respect your skepticism, but I also expect you to keep an open mind until you hear what the results actually were."

He gave a patronizing little laugh. "What was it, a little computer chip that played the voice of God in his head? 'Go stab little blond girls'?"

In a manner of speaking, she wanted to say. She said good-bye and hung up, falling back onto the lumpy hotel bed.

Sam propped himself up on his elbow. "Don't tell me. You mean he wasn't delighted to hear from you?"

"I couldn't help it. I've been up for two hours, freaking out. I couldn't put off calling him anymore. I feel so exposed. Once it's public knowledge, no one will have a motive anymore to keep us from telling what we know, but until then . . ." She looked at him. "I'm just scared."

"I know that," he said quietly. He picked up the little plastic pouch from the bedside table. "You know," Sam sighed, "I've got to tell you, I really wish you had just put this through the system and sent it to the lab, all aboveboard. There'd be a record then."

She sat up and surveyed the room, blandly decked out in ur–hotel beige. She found herself momentarily unable to recall the name of the place they'd chosen to check in, and there was some strange comfort in that, as if the place's lack of distinction were a kind of camouflage for them. She turned to Sam. "I gave it to Susu because I didn't want egg on my face when it turned out to be nothing, like Turturro told me it was going to be. This way, when it turned out to be nothing, it really would be nothing. No residue. No skin off my back. And no Andrew Greer yakking about how I was grasping at straws."

Sam sat up and leaned toward her. "Syb," he said, "look, let's not panic. I'm willing to accept that there's something fishy going on with this implant, because I don't think the government has okayed LSD testing on people since the sixties. I think some drug company somewhere is doing a little extracurricular research or something. And these people are bastards, no question, but they're not the type to off public defenders."

"They offed a chemistry professor," she observed.

"We don't know that," said Sam.

"Oh yes," Sybylla said, her voice small but matter-of-fact. "I think we do."

He brooded for a minute, watching her. "What are we going to do with Thing here? How do you plan on carrying it?"

She smiled a little. "Where's the bag from the drugstore?"

Sam reached under the bed and retrieved a Love bag from the night before. It contained an opened three-pack of Trojans—one of which remained—and the rather less understandable stick of glue. He watched as she withdrew the last condom.

"Honey, I'm flattered, but even I have my limits."

"Oh, you're so vain." Sybylla shook her head. "Now watch this." Carefully, she peeled back the edge of the condom packet and slipped out the latex ring. Then she extracted the implant from its plastic envelope.

"You're not," Sam said, full of admiration.

"I am." The little disk fit perfectly. Sybylla sealed the edge with the glue stick and the packet was intact—a bit worn, just as it might be from riding around in the wallet of a modern single gal, which is exactly where she put it. Sam nodded his approbation.

At eight o'clock, they slipped into 100 Centre Street by a side entrance and presented themselves at the pens.

"Bit early," the court officer observed. "You folks been burning the midnight oil?"

"Something like that," said Sam.

The officer looked from one face to the other and gave an unmistakable leer. "Don't even know if Trent's awake."

"Then wake him," Sybylla said. "Please."

They woke him. A minute later, he was led, bleary-eyed, into the tiny consulting room. Sybylla waited until the officer left.

"There's been a change," she told him, laying her hand on his wrist. "Yeah?"

"I want you to tell me everything you remember," Sybylla said flatly. "The van, the room, the people, everything."

Trent shook his head fiercely. "I can't do that."

Sam leaned forward. "Trent, we wouldn't ask if there wasn't a good reason. This is for *your* benefit. Your defense."

"I want to," he said. "But you might get in trouble."

Sybylla snorted. Her hand tightened on Trent's wrist. Her voice was steely. "I've got a news flash for you, friend. I'm already in trouble, and so is Sam." She paused. "I'm not giving you a choice here, so talk."

Trent studied her. "You believe me, don't you? You didn't used to, but now you do."

"You're right there," Sybylla said grimly. "I apologize that it didn't happen sooner. Now, somebody went to a lot of trouble to put something in your body. I want to know who and I want to know how. I realize you probably won't be able to help me with why." Sybylla flipped up a legal pad and waited, her black felt-tip poised.

His gaze fell to the battered table between them. "I was at my squat, like I told you. I was sleeping, and when I woke up, this van was backing up. The back of the van was almost on top of me. I said, 'Hey!' I was trying to get out of my sleeping bag. And the back door opened and these guys was trying to throw me in the van. One of 'em was big, I remember. Like a weight lifter or something. The other one was just a kid—little scrawny black kid. Had one a those razor haircuts, like, with a pattern on the sides. This kid says to me, 'C'mon, you're going to the shelter. You stink—you gotta have a shower.' I says, 'No way. I'm not goin' to no shelter. I never go to the shelters since I was a kid.' I swear to Christ, one of 'em gives me a needle." He swatted the seat of his pants. "Here. Hurt like shit. And that was it for the van."

Sybylla was scribbling. "What do you mean?" Sam said.

"Next thing I know, I'm in some little room on a little bed. My clothes is gone. I'm wearing some fucking hospital gown. People coming in and out, taking my temperature, taking my blood. I keep saying, 'What are you doing? I want to leave. You can't keep me in a shelter if I don't want to be here—it's against the law!' I know the law. Nobody says a word to me. There's no window in the room, so I can't tell how long I'm there, and plus they're giving me needles all the time, and I know it's heavy-duty stuff because I wake up, I feel like shit."

"Trent," Sam asked, "were you still sure it was a shelter you were in?"

"Hell, I don't know. It wasn't like no shelter I ever seen. Too spick-and-span, for one thing. Coulda eaten off that floor. Then I thought maybe it was a hospital, not a shelter. So next time one of 'em came in, I said, 'You can't keep me against my will 'less I been committed. So you show me the commitment papers or you let me out. I know my rights!' But they wouldn't."

"Okay," Sybylla said, finishing what she was writing. "What happened next?"

"Next." He shook his head. "I don't know. I was in an' out all the time, so it's not like I can remember something happened and then the next thing happened, like. But finally, I sort of realize I'm not in the room

192

anymore. They took me out, right? And there's one bastard on each of my arms and they're walking me down this hall. It's fucking freezing, too. Like the floor's made of ice. And they take me into this room and it's like an operating room or something. So I start screaming holy hell, I swear to Christ. Then I was running and I was in these trees. There was a train, too, but maybe that was later. And the next thing I remember is, I'm over at the hospital." He looked up at Sybylla. "I mean the real hospital. Where you came."

"So you have no idea what happened to you in the operating room?"

He shook his head. "Nah. I don't remember."

"Or how you actually got out of that place? Or the little girl?"

"Nah. If I did that to her"—he glanced up guiltily at Sybylla; it was the first time he had made this concession—"I musta been outta my mind. But I'll tell you one thing. My mind was fine before those people started messing with me. I sure wouldn't stab no kid before they got me in that stinking van."

"I know that," Sybylla said. She reached into her bag and found the implant. "This is what they took out of your arm, Trent," she told him quietly. "Have you ever seen it before?"

Trent stared at the disk, wide-eyed. Slowly, he shook his head.

"In my arm? Where that scar is?"

"That's right."

He stewed in silence for a moment, his mouth tight. Sybylla heard him breathe in fierce snorts. "They had no right," Trent hissed finally.

"That's true," Sybylla said soothingly. "Someone violated your rights, and I'm going to find out why. But Trent, I'm not going to lie to you. They still may not let you off for what happened to the little girl. You saw her up there. You saw the way she looked. Whatever happened to you, you're normal now, but she'll never be normal. It wasn't your fault, but you've got to be prepared that they still might not forgive you. You understand?"

Trent was staring at her, and Sybylla saw that indeed he understood perfectly everything she had just told him. The unfairness of it was coursing through him, even as a peculiar resignation followed on its heels. Finally, he leaned forward, idly touching the white disk in the center of the table. "You find out," he said, his voice so low that Sybylla had to strain to hear it. "For me." He looked up at her. "You find out why."

"I will," she promised.

He sat back heavily, bereft. Sybylla was capping her pen.

"Trent," said Sam, "we've changed the order of testimony this morning. We need your doctor from Bellevue to testify first, because the jury has to hear about the implant from him. Then we'll go back to the original schedule, and you'll probably come on later in the morning. All right?"

He nodded slowly.

Sybylla looked at her watch: nearly nine. "Let's go."

Trent was motionless, the muscles of his cheeks slack as he stared at the table where the disk had been. Even as he had been promised a measure of redemption by Sybylla's belief in his innocence, he had also received the simultaneous blow of accepting that freedom was a distant prospect for him, if a prospect at all. Suspended in the no-man's-land between outrage and outright despair, he looked to Sybylla like a man who had just learned that his life was not merely about to end but, in fact, had ended already.

CHAPTER
TWENTY-THREE

66**D**efense ready to proceed, Ms. Muldoon?"

Sybylla stood up. "Ready, Your Honor. We call Dr. Bruno Turturro."

He wasn't in a much better mood than when they had last spoken, she saw. The doctor even gave her an unsolicited frown as he strode to the front of the room, a gesture she was too tense to return. Her anxiety to get the LSD and the disk into evidence was so strong that it was only with much difficulty that she was able to get the preliminaries down. At his table, Greer was watching smugly, his pencil poised to record the psychiatric absurdities he assumed were coming.

"Doctor," Sybylla began, "what is your area of medical specialty?"

"I'm a psychiatrist. Board-certified in psychiatry and internal medicine by the State of New York."

"Where were you educated?"

Turturro sighed and recited his resumé: "I received my undergraduate education at Syracuse University. I received my medical education at Downstate Medical. I did my internship and residency in psychiatry at Cook County Medical Center in Chicago. I have been at Bellevue for eight years, and am at present chief attending physician of the Department of Psychiatry."

"Do you have private patients as well as your patients at Bellevue?"

"No," Turturro said. "The hospital is my employer. My patients are referred to me—if you will—by the city. Typically men and women who exhibit antisocial or aberrant behavior either in their homes or in public places and then are sent to Bellevue for evaluation. It is my job to evaluate them and to determine treatment."

Sybylla flipped through her notes and made a play of locating the right page. She wanted the jury to know that the preliminaries were over.

"Dr. Turturro, on March the fifteenth of this year, did you have occasion to examine a patient who is now the defendant in this case?"

He glanced, nonplussed, at Trent. "I did."

"Doctor, leaving aside for the moment the question of a preliminary diagnosis, would you describe for us briefly the symptoms this patient exhibited?"

Turturro sat up and crossed his long legs. "The patient was extremely agitated—shrieking, occasionally responding to or interacting with persons or entities who were not present. Limbs were jerking and flailing. The patient also seemed to be exhibiting intense fear."

"I see." Sybylla walked around to the front of her table. "Dr. Turturro, did you have occasion to perform a physical examination of the patient?"

"I did."

"And what did that entail?"

"Oh . . . well, our standard intake exam includes a blood and urine workup, temperature, blood pressure, palpation for internal masses, broken bones, whatever we might be able to feel, since an irrational or nonresponsive person might not be capable of communicating a medical situation to us."

"And you did all that with Trent?"

"Yes."

"Now let's see," she pretended to consult her notes, "what was Trent's temperature?"

The tall man glanced down at his file. "Ninety-nine point two. Essentially normal."

"Any broken bones?"

"No. There were none."

"What about the blood and urine tests. Anything unusual turn up?"

Turturro didn't bother to look down. "I don't know if you'd call it unusual, under the circumstances, but there was a positive test result for lysergic acid."

She cocked her head at him as if she'd never heard the term before. "I'm sorry, Doctor. Lysergic what?"

He gave her a facetious look. "It's more commonly known as LSD, Ms. Muldoon."

The effect was instantaneous. "Hey!" Greer was shouting. "Your Honor, sidebar conference now! Your Honor!"

Coffin put up his hands. "All right. No need to yell, Mr. Greer. Ms. Muldoon?"

Suppressing her smile, she walked up to the bench. Greer was on fire.

"What is this crap?" the DA hissed. "What are you getting at?"

"I don't understand what you're asking." Her voice was innocent. "What do you mean, what am I getting at? It should be obvious that I'm trying to get at the truth."

The DA was crimson with rage. "What's the matter, couldn't find a shrink to say he was crazy? You made your bed with an insanity defense. You'd better damn well lie in it."

"Mr. Greer," Coffin said, "I'm sure you can express yourself without profanity."

Sybylla shook her head. "Ooh, you *are* confused, aren't you? What on earth makes you think I'm pursuing an insanity defense?"

He stared at her, struck dumb, on the cusp of hyperventilation.

"What—" Greer gasped. "You filed notice. You—you notified my office you'd be pursuing insanity."

"Well, perhaps at one point we were considering that," Sybylla said blandly, "but I assure you, we revised our intentions a long time ago when critical evidence came to light. I think I can comfortably state that I haven't once uttered the word *insanity* since this trial began." She shrugged at him. "You can check the transcript if you want, but you won't find anything to indicate such a defense."

"Don't give me that." He leaned close to her and his breath was sour. "You got that witness to say he was nuts, and the surgeon. And the *victim*, for Christ's sake!"

Coffin's normally affable expression tightened. "Curb your lip, Mr. Greer. I know you're angry, and I agree that you have cause, but don't push me." He turned to Sybylla. "I think there's been some subterfuge here, Ms. Muldoon, though I can see you've stayed within the law." He eyed her. "Just. Now, do you mind my asking where your defense is going? This might be a good time to show a few of your cards."

It was inevitable, Sybylla knew. "Your Honor, there is ample evidence, including physical evidence, to indicate that my client was exposed against his will to a dangerous mind-altering substance that had a direct causal effect in relation to the crime with which he's been charged."

"Oh, come on." The DA was sneering. "Insanity was bad enough. Now you want us to believe that poor innocent Trent had acid dropped *on* him?"

Sybylla kept her eyes on the judge. "As I said, Your Honor, *ample physical evidence*. The prosecution witnesses Mr. Greer referred to a few moments ago were describing an assailant who was suffering from the effects of a hallucinogenic drug."

"If you persist with this," Greer huffed, "I'm going to bring you up on disciplinary charges. You have willfully subverted the prosecution's ability to prepare its case, and I'm going to need time to consider this so-called evidence."

"Why don't you take a moment to hear it first?" Sybylla shot back. "Or would knowing the actual evidence cramp your style?"

"All right." Coffin's voice was paternally brusque. "Now, Ms. Muldoon"—he turned to Sybylla—"you know as well as I do that intoxication is not grounds for acquittal. If it were, the prisons in this state would be a lot less crowded than they are."

"But *involuntary* intoxication, I think Your Honor will agree, is a different matter. Defense can prove beyond question that this intoxication was inflicted on the defendant while he himself was a victim of kidnapping."

"Oh, this is hysterical." Greer snorted. "This I've got to hear."

"And so you shall," Coffin said. "And so shall I. I must say, my curiosity is piqued. But, Ms. Muldoon, keep it aboveboard from now on. That's a warning."

"Yes, Your Honor." Sybylla tried to sound contrite. She couldn't resist a wink at Greer as they returned to their tables.

"Dr. Turturro," Sybylla took up her pad again, "the behavior you described a few minutes ago—flailing limbs, talking to people who weren't there, the fear you mentioned—are they the kinds of behaviors that a person under the influence of a hallucinogenic drug like LSD might experience?"

She'd phrased it narrowly enough. Turturro took a minute to conclude that he couldn't get out of her box. "Yes," he said stiffly. "Might."

Sybylla nodded. It was time to move on to the disk. If she asked Turturro about the time frame now, he would take the opportunity to rain on the LSD theory, and rain so hard that even the introduction of the implant might not counteract the effects.

"Dr. Turturro—" Behind her, there was movement. One of the DA's minions was coming up the aisle. Miffed at losing her train of thought, she started again. "Dr. Turturro, did you find anything when you palpated the patient?"

"Well, we—"

"Your Honor!" Greer was again on his feet, his face ashen.

Asshole, Sybylla thought. What now?

"Your Honor." The DA leaned forward over his table, one arm braced on the stack of files before his seat. He seemed unconvinced by what he was about to say. "Your Honor, I have to express my deep apologies to the court, but I have an emergency to attend to. I need to leave the courtroom for a short time."

"*What?*" Sybylla exploded. "Can't we finish with this witness first?"

"Absolutely not," Greer hissed at her. "I have to leave immediately."

"Your Honor, this is outrageous. I demand to be allowed to finish."

"Ms. Muldoon," Coffin said, sounding a little surprised at her, "your colleague has an emergency. Emergencies aren't always convenient."

Even amid her fury, Sybylla felt the rebuke and blushed.

Coffin turned to the DA. "Mr. Greer, how much time do you need to deal with your emergency? Would an hour be sufficient? I'd like not to have to interfere with the defense unnecessarily."

"An hour is fine," Greer said. Sybylla's eye fell on the small white square of paper in his hand, the note his aide had delivered. She'd give anything to see it, to be reassured that the so-called emergency was bona fide.

"Court will recess for one hour," Coffin announced. "Jurors will return to the jury room. As usual, ladies and gentlemen," he addressed them, "do not discuss the case amongst yourselves." He stood and strode out.

Sam reached up and took her arm, tugging Sybylla down. She stood rigid, watching Greer take off out of the room like a weasel under the gun. "Syb," he whispered, "sit down." She sat, fuming. "Ease up, all right? It's a family thing. Or an office thing."

"It's a Trent thing," she whispered fiercely to him. "Isn't it obvious?"

"C'mon." Sam smiled. "What'd he do, send a secret signal out to the hall? 'Stop the trial. I want to get off'?"

"Yes," she hissed.

The court officer came for Trent, standing silently behind his chair. Trent turned to her. "Do I have to? I'd rather stay here."

"I'm afraid you have to," she said, finding a semisoothing tone for him. "Maybe they'll give you some coffee or something. We'll get back under way in an hour."

"All right." He nodded, glum.

"Don't worry," she told him.

Trent smiled weakly at them as the court officer cuffed him and led him away.

"Coffee's not a bad idea," Sam said after he'd gone. "Why don't we take advantage of the break?"

"It isn't a break," she whispered. "Something's wrong. Can't you feel it? Somebody knew where Turturro's testimony was going and got it stopped. Or at least bought a little time."

"Sybylla," Sam said, his voice unusually stern, "now that is really over the edge. Just cut it out."

She looked at him blankly, then turned to her notes and began to read over her remaining questions for Turturro, the black ink smearing her palm as it moved across the page. With a sigh, Sam went in search of coffee.

When he returned, half an hour later, the players in room 1608 were almost exactly as they had been when Sam left them—the DA, judge, defendant, and jurors absent, the victim's family and friends shifting and talking softly in the row behind the prosecution table, and Sybylla still scrawling, her head down. He took his seat quietly and gave her a bright "Hey," hoping her mood had passed.

"Hey," she muttered in response. "Where you been?"

"Cafeteria."

"Hear any buzz on the DA's so-called emergency?"

He smiled at her. "Nope. Not a thing."

"Fancy that." She flipped a page of her legal pad and continued writing. "You see Turturro?"

"Out by the elevators. Having a smoke."

"Hmm." She paused and massaged her palm. "Christ, how much longer?"

"It's only been thirty-five minutes, Syb."

"He'll be late," she said dryly. "If Coffin gave him an hour, he'll take two. Then it'll be time to break for lunch. By the time the jurors get to hear about the implant, they'll be so distracted by stops and starts, they won't be able to take it in."

But in fact, Greer wasn't late; indeed, he reentered the courtroom a good fifteen minutes before his allotted time had passed, walked purposefully down the aisle, and beckoned to the court officer, who huddled with him. Then, with a nod to Sybylla and Sam, the DA took his seat.

"I guess we're on," Sybylla said quietly, watching the judge emerge from his chambers.

Coffin took his seat. He looked rested, she thought, as if he had grabbed a catnap during the recess. "Mr. Greer? Do I understand correctly that you're now ready to proceed?"

"I am, Your Honor," Greer said. "I apologize once again for the inconvenience."

"All right, then. Bring the jury in, please. Carl, go get the defendant."

Sam leaned over. "See? Everything's fine."

Except that it wasn't fine. Her eye fell on the end of Sam's ballpoint pen, his fingers curled around it in a tight grip. He had black wiry hairs on his fingers; she'd never noticed. They were oddly unmoving, Sybylla thought. She had no opinion about them at all; they were simply there to be observed, moving up and down with the fingers and the pen as it drummed a steady beat on the tabletop. How could she have no opinion about the hairs on Sam's fingers? Wasn't he the person she slept with? Wasn't her life tied to his now, with circumstances that bound them and affection that bound them just as tightly? Dimly, the jury filed in. They were all waiting.

Somebody was shouting, and Sybylla really wished they would stop. It wasn't a delicate kind of shouting. It was disorganized and abrasive and really a pain. Other people were joining in. It was going from bad to worse, she thought, like a chorus of stray dogs picking up one another's howls. She looked up at the door that led back to the pens, the door behind which Trent had been taken. Sam, his face still and stiff, was looking, too. His pen had stopped drumming, Sybylla noticed.

"Hey!" It was Coffin, yelling at one of the court officers. "Hey, get back there and find out what's going on."

"What's going on?" Sybylla found her voice, grasping Coffin's words. "I don't know." Sam shook his head. "Sounds like a damn riot."

"We've got to—"

"What?" he said fiercely. "We've got to *what?*"

"It's *Trent*," she heard herself yelling at him. "Don't you see that? It's *Trent.*" He stared at her. "I'm going."

"You're not." He made a stab at grasping her hand, but when that failed, he plunged after her through the chaos the courtroom had become, the spectators pale and fearful, the officers clustered around the door, going in and coming out, with reinforcements arriving in waves from elsewhere in the building. Every time the door cracked open, the screams sailed out. "Let me back there," she yelled when she reached the men.

"No way."

"It's my client," Sybylla yelled. "Let me in."

The cluster eased as the door was pushed open again. "Let her in." It was Carl, Judge Coffin's bailiff. "It's all over, anyway."

"Come on." Sybylla grabbed Sam's wrist and dragged him into the dank hallway.

"This way," Carl said. "I'm real sorry. But it looks like it was a quick thing. Didn't suffer, I mean."

Sybylla bit her lip. "Who found him?"

"I found him. I went to bring him in; he was flat on the floor. Paramedic's with him now, but I seen a lot of bodies, and there's no chance, I'm pretty sure."

They rushed past cells, nearly all inhabited by one or two prisoners apiece. The sounds were unearthly, and she fought an urge to press her hands over her ears.

"They hear it," Carl explained. "They don't get information passing along, but they get the urgency. People go nuts. Can't shut 'em up. You hear it out in the courtroom?"

"Yes," Sam said shortly.

When the corridor turned a corner, it was clear that they had reached ground zero. The cell door was flung open, and guards were crowded just outside the bars, watching the paramedics give hopeless CPR. Sybylla, drawing near, saw the stark white of Trent's exposed chest, his ribs standing out in bold relief on either side of his torso. He looked so young, she thought dully. He looked like the little boy he seemed to have remained, his growth stunted by poverty. One brown shoe, untied and half twisted off, poignantly accentuated the image. The paramedic tipped up his chin and breathed with aggressive optimism into his mouth, then pumped Trent's chest in a purposeful rhythm, but the intense concentration on the man's face was tempered by the crisp shakes of his head. He was letting his partner know that it was finished, even as he continued to try.

"All right," the partner said finally. "Let's stop."

With a deep sigh, the paramedic rocked back on his heels. "Sorry, folks."

There was a murmur of approbation from the ranks. Sybylla stepped close to the body, letting its smallness strike her anew. Trent's eyes were open wide, their deep brown irises contemplating the grimy ceiling of his cell. What a miserable last sight, she thought. But it had all been miserable for Trent, hadn't it? Beginning to end—all the worst that life had to offer. She wiped furtively at her eyes. Her hand came away wet.

Sybylla turned to Carl. "What happens now? I mean, to him?"

"They'll take him over to the morgue at Bellevue," the officer said kindly, as if she were indeed the next of kin.

"What about an autopsy?"

"Oh, I don't know about that. They usually only autopsy if the circumstances of death are suspicious."

Her eyes widened. "A man dies in the middle of his own trial, you don't call that suspicious?"

"Well now," the officer said carefully. "I'm not a doctor, but I've seen a lot of murder, and believe me, this isn't what murder looks like. This body has natural causes written all over it."

She turned to the paramedic. "What do you think?" He was zipping Trent into a body bag. Sybylla looked away, selfishly wishing she might have been spared this last vision of him: his narrow, bony chest, stark white against the paramedic's large black hand, the unfurled laces of his poor shoe, his eyes gazing so pointlessly upward.

"Looks like a heart attack," he said shortly. "That's what it looks like."

"Bit young," she said. "Isn't he?"

"Oh, I don't know," the other paramedic chimed in. "Congenital heart defects, inherited hypertension. Stress."

Sam had laid his hand on her shoulder. Sybylla shook it off. "I'm going to have to insist on an autopsy."

The paramedics exchanged glances. "There's nothing here, miss," one ventured.

"Even so. I'm his attorney and I think an autopsy is warranted."

She watched them finish with him. One of the paramedics found some paperwork for her to sign. Sybylla bit her lip as Trent's face disappeared beneath the green plastic and they wheeled him out.

"All right," she said to no one in particular. "Let's go."

Word had clearly reached the outer chamber. Sybylla and Sam met tired, contemplative faces when they emerged from the pens and returned to the defense table. Judge Coffin had waited for them to dismiss the jury and formally terminate the case known as *People of the State of New York* v. *Trent.* Now he waited no longer.

"Ladies and gentlemen," he addressed the fourteen men and women, "I'm sorry to say that, in the last few minutes, this trial has come to an abrupt conclusion. It isn't the conclusion I'd like it to have reached, but it's a conclusion nonetheless. In our system of justice, a criminal case dies with a defendant, and the defendant in this case has indeed passed away. In legal terminology, this is known as an abatement by death.

"So now it falls to me to thank you for your good attention and for the integrity I know you would have brought to your deliberations. You are free to go. This court stands adjourned." He rapped his gavel and stood.

The roar was deafening as the reporters leapt over one another, some in the direction of the Barrett family and some in the direction of the door. An unseen limb jostled her as she reached down to the floor to feel for her briefcase. Behind her, something was blocking her light.

"Ms. Muldoon?"

So kind of him to take a moment out from this global adulation.

She looked up. "Mr. Greer."

"I'm sorry it worked out this way."

"Oh?" She peered up at him. "Which way is that?"

He frowned. "I'm sorry your client has passed on."

Passed on—a euphemism more suited to peaceful deathbeds than to the filthy floor of a holding cell.

"Yes, I'm sure you are sorry."

He let her sarcasm pass without comment. "I wanted to offer my condolences, though, as you know, I did not consider Trent to be an exemplary human being." He paused. "I hope we'll meet again, and perhaps under less adversarial circumstances." He turned his broad back to her.

Abruptly, Sybylla caught his arm. "You listen to me," she heard herself say, though she did not recognize the voice. "If I ever—*ever*—find out that you or your office had something to do with this, I will make *sure* that you never get closer to Albany than a tourist pass at the statehouse."

"I beg your pardon!"

"Sybylla!" Sam yelled, horrified. "Don't." He yanked her arm.

Greer was shaking his head in wonder. "I don't have a clue what you're talking about."

"Oh, don't you," she spat.

"Listen, Ms. Muldoon. I'm going to tell you something. As a favor to your father, I'm going to pass on a little bit of advice. You're not the first public defender to suffer career burnout. It's happened to better lawyers than you, and it has nothing to do with your value or your commitment to the law. Give yourself a little break. Try some other kind of legal work for a while. You can always come back. A couple years of corporate work or academic work, they wouldn't kill you." He gave her a pseudopaternal nod. "Take my advice. You're a little young to be this paranoid."

Stung, she took a step back. Sybylla could hear Sam breathing heavily behind her.

"I hope I am paranoid," she told him, finding her voice. "I truly hope that's all it is. But if it isn't, I stand by what I said. I'll have every muckraker in the city rummaging in your closet."

Slowly, his face eased into a smile, almost tender, as if she were one of the floral-framed cherubs on his desk. "I'd be careful about that if I were you," the DA said. "You can't be too sure whose suit of clothes you'll end up finding." Then, with a curt nod to Sam, he set off into the arms of the moral victory that was his to claim.

CHAPTER

TWENTY-FIVE

"I hope you're not too disappointed," Sam said, a mite sarcastically, as he held back the door for her. "Of course it was a delight, hanging out in the morgue with you, and I never actually got to see somebody get disemboweled before. But I hate to think how shattered you must have been when it turned out to be a perfectly legal cardiac arrest."

She turned west on Twenty-eighth Street and tried to ignore him. It was evening. They had spent imponderable hours in the basement at Bellevue, and she just wanted to breathe fresh air.

"Why are you going on about this? He's just plain *dead,* Sybylla."

She turned on him. "I know that. I fucked up and he's dead."

"You fucked up. How did you fuck up?"

"I don't know yet," she said, swallowing. "I'm going to find out."

"Fabulous. I suppose this means more hanging out in hotels and running away from bad guys." She was glaring at him. Suddenly, he softened. "Syb, listen. Of course you feel terrible, but it wasn't your fault. And you *didn't* fuck up. In fact, Trent remains technically not guilty."

"Oh, great," Sybylla sneered. "Let's go back down to the morgue and tell him."

"At least now things can get back to normal," he said quietly.

Sybylla stared at him. "What are you talking about?"

"Well, it's all over, isn't it? Our drug company friends won't care about their implant now. The trial's over—it won't mean anything to anyone."

"It means something to me," Sybylla hissed. "Like my life."

Now it was his turn to stare. "Sybylla, you're not serious. Nobody's going to harm you—harm either of us. The implant's just a random *object* now; it has no context. It isn't news anymore. Even if someone was following you until today—which I'm still not entirely sure is the truth— there'd be no reason to keep doing it. Don't you see that?" She said nothing, her expression stony. "You can go back to your life now. Back to your apartment and your routine." He waited for a reaction. "Sybylla," he insisted, starting to sound angry, "I'm telling you, it's *over.*"

"You seem very sure about this."

"I *am* sure," he said, ignoring her tone.

"I'm not." She turned and began to walk away, furious at him but— rather disconcertingly—sort of hoping he'd come after her.

He did. "You know, Sybylla," Sam said, "I never thought I'd agree with Andrew Greer about anything, but there is a definite air of paranoia about you right now."

"Is it still paranoia if it turns out to be true?" she said archly. "If you're so sure you're not in danger, then why are you coming with me?"

He shook his head, noting the Twenty-eighth Street subway station, her apparent destination. "I'm not coming with you—wherever you're going."

"Bye, then." She tossed the remark over her shoulder as she descended the station steps.

"Good-bye to *you*," he howled down at her from the sidewalk, a gesture that invited the bemused attention of her fellow travelers. Sybylla gritted her teeth, slipped a token into the slot, and moved through onto the platform.

It felt safe to be in a crowd—*safer*, at any rate—and for possibly the first time in her life as a subway rider, she regretted having to extricate herself from the packed car. A drizzle had set in during her ride uptown and the cheap umbrella hawkers were pushing their wares by the back door of Bloomingdale's. Sybylla walked east, bought a cup of soup at a delicatessen, and grimly eyed the evening edition of the *Post:* GOD SAYS GUILTY: WILD MAN DIES DURING TRIAL.

She hoped they were not claiming to have interviewed God.

Bennis sat placidly in the rain, his legs crossed under a blanket, his expression blankly bereft. Sybylla made her way through the small shantytown, weaving among the hostile and curious and apathetic men who watched her pass. Somebody had taken over Trent's squat, she noted, his small body of about Trent's length and heft asleep beneath the tarp, a bit of sandy hair protruding. It was an oddly disturbing sight, with its queer implication that an endless chain of Trents was on call to fill one another's shoes and sleeping bags, waiting only for death to move one step forward in the queue. She wrapped her coat tightly about her, and spotting a relatively unsoiled bit of sidewalk, she took a seat by Bennis.

"Hello," she said. She reached into the brown paper bag and extracted the soup. Bennis took it without comment.

"I know about it. If that's why you're here."

"It was very sudden. I don't think he suffered," she lied.

Bennis shrugged, as if the question of suffering was moot.

"I woulda testified. I was ready."

"I know. And I think Trent had a real chance of acquittal. But it never got that far." Bennis said nothing. Sybylla glanced over at Trent's squat, whose current inhabitant was now stirring. "Somebody moved in?"

"That's Paul. Guy who was here when they took Trent away. I hadta let him. Some guy went off with his stuff one time he wasn't here, and I knew Trent wasn't coming back." He shrugged.

"You said Paul was cr—that he wasn't right in the head, didn't you?"

"Yeah. He's better when he takes his pills, but usually he forgets." Bennis smirked. "Like now. He's kinda—"

Her intake of breath was sharp as ice. Her eyes were riveted on the small body, righting itself and shrugging off the heavy blanket. It stood barely five foot four, and it couldn't have weighed more than Sybylla herself. It belonged to a man who looked hauntingly like the body she had seen unfurled on a stainless-steel table only an hour earlier.

"Jesus."

"Yeah," Bennis commented. "It's something, ain't it? At first, it was some of the other guys saw it. I didn't see it. I didn't see what they was talking about. But they coulda been brothers, eh? Except, like I said"— he leaned forward—"Paul ain't normal."

"Um-hm." She was still staring. The small man's arms were jittering. His head cocked to the side in a regular rhythm, and a steady stream of staccato gibberish emerged from his throat, an angry, rasping dialogue in an unknown language and with an unseen partner.

Bennis was reaching into a paper bag at his feet. "Hey." He shook half a wax paper–wrapped sandwich at his neighbor. "Hey, Paul. Here's yer dinner."

The man responded to his name and drew near, gradually focusing on the sandwich Bennis held up to him. As he leaned down, Sybylla saw that the resemblance was indeed superficial; close up, the features were less delicate than Trent's, and the nose had been conspicuously broken. But the similarities in body shape and size and in facial coloring were indeed remarkable. From far off, they might well have appeared interchangeable.

"Paul," she said suddenly, without thinking, "you knew Trent, didn't you? You were here when Trent got into the van, weren't you?"

He fumbled with the wax paper and shoved the sandwich into his mouth. A bit of withered bologna flapped over his lower lip, and Sybylla held her breath against a wave of nausea. He chewed diligently, his eyes locked on the ground.

"Paul?" she tried again. "Can you remember what the van looked like? Did it say anything?"

No response but the sickening sound of masticating food.

Bennis was laughing. "I told you. He ain't all here. Besides, I saw the van. There weren't nothing on the side. Least the side I could see. It was just a white van, like you'd see anywhere. You don't know nothing, Paul, do ya?"

Paul stopped chewing. His eyes drifted lazily from the ground to Bennis, then from Bennis to Sybylla, where they lingered with an expression that was almost intelligent. He dropped the empty wax paper on the ground and took a step forward. Automatically, she recoiled from his stench, but something made her stand her ground. Bennis was still laughing softly, like background music. Paul reached both hands forward until his palms, ingrained with the blackest dirt, were only inches from her face. Then, suddenly, those hands turned to each other and gripped as if they were long-lost friends, tightly and firmly. It was a little like the overhead gesture that athletes make in victory, Sybylla thought, or a man shaking hands with himself after a long absence.

"Hands," said Paul rather insistently. "Hands, hands."

"Thass right." Bennis laughed.

Paul reached his two hands out to Bennis, and the older man, still grinning, shook his head. "Sorry. Got no more. No more food. Try down the row. Mac might have something for ya." The slight body straightened. Sybylla watched Paul turn and shamble away, off down the sloping street, toward the cluster of homeless men at its foot.

"You take care of him," she observed.

"Sure." Bennis shrugged. "No one else does. He wouldn't eat if nobody told him to, you know?"

She nodded, then climbed to her feet. "I have to go, Bennis. I just came to tell you about Trent."

"Sure." He was somber again. "Okay."

"And thank you for wanting to testify. It would have helped. I know."

He sighed deeply and absently rubbed the mouth of his bottle with a bit of sleeve, then placed the booze on the pavement by his hip. Resting nearby, Sybylla saw a bit of the cord that normally terminated at Davis's foot. Davis, she now realized, was not here. "Where's Davis?" she asked, but the man only grunted. Escaped, it might mean. Or dead. She didn't really want to know. "I didn't have a chance to pick up some cigarettes." She fished out a twenty from her purse. "Take care of yourself, Bennis." He reached out to take the bill and nodded, but his eyes were unfocused. "Good-bye."

She walked down to First and then up a few blocks, deep into the heart of a Yuppie enclave: dry cleaners, sushi bars, gourmet essentials. In front of a Blockbuster Video, she grabbed a cab that had stopped to disgorge two women in business suits and Reeboks, and then she headed across town to her own, not dissimilar neighborhood and disembarked in front of the Korean grocer.

Mr. Ko nodded gruffly as she reached the register with her load of salad and ice cream.

"How are you?" she said politely, unloading her things.

"All right." He weighed the salad. "Business bad."

"I'm sorry to hear that," Sybylla said, though she couldn't imagine it was true. The market was always busy, as far as she could see. Still, it could hardly be as busy as Ko and his family, who were never, it seemed, idle in pursuit of their American dream. He was shoving her ice cream into plastic bags.

She looked out the door at the evening pedestrians. It was warm tonight. Spring had finally arrived, and people were enjoying the change. There seemed more couples than usual, strolling and stopping to look into the overburdened windows. One particularly well-scrubbed pair had paused before the market and were eyeing the mound of coconuts stacked outside. They were holding hands, just the entwined fingers visible, protruding from their jackets. Sybylla found herself looking at those fingers and then staring at them.

"Twelve dollar, fifty-two."

Sybylla turned to him, perplexed. "Mr. Ko?"

"Twelve dollar—"

"Mr. Ko, remember you said how that van parked in your space? Remember? When they picked up the woman from the alley?"

"Twelve fifty-two. I got customer."

"Yes." She fumbled for the money. "You said you spoke to them. Can you remember what the van looked like? Did it say anything on it?"

"Sure." He took the money. The drawer of the register popped out. "I write it down. I was angry. I tell them, 'I call police if you don't get out of my space.'"

"You wrote it down?" Numbly, Sybylla accepted her change. Ko lifted the plastic sorter that held small bills and coins. Underneath, she glimpsed a wad of personal checks and credit-card receipts and twenties, then the folded bit of white paper he grasped between thumb and index finger and passed to her, even as he waved forward the next in line. She couldn't help herself. With imprecise fingers, she unfolded it and read the scrawled digits of a New York license plate and below them three words that were chilling in their benevolence: Helping Hand Services.

"Hiya." She was perching in Steiner's doorway, shoulder to the door frame.

He looked up from his brief and gave her a "can't win 'em all" shrug. "Too bad, Syb. Keep trucking, though, eh?"

"What?" It took her a minute to remember which tragedy he was referring to. "Oh. Yeah, I know." She nodded. "Poor Trent. He never caught a break."

"For which you're not responsible, Sybylla." He gave her a semi-serious glare. "Are you listening to me?"

"Hm?" She hadn't been, exactly. "Listen, boss, do you still have your magic man at the DMV?"

Steiner frowned. "Who wants to know?"

"Just a little matter." She shrugged, trying for nonchalance. Her coffee, however, was trembling in the mug. She was a lousy liar, and she hated lying to Steiner.

"You know"—he flapped shut the file cover—"we may be poor around here, but we do keep a few inspectors out in the shed. Why don't you go lasso one?"

"It isn't a case, actually. I'm a little embarrassed."

"Oh?" Steiner folded his hands. "Tell me more."

Sybylla sighed. "Well . . . these friends of mine were driving on Third Avenue and they got rear-ended by this white van, and the van left the scene of the accident even though there was visible damage to my friends' car. They wrote down the license plate number, but the police haven't done anything, so my friends asked me if they can sue these people who own the van—they're real pissed about it, see? But they also said they thought this might be some kind of charity van. So what I thought was, you know, if it turns out to be just some asshole's van, then yeah, I'll send them over to the civil division. But if it really is a charity, then I'm going to advise them to drop it."

"Equal justice," he observed.

She grinned. "Yeah, whatever."

"I think I was wrong about you, Syb." Steiner shook his head. "Obviously, you have time on your hands. I was *going* to suggest you might be ripe for some vacation."

She made a face at him. "Oh, don't worry about me, boss. I'm as overworked as anyone else around here. It's just one of those stupid things, you know? It's been sitting on my desk for a couple months, but one of them called me yesterday and asked about it again. So, like I said, do you still have that guy at the DMV?"

"Officially? I never had a guy at the DMV. Of course. Unofficially, I once represented a guy from the DMV. Bonked a drug dealer on the head with a two-by-four. Sweet guy. Yeah, I still talk to him from time to time."

Sybylla reached into her pocket and handed him the number. "I'd really appreciate it."

After a moment, Steiner shifted in his seat. "Syb, don't take this wrong, but I was serious about your taking a little time off. There's no reason you'd have to relax if you didn't feel like it. Your dad's confirmation hearings are supposed to start next week. Don't you want to be there?"

The question took her aback. Of course she wanted to be there. The opportunity to watch the checks and balances in action was indeed tempting. Not only would she have a ringside seat at history in the making, but there might be a chance to tell Senators Simpson and Specter exactly what she thought of them. There was, however, the small problem of her father, who had not actually invited Sybylla to attend his moment in the sun. Still, Sybylla knew that her father truly didn't like to be angry with her. Were he not busy in Washington being herded through the corridors of power, she suspected he'd have been on the phone to her by now.

"Maybe," she told him finally. "I might leave town for a few days."

"Hey," he shrugged, "it's nothing to be embarrassed about, you know. You can disagree with his politics and still support his candidacy. He's your dad, after all."

"Yeah." She nodded vaguely. "Boss, about the license plate thing . . ."

Steiner rolled his eyes and picked up his phone. "We'll stick this one in the favor bank, I take it?"

"Absolutely. You've almost earned a new washing machine."

"This'll take a few minutes," he said, his implication apparent. Then to hammer it home: "Don't wait."

Sybylla turned and left. She hated to involve Steiner even more than she had hated banishing him from her earlier discoveries about Trent, but her initial attempts to make sense of the Helping Hand information had come to nothing. The charity was not registered in New York, the city's Social Services network had no record of the organization, and the harassed woman at the Guild for the Homeless did not sound concerned by the possibility that somebody was removing homeless men and women from their squats. "Excuse me," Sybylla had said finally, her admittedly short fuse exhausted, "but don't you care that people are being taken off the streets?"

"Of course we care." The woman sighed. "Don't you understand? We're all *for* removing the homeless from the streets. That's what we *advocate*."

"But nobody's ever heard of this organization," Sybylla insisted. "Doesn't that concern you?"

"Well, I suppose so," the woman said shortly. "Perhaps if I had some free time, I'd spend it being concerned about a charitable organization picking up homeless people. But frankly, I'm too busy worrying about the homeless people who *haven't* been picked up—the ones who are starving and getting beaten up and having babies in doorways. Now, is there anything else I can do for you?"

She had thanked her, hung up the phone, and proceeded to plan B.

When she reached her office, she found her own chair turned, its back to her and a convention of black curls meeting where her own head usually rested. Time to face the music. She set her jaw.

"Who's been sitting in my chair?" said Sybylla dryly.

He swung it around, leisurely, till he faced her. Then he gave her a winning smile, as if nothing untoward had passed between them. "Hi, you."

Disconcerted, Sybylla headed for the room's only other chair, an institutional and graceless wooden number.

"Syb, I'm sorry about yesterday."

"Oh?" She set her bag on the floor.

"I mean, I really felt so relieved the damn thing was over. Awful about Trent, of course, but I thought, Well, now we can relax, you know? It didn't occur to me you'd feel differently."

"But I did." Her voice was matter-of-fact. "And I do."

"Well, I don't like to point this out, but you appear to be alive today."

Alive, yes, but hardly well rested. She'd spent a miserable night, sleeping poorly and waking at her building's every creak or hiss.

"So," he pressed, "you feel better?"

Sybylla relented. "A bit, maybe."

"And you forgive me for being a cad?"

Who could ignore such a request? She felt herself smile. Sam smiled, too.

"I like this chair," he said with studied seriousness. "It's much nicer than my chair. Can I have this chair?"

"No. You may not. But you may visit it whenever you wish." She set down her coffee.

He smiled. "You going to Washington next week?"

"I don't know. Maybe." She smiled. "Steiner wants me to go. Maybe he wants me to get Teddy Kennedy's autograph for him."

"Do *you* want to go?"

"Sure." Sybylla shrugged. Sam was rocking side to side, hypnotically, in her swivel chair, his eyes steady on her face, and now she noticed, too, that his hand rested on an open file on her desk, and the file was Trent's. He had been reading when she came in. Openly, without any attempt to hide it. Sybylla frowned. "I see you've been looking through the file."

He looked down at it, as if he was surprised to see it there.

"Oh. Yes. I don't know, I just felt curious."

"About what?" She cocked her head.

"Oh . . . you know, if there was anything I missed. Anything I could add to help us understand what happened."

"What do you mean, what happened? Is there a question about what happened?"

"Not really," he said carefully. "I just thought, you know, I'd take a run through the file and see if anything jumped out at me." He shrugged.

"And did anything?" Sybylla asked coolly. "Jump out at you?"

He shook his head. "Not really. I did wonder about one thing, but otherwise, no."

"And that one thing?" She crossed her legs.

He leaned forward in her chair and flipped open the file, rummaging through the loose sheets of legal-sized paper. "Where is it? From the notes you took when you talked to Trent in the hospital. There was this weird thing you wrote. Um . . ." His finger skimmed the sheet. "Oh, here. What does this mean? 'You men at ease'?"

Sybylla smiled. She had been expecting something terrible. A wild oversight, the true villain leaping from his secret lair in her own notes.

"Oh, that." She shook her head. "That was just something Trent said about the place he was held. Actually, I think he said it was something *they* said. The people at the place. I thought maybe it meant it was a Veterans Administration hospital, like where the doctors told the patients to be at ease when they came through on rounds or something. I made some calls about it, but Trent wasn't even a vet, so, you know, it was a washout. Besides, doctors don't say that to patients. Even in VA hospitals."

" 'You men at ease'?" he said, testing the sounds in his mouth.

"That's what he said."

"Oh no." Sam grinned. " 'You men at ease'?"

A flash of impatience crossed her features. "I told you, that's it." He threw back his head and laughed. "What's so funny?" Sybylla demanded.

"I'm sorry. It's just . . . Don't they teach the classics at Yale Law?"

"What . . . the classics? Why would they teach the classics? Which classics?"

He laughed even harder. "The classics. *The* classics. Aristotle. Aeschylus."

"Why would they teach that stuff at law school?" she asked.

He shook his head, buoyant. "No, they don't, of course. But at Harvard, my first year of criminal law, my professor had a classical bent, and he went on and on about this. The question even turned up on the final, I seem to remember."

"*What* question?" she practically yelled at him. "What does 'this' mean? And what does it have to do with 'You men at ease'?"

Sam sighed and leaned forward across her desk. "Not 'You men at ease.' Eumenides."

She was utterly lost.

"It's spelled E-u-m-e-n-i-d-e-s. Otherwise known as the Furies. They're the spirits of justice. They pursue the wicked criminal to the end of his life." He gave her an apologetic look. "I'm sorry. I'm not really such an intellectual snob. It's just I happen to know about this. The Furies tormented Orestes after he killed his mother, Clytemnestra. She had killed Orestes' father, Agamemnon, in revenge for *his* having killed Orestes' sister, Iphigenia. He did that to get his army a good wind to sail to Troy, where he hoped to kick a lot of ass. Y'follow?"

"Sure," she said, though she didn't. "But who were they?"

Sam laughed. "Oh, just your average mythic symbols of primal justice. Cronus murdered Uranus, the sky, who was his father. He lopped off the old man's organ and when it hit the ground, there was a kind of foam from it. Primal ooze, if you will. And out popped the Furies. Sort of a bunch of screaming ladies howling for retribution. Later, they calmed down a bit. They turned into the Eumenides. More cultivated. It's like they evolved with society from rough tribal blood justice to civilized justice." He held up his hands. "Like us. Civilized justice."

She shook her head. "A lovely thought. But I can't see what any of this has to do with Trent. Where would he hear a word like Eumenides, anyway?"

"Nowhere." Sam shrugged. "Unless he ran into some raving ex–classics prof on his travels. I haven't heard the word myself in years." With a grunt, he propelled himself out of Sybylla's chair. "Okay. I'm going back to my own office now."

"Okay."

"Want to have dinner tonight? We could go somewhere funky. Act like responsible Yuppies for a change."

"Maybe," Sybylla said distractedly. Already, she was trying not to forget the word; Eu-men-i-des, she practiced silently.

"Let me know." He gave her shoulder a friendly pat and left her in her uncomfortable chair, her client chair. Why should this chair be so uncomfortable? she asked herself. People come here; they're unhappy enough to be in this office. They should be comfortable. Eu-men-i-des. She tried Trent's version in a barely audible voice. "You men at ease." Eumenides.

"Here you go," a voice broke into the swirl of her thoughts. He reached out his hand: her slip of paper, now with a scrawl of his script on it. "And let me know if your friends are going to need a doctor to say they have whiplash. I've got a cousin in Queens who specializes in that. Family thing." He grinned. "I get a kickback."

"From Freedom Summer to whiplash kickbacks." She smiled at him fondly. "How the mighty are fallen."

"Hey," he said, leaving, "Jerry Garcia's a tie designer now."

Sybylla sat motionless in her chair for a long moment before letting her gaze fall onto that piece of paper. Then, slowly and deliberately, she eased open the fold and read the name and number he had written.

Why does this not surprise me? Sybylla thought, as if hearing herself from a great distance. She seemed to be losing her capacity for surprise. She closed her eyes for a minute and found herself recalling the strange and oddly enthralling painting she had seen in her father's club: the three calm ladies waiting patiently for a murderer to finish his terrible deed, confident of their appointment with him in Samarra. Justice swift and sure. She thought now, for the first time, how such a theme might appeal to those who shared her father's politics, or his zeal for retribution. How nice it must be to imagine ourselves surrounded by personalized tormentors, ready and waiting for us to act upon our own inherent evil. Before she could talk herself out of it, she dialed the number.

Her call was answered by the curt voice of a vaguely British-sounding man. "Hyperion," he barked.

By pure instinct, she fell into character. "Hello, this is the Hyperion Club, isn't it?"

"As I said." The voice was now not only curt but suspicious in the bargain. "May I ask whom you are trying to reach?"

"Oh, well, I'm writing a piece for *New York* magazine about some of the private firms doing outreach work with the homeless? You know," she lectured, "not everyone feels that Reaganomics was in error on this point. I, personally, think Ronald Reagan was absolutely right when he said the cutbacks in government spending for social programs would mean an increase in private and corporate outreach, and I think it's time some of the city's unsung private charities should be spotlighted."

Silence. He was waiting for more.

"It's come to my attention that one of the most active of these organizations is the Helping Hand program. I see their van working with the homeless all the time, and I wanted to include the people who are steering the program in my article. Now, I'm aware that Helping Hand is affiliated with the Hyperion Club—"

"How," the man cut her off, "do you happen to be aware of that?"

Sybylla paused. A lie should stick closely to the truth, she'd once read somewhere; the more colorful ones were the first caught out. "Oh"—she tried to sound nonchalant—"well, when I couldn't find you listed, I looked up the van registration. Is there a problem?" she said innocently.

"I know nothing about the club's social programs," the marginally British man said shortly, with a special sneer reserved for the word *social*. "Our member in charge of those activities is not here today."

"I see. Well, how can I reach him?"

"It is not our practice to give out members' names and phone numbers. In any case, he would not wish to make any comment." There was a pause. "I'm sure he feels that charitable outreach is best conducted privately, without courting public approbation."

She tried another tack. "Well, may I at least have this member's office number?"

"He works out of state," the man said impatiently, as if there were no telephones beyond the Hudson River. "I'm sorry, but it will be impossible. I wish you the best of luck with your article."

Sybylla took a breath and lost her head. "You're talking about Robert Winston, aren't you?"

Idiot, she howled at herself, but now that she'd said it, she couldn't lose the tiny chance of a confirmation.

"Sir?"

"Where did you hear that name?" the voice was yelling. "Who are you? Who are you? What—"

She hung up the phone and stared at it, numb, her brain utterly empty of complex function. Then she felt herself reach down to her purse on the floor and retrieve her wallet. It was made of pale leather, once stiff and thick but now worn thin and as soft as butter. It won't last much longer, she thought irrelevantly. Her fingers eased open the flaps and searched—past her money and credit cards, past the wad of coupons she never remembered to redeem, past the strange flat disk that had once resided in her dead client's upper arm, to the utterly proper business card that had been passed to her, in time-honored tradition, within the noble halls of a gentlemen's club. There, the name of the business run by her father's old friend was engraved in black on a rectangle of woven eggshell-colored paper. It had a phone number, too, she noted, taking little pleasure in this rather banal fact. And an address in Great Falls that Sybylla knew well enough, having spent the first eighteen years of her life only a short distance away from it—through the dense and sweetly dark Virginia woods, in her father's house.

CIVILIZED

JUSTICE

"The worst part," Sybylla complained into the phone, "is that it all feels so unresolved."

"But hasn't there been a resolution? Death is a rather emphatic resolution, wouldn't you agree? After all, whatever your client did or didn't do, his life can no longer be altered."

"Perhaps he can still be vindicated," she said carefully.

"Vindicated?" Robert Winston asked. "Why? It won't help him, and don't tell me your time isn't needed elsewhere. I'm sure you have many other innocent clients who are alive and who need all your energy to assure their acquittals."

She sighed heavily. "I'll tell you, Mr. Winston, I think this may have been it for me. I wasn't aware I was this close to the edge, believe me, but it's like overnight, my taste for the work has just . . . I don't know . . . *left* me. I woke up this morning and I thought, I just can't face it again. That depressing office, and all of my clients. Their *demands* on me. They just sap my strength. I mean, I don't have anything left for myself. I thought, you know, it would be so great to be able to go to a nice office for a change. With something pleasant to look at out the window. To have a comfortable chair in my office, for God's sake, and a decent desk to work at, and people to work with who weren't so harassed all the time. But most of all, it's this unhappiness people are always bringing through my door. You don't know what it's like."

"No." His voice was noncommittal. "Tell me what it's like."

"It's . . . They come in here, and they're in trouble, and they're so *needy*. They all assume they're the only client I have, and I'm their servant. They bring their kids with them and the kids just look at me like it's all my fault. And I look at them and I think, In ten years, it'll be them sitting in the hot seat on the other side of my desk. Or I'll be in arraignment court waiting for a case to come up and all the faces will start to look familiar. It never stops, you know? You give these people your heart and they're just out the door. But the worst of it," Sybylla confided, "are the crimes they're charged with. It's incredible. It's . . . it's disgusting, some of it. You think you've heard every story. You get used to listening to the most repulsive behavior, and then some new piece of filth drifts across your desk. I had this guy last year—he liked to rape old women. It never made the papers, 'cause his victims never reported it, but the guy told me. He was so proud of himself. I'd just gotten charges against him dropped on some lousy car theft; then he hits me with this as we're riding down in the elevator. And I think, *Why?* You know? I wanted to be a lawyer 'cause I wanted to further justice. I feel . . ." Her voice dropped, as if this revelation was shameful. "I feel I've put in my time now. Five years here. And lots of innocent clients, don't get me wrong, but a whole lot more of the other kind. Because, let's face it, *somebody's* doing these crimes. They're not committing themselves."

"Well," Winston said finally. "That's quite a speech. Quite a change of heart, too, if you don't mind my saying so."

"Yeah. What can I say? It's just time, I think. So I thought of you."

"Of me?" His voice was thick with caution. Sybylla steadied herself, then plunged.

"You once said . . . Do you remember when we met at the Hyperion Club? You said you could always use bright people in the private sector. I don't know how bright I am, but I'm interested. That is, if you're still willing to consider me."

She heard him take it in. "You understand," he told her after a minute, "that much of what we do is desk work. The closest you'd get to a trial is attending voir dire in a consulting capacity. You might miss it."

"I might. Mr. Winston, all I'm saying is that I think I'd like to find out more. I mean, could I possibly step in and see the office? See what consulting work is like? Maybe I could talk to some of the employees. I wouldn't have to bother you, necessarily." There was a long pause. She prodded. "You see, I'm going down there, anyway. To watch the hearings."

"Oh yes," Winston said. "I'm afraid I won't be in the office at all next week. I have some meetings downtown, and naturally, I plan to watch the hearings myself." He let the silence build between them. "But why don't you come down on Monday, anyway. I can have one of my associates show you around and answer all of your questions."

He listened as she leapt at this, her enthusiasm far from comforting. Then he ended the conversation with the kind of good wishes that would befit the daughter of a close associate and set down the phone, decidedly ill at ease.

The devil of the thing was in the timing, he saw. Thus far, he had been able to maneuver the entire Trent affair without bringing harm to Dermot's daughter—he owed that to his friend, and, in a way, to his own history—but with Dermot's confirmation hearings nearly upon them, it was imperative that this situation be properly evaluated for risk as soon as possible, that he be able to separate what Sybylla certainly knew about LRA from what he suspected she knew, and from what he was now beginning to fear that she knew.

Winston shook his head slowly at the telephone, then turned his chair to the window, looking far down the long meadow to the woods, now rousing themselves from the damp Virginia winter.

His loyalty to Sybylla's father had been forged first in friendship and subsequently in bonds even more enduring and complex, through a career that had not adhered to its hoped-for trajectory and through a marriage that had suffered wrenching, unforeseeable difficulties. The bonds could not be broken, Winston knew—at least not without consequences too cataclysmic for either party to withstand. Their fortunes were merged, and now, with Dermot poised to ascend to the nation's highest court, it was the moment of his own triumph, too. Nothing could be allowed to interfere with that.

He would keep his eye on Sybylla until the danger—if there was danger—had met some resolution. He just hoped, for his old friend's sake, that it didn't turn out to be the kind of resolution her client had so recently achieved.

CHAPTER
TWENTY-EIGHT

"You're not serious," Sam observed.

"I'm not?" she said lightly. "I thought I was. Why shouldn't I be?"

"What are you doing going down there? Especially if you have reason to believe they're responsible for abductions. How can you put yourself in that kind of danger?"

"I don't think there's any real danger. I just think it bears looking into."

"Sure. Fine. Let somebody else look into it."

She sighed and intoned: "'In Germany, the Nazis came for the Communists and I didn't speak up because I was not a Communist. Then they came for the Jews and I didn't speak up because I was not a Jew. Then they came for the trade unionists—'"

"All right," he said stiffly. "But I somehow doubt your motives are quite so noble."

She sat up in bed, newly perturbed. "Meaning?"

"Meaning, if you have suspicions, there are appropriate avenues through which to pursue those suspicions. Your insistence on putting yourself in harm's way by taking on this responsibility yourself is absurd. If you think there's something here, you should notify the police or the Bar Association or whatever authorities you think are in a position to look into it. Any other tactic is foolhardy and self-serving."

Sybylla regarded him. "Foolhardy, I might allow. Explain self-serving."

"I can't," Sam said shortly, "because I don't know exactly what you hope to get out of it. But if I had to bet, I'd say it had something to do with your dad."

"How fascinating." Her voice was tight. "Do tell."

He paused to lift Atticus from between his ankles and gently but emphatically deposit him on Sybylla's rug. "You want to embarrass him. You want his longtime friend to turn out to be a crook of some kind, and then you want to hit him with the news just as he's being held up under the microscope. Payback for all these years he's given you grief about the crooks *you* represent. Am I getting warm?"

"If you were," she observed, "I don't think I'd be feeling quite so chilly."

Sam turned on his side and faced her. "I don't have an ulterior motive here, you know. Except that I care for you and I don't want to see you hurt. Please, Sybylla. Trent's dead. You can't help him anymore. I don't want anybody else to get hurt over this."

"It sounds," she said carefully, "as if you believe Trent himself was deliberately hurt."

Sam, suddenly consumed with the floral pattern of her sheets, said nothing.

"Is that what you believe, Sam?"

"Of course not. They said there wasn't a mark on him."

"Maybe they didn't look hard enough. Maybe there was something they couldn't see."

He was staring at her. "Sybylla."

"Yeah, yeah. Wacko paranoid. You told me before."

Slowly, he sat up and swung his legs over the side of the bed. "I'm asking you. Don't do this."

"Why?" she said calmly.

"Because I'm asking you. That's why."

Sybylla sighed. "You know, it's funny. My dad said the exact same thing to me when he was trying to get me to turn over the Trent case to another public defender. But he's my dad. What's your excuse?" Sam shrugged, his face sullen. "What is it about men? You sleep with somebody, and it's like they think you've put them in charge." She felt herself winding up. "You know, every time you think you've made it out of the cave, somebody comes along and clubs you over the head."

"I resent that," Sam said quietly.

"Gee," she spat, "I'm devastated."

They looked at each other for a long minute, each mildly in shock.

"I'm sorry." Sybylla said it first.

"Are you?"

She shrugged. She wasn't at all sure.

"Look. I know I can't help Trent. But I want to know what happened to him. I'm just going to go down, look around. I told Winston I'm thinking of leaving Legal Aid. Want a few of the finer things in life. I'm pretty sure he bought it. Besides, he said he won't even be there." She smiled, trying for levity. "I figure if I walk in and there's a bunch of homeless people tearing around on LSD, I'll know there's something strange about the place. Otherwise, I'll have a couple of high-minded conversations about American justice in the nineties, and then I'll head on into Washington to watch the hearings. All right?"

Sam sighed. "All right. But you won't see a thing. I'm telling you, the days when they were doing all that wild stuff with lysergic acid are long gone. The government got cold feet in the early sixties, around the same time the unwashed masses got ahold of the drug."

"Is that why they stopped testing it?" She crossed her legs on the bed.

"Well, yes and no, from what I understand. For one thing, they found that they just couldn't control the thing, so its usefulness for subversion was really compromised. I mean, at one point they were thinking of it in terms of a 'madness gas' they could spray over the enemy, or some psychosis-causing agent they could slip into a city's water supply. There was even a plan to dust Castro's shoes with it, but the problem was, nobody could predict what would happen. Some people went wild, sure, but others just sat down and wouldn't move. And then, when people outside the sanctioned experiments started using it, something else the government hadn't predicted started happening."

"Which was?"

Sam frowned. "Well, the CIA had viewed the drug as an essentially negative catalyst. They gave it to a subject and the subject tended to experience intense anxiety—what they characterized as a state essentially indistinguishable from psychosis. But when the ordinary Joes started doing LSD, they had a very different experience. Aldous Huxley, for instance—when he first took a hallucinogenic drug, he described a kind of wonderful mind-expanding trip, and of course that's what the majority of recreational users had, and still have. It appeared that maybe the environment had a lot to do with how the drug would take effect. If you gave it in a hospital room with monitors around and people standing over you, the reaction tended to be bad. But if you took it with a group of happy, supportive friends, it was great—generally. Anyway, lysergic acid couldn't be counted on to drive the enemy mad anymore, and there was this whole schism developing between the folks who thought of it as an imitator of psychosis and the LSD prophets who talked about creativity and self-awareness. Also, a few of the subjects in the army experiments had committed suicide, and even the CIA had to consider that."

"So it just stopped?" she asked. "All that research?"

"Dried up, more like. It didn't stop overnight, but the CIA had pretty much given up on LSD as the great white hope. Besides, they'd already done tons of research with the drug. For a while there, they were giving the stuff to everyone they could think of. That is, everyone not in a position to complain or question what was happening—inmates, mental patients, people in treatment for other drugs. You had researchers giving acid to alcoholics, kleptomaniacs, psychotics, even nymphomaniacs. There was one guy who was using LSD to make schizophrenics into assassins through some crazy recipe of LSD and electric shock. Christ, you have to feel for those people." He winced. "But in the end, the government had to wash its hands. It couldn't be seen experimenting with the same stuff all those scruffy types in Haight-Ashbury were taking for fun." He peered at her. "You ever try the stuff?"

"Nah. A few cigarettes behind the stables at Madeira was about as far as I went." She grinned at Sam. "I didn't have a wasted phase like you."

"Oh no?" He reached forward and pushed back the hair from her right ear. "What's this, then?"

Sybylla blushed. "What do you mean?"

"Looks like you tried to pierce your ear at a slumber party or something."

Hurt, she eyed him. "Sorry to disappoint you, but it was congenital."

Sam seemed surprised. "Oh. I'm sorry." He looked closer. "Really?"

"I'm a little sensitive about it, if you want to know the truth."

"Really?" He seemed dense. "Why? I think it's so sweet."

Sybylla frowned. "You do?"

"Absolutely."

She turned away. "Whatever."

"Anyway"—Sam looked at her squarely—"as far as Legal Research Associates is concerned, I don't know what you think you'll find out there, but I can tell you that if anyone's messing around with lysergic acid, it'll be well out of sight. And that's what I'm worried about."

Sybylla sipped her water and tried to look innocent.

"Promise me." His look was intent. "Promise me you won't go poking around. Just let them show you the company health club in the basement and the dental coverage and get out of there. If you still think there's more to it, we'll talk about it then. All right?"

Her face was blank. She didn't want to get boxed into lying.

"Sybylla? Promise me."

Stealthily, she eased her left hand beneath the pillow and crossed her fingers. "Of course." She smiled.

Except that she felt miserable about it the next morning, pausing as she packed her limited wardrobe of clothes suitable for C-SPAN to shake her head in self-rebuke; the entirety of her evening with Sam, indeed, seemed to be reducing in warped retrospect to her unfortunate Neanderthal reference and to those two crossed fingers under the pillow—tension and subterfuge. He had left early that morning, content with the knowledge that Sybylla would soon have the whole of this unfortunate preoccupation out of her system, but the reality was quite different. The reality, she thought, was that one way or another she intended to figure out what disappearing homeless people, obscure elements of Greek mythology, experimental LSD, an ultraexclusive men's club in New York, and a legal consulting firm in a sedate Virginia suburb of Washington were doing in the same confusion of facts and coincidences.

In a refreshing twist, the rental car Sybylla had reserved the day before was gassed up and waiting for her when she arrived at Avis, and she headed over to the West Side Highway, listening to Nina Totenberg, one of her heroines, tactfully approach the thorny question of Dermot's ideological bent in an NPR special on the upcoming hearings. Nina seemed to have a bit of a smirk in her voice, Sybylla thought, as the commentator channeled her exasperation at the nomination of yet another rabid conservative into appropriate journalese. The nominee's history of hobbling entitlement programs, declaring government support for the arts to be constitutionally suspect, and giving women and minorities what-for (Sybylla's first and only confrontation with her father on the issue of abortion had been so bloody and come so dangerously close to a complete schism that neither, wisely, had raised the subject again) oozed out of the static-plagued radio like the irksome disasters that had escaped Pandora's box, and it became increasingly difficult for Sybylla to contain her anger—though whether at Dermot, for creating such a shameful legacy, or at Totenberg, for delineating it so exhaustively, she wasn't sure. NPR, at any rate, was predicting only a perfunctory resistance to the nomination, barring any unforeseen developments in the hearings. The happy band of liberal Democrats would weigh in with righteous nays, of course, but they would be handily outnumbered by their right-minded senatorial colleagues, who had already declared the President's choice to be a distinguished scholar with an unblemished record of advocating the most American of ideals.

From *Law Review* at Harvard, Nina was reciting, Dermot had joined the Manhattan DA's Office, where, due to reasons unrecorded for official posterity but thought to be related to a long-since-addressed alcohol problem, his employment had been abruptly terminated. A short while later, however, he had moved to D.C. and emerged as the Assistant U.S. Attorney at the prosecutorial helm of *United States* v. *Fentano*. Fentano, the listening audience was reminded, was a poetry-loving mob enforcer, an amateur scribbler of verse who was convicted of murdering two undercover police officers. A dapper dresser, Fentano passed the downtime between testimony by reading Dante Gabriel Rossetti and making doe eyes at his avid contingent of female fans. The prosecution's evidence was neither plentiful nor particularly airtight, but Dermot had somehow gotten the jury to convict, prompting a veiled death threat from the lips of Fentano's father-in-law (CEO, as it were, of the family business) and catapulting the young attorney into the realm of the household name—at least in Washington and at least for a while.

Then, Nina Totenberg said mirthfully, there followed a string of similarly stunning wins. Serial killers and psychopaths, sadistic rapists, a publisher of child pornography, even a former city councilman who had attempted and bungled an extortion attempt. Within five years, Dermot had established himself as the man to call on if the U.S. Attorney truly had to win the case in question. In time, Dermot himself stepped up to serve as U.S. Attorney, and from there he leapfrogged into the legal stratosphere. Nina listed some of his more noxious decisions as a D.C. Circuit Court judge: the children of welfare recipients were not entitled to state-funded tutoring to help them graduate; state laws banning assault-rifle stockpiling were unconstitutional; employees dismissed for being physically unattractive were not eligible to sue for damages based on discrimination. It was a simultaneously heady and depressing list.

Sybylla sighed, brooding over the difficult role that lay ahead for her, acting the proud offspring—which she was—without letting any of her real shame over Dermot's legal legacy and agenda leak out. When she had called her father and expressed her wish to watch the confirmation hearings, the proposal had been enthusiastically, even joyfully, received. Sybylla heard the relief in his voice. As angry as he had been over her refusal to drop Trent as a client, she knew he hated feeling estranged from her, even for a short period; their equilibrium, established over years of trial and error, was as important to his contentment and productivity as it was to hers. On the phone, Dermot made no secret of the fact that he was glad the Trent matter was over, in spite of the way it had ended, and he took the opportunity of her call to vent his relief. He would see her in a few days, he said happily, either at the house or at the hearings themselves, whenever she was able to show up. The appointment with LRA was not mentioned, and if he knew about it, he gave no sign.

Sybylla was nearly through the Holland Tunnel when Nina Totenberg declared that Judge Muldoon, a widower, had one daughter, also an attorney.

"Not to mention a card-carrying member of the ACLU," Sybylla informed the radio. "Not to mention a sustaining member of her local NPR station."

Nina, in her silence, seemed neither surprised nor impressed. Sybylla hit the off button and merged onto the New Jersey Turnpike, turning south through the spring drizzle, heading for home.

CHAPTER
TWENTY-NINE

The sign for Legal Research Associates marked the entrance to a long driveway that, past its initial transverse of woods, curved toward the river and abruptly opened onto a large clearing. There, flat beneath the midafternoon sky, a postmodern vision of steel and glass embraced the slight hill like a stingray burying itself in the sand. Sybylla pulled her car into the parking lot and stared at the thing, utterly disoriented at the sensation of finding herself so near her childhood home and yet in such unfamiliar surroundings. Indeed, the last few miles of her journey to the LRA complex had been covered in a kind of wary suspension, as if she was daring the familiar roads and farms of her town to have metamorphosed since her last visit into something alien and excluding. They had not.

As she crossed the Beltway Bridge and turned north along the

Potomac on Route 193, there was the same progression from suburbia to the estates of modestly landed gentry. Horse barns began to proliferate, and tennis courts peeked from behind the pseudo-Colonial dwellings. The town's small commercial center had not grown, but each of its shops bore the unmistakably prosperous signs of a local monopoly. Even the sleek bay horses in the jumping ring of the Madeira School appeared unchanged from her own day, bearing as they did their lithe flowers of southern girlhood. She suppressed a smile. Nothing had changed. Great Falls had only further ossified in its money and conservatism.

Seneca Road, like Sybylla's own road a mere quarter mile away, constituted a relentlessly private residential neck of an already-private community. Houses on Seneca were set far apart and tucked back into the woods for optimum privacy; they perched on the lips of private ponds or overlooked the Potomac and were accessorized by stables and studios. People tended to move here when their priorities had progressed beyond play groups for the kids and access to parking; when they were ready, they came here to pursue their own projects or tend their investments and generally get on with things in comfortably rural peace among their neighbors—CEOs or Arab royalty or incomprehensibly wealthy widows. When drivers crossed paths along this snarl of meandering wooded roads at the edge of Great Falls, the unwritten code called for friendly nods and nothing more.

"Miss Muldoon?" A hand tapped her window, making her jump. She collected herself and smiled.

Winston's lieutenant was Simon Cates, a diminutive and ebullient black man in his early forties. He gushed admiration for Sybylla's father as he pumped her hand, helping her out of the car in an awkward hybrid of chivalric manners and outright hauling. "I've been so looking forward to meeting you," he enthused, somewhat self-evidently. "Your father! You must be so proud!"

Sybylla, who supposed she would be hearing some variation on this theme for the rest of her life, took the opportunity to practice her lines.

"Of course," she gushed. Then, turning to the complex: "What a striking building."

"Isn't it? I'm told Mr. Winston had a hand in the design. He's really a remarkable man. But I gather you've met him yourself," Cates said merrily, as if no one who'd actually met Winston could conceivably hold a different opinion.

"Yes," Sybylla said vaguely.

"Thought I'd give you the tour," Cates said. "Then we'll go back to my office and talk."

He led her into the stony minimalist lobby and then through a passageway of polished granite walls that might have seemed claustrophobic if not for the light beckoning at the end. Into this light they quickly emerged, and Sybylla stopped in surprise. The huge room before them was crammed with cubicles, each bearing only the most transient of personal touches: junk food and cans of soda beside the computer terminals and discarded shoes beneath the chairs. At each station, utterly focused workers wore headsets and stared at the green-glowing computer terminals before them, their hands moving rapidly over the keyboards.

"Jury-pool analysis." Cates spoke with pleasure, surveying the scene like a general overlooking newly vanquished land. "We operate round the clock."

"But what are they doing?"

"Oh, some general population research for our own use, but mainly specific community-analysis surveys for our clients. When an attorney goes to try his case in an unfamiliar jurisdiction, we collect data on the jury-eligible public in the new trial venue."

"What kind of data?" Sybylla asked.

"Everything, pretty much. Educational levels, age distributions. Religious beliefs, political leanings. Feelings on the death penalty, different ideas about justice, retribution, the role of the courts in responding to crime. Ethnic prejudice. You name it."

"You can tell all that?" she said, incredulous. "From a few questions?"

"Oh, but we don't just ask a few questions. We get data on a wide array of fronts and then we use multivariate statistical techniques to analyze it. Community analysis and community attitude profiles are a very distinct component of what LRA can offer a client." He paused. "You seem surprised."

She looked at him. "I sort of expected it to look like a law firm. With people doing legal research. You know, Legal Research Associates." She shrugged.

Cates smiled. "Come with me." At the end of the data center, a stone passageway identical to the one off the main lobby formed a no-man's-land between that building and the next. The complex, he explained, had been designed as four interlocking rectangular buildings arranged around an artfully cobbled courtyard. The space into which they now moved looked for all the world like every blue-chip law firm that Dermot had ever urged her to join. The avid drones who scurried around in suspenders and expensive shoes appeared indistinguishable from first-year associates at any other firm.

"Bit more of what you anticipated, I take it."

She nodded.

"You know, Miss Muldoon," Cates said philosophically, "each trial has its own unique themes—its touchstones, in other words. Our analysts are isolating those themes. Distilling the entirety of the case, if you will, to clarify its most central issues. This is where the groundwork for jury selection is done, and where a theory is developed as to what types of people will be sympathetic to our client's case and what types will be hostile to it."

"You mean like an ideal-juror profile," Sybylla said with a nod.

"Well, yes, but ideal-juror profiles are primitive compared with what we do. They're too inflexible. I'll tell you something. In my entire career, I only once saw a juror who met an ideal-juror profile for that case. I remember her. She was a divorced white mother of daughters, in her early fifties, schoolteacher, daughter of a cop, of Italian descent. She lived in a part of the city that had recently been getting a lot of minorities moving in. She'd been a victim of a nonviolent crime and the criminal had been caught and convicted. There. She was perfect."

"So?"

"So? She got excused. I don't know . . . she knew one of the attorneys from bowling or something. That's what good an ideal-juror profile is."

"But how's what you do so different from that?"

Cates smiled, surveying the intense activity of his domain. "Our approach is to make our case appeal to the widest range of potential jurors. We anticipate the questions jurors will want to have answered and we discern which evidence will have the greatest impact on them. But even as we're broadening the case's appeal, we're simultaneously working to narrow the jury pool, at least to the extent of eliminating those jurors who will automatically close their minds to us. It's a balancing act. And generally, it works."

Sybylla considered. "So some of these guys are deciding which jurors to keep off the panel, and others are deciding how to make the client's case appealing to whoever's left."

"Yes," said Cates. "We also analyze whether a case should come to trial at all, and we design voir dire questions and strategies here."

She smiled. "A full-service salon."

He gave her an odd look. "If you like. LRA incorporates a number of disciplines to realize a common objective. You'd be much mistaken, for example, if you thought of us solely as lawyers in service to other lawyers. There are plenty of lawyers here, of course, but there are even more sociologists, media experts, market research, PR, even a few psychologists. My own view is that we're a model for twenty-first-century legal achievement. There has always been a science to trials, much as there's always been a far more publicized art. But now we have refined that science until there are actually a wide variety of knowable certainties about jury interpretation, and we can't unlearn that any more than we can unlearn disease pathology or treatment."

She looked at him. "Not a very appropriate example, is that? I mean, how can you compare subtleties in jury strategy to something like discovering the cure for a disease?"

"I'm surprised at you." Cates grinned. "Aren't you a public defender?"

"Mr. Winston tell you that?"

"He did."

"Did he tell you I'm a burned-out public defender? Did he tell you I'm dying to get out from under all the human misery my sleazeball clients have loaded me with?"

"Perhaps not as elegantly as you just put it yourself. But yes. Now, shall we move on to the labs?"

"Labs?" Sybylla's ears perked up. Labs, as in LSD? "What kind of labs?"

"Come," he gestured for her to precede him. "I'll show you."

Her heart was racing as she moved through the next stone corridor, expecting a flash of sterile white, if not a vision of homeless people chained in a line to the wall and tripping on acid, but the corridor led only to a benign beige corridor with nondescript doors leading off it.

"This is a lab?" She concentrated on sounding confused, not disappointed.

Cates laughed. "Of sorts. This is our 'directed research' division. We work here with our attorney clients, polishing their courtroom demeanor and their delivery. We also work with witnesses, improving their effectiveness in testimony. And expert witnesses—we work with them, too. Help them simplify really complex technical or medical information so the jurors don't zone out. Something like that can make a big difference in malpractice trials, or liability. Criminal trials, too—forensics can be pretty hairy stuff these days." He opened one of the doors and showed Sybylla a small conference room. A disembodied witness stand stood at one end, and a few feet away, a video camera was poised atop a tripod.

Next were a series of rooms where teams of paid mock jurors were assembled to hear a synopsis of both sides of a trial, with witness testimony live, videotaped, or simulated. The rooms were comfortably appointed, if otherwise unremarkable, but farther down the corridor, Cates headed eagerly for one door in particular, which he opened with obvious glee. Within, Sybylla saw a meticulously constructed courtroom, complete with wood paneling that looked like mahogany and far nicer furniture than 100 Centre Street had to offer. "For a complete mock trial," Cates explained. "That is, if the client is concerned enough to bring his witnesses here and really be thorough about it. We can have one of our own staff present opposing arguments. We can even assign roles of opposing witnesses, you know, really do a convincing job. When we debrief our jurors afterward, they're usually surprised to learn that any of the witnesses they saw were simulated. We can also provide several mock juries and test even very subtle differences in trial presentation."

"What do you mean, 'test'?" Sybylla asked.

"Oh, that's what this is all for." Cates smiled indulgently. "Here, let's go to the jury rooms." He led her down the aisle of the fake courtroom and through a door in the side paneling. It was disorientingly real, Sybylla thought, passing into the narrow corridor beyond. It reminded her of a style of modern painting she had once seen that had been described to her as "superrealist." Everything looked like it was supposed to look—the rabbits had ears and whiskers, the cars and helicopters appeared functional—but there was a weird glow to the images on the canvas. One could not have put a finger on the single element that wasn't quite right, but things appeared somehow, queerly, *too* real, too vibrant. Not dingy enough for reality, she supposed.

"Here we go." Cates flicked on a light.

It was a jury room, comfortably carpeted, its chairs a little too ample to be quite correct. Its table was long and unscarred, and legal pads and pens were neatly stacked at its center, along with a tray of glasses. A blackboard hung on one of the long walls, and a large mirror dominated the opposite one.

"Two-way?" Sybylla guessed.

"Yes. We monitor the jury during their deliberations. We film them, even if the client is able to stay and watch. Then we usually do a highlight video summary in addition to our written report. It's phenomenally effective. We can try out multiple refinements in case presentation, and you'd be surprised to learn what a direct correlation there is with ultimate outcome."

"What do you mean?" She frowned. "What kinds of refinements?"

"Well, all sorts of things. For instance, changes in evidence presented—even subtle ones. Changes in jury composition. Changes in demeanor of the witnesses, not to mention the attorneys. You'd be amazed. Having a male or a female attorney, for example, can make a big difference. Physical appearance. Even clothing. This" —he nodded at the room—"is a laboratory in every real sense. We run our experiment and then we change it a little and run it again, until we get the formula that works."

"You mean the verdict you want."

"Of course." He smiled.

"What if you never do get the right formula?" Cates looked at her quizzically. "I mean," Sybylla went on, "what if you keep changing the lawyer's clothes and his witnesses and his statements and the jury composition, and the jury just keeps ruling against him?"

"Well, there's value in that situation also. In a civil case, our client learns that settlement should be considered very seriously."

"What about criminal cases?"

He shrugged. "Same principle. Lawyers can be much more realistic when discussing pleas once they've run their cases through our system."

Sybylla looked around the room, imagining its comfortable chairs full of eager, arguing pseudojurors. "Where do you find your guinea pigs?"

"We start with the jury pool in the actual trial jurisdiction; then we custom-create a jury pool along the same lines—age, sex, income, religion, whatever. And if we tinker with the recipe here, then our client has that much more information for voir dire." He looked at her keenly. "You seem disappointed, Miss Muldoon."

Alarmed, she looked up at him. "Oh no! It's fascinating. Only I was wrong, you see. I thought there would be more legal theory. I mean, I knew you did research on jury pools and you ran up ideal-juror profiles and things like that, but I didn't know about all this."

"Oh, we certainly do place an emphasis on our voir dire–related services. It's where we feel we're most significantly breaking new ground. This particular service"— he nodded at the room again—"is fairly high-end for most of our clients, not least because it's extremely expensive. But it's far more effective than a simple ideal-juror profile, which is probably what lawyers unfamiliar with LRA tend to associate with our work. The trouble with ideal-juror profiles is that they're notoriously wrong, you see. You can load your panel with middle-aged Native American mothers who loathe law enforcement like you want them to, and they'll rule against you every time." Cates smiled. "No, what we have here is a much subtler art. And this kind of mock run-through is at the cutting edge of it."

Cates turned to her, taking in her serious expression with barely suppressed amusement. "But enough about us. Let's go back to my office now, and we'll talk about you."

Sybylla felt herself sag. She had seen nothing to alleviate the sense of mystery that LRA had held for her. LSD? Homeless people snatched from the streets? Kidnappers and assassins? It felt far indeed from the vaguely distasteful but perfectly legal work being done in this clearing off Seneca Road. If there was more, she saw with intense exasperation that she hadn't the first idea where to look for it. And now it was time to play out her role as the eager applicant. Meeting Cates's gaze, she forced a smile. "Yes, let's," Sybylla said.

"**M**y friend told me to make a point of asking you about something."
She ducked through the door Cates held open.

"What's that?"

"About the health club he imagines you have in the basement. De
rigueur corporate offering of the nineties, so your employees can refine
their cardiac fitness during lunch hour."

"Oh, that's priceless." Cates cackled. They were making their way
through a sumptuous suite of conference rooms and expansive offices in
the fourth and final building. "C'mon, I'm over here."

"What, no health club?"

"I wish Robert Winston was here; he'd love this. No, Miss Muldoon.
No health club, though not for lack of trying. Our chairman has very specific ideas about the interface between work and anything that might be
construed as leisure. Basically, he feels there shouldn't be one. I don't
know what he himself does to stay in the shape he's in, but whatever it is,
it doesn't happen on these premises. As you saw, there is not even a cafeteria in the complex. A private chef prepares simple food for the legal
staff and our hired jurors, and rather more elaborate meals for senior
staff and clients."

They were passing the most massive of the mahogany portals, before
which a prim but faultlessly dressed secretary worked at a ponderous
curved desk. Through the open doorway, Persian rugs stretched into the
distance. "Wow," Sybylla said unthinkingly.

"Our chairman's office." Cates smiled. "Mathilde?" Cates addressed
the secretary. "This is Sybylla Muldoon. Dermot Muldoon's daughter."

"Oh!" The woman's eyes lit up. "I know your father. We're all so excited about him."

Sybylla smiled.

"Would you like coffee?" Cates asked her.

"If your busy chef can spare the time."

The secretary nodded, instantly on top of the situation. Cates steered Sybylla into his perceptibly more modest office and took an armchair opposite her. "You know," he said, grinning, evidently still enjoying her gaffe about the health club, "they've got all those defense contractors and consulting firms over in Langley, and compared with LRA, they're like a summer camp. People go jogging at lunch; there're deer wandering around; volleyball court in the summer. But it's just not what Mr. Winston wanted for his company. We don't come to him anymore with requests for field trips or social events. But there are other advantages to working at LRA, and those of us who do find our leisure elsewhere. So," he said, "in answer to your query, no cardiac fitness in the basement. In fact, this building doesn't even *have* a basement."

Sybylla, tired of all this irrelevant mirth, was anxious to move on. "Mr. Cates, I wonder if I might ask about something else. I'll be very happy to leave Legal Aid if and when I do make the decision to do so, but I can't see leaving my altruism entirely behind. I was wondering, do you have any outreach programs here?" She spied his confusion. "I mean, pro bono work or—"

"No," he said shortly. "No pro bono." He stopped and considered. "Well, I should amend that. The chairman himself very occasionally provides services free of charge for friends, but as to formal programs, no. Never."

"Any charitable endeavors?"

It was too much to ask that he would acknowledge Helping Hand Services, she told herself, but she nonetheless let hope fill the lull as he considered.

"I know we had a blood drive once. Some of us give to the United Way. I don't know if that's what you had in mind."

Bunch of Mother Teresas, she thought.

"Well, that's nice, but I was thinking more along the lines of a real community service. I'm still very interested in helping the homeless, for example. At Legal Aid, we have a program where we go into the shelters sometimes and offer free legal advice. Landlord conflicts, restraining orders, stuff like that. Do you do anything along those lines?"

He laughed as Mathilde arrived, bearing coffee and what looked like petit fours. "Oh, we don't have too many homeless here in Great Falls."

So much for Helping Hand Services. She sighed. Either he was a superlative liar or he truly had no knowledge of the connection.

"So, Miss Muldoon. Tell me, what do you think of us?"

"I think . . . I think there's a lot to take in, frankly. It would be a complete lifestyle change for me." She accepted the coffee cup he handed her.

"That it would. May I ask you something personal?"

"I . . . Of course."

"What is Dermot Muldoon's daughter doing at Legal Aid in the first place?"

Her blood ran cold. She forced a smile. "Adolescent rebellion, I suppose. All I can say is, I've done my time in the trenches. And it wasn't even the clients or the low pay that finally got me. It was the growing sense that I wasn't really using my brain. You don't have to be a genius to defend these guys; you just follow the book. And I'm just getting a little tired of it." She paused. "May I be frank?"

"Certainly." He was sipping his coffee with studied good manners.

"I didn't become a lawyer to follow the book. I want to write the book. I suppose I'm more like my father than I ever admitted. And I'll be honest with you, a lot of what I've seen here today was initially disturbing to me, but I'm already excited about it. I want to watch the mock trials and observe the jury deliberations, and I want to read the community-analysis reports. I want to see how changing an attorney's clothing can affect a trial outcome. And in my work, those case touchstones you mentioned are a subtlety we simply can't afford. We're too busy trying to imply that a witness is wrong or the victim was a participant in the crime. I think it's time to start getting back to what my dad taught me to love about the law, and I think this might be a good way to do it."

He looked at her thoughtfully, his face wearing an expression more serious than any she had seen it wear before.

"But you're aware, I hope, that LRA does have an acknowledged conservative outlook. Working with us might be an about-face for you on many significant fronts."

"Yes." Sybylla nodded. "I understand that. It's odd, you know. The only times I've ever run across trial consultants in the past, they tended a bit more in the other direction. The feeling, as I understood it, was that the prosecution didn't need the added edge of a refined jury-selection technique; or any of the other advantages LRA offers. I mean, seeing as something like three-quarters of a jury pool already feels that if a defendant is standing trial, he's probably guilty, even though they won't admit to presuming guilt. With criminal cases, those consultants tended to work more or less exclusively with defense attorneys."

Cates reached for a pastry. "I'm aware of the trend in our field. But the first thing to acknowledge is that it's a big field, and getting bigger every year as more and more attorneys become aware of the difference we can make to their trial outcomes. There's room for everyone, I think, and certainly I feel in principle that the advances we've made should be available to any attorney who feels they may be of use to him. But our particular company's philosophy is that, despite the tendency to presume guilt that you mentioned, the legal pendulum has nonetheless swung too far in the defense's direction over the past two decades. The unscrupulous use of the insanity defense, for example, the voluminous red tape of admissibility regarding confessions and recordings, it's resulted in an obscene and unjust rate of acquittal. The far left likes to say that it's better to acquit a guilty man than run the risk of convicting an innocent one. We say that's well and good in principle, but in practice it's a little rough on the victims that guilty man will create once he's acquitted and back on the street. Let's face it—we all know there are going to be more victims. The fact is that the chairman has tapped into a nationwide need being felt keenly by our country's prosecutors. They require and deserve an edge to make up for what they've lost, and we are here to provide it to them. Defense attorneys, naturally, are free to go elsewhere to find similar services."

"But prosecutors' budgets are often tight, and your services, as you've pointed out, can be expensive. How do they afford you?"

Cates shrugged. "Most find room in their funding, particularly if the case is a high-profile one. Others use donated funds. And others, if the case is sufficiently compelling to the chairman, take advantage of a sliding fee scale. Mr. Winston uses his judgment in these instances. He likes to work with a broad range of prosecutors."

"I see," Sybylla commented. She looked out the window at the shadows deepening along the lawn. "It's so pretty here. It must be nice to work out here in the country. No subway. No one hitting you up for change all the time."

"Yes," Cates said thoughtfully. "It's very nice."

"I don't suppose you'd tell me who some of your clients are."

Cates shook his head, but kindly. "The chairman promises our clients absolute confidentiality. Files are maintained with stringent security."

"Oh well," Sybylla said jovially. "I just wondered what kinds of clients I'd be working with."

He leaned forward, solemn. "You'd be working with leaders, Miss Muldoon." Cates's voice was creamy smooth. "The next leaders, men and women who are ready to break into the public eye. Even in the short time LRA has been in existence, many of our clients have risen to high elected posts, and I have little doubt that that pattern will continue. Crime is the paramount issue for the rest of this millennium, as I'm sure it will be for the next, and our clients understand that the swift and effective conviction and punishment of criminals is the single-greatest result that their constituents want from them. We are a part of that result, Miss Muldoon. We are a business, naturally. We are paid for our services. But the soul of our endeavor is to help those who are leading the battle to preserve safety in our society." He sat back against his chair. "If you are prepared to participate in that battle, we want you here with us."

She was breathless. Cates sipped his coffee, his eyes on her, unblinking.

There was nothing here for her, she knew. Despite the undeniable wackiness of some of LRA's practices, despite its reprehensible politics, there seemed nothing overtly *wrong* about what she had seen. What had this place to do with any of her suspicions? She'd seen not a shard of anything linking these tidy, buzzing offices to disappeared homeless people or outrageous medical experimentation. It was a bust, the whole thing. And now she had to extricate herself from a job offer she'd expressly sought, without attracting any unwelcome attention from Winston. She berated herself. What a waste of energy. What a waste of time. She tried to smile. "I'll need a few days."

"Certainly," he said, amiably enough.

Sybylla got to her feet. "Mr. Cates, may I use your washroom? I drove here straight from New York, and I'd like to freshen up a bit before I head downtown." She shrugged self-effacingly. "I don't think I'm quite prepared for CNN."

He was affable. "You look fine, but certainly. I'll just show you to the ladies'." He stood. The telephone on his desk rang with a low purr. Sybylla watched him look over at it, then frown. "Oh dear"—he seemed to address the telephone itself—"I think this may be the call I've been waiting for."

"Well, don't worry. I can find the ladies' room on my own."

He was already edging toward his desk. "Mathilde will be happy to direct you. And do come back so I'll have a chance to say good-bye before you leave."

She turned on her heel. In her wake, she heard his professionally modulated enthusiasm: "Norman, yes, I've been looking forward to your call."

Sybylla stepped out into the carpeted hall. Her conscience was clear, her motive no more suspect than a genuinely demanding bladder and the need for a little fresh lipstick, but the banality of her calling fell away as she approached the massive mahogany desk and realized that its occupant was absent.

"Mathilde?" she called, but not too loudly. Probably copying something, or on an errand, or using the bathroom herself. Sybylla frowned, looking into the tantalizingly open doorway of Robert Winston's office. She would just wait a minute. "Mathilde?" she repeated, softer still. Just for show.

Well, after all, Winston probably had his own bathroom, didn't he? And a lady in distress would quite understandably head for the nearest plausible powder room, wouldn't she? And if she just happened to get a glimpse of his inner sanctum while en route to the loo, that would be something of a nonevent, wouldn't it?

Shut *up*, she yelled at herself. She stepped into the office.

It was almost absurdly large. Sufficient for cocktail parties or rugby scrimmages, with a glass wall overlooking the long lawn and the rim of dense green forest beyond it. Winston's desk was also long, a drawn-out arc of dark stone, so polished it positively glared. Atop the desk's expanse, all was in minimalist order: no papers, no files, nary a paper clip. Of course he would be a compulsive, she thought grimly.

In one far corner, a glimpse of metal. Sybylla quickly crossed the room and gazed upon the brave new world of the bathroom, a spectacle in stone and steel, its surfaces pristine, its fixtures warmly dull. There was something in this marriage of primitive materials and high-tech sleek that mirrored Winston's persona, she thought, taking in the subdued gleam of the sink's curve. Masculine to a fault, utterly modern. Overhead, pin lights came alive on a dimmer switch, bathing the small room with warm illumination. Unthinkingly, she ran a nervous finger over the rough stone of the backsplash, and its grainy puckers sent chills up her arms. Black soap rested in a steel dish that looked like a piece of sculpture. The man who washed here, she thought, took his hygiene seriously, but he didn't fuss about it.

Just beyond the sink area, one corner of the room was taken up by a kind of closed-off booth. Shower? she thought, involuntarily stepping forward. Peering through the small window the booth's door afforded, she saw a wooden seat that folded up against the wall by a hook and eye. Indeed, she noticed now, the interior walls of the booth were wood, as well. It's a sauna, she realized.

Abruptly, uneasiness filled her.

Winston had a private sauna.

The man who did not favor leisure on the job. The man who did whatever it was he did to stay in shape somewhere else. The man who begrudged his employees a few lousy Exercycles in the basement for them to use on their lunch hours had a sauna in his office.

But of course it wasn't a sauna. It was an archive, camouflaged and utterly private, and somewhere within it lay a repository of records, and in those records—her thoughts raced—lay the one specific record delineating the relationship Trent had to this place. A document that explained when, how, and, above all, *why* somebody had sliced open her client's arm and inserted a chronic case of insanity.

She did not want to think about what she was going to do.

Sybylla pulled the wooden handle of the door. It was heavier than she had anticipated, resisting her as she pulled it open and stepped forward onto . . . Sybylla looked down. Weren't saunas supposed to have wooden floors? This floor was smooth black stone, so highly polished it actually reflected up. The light had come on automatically and now revealed the sauna's rather significant lack of stones, which normally, she knew, were fixed in a wooden crate and heated electrically to generate intense heat. Unthinkingly, she reached forward to touch the hinge of the small wooden seat and found the latch stuck stiff and tight, as if it had never been *un*latched.

Turning, Sybylla found a little glowing screen beside the sauna's door, lit pale blue around its rectangular border. Along the base of the screen, an alphabet of letters were displayed, each one in a tiny square, and above them a line of text blinked brightly: PLEASE ENTER PASSWORD.

Now this is where the alarms come in, Sybylla thought, thinking of Cates for the first time since she entered Winston's office. Nice Mr. Cates, on the phone with his client, but perhaps beginning to wonder just how much freshening up his new friend was planning to undertake for CNN. She was pushing the envelope of a normal pee-and-primp, it occurred to her, but she had another minute, perhaps two, before a well-mannered fan of her father would consider busting into his boss's bathroom to reclaim her.

She squinted at the screen, biting her lip. Not that she was even thinking of trying a password, Sybylla told herself firmly. It would be insane. Suicide. Besides, it wasn't as if her automatic search for a likely password was turning up any nuggets. She tried to remember if her father had said anything about Winston being married, but she canceled her internal data search when she recalled that spouse, child, and pet names were particularly obvious bad choices for secret passwords. But at the same time, she remembered with a sinking heart, you weren't supposed to choose as a password any plain English word, either, because some hackers had programs that ran the dictionary against your computer until it hit the magic button. So no garden-variety word and no near-and-dear moniker, either. What was left? Numerical or alphabetical gibberish only, and she didn't stand a chance against that. For a long moment, she stared at the blinking characters, feeling their regular pulse begin to lull her a bit. Numerical or alphabetical gibberish, she thought hopelessly. Or a foreign word, of course. Or perhaps a foreign word transliterated into English—*that* might slip past a dictionary code-breaker. But there wasn't much help in that little inspiration.

Or was there? She had vowed not to forget the word Sam had taught her, and yet now she stood before the blue screen, willing her tongue to untwist itself and speak. The Greek word. The word Trent had mauled so oddly, making her think of doctors shouting orders at their patients. Ten hut! About-face! *You men at ease.*

Eumenides.

Her stomach clenched. She knew it was right. She felt the key slip into an imaginary lock and heard a whoosh as—what? As the sauna's back wall would suddenly lift or pull aside to reveal a wall of files. And one would be titled "Trent" plain as day, placed carefully between the file marked "Trelawney" and the one marked "Trentano," and she would slip it easily out and into her purse, then go and bid farewell to nice Mr. Cates.

Eumenides.

She wiped her palm against her skirt and raised her finger to the screen. Blue light jumped out at her nail, giving it a sickly hue. Don't do this, her sane self said.

E, Sybylla pressed. PLEASE ENTER PASSWORD disappeared and *E* took its place. *U,* and the *U* jumped up beside it.

M, E, N, she touched, whispering the letters as she found them, willing them to be correct. *I, D, E* . . . She paused. So far, no sirens. Was it waiting for her to finish before it decided she was an intruder? Or could she infer from its silence that, thus far, she had done nothing wrong? Spinning with this thought, she rashly pressed the last letter, and to her astonishment, the entire string of letters disappeared and was replaced by two simple, cataclysmic words: STAND CLEAR.

Stand clear? She froze. Clear of what? Did the wall covering the file archive swing wildly? And if so, in which direction? She spun around to watch it, abruptly losing her footing as the floor suddenly gave a tremor beneath her feet. The tremor was followed by another tremor, and then came a sickening sinking feeling, but when she twisted to look back at the screen, she saw to her horror that it had somehow raised itself a good five feet above her head, and was rising even higher with every passing second. What was it doing up there? she thought dimly. Why was it lifting itself up like that, like the chandeliers at the Metropolitan Opera as the houselights dimmed? And why, she noticed now, was the rest of the room rising with it, until the wood paneling and the light in the ceiling and the little seat that had never been folded down from the wall looked like the very top of a chute as it might appear to somebody way down at the bottom?

But I *am* at the bottom, she suddenly understood. Or at least on my way there, sinking heavily and steadily into the earth. The sauna wasn't a high-tech archive at all. *You idiot*, she told herself. *It's a goddamned elevator.*

It stopped with a jolt, the little rectangle of polished stone beneath Sybylla's feet slipping neatly into place. Three of the walls now surrounding her were of the same black material, and the space was so grave-like, so incalculably deep and dingy, that it escaped an aura of utter claustrophobia only by virtue of the halogen light set flush into one of the sheets of stone. By its illumination, Sybylla examined her options—or, more accurately, her option.

This was the wall at her back, which, on close examination, had turned out to boast a narrow door unadorned by anything so obvious as a doorknob. As her only discernible means of escape, the door obviously bore serious consideration, but she hesitated to make use of it, since she hadn't the faintest idea where it led, and it didn't take long for her imagination to provide her with an array of distressing possibilities. Although she had no notion of how to make the elevator reverse its course and return to the aboveground level, Sybylla somehow felt closer to that possibility in here than she did when she thought about going out there. In here, at least, she could crane her neck and make out the speck of light embedded in the sauna's roof, and find the glint of the never-used hook and eye.

But she had no choice, no real choice, and she understood that only too well. Beyond the door lay what she had come here to learn. Slowly, experimentally, she planted her palm against the smooth and chilly surface and pushed. It swung out barely an inch. Sybylla planted her eye to the crack, blinking at the brightness of the light. For a minute, her vision swam, and she had a passing terror that she had somehow contracted a kind of snow blindness, a whiteout that had blanked out the world, but gradually she came to understand that she saw nothing but white because there was nothing but white to see. The floor, the far wall some feet away, both were painted glaring white. There was no sound. With a deep breath, Sybylla pushed farther, willing herself to step out of the elevator, buoyed by faith.

It was a small room, though after the elevator, it managed to feel luxuriously airy. Set in the wall to her left was a small pad bearing a single black button and the word *Activate*, an instruction Sybylla regarded with some relief, since, at the very least, it seemed to address the mystery of how to return topside. Turning to her right, she could make out a second, rather more conventional door, and now she moved to this portal, steeled her nerves again, and repeated her cautious inch-far push. This time, there was a good deal more information to assimilate: a corridor, its walls white and its floor that same glossy polished stone, the unmistakable clatter of foot traffic and voices, and above all the temperature, which was cold. Very cold, she noted. Cold as in a cave. "Like the floor's made of ice," Trent had said. With a flash of apprehension, the memory caught Sybylla by the throat.

Out in the corridor, two pairs of feet passed in quick matched strides. She crouched behind the door and planted her eye to the crack. A man and a woman, both wearing white lab coats, both carrying clipboards. Did they all come down in the elevator? Sybylla wondered. Or were there other elevators, elsewhere in the LRA complex? And were the elevators as well hidden as Winston's, or were they common knowledge to the staff upstairs?

A second pair of feet sounded its warning and she let the door fall back again. These feet, clad in leather shoes with a one-inch clacking heel, belonged to another woman in another white coat. It was clear, she thought, that she was going to need a white coat to stand a chance of passing anonymously here.

With her ear to the crack, she listened for footfalls over the crash of her own heartbeat; then, in direct violation of her far better judgment, she stepped carefully out into the corridor. The door fell shut behind her with a sickening clack.

Clack, as in locked.

She stared at it. The door was nondescript enough, with a chrome handle and a small sign that read RESTRICTED. It had locked automatically and irreversibly, cutting her off from the very dubious comfort of a known escape route, albeit an escape route to a place where her fraudulence and intrusion might well have been discovered by now. Sybylla swallowed. Wherever she was going, she clearly wasn't going back up there.

The approach of footsteps jolted her out of her paralysis. Willing herself not to run, she turned in the direction the man and woman had headed, desperately arranging her features into a mask of normality. The first door she passed was closed and marked UTILITY. The second said LOUNGE. Apart from the temperature, it was looking pretty banal, she had to admit. The corridor was approaching an intersection, coming to a T with a slightly wider and, from the sound of it, more traveled one, but just before the corner, she noted a sign that cheered her considerably. LAUNDRY, it read. The door wasn't locked. Inside, two industrial-size washing machines were humming, churning loads of white material and suds. Sybylla took a lab coat from a pile of clean folded garments and slipped it on.

Now, with bravado if not confidence, she set out again, turning the corner and letting herself fall in with the sporadic foot traffic up and down its long length. There was an uneasy quiet to this place, it seemed to her, a human abandonment paired with some baffling productivity, as if, those few workers she had seen aside, the curious facility she had invaded somehow managed to run itself. To her relief, however, she saw that there was nothing in her disguise that automatically marked her as an outsider. Indeed, the first time she braced herself to make eye contact, the other eyes' owner merely nodded at her and moved on, continuing with his ardent sentence in progress (". . . *told* him, it's not the mix; it's the V blender acting up again. He said . . .") while his companion pursed her lips in thought. As her immediate fear of discovery subsided, she gradually became aware of a low drone, building as her footsteps took her nearer its source. It seemed at its peak to her right, and she slowed to peer curiously into a long room off the corridor, packed with large machinery that churned an abrasive, gravelly sound. Whether it was one great machine or a series of merely large and distinct automations was beyond her ability to tell, but the cumulative effect of all of the room's chugging, churning technology was daunting. Moving through it, seeming almost to tend it, she thought, were men in white coats, clutching clipboards. They moved from point to point within its maze, pressing buttons and writing things down, performing minirituals like pilgrims making the stations of the cross. One of them glanced up at her, his face pinched. Sybylla wilted in paralysis, waiting for the shriek of accusation, but it never came. She was evidently unremarkable here, she thought, letting a long-held breath hiss through her gritted teeth.

Farther along the corridor was an expansive lab, white and aggressively clean, with gleaming stainless-steel counters and immense amounts of glittering glass. Here, too, Sybylla paused, watching the methodical and purposeful activity, and letting herself make the sad association with Susu's lab at Yale, which she'd visited once or twice to drop off a message or pick up her friend for dinner. She remembered the focused intensity with which Susu worked, her thin shoulders hunched forward over the work surface, her dark brow furrowed, and realized with an unwelcome clarity what a simple thing it must have been to take her unawares in her NYU laboratory as she sat, absorbed in whatever her project might have been. The implant Susu had analyzed for Sybylla, the "wild" item whose threat to her neither of them had realized . . . it might have been made here, she thought, looking around with new wonder and resentment, though it was nearly impossible to imagine these sober, industrious scientists looking so consumed over the task of synthesizing LSD. Whatever this place was, it had clearly traveled far from community-analysis reports and voir dire strategies.

Turning, she continued to make her way up the corridor. Was it a government thing? she wondered. Something unpopular like germ-warfare research or weapons design? Difficult to place openly in a community? She wouldn't put that past either the government or Winston, Sybylla thought: a congenial and discreet tenant-landlord arrangement in exchange for some of that insider prestige he seemed to crave. Or was it some ultrasecret branch of a drug company, putting the final touches on their cure for cancer or AIDS well out of the prying gaze of the press? But no, she decided coolly. There was nothing altruistic or humanitarian about what was happening here. Even drug companies, not known for overflowing with the milk of human kindness, tended not to hide such happy lights under a bushel, let alone underground.

Sybylla was, by now, entirely disoriented, having lost track of the rights and lefts she'd taken since leaving the elevator room. Ahead, the wide stone corridor reached another T, branching out to unknown facilities and stopping directly before a door that read, somewhat bafflingly, RETENTION AREA.

She frowned.

"Heads up," a voice said, making her jolt. Sybylla turned. The man stood behind her, big, blond, and sickly pale, like a surfer whose endless summer had in fact ended. He carried an institutional plastic tray laden with two cups of coffee, two wedges of pie. *So there is a cafeteria,* she thought, as if this insight were her most pressing concern. Evidently Robert Winston's work ethic terminated at ground level.

"Yo, babe," the surfer said. "You look lost."

"I am. Kinda," Sybylla said, stepping aside. It was true, after all.

"You new?" he asked, affably enough. Sybylla felt her guard slip, just slightly, descending from ongoing terror to mere wariness.

She gave him a facsimile of a grin. "That obvious, huh?"

"Well, come on." He shifted his burden onto one arm, drummed a pattern on the security keypad by the door, and hoisted it open for her. "You seen the rooms yet?"

Sybylla shook her head. "Maybe you could show me."

She followed him in, pausing as he delivered half the contents of his tray to a heavyset orderly behind a desk and walked on. The corridor was narrower here, and dimmer than the main artery she had just left. On one side, she briefly saw a medical examining room with a paper-covered table and glassed cabinets full of syringes, medication, and supplies. "We do intake over by the garage," the man said, coming up behind her. "This is for maintenance. You know, any little stuff that comes up."

It seemed worth the risk: "What kinds of little stuff?"

"Oh, infections, lacerations. We took a growth out of somebody last month. But nothing heavy-duty. There's special facilities for that, little farther along the corridor, and there's an OR for the procedure."

Procedure. Sybylla was still digesting the word as she passed the next doorway. She stopped, her eyes widening in amazement.

It was a beauty parlor.

Only a few feet away from her, a middle-aged woman sat rock-still in a barber chair, looking expressionlessly into the mirror. Her hands were folded calmly in her lap and her thick ankles were demurely crossed. She wore a plain white smock, institutional in its utilitarianism, and simple slippers on her feet. On a table beside the chair, an empty bottle of hair dye stood in a pool of gray glop. Hair dyed gray? Sybylla thought vaguely. She'd never known a middle-aged woman to dye her hair *gray*.

"Gotta move this one," the surfer said jovially. "C'mon with me." He stepped past Sybylla and gripped the strange woman by an arm. She did not resist, but rose slowly and let herself be guided down the hallway to a beige door, indistinguishable from the long line of perhaps twenty such doors that punctuated the hall. A narrow peephole had been cut into the steel, affording a view of the room inside. "Hold it open, would ya mind?"

Sybylla caught the door and watched the surfer lead his charge inside. The room was tiny, she saw, barely large enough to contain an institutional bed, a low table and chair, and a toilet. Overhead, the light glared, reflecting off the gleaming stone floor. It was freezing. Involuntarily, she shuddered.

"You get used to it," the man said. "I used ta wear a sweater under my lab coat. Don't even feel it now." He turned the woman and gently pressed the tops of her shoulders. Obediently, she sat on the bed. " 'Kay, honey, lie down. We'll shut off the light and you can go off to sleep. Sound all right?"

Dreamily, the woman nodded. The orderly shut the heavy door behind them.

"She's so compliant," Sybylla observed, unthinking.

"Yeah," he said affably, "that's when you know the treatment's taking. They just, like, shut off. You shoulda seen this subject a few weeks ago. She was screaming about how she was Ronald Reagan's mistress. She kept yelling, 'Nancy had my baby killed! Nancy has the Secret Service following me!' "

"Wow," Sybylla said, for lack of anything more incisive.

"That's nothing. Want to hear something wild?" Without waiting for her answer, he motioned her farther down the hall to one of the other doors and flicked on a light and an intercom. "Go on," he urged, and Sybylla peered into the peephole. Inside, a lanky man sat on the edge of his bed, jerking rhythmically. His arms were wrapped around his sides in a canvas restraint and his face, weathered and lined, was beet-dark. Sybylla could just make out the low sputter of his voice in full, inarticulate tirade.

"Can't hear what he's saying," she said.

"Guess you missed the show." He shrugged. "Sedative must've kicked in. *Finally.* Yesterday, when he came in, he was just about bringing the roof down. Kept it up all night, the bastard. Wanted us to know that the Altarians would be along to collect him momentarily and they wouldn't be too happy about our picking him up. He was lined from head to foot with tinfoil, too." He closed the cell door and turned to give her a curious grin. "Too bad you didn't get to see it. Pretty funky."

She tried to smile.

"So, where'd they find you, anyway?"

"Find me?" Sybylla said carefully, trying for nonchalance.

"You know, where'd they recruit you?"

"Oh . . ." She thought frantically. Career guidance counselor? Job fair? She somehow doubted it. "New York," she managed finally. How could that be wrong?

The man gave her an oddly sympathetic look. "Don't want to talk about it, do you? That's all right," he reassured her. "Some people don't. Lotta grim stories down here, but don't worry about it, nobody's going to press you."

She was lost. "I appreciate that" was all she could think of to say, since indeed she did appreciate it. "Um, do you mind if I ask you the same question?"

"Not at all." His voice was kind. "Girlfriend of mine, in college. She got carjacked one night, coming back to the dorm from doing her laundry."

Sybylla stared at him, her head spinning at the non sequitur. His girlfriend got carjacked? That was supposed to explain why he was herding zombies around an underground facility? To make matters worse, he seemed to be waiting for some response.

"That's terrible," she managed finally.

"Oh, it was. I took a leave from school to attend the trial. I was there, like, every day, from jury selection on, and, y'know, I had just total faith in the system. I mean, it never occurred to me those guys were gonna get off, but of course they did. Two of the jurors, they just wouldn't budge. And why?" he said, the bitterness still evident in his voice. "Not because of anything in the evidence." He shook his head. "They just decided the defendants didn't look guilty, and that was it. Like, from the very first day of the trial, they'd already decided. This one juror gave an interview to the press. All she said was, 'I just couldn't see it. I just couldn't see it.' That was the level we were dealing with."

She was still staring. "Must have been awful."

He turned and leaned back against the cell door. "So anyway, then I got a call from this man, a friend of my dad. He was always interested in me, from way back. We used to talk about politics," he said happily, leaving Sybylla in little doubt of what breed of politics those were. "Helped me get into Princeton, too. Turned out he was a club mate of the chairman's. Anyway, he told me a little about what was going on, and it all just kinda fell into place. You know?"

She nodded dumbly, as if she did know.

"So when'd you start?"

This one felt a bit easier. "Today."

He nodded. "You been to see Mace yet?"

Sybylla frowned. Should she say yes? "Um . . . Mace?"

"Oh, shit." He glanced at her. He looked sheepish. "Look, I'm sorry. I really have to be a little more discreet about the nickname. He's got a major temper, as you'll soon find out. If he ever heard I'd called him that, it wouldn't be pretty. I mean, everybody does call him Mace, but not to his face, if you know what I mean."

Sybylla didn't, but she didn't say so.

"I meant Dr. Hofmann, of course. He likes to see everyone their first day."

Then I guess he saw me, Sybylla thought. "Yeah, I'm pretty sure that was the guy I saw."

"Short guy? Little hands? Had sort of a high voice?"

"Yes." She nodded, trying to look emphatic. "That's him."

"Piece of work, huh?"

She gave him a look she hoped was noncommittal.

"He's like the class nerd who grew up and invented the hydrogen bomb, and kept world rights." He finished locking the cell door behind him and turned to her, newly genial.

"Wanna stay, have some coffee with us?"

"I don't know. My first day and all. I think I better keep busy, you know?"

"Sure," he said warily, as if any woman who turned him down must merit suspicion.

"Another time, though?"

"Fine." They'd reached the orderly's station just before the door, and the surfer picked up a clipboard on the desk. "Buzz her out, Jake."

Jake, rousing himself from paperwork, buzzed her out, and Sybylla stepped with relief into the hallway and closed the door, her eye falling on the sign that read RETENTION AREA.

Retention, my ass, she thought viciously, turning and continuing along the corridor.

Just before the next intersection, she passed the "special facilities" the surfer had alluded to, though *special* took on considerable irony as she gazed, perplexed and repelled, through the long observational window. She felt her entire body go numb, her face cemented into revulsion. The entire right side of the corridor was consumed by a long area marked TREATMENT, its interior plainly visible, as if there was nothing so terrible within, as if—in other words—its row of beds were not filled with "subjects," their eyes covered and their ears plugged with audio speakers. Arachnid webs of electrodes were splayed over their foreheads, and their mouths, grimacing, teethed on what looked like bits made of plastic, making her think of electroshock therapy, circa 1950. There were no restraints fastening them to their beds, and no attendants standing over them. Why didn't they get up? she thought hopelessly. How could they just lie there and take this . . . whatever this was? She shook her head, utterly at sea, and stepped back from the glass.

At the far end of the row, through the glass of an adjacent door, she saw what looked like an exhaustively appointed emergency room. It was immaculate and empty, and Sybylla moved down the corridor and stepped inside with caution, noting a small operating room adjacent. Whatever else these people were doing to the "subjects," she couldn't help thinking, they were evidently taking medical care seriously. Then again, her saner voice responded, so did the Nazi doctors.

"Thought this one was all squared away," a voice said. Sybylla, looking around, caught the blur of two white lab coats and heard the door to the corridor slap shut. Without thinking, she dove behind the operating room door and crouched, cursing her nerves. It would have been better to bluff, she scolded herself. It had worked so far; she could have claimed to be lost, a new recruit wandering the halls, but now she was stuck here, branded guilty by her guilty response. She tried to hush the rasp of her breathing and listen.

"Didn't we just do this guy? What, two, three weeks ago?"

"Yeah, but we underdosed, apparently. The treatment never took, and then he started reexhibiting a few schizophrenic tendencies. Last night, he had a full-blown episode, so we weighed him and found out he'd put on a few pounds since we got him."

"That shouldn't make much of a difference." The voice was gruff.

"Nearly twenty pounds, actually. Guy was half-starved. And maybe the chemistry changed. You never know with these people. They're not exactly prime specimens. Anyway, it's not the first time we've had to tinker. Just remix the implant, reopen the incision, and try again. Look," the man said to his apparently dubious interlocutor, "they can't all be success stories, at least not right off the bat. We get it wrong sometimes, too."

"But this wrong?"

"Oh, this." The guy laughed. "This is nothing. We had a guy a few months ago, wasn't even schizophrenic."

Sybylla, whose ears had seized on the word *implant*, now stiffened. "You're joking."

He was laughing. "Wish I was. Actually, it isn't funny. One of the research assistants got slashed up with a scalpel; then the guy somehow got out."

"Out as in . . ."

"Yeah. As in out."

The two men were moving past her and on into the OR. Sybylla heard them begin to move around inside, shuffling instruments, ready-ing the facility. In her tension, she felt her calves begin to cramp, and she winced in pain.

"Never seen Hofmann that bad, though I can't really blame him. You'd think the intake people could recognize a psycho by now."

"You'd think," the other man agreed. "That about it?"

"Yeah. Pretty straightforward. Oh, listen." He chuckled, and Sybylla heard the unmistakable sound of a human commotion moving in their direction. "That's our boy."

She sank farther back behind the door and listened, trying not to re-act as a shrieking, writhing man was hauled past. One foot hit her door, bouncing it against her knee and away from her. With a sharp reflex she hadn't known she possessed, she caught the bottom corner with an index finger, preserving her camouflage by a fingernail.

"The mayor!" the man was screaming. "I got the mayor on my side; he saw what you did! I'll call the mayor!"

"Of course, you should," came another voice, making no attempt to sound soothing. "The mayor's over here. You just lie down here and hold still, I'll bring hizzoner in."

"He saw what you did! They got a bug on me, goes right to Gracie Mansion! Mayor knows where I am, ever' second!"

"Sure, that's right. We all ready here, folks?"

"Get the door."

She closed her eyes, feeling the rush of cold air as it swung away from her and hearing it snap shut, separating her from the screaming within. Slowly, Sybylla rose, dazed and unsteady. The man was howling on the other side of the door. *Bad people,* Trent had said.

Trent, the textbook schizophrenic who wasn't a schizophrenic at all.

She did not know what else there could be to see, or how many more of the frontiers of science awaited her discovery, but Sybylla was sud-denly overwhelmed by the cumulative horror of what she had witnessed. It wasn't only that there were civil liberties being violated here left, right, and center, or that the impressive medical technology this place boasted did not seem to be dedicated to benevolent purposes. What wrenched her, she thought, was the banality of all this evil, the humor and matter-of-factness with which this subterranean cast of characters—technicians and orderlies and doctors—exercised their obscurely focused will over the so-called subjects. Whatever other discoveries awaited her here, she suddenly cared less for them than for the prospect of real air and the safety of her own rented car, putting greater and greater distances between herself and this place. I'll keep walking, she told herself, not rushing, but walking, and look for anything that suggests an elevator or staircase. The maze couldn't be infinite, after all; it was a wonder she hadn't found the escape hatch already. But above all, she'd amassed enough information to ensure nights of sleeplessness, and while she still could leave, it was time to do so.

Except that Sybylla's feet seemed to have glued themselves to the floor with an instant, intractable potion. Dimly aware that they had stopped moving, she sent them a halfhearted spasm and then gave up on them, the better to concentrate on the door before her, which she was staring and staring at. JURY ROOM, it read.

Jury room? For a strange, disjointed minute, she questioned whether the past hour had even occurred, whether she wasn't, in fact, still upstairs on her tour of LRA, admiring the cutting edge of trial consulting as shaped by the visionary hands of Mr. Robert Winston. Her job interview, the elusive ladies' room, the sauna that wasn't a sauna . . . perhaps she had conjured it all in one great gush of imagination, like the soap-opera character who dreams an entire season because one of the leading actors wants to return to the cast.

Dimly, she saw her own hand reach for the doorknob, and before she could stop herself, it turned, taking the door with it. Her feet carried her thoughtlessly forward, into a room identical to the one she had seen only a short time earlier. Carpeted an indifferent gray, it contained a long table laden with legal pads and glasses of water. A blackboard filled the far wall, and a mirror stretched the length of the wall to Sybylla's left. The ceiling was low, but the light was as bright as it had been everywhere on the underground level, making the complexions of the people strangely pasty and green.

The people, Sybylla noted. The same people who had turned in unison to meet the sound of the opening door and were now staring at her with open, expectant faces. Her gaze fell to their hands, which, as in da Vinci's *Last Supper,* seemed to have been caught in the act at a charged moment of the proceedings; pencils were poised, a glass half-raised to a waiting mouth, a finger lifted in emphasis of some now-interrupted statement. Her eyes swept over their faces. They were young and old, but mostly of an unplaceable middle age, gray-haired and red-haired and black-haired, stocky and thin. They were dressed well or plainly, in tailored or cheap but neat clothing, and they sat in a variety of postures, from limp to alert and stiff. They have nothing in common, Sybylla heard herself reason. Nor should they. Aren't they a jury, drawn from the general populace to sit in judgment on their peers? Education and politics and class aren't meaningful here, or at least they shouldn't be. And so conscientious! If I was ever in trouble, she thought absurdly, taking in the scribbled-on legal pads, the blackboard with its diagram of a crime scene, the fat and well-thumbed binder of documents entered into evidence in the middle of the table, I would want a jury like this one—so diligent, so intent on getting it right.

Except that these people were all, somehow, *not right,* she discovered, looking from face to face. They looked at her, she saw, as if they had no real curiosity about who she might be or what her purpose was in intruding on their deliberations, and even now, not one of them had uttered a word or a sound in reaction to her sudden, baffling appearance. But that's because they're not real. It came to her suddenly. They're real, but they're not . . . real.

She heard breathing. Someone cleared their throat, a hand twitched, and still Sybylla understood that the men and women had been so altered that they had resigned their souls in some ultimate, unchangeable way. Lost, she understood. They had lost themselves somewhere, put themselves down for a minute and returned, to find another person in their place. Or not a person at all—a nonperson. Someone who looked like a person should look and behaved like a person should behave, but who wasn't whole somehow. Looking at them, it was difficult to believe that any of them had ever been whole, their faces were such blanknesses—empty canvases wiped clean of a single idea.

One idea. Beginning as a pinprick in her own thoughts, smearing and spreading into horrible chiaroscuro. Rigid, Sybylla felt the undiluted evil of this place overwhelm her as the disparate pieces of Trent's story flew into place, bringing the terrible things she had seen today into an awful, rational order. Struck dumb in its grip, she could barely hear the voice sputtering to life over an intercom, filling the room with rage and howling: "Who the fuck are you?"

CHAPTER
THIRTY - TWO

Her stomach clenched. She spun, finding only the cool surface of the mirror, masking whatever was behind it.

"Did you hear me?" the voice demanded. "Identify yourself."

"I'm—" Sybylla, she'd almost said. "I'm sorry." She was buoyed by the sudden hope that she could talk her way out of this. "It won't happen again."

"It certainly won't," the voice said, "but that doesn't excuse your being here now."

"I'm new," Sybylla said, using up her only other proven line. Her eyes darted from end to end of the mirror, not knowing where to focus. "I just . . . I'm sorry, I don't know my way around yet. I got lost. I . . ." Shut *up*, she told herself. You're making it worse.

"That may be. But Eumenides relies on the integrity of its team members. We each have our jobs to do, and the success of the project demands that we not tolerate this kind of unauthorized intrusion into one another's work. I'm sorry you seem to be getting off on the wrong foot here, but I'm going to need your security clearance code. This will have to be reported to Mr. Kolb. Now, what is it?"

Sybylla, who had been utterly distracted by the unanticipated appearance of the name Eumenides and had thus failed to follow the rest of the man's speech, now dimly realized that she was being asked for information. "I'm sorry, what did you say?"

"Your security clearance code."

The Eumenides Project. "The spirits of justice," Sam had said. She looked at the pasty-skinned men and women around the table. The spirits of justice, American-style: they were jurors. Manufactured jurors.

262

Street people, with no ties to other human beings and no firm hold on reality, the weakest and most vulnerable and most expendable members of society, they had been brought here and roughly fashioned into these strange quasi-normal approximations of jurors. But why?

"Young lady! Your security clearance code, right now."

She looked up at the mirror. "How can you do this?" she heard herself ask. "How can you do this to these people?"

"Stay right where you are," the voice boomed. "Don't *move*."

Move, Sybylla repeated to herself, testing the concept. *Move* seemed like a pretty good idea about now. With a glance back at the queer, inert bodies around the table, Sybylla tore out of the cramped room and took off down the corridor, her feet slapping at the stone floor. The walls fled in a white blur on either side. Behind her, she heard the unmistakable clatter of a door being flung open, indecipherable yelling, the sound bouncing off the shiny surfaces. She rounded a corner into an unfamiliar stretch of hallway and risked slowing to read the signs, hoping unrealistically for a blinking, glaring EXIT demarcation, but the doors along the left bank of the corridor were individual offices bearing only surnames.

The corridor had exploded in fiery red lights and a siren had been activated, its shrill bleat punctuated by an angry voice over the PA system, informing her that she was supposed to stop where she was and go no farther. Except that they don't know where I am, Sybylla thought. At least, not exactly. She'd made it into this little stretch of the corridor unaccompanied, and while her pursuers might reasonably and rightfully assume that she hadn't gone far, the string of offices on the other side of the hall might buy her a few minutes to think. She headed to the last one, noting its name—Hofmann—and recalling through the blur of her panic that Hofmann was the personnel director, or something like that. He won't be here, she thought, willing it to be so. Turning the knob, she opened the door and stepped inside, listening hard for the sound of her pursuers passing her by.

But the room was silent, utterly still, and black. Icy, too, Sybylla thought. She felt behind her for a lock, found one, and threw it, the bolt sliding with a satisfactory snap into its place. With her ear to the door, she could only just barely make out the rhythmic howl of the siren and the shouts of someone looking for her. A guard, she imagined, not unreasonably. With a gun and a private penal code. Nobody knew she was here, Sybylla realized. Indeed, since leaving Simon Cates's office at LRA—it seemed like years ago—she might have dropped from the face of the earth. She could die here, she thought, pinched with terror. She could die here, and no one would ever know.

It's this darkness, Sybylla scolded herself. It already felt like a tomb, so black and cold and deep in the earth. She would have to get a grip on herself if she was ever going to think her way out of this mess. Reaching up, she quickly located a light switch by the door, flipped it, and stepped back to look around the room.

The place seemed standard enough: large heavy desk, a comfortless low couch, three walls of bookshelves lending a distinctly claustrophobic mood. Indeed, she reflected with a curious detachment, this was the first moment since entering the underground level that she had actually felt anything like claustrophobia, but now it seemed to combine with the chilly air and the shiny stone floor to produce its own specific discomfort. For a moment, she indulged an instinctive urge to cover her eyes and breathe deeply, and it took a long moment to recover what few of her wits remained. When she parted her fingers at last, her gaze seized immediately on the telephone.

I'll call Sam, she thought wildly, snatching it up. Then: No, if I'm going to go through the explanation of where I am and how my rescuers can get here, there had better be a tape recorder running, because I might not have time to run through it two or three times. Now, to get an outside line, most places wanted you to dial nine, didn't they? She held the silent receiver to her ear and pressed nine, only to hear the phone erupt in strident beeps. Not nine, apparently. Sybylla pressed one, another likely candidate, and the same thing happened. Finally, with zero, she reached an authentic-sounding dial tone and punched in the emergency code with a racing heart. Surely she was cutting it close to the bone as it was; whoever was looking for her must already have narrowed her position down to this part of the complex, and the scrape of a passkey at her door was probably imminent. The phone rang lazily, droning over and over. Sybylla twisted the phone cord with a wet and tensing hand. Pretty laid-back for emergency dispatchers, she told herself, straining for levity. To distract herself, she let her eyes run over the bookshelves, picking over the stacks of journals and the unruly mounds of neglected correspondence. The books she managed to discern in the gloom were treatises on virology and chemistry, genetic engineering and abnormal psychology. Bizarre reading for a personnel director, she observed vaguely, but then her gaze drifted upward again, and that thought, along with every other thought in her brain, shattered in a heap.

It was up there, pushed back to the surfaces of books laden with years of dust, that she caught the flash of a framed photograph. Covered, as it was, with a film of grime, Sybylla had to strain to make out the figures in the picture, four of them, and claw from that unfamiliar scene the single thing that was screaming at her, the thing she recognized.

In her ear, the phone clicked. "Who is this?" a voice demanded.

She stepped over to the bookshelf. The frame was so far back toward the wall that she could barely pick out the dull gleam of its edge now. Sybylla looked around for a chair.

"Who are you? Who's using this phone?"

So hostile, this dispatcher, Sybylla thought distantly. There was a chair a little farther along the bookcase. She dragged it toward her a few feet and stepped up on its seat, the telephone still clutched in her hand. She felt like an elevator rising, shelf by shelf, her eyes straight ahead, so that when she drew level with the photograph at last, there was a sense of having reached the apex of something, or its termination. There simply was nowhere further to go.

"Identify yourself immediately," somebody was yelling. "Why are you using Dr. Hofmann's line?"

She dropped the phone. The voice had begun to bother her.

It was interesting, Sybylla thought. All these years, she had looked at the picture and just assumed—assumed, as if it was only too obvious!— that the hand around her father's shoulder had been her mother's, and the hand around her mother's upper arm had been Dermot's. Curious, she thought dimly. She examined the tangle of limbs as clinically as if she was analyzing a game of Twister. But it had always been Robert Winston with such a protective hand above her mother's elbow, and the fingers on her father's shoulder belonged not to her mother but to this strange man she had never laid eyes on before. What were these people doing intruding into somebody else's life like this? It was too strange. She shook her head with a sick, inappropriate giddiness. All this time, and now somebody had invaded the cherished image of her parents, creeping into her past and stealing it. She thought of the copy of the picture that sat beside her own bed and wondered if the change had occurred there, too, stealing into the old emulsions like the decaying visage of Dorian Gray. Was the photograph waiting in this altered form to greet her when she got home?

"*If* I get home," she said, surprising herself by saying it aloud.

Mesmerized still, she held up her hands to the picture, making a three-sided frame with her fingers and bringing it close to the grimy surface until the picture became finally familiar: her father, her mother, their arms around each other in newly wedded happiness. Her parents. The picture on the desk in her father's study. The picture by her bed. *My picture*, Sybylla thought childishly, beating back at hysteria, as if its apparent theft were the worst implication of discovering it in this place.

That man on the phone was going berserk, it occurred to her. Down there on the Persian rug, the black telephone receiver was practically vibrating with rage. With a sudden gasp, she looked around and seemed to see herself in this paralysis, up on a chair in somebody's office, with Winston's security force in hot pursuit—now *very* hot, she guessed—and no help on the way. Philosophical appraisals of the art of photography could wait, Sybylla told herself. First, I'd better save my life.

Miraculously, the hallway was clear, but the door to Hofmann's office had barely clicked shut behind her when she heard the clatter of shoes against the stone. Sybylla sprinted away from the sound, her pounding feet taking her farther down the corridor, away from the treatment area and the jury room. There were fewer doors here, and she had enough functioning neurons left to wonder if she had put the main area of the underground level behind her, leaving only storage areas or other dead-end spaces ahead. Only a small cluster of signs was now visible as the corridor seemed to be approaching a terminus. She panted as she ran, straining to make out the nearest sign, which finally came into focus.

INTAKE.

Intake, Sybylla thought. The surfer had said something about intake, hadn't he? He had said that intake was done over by the garage.

Her heart leapt.

The corridor turned sharply, cutting her off from their sight. GARAGE, the first door read.

Sybylla threw her whole weight at it, and it swung away from her violently, bashing into the steel bar of a railing.

No elevators, Sybylla thought disjointedly. They drive to work.

The room beyond was long and narrow, with cars concentrated near the door. Far down its length, it merged into a yellow-lit tunnel that curved into hidden darkness. Her white lab coat would stick out like neon in there, it occurred to her; she clawed it off and flung it behind, sprinting toward salvation and assuring herself, illogically, that once she had rounded that curve, her pursuers would forget about her and go away. She reached its rim and was about to slip into the yellow passage when she made out the specific drone of an approaching vehicle.

"*Shit.*" There was a Dumpster, wedged into a corner at the tunnel's rim, and Sybylla dove behind it, crushing her cheek to its dirty steel surface. The roar of the imminent arrival drowned out all other sound, and Sybylla squeezed her eyes shut as the headlights swept over the Dumpster, but when the light passed on, they opened involuntarily. A door was slammed, then a second one. Sybylla couldn't see anything, so she raised herself one tiny inch and slowly, extremely slowly, turned her head back in the direction she had come.

It hadn't been a car, she noted with absurd calm. It had been a van. In fact, it had been *the* van.

A black hand clasping a white hand. The words HELPING HAND arcing over them in a grim parody of selfless outreach.

There were four men by the garage door, all clad in dark uniforms, and two, she noted grimly, were carrying guns. But they appeared to have been distracted in their pursuit. They clustered around the van's driver's side door as it opened and a man in a black leather coat emerged, large and heavy, his round head squarely affixed on outsized shoulders.

But of course. She nodded with a certain forlorn satisfaction. *Of course it would be him.*

The men who had been following her stood before him, gesturing wildly, their voices indecipherable barks in higher and higher decibels. He grew more visibly enraged.

Susu's admirer. Sybylla shuddered in bleak recognition. The StairMaster man. Her fear burned acid down her throat.

He had taken charge of the situation, obviously. Paralyzed, Sybylla watched, listening to the crazed but indecipherable staccato of his orders. Half of the security guards headed for the garage door, presumably to search elsewhere in the complex, and Sybylla wondered if they hadn't, after all, seen her enter here. The other half began to inspect the cars near the door, stooping to look beneath them and peering into backseats. The man himself did neither; instead, he went to the back of the van and opened it up, angrily ordering whoever was inside to come out.

Two legs appeared first, clad in metallic warm-up pants, then a matching jacket punctuated by enough gold jewelry to adorn half the women of Manhattan—the same women he'd probably snatched them off of in the first place, Sybylla found herself thinking grimly. The man— no, *boy*, she corrected herself, offering up excuses for him even under these fairly incriminating circumstances—hopped lightly onto the cement floor and stretched luxuriously, as if the people around him were not in varying states of alarm. So these were Cleve Rivera's new friends. Sybylla shook her head. The ones who had hired him a "real" lawyer. She watched him reach back into the van and withdraw the restrained arm of a writhing street person, his face obscured by filthy, matted hair. The guy was crowing some high-pitched and erratic communiqué, sending out the call to any of his kind who might be in earshot. He looked dreadful: shoeless, with sagging and shredded pants, a sweatshirt unzipped to his navel, and skin so filthy that his race was not immediately apparent. Basket case, she thought to herself. Textbook schizophrenic.

She returned to her crouch and looked longingly at the tunnel, only a few feet away. It was only a matter of time before the searching guards reached her position, and the memory of Trent's and Susu's shared fate did not augur well for what they would do to her when that happened, but still she could not overcome her fear. A distraction was her only real chance, it seemed to her, but it hardly looked as if one would be forthcoming. For what seemed like a long time, she stewed in this terrified paralysis; then, finally, she forced herself to creep to the end of the Dumpster and peek out.

A hand fell on her ankle. Her gasp was the loudest sound in the universe.

"I warned you." His voice was a whisper. "Didn't I warn you?"

She turned. "Yes." She nodded, her voice soft but unreasonably calm. "I remember."

"You didn't pay me no mind, did you?"

Sybylla turned to him. "Cleve, I don't know all the details about what you're mixed up with here, but it's bad. Worst thing you've ever done. Even a real lawyer won't be able to help you too much."

He actually considered this for a minute, but then he grinned. "Well, so what? Least I'll see the sun rise tomorrow."

This, it seemed to Sybylla, was meant to refer to her own prospects.

"Cleve"—she shook her head—"you remember the times I helped you? I got charges against you dismissed three or four times. I got you a place in that hotel on the West Side. I even got you a job."

He sneered. "Shit job. Going around to the shelters, making shit for pay. I'm making some real money now."

"That's not gonna matter when you get life without parole for being an accessory to multiple kidnappings."

Cleve shrugged. "Can always make a deal. Stuff I know."

"Fine. And I'll say you helped me, too. That'll pull some weight."

He shook his head at her. "No way." His hand tightened on her ankle. His other hand, she noticed now, clutched her discarded lab coat.

"You find that near the door?" she asked him. Cleve said nothing. "Maybe the person who left it went up that way." She indicated the end of the garage farthest from herself.

He grinned. "I don't think so."

Sybylla felt tears pooling behind her eyes. So this is it, it occurred to her then. All of my life, all of the good I've tried to do, it comes to this moment, and none of it will make the slightest bit of difference tomorrow. I gave this worthless kid the benefit of everything I knew, my education and my compassion, my convictions and my raw effort, and he'll deliver me to my executioner as thoughtlessly as if I were a roach on the pavement.

"Cleve." Her voice wavered and broke. "Please. Help me."

Something in his smile froze. They stared at each other. Almost imperceptibly, his fingers moved on her skin, and then there was a sudden rush of air as he released her. Still clutching her white coat, he retreated to the rear of the Dumpster and rose, making his way back toward the van. Stunned, Sybylla watched him leave her, uncertain as to what it meant. The security guards were clustered now around the StairMaster man, over by the doorway leading into the complex. As Cleve passed them, a hand shot out of the group and grabbed his arm, sliding down it to find and remove the bunched-up white garment. The bodies seemed to fall away, leaving only the short, stocky man, who pursed his lips at the thing and then looked curiously up at Sybylla's former client. He asked Cleve something then, but she couldn't make it out.

Cleve shrugged, then pointed up in the other direction of the garage.

The stocky man stood with his back to her, facing Cleve. He held the lab coat up and shook it angrily. "—sure?" Sybylla caught.

His other hand was holding a gun.

"—found it," she heard him say.

The short man stepped forward and bashed Cleve's face with the gun. She flinched.

Even from this distance, she could see the blood erupting from his cheek. She wanted to stop it. She really did. But she couldn't move.

It was easier to hear them now at least. The short man was shouting, his gun rising and dropping in punctuation to his words. "*Told* you," she could make out. "Last time you fucked up, I *told* you."

Cleve shrugged, his hand to his wounded cheek.

"You *put* us in this shit," the man raged. "Now you tell me where she is."

Sybylla could see him hesitate. Then he whined, "I found it up there. I *told* you."

The short man raised his gun. "Wrong answer," he said emphatically, then fired. The body dropped. An instant later, the crash filled the universe, blowing with a deafening thunder through the hall of cars. Flooded by raw terror, Sybylla slipped past the rim of the tunnel and ran.

When the long uphill road finally surfaced, the first intake of real air that hit Sybylla's straining lungs felt unbearably sweet. To the best of her ability to hear—an ability somewhat compromised by the rasp of her breathing—she had not been followed up the narrow two-lane passageway. Nor was there anything dreadful waiting for her ahead, if you didn't care to count the darkness or the dense rain that had apparently begun since she drove her car to the LRA parking lot, readying herself for a job interview and ruminating on her bizarre, unfocused suspicions. That seemed another life ago now, and the life she had led before that—as an adult woman with a career, a cat, and an exercise class—felt incalculably distant.

The thing to do, she told herself, was live through the night. Living through the night seemed as ambitious a goal right now as winning *New York* v. *Trent* had been only last week. How it might be accomplished, she wasn't at all sure, but the first step was a fairly easy call, and that was to figure out where she was. The woods all around her were drenched with pounding rain and her vision could not penetrate far into the gloom, but she used what little illumination there was to concentrate on the gravel drive underfoot, moving as swiftly along it as she could. How quickly and how irreversibly the world had shrunk to this, Sybylla thought—this thin slice of recognizable terrain in the midst of otherwise universal and unknowable horror. She had no choice but to follow its thread through the maze, blindly trusting it not to lead her to a Minotaur.

And it did not. In a few minutes, when the rain clouds obligingly parted, she saw that she was in a clearing and moving quickly alongside the great rusting carapace of a freight car, marooned at the side of the steel rails. But I know this place, Sybylla thought, deriving some amazed comfort from that. The car had been here for as long as she could remember, though she had seldom come this far along the tracks during her brief teenage flirtation with jogging. Indeed, she had most often headed in the opposite direction, following the tracks and their wide margins of gray gravel in the direction of town, measuring her mileage by the markers of the railway line.

The freight line was little used now, but long, leisurely snakes of cars did occasionally come through, waking Sybylla—who did not sleep deeply enough to ignore their distinctive rumble—whenever she was home visiting her father. She had no idea what the cars carried, but she had always found something inevitably romantic in this vestige of the national circulatory system, this steadfast progression of vital goods moving over iron railings through the American night, connecting the woods near her house to Washington, Baltimore, and the north beyond. It would have been Trent's good fortune to meet one such train in this place, moving slowly enough for him to catch a ladder or a car door that lay ajar, and all through the prism of hallucinatory perception that had been placed carefully beneath the skin of his arm. She marveled at the links of chance that must have brought him from this strip of Virginia railroad to a freight yard hundreds of miles north in the city he knew as home. Chance. Or sheer will. Sybylla shook her head as an eruption of lightning flashed overhead. Or simple, unalterable fate.

Another drone, that of the swollen and rushing Potomac, now joined the falling rain and gradually overwhelmed it. Sybylla left the access road and slipped into the woods, reoriented and anxious to put distance between herself and her pursuers. The riverbank, near and familiar from a lifetime's exploration, was her beacon, and she quickly made her way to its edge. Here the sound was deafening as incalculable pounds of water spilled over the boulders that gave Great Falls its name—the same spectacle George Washington had once planned a canal to circumvent, and the same spectacle that thousands of modern Washingtonians now came to picnic beside in summer. She stood for a moment to catch her breath, then turned downstream.

There was a footpath in the woods, just here, where Potowmack and Elm islands overlapped. She gave in to the intensity of her satisfaction, allowing herself one small smile of relief as she darted back into the darkness. This was a neighbor's field, well remembered for the sweetness of its autumn apples and the foxhole into which she had once stumbled, wrenching an ankle. A short dash through a grove of sycamores and she could make out the wonderfully reassuring flicker of the streetlamp over her father's mailbox. Sybylla began to run even faster, making for the safety of that light.

Except that there was no safety. She knew that. In all likelihood, the man in the black leather coat already knew that she was no longer in the complex, and her father's house was the first place he would look after reaching that conclusion. This was no haven for her, but neither could she leave without going inside. With her rented car marooned and unreachable in the LRA parking lot, her only means of transportation was the ancient Volvo she had driven in high school, still stabled in the garage behind her house. To the best of her knowledge, the car was only driven during her visits home, and the fact that Sybylla could not be overly optimistic about its automotive health did not brighten her general outlook.

She dashed through the circle of light from the streetlamp and up her own driveway. Her frantic fingers nearly botched the house's alarm code, but after a long second, she heard the reassuring double beep of the security system agreeing to admit her. Inside, the warm familiarity of the entrance hall brought her up short, standing as it did in such terrible contrast to what she had seen tonight. And all of the years it must have been going on! She shook her head in disbelief. So close to where she and her father had lived their routine, unsuspecting lives—it was almost unthinkable. Robert Winston had built an empire and a conspiracy that had hovered at her doorstep for God knew how long before seeping over it like an encroaching pestilence. Now this man, whose name she had never even heard until a few months before, stood solidly between herself and the rest of her life. Sybylla was soberly realistic about what had to be done.

There was no sanctuary for her after this, Sybylla knew. Not in New York and not here in Virginia and not anywhere else. Only one person could intercede for her now, and though she and Dermot had disagreed on nearly every topic they had ever debated, Sybylla knew that when her father learned what his friend had done, his outrage would match her own and he would put that outrage to good purpose. He would not believe her at first, of course. She knew well enough how preposterous her tale would sound. But the implant was tangible proof and she still carried it, wedged into the billfold of her wallet and looking for all the world like something else a nice girl should not be carting around.

In the kitchen, she had to riffle the miscellaneous drawer of half-used pads and worn-down pencils and random mysterious gadgets until she found the key, still threaded on her old Madeira School key chain. Clutching it tightly, she was turning to run when her eye fell on the closed door of her father's study. Without warning, the photograph reconstituted itself before her eyes, and Sybylla was abruptly flooded with a compulsion to see the image again in its familiar form, framed in the good silver frame on Dermot's desk: the picture she had sneaked in to see as a child, examining the beautiful face of the mother she had not known, her stern father's unsuspected capacity for happiness. She needed to see it again now, to reassure herself that the aberrant image she had seen in Hofmann's office had not actually been some shameful warp of her own. The rain was still sheeting down and thunder rumbled somewhere, not close by. She had been in the house barely a minute. There was time, an untrustworthy voice assured her. Of course there was time.

The heavy door swung easily on well-oiled hinges. Dermot's study was thick with books and journals, mostly double-lined on the shelves and stacked on a low table in front of the couch. The desk, though, was fairly clear, a testament to the fact that her father seldom used it to read at or write at. He had never mastered a typewriter, let alone a computer, and his general method of home research and work was to dictate papers to his clerks and secretaries on a portable microphone, the text delivered from a comfortable slump on the soft tapestry-covered sofa. A desk, in this scenario, was merely a prop and nothing more—a piece of furniture that was there for no other reason than that a study like Dermot's was supposed to have one. Apart from the photograph, its surface bore only an antique lamp and a small bronze of a dog, given to him by his staff at the United States Attorney's Office when Dermot was first elevated to a judgeship.

Sybylla walked gingerly around the desk, as if intent on sneaking up on the picture, taking it by surprise before it could alter itself. In the darkness, the image was faint, so she flicked on the lamp and held the picture beneath its glow. They were still there, those two people she had always known, the man beginning to go prematurely gray, the lines from the nose to the corners of the mouth foreshadowing their later depths, and the woman shyly lovely, with Sybylla's own eyes and the lips she had so coveted for herself as a teenager. My parents, she thought fiercely, as if that fierceness could reclaim them. But already their suspicious hands looked awkwardly, impossibly twisted. That masculine hand on Dermot's shoulder could not be her mother's. The fingers on her mother's arm did not look like Dermot's.

The picture itself did not reach the edges of the frame, she noticed now for the first time. There was a mat—some dark color, and rather wide, as well. Thoughtfully, she traced those extra inches with a finger, running it around the four sides of the glass. Then she reached for the frame and turned it over, fumbling at the back and stupidly striking the terms of a pointless agreement with herself: if they were there beneath the obscuring mat—those two extra figures, those interlopers—then she would believe what she had seen tonight. If not, it would all have been false, a creation of her fancy and her paranoia in unconstructive partnership. They would not be there. She forced a hoarse little laugh from her dry throat.

But they were. Of course they were. And actually brighter than the figures of her parents, too, as if their long sojourn beneath the mat had protected their potency as well as hiding them from sight. Winston and the strange small man grinned smugly at her now, flaunting a kind of youthful arrogance that she could not remember ever having felt herself. Her father had chosen to keep the images of these two men from her, or perhaps, it occurred to Sybylla, from himself. For whatever reason, he had banned them from the version of the memory he wished to retain, without excising them outright. An allegiance to the ultimate truth, she reflected, suitable for a Supreme Court justice.

With a heavy heart, she began to shove the picture and the mat back into their frame, but they stuck. Sliding the pieces apart, she tried again, only to find that the motion was blocked at the same place. A bit of yellow paper protruded from the edge of the frame, and Sybylla pulled at it now, anxious to remove the impediment and cover the tracks of her prying, but the paper seemed wedged. With a sigh of exasperation, she reached in and yanked it free, frowning in surprise when a sizable wad of paper came away in her hand. For a moment, she simply stared at it;

then, shifting the beam of light, she saw that it was paper from a legal pad, several sheets folded over three or four times. The paper wasn't pristine; it looked as if it had been folded and unfolded many times. Without thinking, Sybylla set it down on the surface of the desk and smoothed it open, taking in the general impression of her father's distinctive script, laid out in inks of varying colors. It was a list, she saw vaguely, added to in blocks of two or three entries at a time, judging from the consistency of ink. It was a list of case titles, followed by dates. "*State of Oregon* v. *Lambert*," read the first one she focused on. "1981." "*State of Rhode Island* v. *Bennett.* 1982." Four pages in all, scrawled in a jumble of names she had never heard of and dates that meant nothing to her. Signifying what?

It made no sense to her. A list of cases Dermot had written about? A list of cases he wished he had tried himself? Cases with constitutional flaws or innovative bits of lawyering? But if it were indeed any of these innocent things, why hide the list so oddly, excessively guarding it from discovery? Sybylla shook her head and turned the sheets over, following the dates back into the past, until the very first entries in the early seventies. At the top of this page, three words appeared in a heavily doodled box, as if the writer had penned them and then sat staring at them, trying to contain them within a cage of ink while he decided whether or not to continue. Three words. She wanted to swallow. She wondered if she would ever be able to speak again. Three words that changed everything and would never allow the world to return to its prior innocence. Those three words were: "The Eumenides Project."

CHAPTER

THIRTY-FOUR

—⁓—

There was a bad cramp in her foot, tensed on the accelerator pedal, and slowly the insistence of this ache made its way into the hiss of Sybylla's thoughts, gradually silencing them. By which time, she dully noted, she had crossed the Potomac six times and circled the city thrice by its ring road.

She could barely make sense of the exit numbers counting down and counting up again, the déjà vu of passing the same signposts with precisely the same chaos in her head, this time as the last, and as the time before. *Maryland equals life,* she had mused as she drove, overtaken by the associations she had grown up with. The Maryland suburbs have the National Institutes of Health, the biotech firms, the medical research facilities. *Virginia equals death.* The Virginia suburbs have the CIA, the Pentagon, the defense contractors. And the Eumenides Project, Sybylla thought grimly—the newest outpost of destruction in the Old Dominion. *Life and death.* Over and over, she had crossed into and out of these boundaries, flitting between the extremes, her own alternate futures.

How she had managed to cover so much ground safely in these ravaged predawn hours, she couldn't say, yet the Beltway was beginning to fill with its familiar congestion of morning commuter traffic and she was still here—still clutching the laced black leather cover of the steering wheel with white knuckles and still nervously fingering the dubious prize of her night's work. The list—her father's list, the Eumenides list—sat unassumingly on the seat beside her, as nonchalant as if it were a scrawled sheet of driving directions.

If only it were that, Sybylla thought. Though she had spent hours locked in a kind of logical combat with the very existence of the thing and still had no real understanding of what it represented, she had not succeeded in explaining away the one very central reality it implied: he knew. Dermot knew. All the years she had pedaled her bike home from school after field hockey practice, opening the door to an empty house because Dermot hadn't yet returned from the city and trailing leaves and dirt from her sneakers up the stairs to her ridiculously pink bedroom, her father knew. All her years at college and at law school and all the years since as Dermot rose and rose to his present heady heights and she worked her tiny cog in the great unwieldy and maddening machine of so-called equal justice, he knew.

He knew that less than a mile from the quiet, ample house where he studied and wrote and slept soundly and even entertained, people were being abducted, imprisoned without benefit of any legal process whatsoever, and experimented on in an aberration of medical research. And he knew, too, that Trent's terrible crazed act had somehow been linked to this monstrous injustice. Dermot had not asked her to decline the case because of his own approaching nomination, Sybylla realized now; he had asked her to compromise her principles and her career and her duty as a lawyer in order to protect the repulsive man he somehow thought of as his friend. And the worst of it was that Dermot's awareness of the Eumenides Project made him an accessory to each and every one of the crimes Winston had committed, including the murders of Susu and Trent. The pain of that was nearly unbearable.

Noting the next approach of the Beltway Bridge, she shook herself out of her trance and edged into the compression of traffic on the G.W. Parkway, following the Potomac toward downtown. Glancing into the cars on either side of her and taking in the dull expressions of commuter drudgery, she felt an almost-physical ache of jealousy for even the most frustrating of workaday headaches. How she wished her own driving ruminations were about a sabotaging coworker or an implacable boss— instead, she had spent this endless night looking longingly yet fearfully in the direction of the capital she circled, feeling it simultaneously pull and repel her. Even as the city signified to her the belly of Winston's beast, she knew that there was no other possible destination for her. The unfathomable fact of her father's complicity did not affect his status as the only one who could help her, though it certainly made that help a mite harder to take for granted. And if he *was* going to help her, he would have to do it fast, because as soon as she appeared in the hearing room at the Senate, her exhausting but apparently successful evasion would be moot—Winston, along with the rest of the country, would know exactly where she was.

Pulling her car onto one of the scenic overlooks above the river, Sybylla turned off the gas and tried to rest for a moment, but her frustration would give her no peace. She could ruin her father, she realized suddenly with a rueful clarity. With a phone call, she could ignite a scandal that would spread to unknown distances, claiming careers of people whose names she didn't even know. Bleakly, she touched the yellow sheets of paper, then, needing air, opened her car door and walked to the edge of the overlook. Before her, only a few miles downriver, lay the city, pale in the early light. She had never felt so utterly and desolately alone.

But *not* alone, Sybylla thought suddenly. She remembered, long, long ago it seemed, that she had promised Sam she would phone him after her visit to LRA. If only she had spent last evening with him in New York, resisting her fatal temptation to prowl about in Winston's imagined secrets. If only she had taken Sam's good advice and let it all go. She allowed her regret to propel the fantasy of how they might have spent these terrible hours just past, imagining the conversation they might have had and the restaurant they might have gone to. Afterward, Sybylla thought, they would have looked at each other and maybe kissed, and maybe gone to her apartment or his and stayed up late. To her own surprise, she caught herself smiling at the specific memory of the specific smoothness of his curling black hair.

She checked her watch: 7:00 A.M. Sybylla grabbed the sheets of paper from the passenger seat of her Volvo and headed for the overlook's bank of pay phones. The number rang four or five times before he answered, and then not with the conventional "Hello?" but with a more dubious greeting: "If you think I'm going to forgive you for not calling me last night just because you call before I can work up a real bad temper, forget it. I'm still mad."

At the sound of his voice, relief swept her. Then she remembered herself. "Sam, I've seen the most terrible things. I have to tell you."

She heard him chuckle. "Terrible things? What, no Jacuzzis in the executive lounge?"

"What? What are you talking about? *Jacuzzis?*"

"At LRA. Isn't that where you were going when I last saw you?"

"Sam," she was shouting, *"listen* to me. I saw the place where they're making those LSD implants. They're . . . Sam, they're kidnapping people right off the streets—homeless people with mental instabilities. They're taking them there and"—she stopped, aware of how it would sound—"making them into jurors. It's . . . I think it's a way of fixing trial outcomes. I saw a room where they were all sitting around a table, just like a real jury, but they're not a real jury. They're just people with new haircuts who are on LSD. I think it's been going on for *years*. My dad—"

"Whoa!" he shouted. "Jesus, Sybylla, forget the LSD. What drugs are *you* taking?"

She paused, regrouping her wits. "I'm not making it up. It's all happening, not very far from my father's house, in an underground laboratory. Look, I don't know if you can picture this, but there's a whole network of roads in the woods. One of them, Seneca Road, leads to the consulting firm, but another turns into a tunnel that leads to a subterranean level of the same complex. Inside, there are laboratories and prisons and medical facilities and these tr—" She felt herself stumble. "*Treatment* rooms." She was gesturing at him, as if he were there. Her hand slapped the side of the pay phone in frustration. "Sam, they call it the 'treatment.' First, they give these people an LSD implant and then this process involving some kind of hypnosis and electric shock. Then they clean them up a bit and change their hair color and, I guess, *program* them with new identities. And then they're turned into jurors and sent to trials. I'm not sure *why* but—"

"Why would help; why would be nice, I'll grant you that."

"I'm sure it's to get convictions. Guaranteed convictions for high-profile criminal cases. The kind with a political payoff for the prosecutor."

"Why go to all the trouble?" She heard him laugh. "Juries convict all the time without benefit of LSD or hypnosis or electric-shock therapy."

Sybylla shut her eyes tightly. Of course he didn't believe her, and how could she blame him? She barely believed it herself, and she had seen it with her own eyes. She took a breath, steadying herself.

"Besides," he was saying, "trials are easy enough to fix as it is. You just pick a likely prospect on the panel and then buy his vote. Why go to such"—he paused, evidently searching for words that wouldn't offend her—"colorful extremes."

"Because that juror lives to tell about it," she shouted. "Because the kind of person who would accept payment for throwing a verdict is also the kind who'd pose a potential security risk, and for the remainder of his life, too. But the people they're using . . . Sam, they're homeless. They're invisible, right? So no one notices when they disappear from the street. And after these LRA people are finished with them, no one's going to notice when they never turn up again."

There was a long pause. Sybylla stood, listening to the sound of her own breath. Finally, she heard him sigh. "Honey, I don't think I can take any more of this right now. I can tell you're upset, but I just can't listen to you."

"Sam," she heard herself plead.

"*No.* Please don't tell me anything else. I . . . We'll talk about this later. I'll call you, all right? Are you at your dad's house?"

"No." She leaned forward. Her forehead touched the cool metal plate on the pay phone. "I'm . . ." Something was stopping her from giving her location. Some unidentifiable restraint was preventing her from telling him. She hadn't time to analyze it. "I've been driving for hours. Sam? I know how this sounds, but just think, all right? We knew somebody was making those things, and we knew one of them wound up in Trent. We didn't know why. But this is why. This . . . juror thing." Hearing nothing, she took a breath and continued. "I went to LRA. They gave me a tour and an interview, and I just sort of happened to wander into Robert Winston's office. You know, my father's friend, the one who created the company. And there was . . . Well, it's kind of a long story, but there was something wrong and I *knew*."

"You knew *what?*" he exploded. "Sybylla, are you telling me you did something illegal?"

She shrugged at the wall. "Not exactly. But sort of."

"Have you completely lost your mind? Do you know what they'd have done to you if you'd been caught?"

But I *was* caught, she nearly said.

"Do you know what they'd have done to your father?"

Sybylla frowned. "Why is my father suddenly so important to you?"

He paused, then said carefully, "He isn't especially important to me. He's important to you."

It took a moment to quell her uneasiness. Her voice, when she spoke again, was subdued. "Sam, my father knows. He's known for years. He kept a list of case titles."

"A list of case titles? I've got at least ten lists of case titles in my office right now. A list of case titles doesn't mean a damn thing, and you know it." His voice was snide.

"All the titles were in my father's handwriting, Sam. They were added at different times, with chronological dates all the way back—twenty years or so. And the first page had a heading. Can you guess what it was?"

"Haven't the faintest." He was surly.

"The Eumenides Project. *The Eumenides Project*, Sam. Remember what you told me? Remember what Trent said? He said he kept hearing people say, 'You men at ease,' in the place those people took him. The same place, Sam. I was there yesterday."

She listened, her ear tight against the receiver, willing him to understand, to believe her. "Sam," she said, unfolding the pages, "I remember some of these cases on the list. Precedent cases, some of them. You remember that case with the defendant who'd been out on prison furlough when the crime occurred? Prosecutor rode that one all the way to the Senate. And the Utah case where this guy served his sentence for child molestation, then got out and murdered a kid like a week later? The prosecutor for that one's now the governor of Utah. They were all violent crimes, and they were all convictions. Look, there's no other explanation for this, I'm telling you. Either Winston is just manipulating trial outcomes because he wants to and he can afford to or else this is some kind of service he's providing to somebody. And the first date's, like, 1970." She squinted at her father's writing. "It's *Louisiana* v. *George Washington Dunay*. And the most recent one"—she was flipping the second page over, scanning it down to the bottom with a shaking finger until she arrived at the final entry, written in blue ballpoint—"the most recent one was only a couple months ago. *New York* v. *Larry Randolph Jackson*." She paused, suddenly dizzy. She read the line again, and then it hit her.

After a minute, his voice wormed through. "What is this, some kind of joke?"

At least he finally seemed interested, Sybylla noted, still staring at the line. And why not? *New York* v. *Larry Randolph Jackson* had been his own case, after all, the case whose voir dire had afforded Sybylla her very first sight of him. She remembered it easily, even today, her vision of the courtroom crisp and sharp. She had been so impatient that morning, anxious to receive her dismissal and leave. Why had she been in such a hurry? she wondered, trying to pull back the rest of the scrim. It was Trent, she recalled now. Trent, who had just been arrested and was over at Bellevue, howling like the textbook schizophrenic everybody assumed he was. Strange, Sybylla mused, how both Sam and Trent had come into her life on the very same morning. Fortuitous, maybe. Or maybe just strange.

"Sybylla?" she heard him say. "Are you still there?"

The funny thing was that she had never really questioned his appearance at all. Unlike some of the other single women she knew, Sybylla had not been so traumatized by the pressure to pair off that she was actively on the lookout for a mate. Life was complicated enough with the myriad responsibilities and meager satisfactions of being a Legal Aid attorney, and the dating game seemed such a bizarre and pointless ritual of resumés exchanged and uncomfortable questions about communicable diseases. Then Sam had materialized, improbably descending to the squalor of Foley Square from his comfortable situation uptown. He had moved into the office next door and pursued her romantically, even petitioned for the entirely subordinate role of her assistant on the Trent case, and she hadn't bothered to hold any of this up to the skepticism she reserved for everything else in her life. Why? Was it such an ordinary thing to toss an apparently thriving career in a cushy corporate firm? Was a major pay cut an everyday occurrence? Why would a rising young attorney want to drop his own workload to play second string on somebody else's case? And did it make sense that a man so handsome and charming should arrive in her life entirely unencumbered by a girlfriend, let alone a wife? He had seemed so suited to her, too, almost as if he had known her before they had met—known her interests, known what she would respond to in a man.

And yet he had never been particularly encouraging of her efforts when she set out to discover why their client had suddenly, freakishly stabbed a little girl, a fact that now stood out in bold contrast to Sam's otherwise-affectionate, supportive demeanor. He had been dubious about the implant from the first, and downright dismissive when Sybylla hinted that Trent might have been murdered. He had never encouraged her to investigate her suspicions, nor offered to help her do so in any way. Only two days before, indeed, he had responded to her theory that LRA had been somehow responsible for Trent's abduction by accusing her of acting out an Oedipal struggle with her father, and now he was more disturbed about her subterfuge in gaining entry than he was about what she had discovered.

Larry Randolph Jackson. Sybylla's gaze returned to the page in her hands. The "Old Spice Rapist," so christened by the press long before an actual defendant had been arrested. The case had been a moderately high-profile one, Sybylla recalled. Not a Son of Sam or a Wild Man, but amplified nonetheless; it was not out of place on her father's list. She remembered Sam's hand on the man's shoulder, so comforting. What a compassionate attorney, she had thought then. An attorney devoted to the almost-holy principles of innocence presumed and a fair, decent trial for the accused. But if there had been one of those zombie jurors on his panel, how could he not have known it?

Sybylla's eyes closed. How could he not have known?

She heard rather than felt the breath escape her lungs.

"Are you there?" he was saying. "I think the line—"

With a shaking hand, Sybylla hung up the phone.

Just inside the main entrance of the Capitol, Sybylla gave her name to one of the security guards and told him she had come to watch her father's nomination hearing for the Supreme Court. The man's response was both dubious and formal until he checked her driver's license and made a phone call; then it became instantaneously deferential. She was given a small room to wait in, offered a cup of coffee in a china cup with the crest of the United States Senate on it, and assured that Ms. Baily-Stein, hospitality liaison for the Justice Department, would be along to assist her very soon.

Sybylla dropped heavily into one of the plush armchairs, trying to excise Sam's betrayal from her thoughts, trying to concentrate on the task at hand. She had no idea of how she would confront her father, or what she would say, but her greatest concern was that her immense anger would ignite the extreme fragility she was now feeling and that she would burst shamefully into loud tears the minute she saw him. This would not do. Sybylla shook her head firmly. It was not about herself and her father, two strong-willed people screaming ideology at each other over their breakfast table, acting out the ancient schism of generations. This was not *personal*. It was about men and women, kidnapped, mistreated, and killed. Real people—vulnerable and hidden people who had no voice and few advocates. She felt like a Resistance member, or an OSS spy, determined to smuggle the secret plans or the schedule for the invasion out of enemy territory, not because she was brave, or noble, but because the individuality and subjectivity of her character had been displaced by an almost-mindless drive to get the thing done: she was all message now, and no longer messenger.

"Miss Muldoon?" An artfully coiffed woman was leaning through the open doorway.

"Yes." Sybylla got to her feet.

"I'm Helena Baily-Stein." She stepped gracefully forward. "What a delight. I'm so pleased you were able to come."

She must moonlight as a professional hostess, Sybylla thought.

"Wouldn't miss it," she managed, taking in Helena Baily-Stein's flawlessly conservative attire: light tweed skirt, cream blouse, plain bolero jacket. Sybylla cringed in her day-old and traumatized clothes.

"You must be so proud of your father. I've never seen a nominee sail through so smoothly. He is a very eloquent, very brilliant man." She ducked her helmet of blond hair a mite closer to Sybylla. "I was fortunate enough to meet him last evening at a cocktail party across town. A very charming man, too, as I'm sure you know."

She forced a smile. "That's my dad. So, is it all right if we go up? I'm anxious not to miss any more of the hearings. I couldn't make it yesterday or the day before. My job, you know."

"Of course." She nodded amiably, pulling back the door for Sybylla. "You're an attorney, too, I think. Do I have that right?"

"Public defender." Sybylla sighed without any particular relish.

"How fascinating," she heard behind her. "This way."

They climbed the wide flight of marble stairs, their heels clacking against the stone. Sybylla pressed her hand against her leather handbag as she walked, hearing the muffled crinkle of the list against her hip, reassuring herself that it was still there. Around her, activity swarmed. Washington attracted such busy people, she thought blandly. Such purposeful people, walking so quickly, talking so avidly. The women all seemed to have been issued with the same tiny waists, long legs, and sprayed-in-place ash-colored hair, and the men all had hearty handshakes and an easy recall for names, something that had always eluded her. Sporadically, making her way down the hall to the main hearing room, she saw people she recognized—A-list senators or distantly familiar faces she had watched on C-SPAN, delivering their impassioned speeches to huge empty rooms—but more often the faces belonged to those who performed more hidden legislative functions: the scurrying aides, the weaving lobbyists, and those quintessential examples of indigenous fauna, the power brokers who rarely emerged into the public eye. Passing through the crowds, Sybylla thought she could discern this last group by the physical positions they held among the others, backs to the wall, two or three or four serious, nodding men leaning in to catch the sotto voce snatches of their guidance. It was a job without a title, a salary, or any kind of stated purpose, but she understood that without the shaping and linking these men performed, the system might disintegrate—or at least begin to resemble its on-paper modus operandi, which, she supposed, pretty much amounted to the same thing.

Press packed the hall around the hearing room doors, and Sybylla's passage through the sheer wall of bodies did not go unnoticed. The word *daughter* began to spark around her as she moved, building to a rumble as people turned to watch her approach and then stepped back to get a better look. Involuntarily, she felt her hand reach up to smooth her hair, unwashed and hanging loose. Helena Baily-Stein knocked gently at the door, which opened a few inches for her to whisper her mission; then, gingerly, the heavy thing was eased back for them to slip inside. "Careful," she said as Sybylla followed her, indicating the heavy cables snaking everywhere underfoot, linking the television cameras to the lights and microphones. Few eyes did not turn to examine the new arrivals, and Sybylla felt her face grow uncomfortably hot. She lifted and placed her feet with care, walking behind the liaison to the front row of chairs, where, to her numb surprise, a seat had been readied for her, its gilt-edged RESERVED sign still in place.

"This is you," the liaison whispered in Sybylla's ear. "I'll touch base with you when the session ends, see if you need anything."

Sybylla nodded, utterly cowed by the glowing red light on top of one of the television cameras, which had swung in her direction. She was pretty sure she knew what that red light meant.

And then Helena Baily-Stein was gone, leaving four feet of space between Sybylla and her father's broad back. Almost near enough to touch, she thought. Near enough, at any rate, to pick out the tiny vertical lines of eggshell blue in the dark cloth of his jacket. The men on either side of her rose politely as she approached but did not shift their eyes from the action. She took her seat carefully, holding her bag across her lap.

The scene was at once familiar from watching previous hearings on television and utterly, bizarrely alien to her now, with the little desk of the nominee placed squarely before and beneath the raised shelf of seated examiners. These blank-looking men—the Thomas hearings had managed to lob only one woman onto the committee—frowned down at Dermot, either in ideological distaste or, among the conservatives, a pantomime of stern open-mindedness. Today was day three of Dermot's occupation of the hot seat, and while it could reasonably be assumed that the senators had at least begun to make up their individual minds about the nominee, they seemed reluctant to abandon their semblance of active deliberation until the bitter end.

Her father was in the middle of a defense of one of his earliest opinions, an argument that civil rights protection did not extend to people of very short or very tall stature in cases where companies—such as airlines—required certain height parameters. His hand, pressed flat on the table's surface before him, lifted and lowered gently in a civilized emphasis, and his voice had a subtle, persuasive undercurrent. He really was good, Sybylla thought, tuning in to the links in his argument above her own churning thoughts. He collected strands from a vast canvas of civil rights law and then wove them seamlessly together, anticipating challenges and then disarming them with a breathtaking assurance. She found herself regretting—not for the first time—that Dermot had never accepted any of the academic offers that had come his way over the years. He would have been a gifted, captivating teacher—that much was clear—and academia might have relieved him of the strain to ascend that he had always labored beneath and suffered because of.

But of course that had been the point all along, hadn't it? To be sitting precisely in the otherwise-undistinguished seat he occupied this morning, fielding these endless questions from the men and the woman who had made up their minds about him long before he opened his mouth on the first morning of hearings. It had been about this, all the way back to the beginning and every day since. As the poor Boston boy with smarts enough to get himself to Harvard, the scholarship law student, the reeling drunk dismissed as an ADA but then salvaged by the conviction he'd won in *Fentano*—this had been the only consistent beacon in her father's life.

Above, the panel seemed to be having a friendly skirmish over who was due to ask questions next. The affected parties preened charmingly for the cameras as they deferred to one another, and the chairman took the opportunity to banter a bit, offering an endearing little Irish fable about the limits of civility. Dermot turned in his seat and caught her eye. He was smiling, calm. *Hello*, he mouthed, and she suddenly understood that he was beyond pleased to see her here; her presence represented a kind of completion for him, that his disparate works had come together, somehow, at the moment of his triumph. It was more than public relations—devoted daughter worshipfully in attendance. It was something deep and complicated but strangely pure in his character, as if his more humble pride in Sybylla tempered the admitted arrogance that had driven his career to this shining apex. She felt her heart throb for him, for what she was going to do.

There was no conscious plan. Numb, her eyes locked with Dermot's, Sybylla felt her fingers unzip her bag and withdraw one small corner of the list. As if from a great distance, she watched his eyes fall to her lap and linger there, expressionless. Then they closed. The muscles in his face gave way with a great release. Her mouth opened. In that instant, she saw him age from a robust man of sixty to a fragile husk, and she hated herself.

Dermot turned back to the committee. His shoulders sagged and his head was down. From the corner of her eye, she watched two or three of the photographers notice his change of demeanor and focus their telephoto lenses. "Muldoon Begins to Show Strain," she captioned their efforts grimly. The panel had sorted itself out now. The members were tittering at one another's clever remarks, then reestablishing their serious, committed faces for the work still remaining. "Judge Muldoon? Shall we continue?"

He sighed audibly. "Mr. Chairman," her father said, "I wonder if I might request a short recess at this point. A few minutes . . ." The difference seemed glaring, Sybylla thought. It was incredible to her that no one on the dais before them appeared to be reacting. Instead, the audience rustled in anticipation of being allowed to get up.

"Well"—the chairman seemed surprised—"I suppose—yes, why

not? We're about due for a break. We'll convene again in thirty minutes. Gentlemen? Senator Tine?" He rose. The room eased into chatter. Dermot did not move.

After a minute, Sybylla stood and stepped close to him. "Daddy, we need to talk."

"Not here." He jerked to his feet. He took her wrist, a little harshly. "Come with me."

Sybylla let herself be led, an awkward smile on her face, past the crowd of well-wishers and reporters. She felt a little ridiculous, a woman instantly regressed to the age of five, but she knew herself to be suspended from the possibility of any real action. She walked behind him, her eyes firm on the back of his gray head. Even now, she wanted it not to be true.

Dermot's obvious goal was the small side door ahead, marked PRIVATE. He moved with speed and purpose and people parted in deference before him, so it was with some surprise that Sybylla found herself stopping only a few feet before the exit. She looked up. A tall person had stepped before them, a person who smiled, first at one, then the other.

"Dermot," said Robert Winston. "Splendid. So splendid, that last argument." He turned to her. "And Sybylla. How good to see you here, too."

She said nothing. She could not have said anything.

"Let us pass, Robert." Her father's voice was quiet, terribly controlled.

"Our Mr. Cates was so very impressed with you, Sybylla," Winston went on, ignoring him. "Wants to turn over our whole operation. Of course, I'm still not entirely convinced that such a devoted advocate for the accused would want to jump the fence, but naturally that will be for you to decide." His gaze, locked on her own, hardened visibly. "You'll have so many decisions to make, my dear. You're at a crossroads in your career, not to speak of your life, aren't you? So much to gain, so very much to lose."

"That'll do, Robert," Dermot snapped. "Now let us by."

The man shrugged and smiled, then stepped back. "So nice to see you, my dear."

She stepped carefully by him, holding her father's arm. Dermot closed the door behind them.

A small group of men were talking at the far end of the moderately sized room, sitting in a cluster of armchairs. Dermot asked for privacy and they scattered with obedient nods. When they had gone, he sank onto a couch and leaned forward, his head in his hands.

"Daddy," she began.

"*No!*" he said harshly. "I'm going to ask the questions here. And I want short, truthful answers. No moralizing, you understand me?"

"There are moral issues involved," Sybylla observed.

"Exactly what do you know?"

It came out surprisingly fast, a dry, colorless recitation, as if she was relating a school science project: "I know that LRA is a cover for what your buddy Robert has been doing with homeless people. I know he's been lifting them off the streets and doping them with LSD and somehow programming them to be jurors. My guess is, jurors who convict according to instructions. I know it's been going on for years, and I know that you know about it." She shook her head. "Daddy, how could—"

"*Wait,*" her father thundered. "Just wait."

Abruptly, rage filled her. "No, I won't wait. Even if I was inclined to be patient about this, I don't have the luxury. These people know I was in their fucking lab. I watched somebody get killed last night. I'm in real trouble now, and I need help."

"Oh, this is ironic, Sybylla." He was shaking his head. "All these years, I've offered you help. I've fallen all over myself to be of aid to your career, and you've spurned it at every opportunity. Now you're here at the most critical moment in my life, throwing your needs in my face because suddenly I'm the only one who can help, and I'm supposed to forget where I am and what I'm doing and everything it's taken for me to be here today, merely because you ask."

"You talk as if this is still about my career. I'm trying to stay alive here!"

He looked up, his face pained. She saw that he believed her.

"Daddy, you've been protecting them. It's so horrible." Dermot shook his head. "You have. You were making this list of cases the whole time. Winston was obviously keeping you informed. How could you be a party to this? Even setting aside the obscenity of what they did to those people, how could you advocate jury tampering? You taught me to revere the law. I thought that was something we shared. I thought—"

"You don't know," he cut her off, his voice tight. "You don't know everything about this situation."

Sybylla looked away. "I know that you asked me to drop Trent as a client because of it. I thought it was because you didn't want your name associated with Trent's defense, and you let me believe that was true. And I wanted to do what you asked me to do. I would have done it for you—that's the irony, you know? I wanted to help you." She was shocked at the sob erupting in her throat. "I was so proud of you. But all the time, you were only protecting that man out there. That *Mengele*. How could you ask me to compromise my principles for *him*?"

"You think you have all the answers, but as usual, you've chosen to view a complex situation as if it were a simple one. There's history here, Sybylla. You couldn't possibly—"

"So tell me!" she shouted, losing her cool. "We're both here. We're alone. The door's marked Private. Tell me what's so special about Robert Winston that I'm supposed to cancel my sworn commitments to protect his crimes. Tell me about this so-called history that permits you to be a party to kidnapping and murder." She nodded at the door. "Out there, you're the next Supreme Court justice, but in here, you're just like any of my clients, innocent until proven guilty. And believe me, even more than my clients, I *want* you to be innocent. So come on. Let me have it."

Dermot got to his feet. "Not now."

"We're not exactly on a relaxed schedule here. Winston's already killed three people because of this. I don't think he's going to stand on ceremony."

He seemed perplexed. "We'll have dinner tonight. We'll talk."

"I'm not sure it can wait till tonight."

He looked grim. "Well, I'm not sure I have any more time to talk with you right now. There's the little matter of the rest of the country expecting me back in their living rooms in a few minutes. Look"—his voice became more placating—"don't think for a minute that I don't take this situation seriously. I do. But remember that you're my daughter, and it counts for something. Believe me." He nodded reassuringly, as if he was trying to convince himself. "Sybylla, believe me that you are in no danger. Just use that other exit." He nodded at the far end of the room. "No one will follow you. Go back to the house and wait for me. We'll have dinner at L'Auberge. We won't be bothered there. And I'll tell you whatever you want to know."

"And Winston?" Sybylla asked, softening.

"Leave Winston to me."

Slowly, she got to her feet and slipped the strap of her bag over her shoulder.

"Sybylla."

She turned to her father. His hand was outstretched. For a minute, she thought he wanted her to shake it.

"The list."

Something inside her recoiled. It was her evidence. It was her proof that everything she believed was indeed true. She felt her fingers tighten over the leather.

"No."

"Give it to me, Sybylla."

She remembered this voice. It was the voice of enforced curfews and punishments meted out for teenage infractions. She had not heard him speak to her this way for a decade, at least.

"Why?" she asked.

"Because it's mine. Because I am your father and I'm asking you."

She bit her lip. "I'm sorry. I don't think that's good enough."

He reached out and took her wrist, squeezing it firmly. "Listen to me, Sybylla. When you were a child, your stubbornness was a mark of precocity, and I was glad of it, but now your stubbornness is based on ignorance. You've been engaging in a very tiresome adolescent drama for years, but now it's time to put away childish things. Whatever else you may think about me, or think you know about me, I am still your father. I may be the only person in this world you can trust. Do you understand? Now, please, give me the list."

There was a knock at the door to the hearing room.

Sybylla unzipped her bag and handed her father the papers. He took them without a word and placed them carefully in his inside jacket pocket.

"I'll see you late this afternoon, or early evening. Back at the house."

"Do you think I'll be all right until then?"

She caught his flicker of hesitation. He nodded. "I know you will."

"All right, then."

Sybylla watched him turn to reenter the hearing room; then she went in the opposite direction and slipped out the second door into a narrow, little-used corridor. The wide main hallway of the building was not difficult to find, and she merged easily with the moving crowds, descending the stairs to the front entrance.

Perhaps her father had been right, she thought, clearing the huge doors without any obstacle and descending the long flight of exterior steps. The spring day was open and blue and seemed eminently unthreatening; looking down the Mall, she could see that the city was teeming with tourists, vast shifting crowds alighting from their tour buses and families posing for snapshots before the Capitol dome. In the face of such happy ignorance, her own exhaustion flooded her and she thought longingly of her house, craving sleep with a heady, physical intensity. And a bath. By the time she reached the lot where she had left her Volvo, Sybylla could almost feel the good hot slide of her legs into steaming water. So avid, in fact, was her focus that she failed to notice the man who dipped between two parked cars and into her path, momentarily blocking the sun. No matter. He noticed her.

The pain was searing but mercifully brief, beginning in the tensing thick muscle of her thigh and spreading more quickly than thought. Accordingly, she was barely aware that something had happened before it had finished happening. Hands caught her as she fell.

CHAPTER

THIRTY-SIX

In addition to the many more noteworthy inconveniences it had wrought in Sam's life, the Trent case had created such a glut of his other work that he had barely made a dent in the backlog by lunchtime, and his mood, when that hour rolled around, was far from buoyant. True, the now undeniably insane occupant of the office next to his was absent, but

Sam's perplexity and rage at Sybylla now took the opportunity of the midday pause to assault him with renewed vigor.

Because things between them had seemed to begin so well, Sam thought bitterly, sifting his out pile into order. When he had cleared enough space, he extracted a by-now-soggy tuna on toast from its greasy bag and forlornly unpeeled the wrapping. There was something in Sybylla's brittle sarcasm that moved him, so blatantly did it mask her very real vulnerabilities, and when she had relented and allowed him to enter her life, he had found that life to be pleasant and pleasurable and, above all, interesting. His own parents' marriage had been based on conversation, a constant hashing and rehashing of subject matter that ranged far and wide. His father, a physician, and his mother, who painted, seemed to have mastered the cardinal rule of successful disagreement, which was that it was never, never to become personal. Growing up, Sam remembered furious exchanges about current events, lessons learned in school, biomedical ethics, the relative value of Northern versus Southern European Renaissance painters, as well as equally avid fights over the correct etiquette of toothpaste-tube squeezing. The boys were encouraged to mine the newspapers for more verbal fodder, and virtually nothing was off limits.

Years later, when Sam finally got around to wondering why he had developed such a bad habit of running through girlfriends, it had taken some time to distill the considerable list of women into a sensible order. Superficially, the women had seemed wildly disparate; there had been pretty ones and ugly ones, sweet ones and nasty ones, women who ran rings around his own considerable intellectual gifts and women who, to be blunt, had not been bright. There had been women who wanted to marry him and women who probably wouldn't remember him at all if he crossed their paths tonight, and a good number who fell between those extremes, but none of them had ever been quite right for him, because none of them, he realized finally, had truly understood how to talk.

Not so Sybylla. He smiled ruefully, taking a bite of his undistinguished sandwich. If there was one thing that woman knew, it was how to use her larynx. He remembered something Steiner had said about Sybylla that first day Sam had started at Legal Aid: "She was raised to argue both sides of anything." Sam's smile slid helplessly into a grin. A woman like that, he could talk to for a long, long time.

Except. He caught himself.

Except that she was stark raving mad. Small detail.

The inescapable resentment that had lingered since she'd hung up on him that morning flooded his limbs, and he shook his head. It had begun so gradually, Sam thought, with only a few small moments of paranoia. He shook his head. Those should have been a warning, but he had blindly received every word she told him, ignoring the obvious possibility that she was engaged in some crazed and personal adventure. People following her, the old woman from her street who had obviously moved on, her friend's tragic death—she seemed to have woven everything into some great conspiracy around herself. Not that the Trent case was devoid of mystery. Certainly, it begged some measure of contemplation when a man wreaked an act of extreme violence upon a child who was a stranger to him. But even ensconced in his corporate firm uptown, Sam had managed to keep up with current events in the city he loved, and the truth was that the modern crime had a nasty, random, seemingly fathomless smack to it. People today did terrible, inexplicable things to folks they had never met—all the time. Sybylla might need to find rational order in every aspect of the world around her, but Sam's attitude was that shit, occasionally, did just happen.

Admittedly, it seemed to be happening to her a lot, but now, painful as it was, Sam found himself forced to contemplate the possibility that some of the perils befalling her might have sprung from her own fair hand. Trent's trial, Sybylla's first truly high-profile trial, had been imminent when Sam moved to Legal Aid, and he saw now that the pressure must have been terrific. The frustration of being made to abandon the most plausible defense for Trent undoubtedly made things worse, and the catapult into the national spotlight after Dermot's nomination could only have pushed Sybylla over the edge. Sam didn't fault her, exactly. But he couldn't excuse her, either.

When had he begun to doubt the weave of paranoid fancy she'd produced for him? With the implant? What, after all, did he really know about that? The thing looked like a damn Alka-Seltzer. It might even *be* an Alka-Seltzer, for all he could tell.

The lab report? It was proof of nothing. Distasteful as it was to imagine, she might easily have created it herself.

Not that he took any great delight in ascribing such actions to Sybylla, but there was no getting around it: her histrionics had become so screeching by now that she appeared to him as certifiable as Trent obviously had been. Since his death, she seemed to have turned some corner in her paranoia, fixating on her client's nonsensical "you men at ease" (persuasive evidence of *his* mental illness, Sam clearly saw, which Sybylla had bizarrely imbued with weighty significance) and her father's friend, the one who ran the consulting firm.

And so it had unfolded, deeper and deeper into the mesh of her fearful distortions, until her phone call this morning. Sam sighed audibly. He had been truly shocked by what Sybylla claimed to have done. That she, a member of the bar, would commit such blatantly illegal acts was simply astonishing to him; indeed, the thought of her sneaking around the LRA facility nearly rivaled the outrageousness of her claims of what she had seen.

With those claims, however, Sybylla had finally gone too far. Homeless people snatched from the streets? LSD and electric shock? Underground laboratories? By the time she got to the Old Spice case, roping Sam himself into the great detailed swirl of her paranoid delusion, it was clear how thoroughly she had exceeded any vestige of self-control.

But even as he responded with outrage to her accusation of his complicity, Sam understood that the moving force behind this mess derived from an entirely different quarter in Sybylla's life, a quarter—as it happened—much closer to home. He saw that at the center of Sybylla's mesh of accusation and irrational fear lay a classic, terribly ordinary father-daughter struggle that had been allowed to spin horribly out of control. He saw plainly that she admired and loved her father, and yet Sam had to admit that Sybylla also appeared determined to subvert Dermot's nomination, even if it meant sacrificing her own professional integrity in the process. The announcement of the nomination, indeed, seemed to have marked the onset of her most outrageous pronouncements and actions, and when her wild story finally came around to Dermot's so-called list that morning, he had suddenly seen the situation for what it was. He had seen, in other words, that he himself had been only a bit player in this drama, which actually was a two-man show starring Sybylla and her father. Closing his eyes for a moment, he imagined her in Washington, clutching her little list, armed to destroy her father's nomination and ruin his life, and Sam shuddered for her, for the shame she seemed determined to bring upon herself. But even at the very moment he had received this insight, Sybylla had hung up the phone on him, cutting off whatever chance he might have had to make her see reason.

Well, that was the end, then. Sam shook his head. He had reached his limit. Sybylla's roller coaster might continue, but he himself was getting off right here. Anyway, it wasn't as if the decision was his to make; the whole situation was obviously out of his hands, and however it might feel right now, that was probably a very fortunate thing. Whatever wrench she might have thrown into his personal life, he still had a career, and, he liked to think, a worthy one. A wave of resentment returned to him as he replayed once again her outrageous implication of his complicity in her fantasy conspiracy, and he bit angrily into his depressing sandwich. Granted, Sam was nobody's idea of an experienced trial lawyer—indeed, the Old Spice trial had been his very first voir dire in a criminal case—but even so, he didn't imagine he'd miss a doped-out and preprogrammed juror if he or she passed through his jury box. Absurd. Completely, irredeemably absurd.

As if it were necessary to confirm this, he found himself eyeing the bank of filing cabinets across from his desk. Sam was an assiduous and exact filer. He knew precisely where the case file was, could even visualize the manila tag, his own spiky blue script: *Jackson, Larry Randolph,* and inside, the wedge of loose yellow legal-pad pages that comprised his voir dire notes. He had kept them, he remembered now, in order to learn from them later, when he'd become more expert at jury selection.

Sam frowned in irritation. Now he had to look at them, of course. The idea of doing so, planted with the dubious sensory accompaniment of bland tuna fish, was becoming so irksome as to be unignorable. He pushed back his chair and stepped around his desk, muttering under his breath. Then he took the file back to his seat.

They weren't in any particular order, those pages, and his scrawled notes described not only the twelve jurors who had ultimately been seated but the many others who had been dismissed for cause or as a result of his or Greer's peremptory challenges. He remembered nothing of them now, despite the occasional scrawled gut appraisal: "Seems too eager to get on," or "Looks afraid of dft." The names, ages, occupations, and neighborhoods flew beneath his gaze, blurring into an indistinct evocation of the megalopolis: bakers, stockbrokers, real estate agents, welfare recipients, bartenders, newsstand owners, sanitation—

Newsstand owners. Sam concentrated. He did remember that one, Wade Jones. Big man, a little grizzled. He'd been approved by them both, himself and Greer, and he became jury foreman. Sam reread his notes: "62 yrs., has newsstand Warren and B'way, city-born, reads 'every' paper, not crime victim, two daughters, 1 yr. college." Well, it wasn't much, was it? Not enough to tell if Mr. Jones might have made him the fall guy in a vast jury-rigging operation, certainly. He read the brief, cryptic shards of information a second time. The newsstand at Warren and Broadway was close, barely a stroll. Too close, Sam thought, becoming enraged with himself as a compulsion to have a peek at Mr. Jones grew within him. "Damn," he said aloud, addressing his now-forsaken tuna sandwich. Already this was eating at him. He pushed the remains of his lunch into the wastebasket and reached for his jacket. "All right, then." He could use a paper anyway, right? So he would just walk on over to the newsstand and ask his former jury foreman if he was a zombie from an underground laboratory, or, failing that, if he'd happened to notice any such zombies on the panel he'd chaired. Once I've performed that idiot task, Sam assured himself, I can forget about this lunacy and its unfortunate author and get on with my own business.

Ten minutes later, he rounded the corner of City Hall Park and spotted the stand, festooned with tabloids and fashion magazines, the lurid covers of skin mags discreetly lining the interior of the booth. Sam watched the seated man inside carefully as he approached, feeling increasingly silly as he began to swim into familiarity: the dense and tall body, the round head and large ears that protruded from his cap, a narrow, straight mouth surrounded by a bristling beard. Embarrassed, Sam jiggled the change in his pockets and pretended to study the newspaper covers as he tried to decide his next move. He just couldn't do it; he bit his lip. He couldn't bring himself to ask this completely unremarkable and hardworking New Yorker about Sybylla's demons. Sam frowned down at the *Village Voice* (city Housing Authority scandal) and *Newsday* (bodies in a landfill on Long Island) and the *Daily News* (Donald Trump's love life). The afternoon edition of the *Post,* he noted grimly, boasted the very subject matter he wished most to avoid—a photograph of Dermot Muldoon before the Judiciary Committee, his face lank and pale. MULDOON BEGINS TO SHOW STRAIN, the text read. And above his right shoulder, the blurry upper half of a body with which Sam had recently been on intimate terms. So at least he knew where Sybylla was, Sam thought grimly. He reached defiantly for Donald Trump.

"Thanks," a voice said. Then: "Hey, it's you."

Sam looked up. The man was grinning at him. "I'm sorry," Sam heard himself say, apologizing for his own ridiculous subterfuge. He finished with a shrug.

"Don't blame you." Wade Jones grinned, misunderstanding. "Your line of work, you probably see lots." He nodded, agreeable. "Mine, too."

"Yes." Sam rolled the paper in his fist.

"It was that case. The black guy raped all those women uptown. You defended him." He said apologetically, "Sorry about that. Just . . . what we had to do, y'know?"

Sam frowned. "I'm sorry?"

"The . . . we convicted him. *You* know." He smirked, bashfully proud. "I was jury foreman."

"Ohhhh." Sam nodded. "Of course. Mr. Jones. Of course I remember you. Well, nice to see you." He wanted to quit while he was still ahead of the game. He took a step back, ready to turn.

Ignoring the hint, the newsstand owner continued, "Thought I'd take the opportunity, you know. I looked for you after the trial and everything, but you must've gone already. Just to say I was sorry and all."

Sam frowned. "Why should you be sorry? You mean because of the guilty verdict? You don't have to apologize for that. It was your job to render a verdict. You can't please everybody with a decision like that."

Jones paused to give change to a woman in a long raincoat. "No, I know, s'just . . . well, you did a good job and all. I mean, defending the guy. It wasn't, like, an easy verdict and everything. The way you talked about how those women hadn't really seen the man, only smelled him? And hell, *I* wear Old Spice; my daughter gives it to me every Father's Day, Chrissake. So I just kept thinking, you know, that it could have been me."

Sam sighed. "Well, identification is always an inexact kind of thing—especially when people have been traumatized. Sometimes, under stress, it's all they can do just to zero in on one aspect of how a person appears—a scar, a hairstyle, something in the voice. In this case, it was the smell. Quite frankly, there were several troubling aspects about that case, but they're being taken up on appeal, and they don't reflect at all on what the jury did in its deliberations. They have to do with what I was and was not allowed to tell the jury. So you needn't be sorry in the least—that's what I'm trying to say. You went into the jury room and you fought it out among yourselves and arrived at a verdict."

"Well, yeah." Wade Jones nodded. "But I mean, no, that's what I wanted to say I was sorry about. Because we didn't really do that—deliberate like that."

Somewhere at the base of Sam's skull, a tiny flicker of pain popped to life. He ignored it.

"You didn't deliberate?"

"Well, not too hard. See, some of us felt like we didn't want to beat our heads against the wall. No point, like. So when we saw the lay of the land, we just sort of said okay." He set his jaw and let his eyes drift right. "I don't mean we started out to do a rough job. I was foreman and I ran it according to the rule sheet they gave me. First vote was seven to five to convict the guy, so we set down to talk about it like we're supposed to. And people seemed willing. It was two in the afternoon or something, so nobody was going to work that day anyway, and we started to say, right, this is why I think maybe he's guilty or this is why I'm not sure, because of the identification and all, and everybody's doing this except this one lady on the jury who's just sitting there smiling at us. So finally I says to her, you know, 'Miss, what do you think?' And she just starts talking about the crime and what these women went through and how the police would never have caught the guy if that one victim hadn't seen him on the street and followed him even though she was scared, and this was like a testament to her bravery and all, which it *was.* I mean, we're all sitting there nodding like we're all suddenly convinced that this guy was the *right* guy, which is the thing we're supposed to be *deciding.* Right?"

"Right," Sam said. It came out sounding like a question.

"So then she starts to talk about how the city never used to be like this. It used to be that a violent crime like that would be a really rare and terrible thing, but now we're just so calm about it. Like we're sitting here thinking about the teeny tiny little chance that this wasn't the guy who raped all those women, when the women themselves say it is, and what an insult that is to the people who got hurt and then did everything right by telling the police and agreeing to testify about it, not to mention helping them catch the guy and probably saving a lot of other women from having the same thing happen to them. And, I don't know, the more she talked, the more the rest of us start to think about other crimes we read about, or that happened to people we know, and we all start telling each other about those crimes. You know, a friend of this gal my wife works with got raped in an elevator in her building in Queens and nobody ever caught the guy. Somebody else starts talking about a little girl who turned up in some ice cooler in Brooklyn, dead, and they don't even know who she was. And pretty soon it's like we feel that we got this chance to do one small thing right. I mean, they caught the guy, and they put him on trial, and all the victims were there saying what happened to them, and what are we gonna do? Send him home just like that?"

Sam sighed. "But I still don't see . . . Look, maybe it wasn't a deliberation like in a film. So you didn't draw diagrams and act out the crime or anything, but you still deliberated. This lady was just very persuasive. She persuaded you."

"Yeah, but she didn't." He turned to reach above his head for a *Penthouse,* which he passed to a man in a business suit. "All she did was make us stop thinking about all the . . . the main issues that was raised by you in the trial. And after she was done with this speech, I still felt like I wanted to talk about those things, but she said she wasn't ever going to change her vote. That was it. So if the rest of us wanted to keep talking, she didn't mind, but it was done for her. And by then, most of the people on the jury felt the same way as her, and there was only two or three of us left who wanted to keep talking, anyway. So we just looked at each other and said what the hell. You know? There wasn't any point going on with it. The best we coulda had out of that situation was a hung jury or something, and what's the use of that? So we just said fine, okay, and we stopped. But I felt bad about it, and that's why I wanted to say something to you."

Sam thoughtfully tapped his rolled-up paper against his other palm. "Well, thanks, Mr. Jones. I appreciate your honesty. But you still don't have to apologize. Juries are made up of ordinary citizens. That's the whole point of our legal system, that the people who judge us are just like us—our peers. We can't go expecting jurors to be superhuman. We just have to do the best we can with normal folks."

Wade Jones chuckled, revealing a blackened front tooth. "Yeah. Except this lady wasn't my idea of normal. You remember her?"

The little flicker of pain had descended Sam's neck. He still ignored it.

"Not really. It was a while—"

"Reddish hair? I mean bright red? And sorta white skin? Looked about in her sixties?" Sam smiled blankly. Discreetly, he checked his watch, anxious to get back to his desk. "All during the trial, this lady never said a word. You know, when they sent us out so you could talk about things without us hearing. We'd be chatting in the hall. Our kids, our jobs. Never the case or anything, but, you know how it is—chitchat. Current events. She just smiled, said yes or no, thanked you when you offered her a seat. I'll tell you the truth, she gave me the creeps after a while, the way she kind of watched. But I never changed my mind about her. You know, about her *type*." He paused. "Let me explain something to you, Mr. Larkin. I'm pretty good at reading people, and the truth about people is, there's not much more than a few types, no matter what they say about the gorgeous mosaic and that crap. Long time ago, after my first couple years in this business, it got so I could see somebody coming up the street to my stand and I'd know what paper or magazine they'd be after. You got your *Nation* or your *National Review*, see? The fashion mags or the skin mags or *Variety,* you can tell. I don't mean I'm never wrong, but most times I can tell when some kid's gonna try and hold me up or he's gonna buy a copy of *Spin.* And I'm telling you, this lady I got totally wrong."

"I suppose," Sam said vaguely, rubbing his neck. He didn't really see where this was going, but agreeing with the man seemed like a good exit line.

"You, too, you don't mind my saying."

He looked up, frowning.

"See, I only paid attention to this woman because you don't see too many like her anymore. Used to be her type all over the city. Your basic old lefty New Yorker, you know? Kind that used to run the Democratic clubs and run around registering people to vote? I gotta laugh. I had an aunt like that. Set up a table in front of Saks for the Urban League. Now, this lady on the jury said in the question and answers that she was retired but she did volunteer teaching with people who couldn't read. And she was wearing one of them red ribbon things that the movie stars wear, and singers. For AIDS, you know? So all the way through the trial I'm thinking we're gonna get back in that room and it's gonna be her saying that he looks like such a nice caring person, he couldn't have raped all those women. Or that he must've had a lot of pain in his life to get himself in this trouble. That kind of garbage. And here I'm thinking, you know, that maybe this just isn't the guy. Not that he's such a nice man or he must've been abused as a kid, but maybe they just picked the wrong *guy*, like you said." He shook his head. "I'm telling you, in the question and answers, I remember I thought that DA was just a moron to let this lady on. She looked all right. I mean, she wasn't wearing love beads or nothing, but you could tell." The man paused. "*I* could tell. Like I said, I know my types. I just asked myself, What's that DA doing letting a lefty like that on the panel? You'd think a person gets to be DA, he knows a thing or two about people. 'Specially a DA who's all fired up to run for governor. I had to shake my head, but then it turned out he was right about this lady all the time. You and me"—he nodded conspiratorially at Sam—"we was wrong. See what I mean?" He was waiting for Sam to agree.

"I guess. Yes, we were wrong."

"It was some show. We got back there, it was like she was this totally different person from what I thought. One minute she's the nice quiet lady with a red ribbon for the AIDS victims, teaches underprivileged people how to read, and then suddenly it's like that person stepped out for a smoke and Nancy Reagan moved in. Had us all revved up about the criminals and how we had to do our job, that's why we were there. I'm telling you, I don't get surprised by people much anymore, but this lady got me by the short hairs, you know?"

Sam nodded. His head was on fire.

"You all right?" said Wade Jones.

"I have to run," Sam said, his voice flat.

Wade Jones shrugged. So run, he was about to say, but Sam was already running.

CHAPTER THIRTY-SEVEN

"Where *is it?"*

She was still groggy when she felt his big hands reaching down to draw her up from the narrow couch. She did not know how long she had lain in the same comfortless position, wanting vaguely to move but unsure of how to begin, and oddly calm about the whole situation. She peered at him now, and the dimly remembered or fleetingly observed physical characteristics reconstituted themselves: closely cropped dark hair, a negligible neck, and a sneering down-turned mouth that would have suited somebody else's image of the hero in a romance novel. He was grinning at her, saying something asinine like "Upsy daisy" as Sybylla was settled against the back of the couch and her feet found the floor. She felt the cold and shuddered at it.

"Where is it, Sybylla?" She looked up. Robert Winston sat at ease behind the desk in Philip Hofmann's subterranean study, her own purse's contents arrayed before him on the desk. Amid the keys and wadded Kleenex and random ATM receipts, and beneath the dull silver of her Visa card, she could make out one red corner of the condom packet—unopened. She bit her lip to keep from showing her relief.

"Time is short, Sybylla. I wish it were not, but that is the reality of our situation. I must return to Washington for a cocktail party, and I haven't leisure to visit with you."

Cocktail equals evening, she thought wildly. It's evening.

Across the room, Winston appeared to relax, slightly but perceptibly. He even smiled his unsettling smile. "You are perhaps thinking that you will not tell me where my property is. Let me assure you, Sybylla, that ultimately you *will* tell me. Can we not, then, skip all the unpleasantness that must occur between this point and that? It will save you considerable distress, and me considerable time." He glanced at his watch. "And time is precious, my dear. More precious, perhaps, than it has ever been to you before."

Then, to accentuate his point, he made the introductions. "My associate, Mr. Kolb. I don't believe you two have met."

Sybylla smiled bleakly and found her voice. "Not formally. But I think he's been in my drawers, so to speak."

Winston nodded. He wasn't bothering to deny it, and that, Sybylla grimly understood, meant that she would never be safe again.

"Looking for my own property, yes. I regret the inconvenience." He was leaning back a little in his chair. He seemed not to be in a hurry to speak, and when he did, at last, it was to express an unanticipated regret.

"You know," said Robert Winston, "I am sorry to see you here. I mean this with all sincerity. Your being here—your sitting there on that couch—means that every one of the many precautions I took to prevent this has failed, and naturally I accept responsibility for my part in that, though you, too, must bear a certain degree of guilt for your sheer pig-headedness. I think you'll agree that I sent you many warnings, Sybylla. I assumed that a simple request from Dermot would end the matter, but I failed to realize the extent of your willfulness where your father is concerned. I can tell you quite candidly that if a child of mine had refused my specific request, I would have given her the back of my hand without delay."

"If that's your idea of childrearing," Sybylla said dryly, "I certainly hope you don't have children."

The briefest flicker of distaste crossed his face, but then it was gone. "I didn't think you would prove so recalcitrant. I never imagined that you would allow your allegiance to a thankless client to carry more weight than your own father's wishes."

Declining the guilt, Sybylla rallied.

"Well, Mr. Winston, I'm sorry to be here, too. I hate to think I'm adding to your already-impressive list of felonies. Let's see, we're already looking at abductions in multiple figures, aren't we? Plus jury tampering on a rather ambitious scale. Not to mention unauthorized medical experimentation on human beings, of course. And then there's the little question of where all those people go after they finish subverting American justice. Where *do* they go?"

Winston tapped a cheek with his forefinger and sighed.

"What is your vision exactly, Mr. Winston? Throw out the entire concept of trial by jury and install trial by Winston?"

Amused, he shook his head. "Not at all, my dear. I have no wish to stand in judgment on my fellowman, though I doubt you'll believe me. I do, however, feel that many aspects of our system of criminal trials are outdated, and the concept of trial by jury is perhaps the most outdated of them all. The fact is that with certain of our modern forensic sciences, the ability to discern guilt becomes fairly absolute. DNA analysis, for example, can prove a rapist's identity beyond a shadow of a doubt. It could not even have been imagined fifty years ago, and yet it is in common usage today."

"So what's the problem? With all this proof running around, you should be satisfied."

"Ah," Winston said. "But this is precisely where we run into the problem of the modern jury." He paused. "I want you to think about something, Sybylla. I want you to think about what you look for in a prospective juror. Can you tell me that?"

"Certainly." She heard the righteousness in her own voice. "I'm looking for someone who is open-minded. Who hasn't already made up his or her mind."

"Which translates, if I may take the liberty of saying so, to someone who is both stupid and ignorant."

She shifted uncomfortably in her seat.

"More than a little accurate, isn't it? After all, you can't have jurors who know anything about your case beforehand, which means that people who read the newspapers or even watch the dross that passes for television news are out. And pity the poor defendants of highly publicized cases who have to round up twelve bona fide idiots for their trials. Twelve people who had never heard of Oliver North sitting in judgment on his actions—preposterous! And *stupid*. More often than not, legal scholars can't make any sense of jury decisions. It's as if the panel simply got tired and flipped a coin, and naturally they don't have to justify their conclusions." He smiled at Sybylla. "I hope you've never made the mistake of asking one of your panels why they voted the way they did. Most distressing. They say things like 'The defendant looked so sweet,' or they didn't like the victim's hairstyle. Points of evidence? Occasionally. Points of law? Never. And this is our system. These are the people we look to for justice."

"But from what you describe," Sybylla objected, "they convict inappropriately just as often as they acquit."

"That is not what I describe. I describe a system in which defendants who have any intelligence at all forgo plea bargains in favor of jury trials because they know that a good defense attorney can so confound the average jury with one tiny inconsistency of testimony that they will acquit. And those inconsistencies may abound—by the time a case comes to trial, memories have grown dim and witnesses are nowhere to be found. So the lesson is that a jury trial is the best way to avoid conviction. Is that fair?"

"It's fair for a defendant to be confronted by his accusers. It's fair that there should be evidence for his having committed the crime he's charged with."

"But what evidence is really good enough for the modern jury?" He was watching her with a fixed but impassive gaze. "They are too used to the idea that reality is malleable, that it can be altered at will, like television. It's something that must be faced, Sybylla. It's a sad fact, but we can no longer trust juries to do what they are charged with doing. Perhaps it is simply too difficult a task, or perhaps our fortitude as individuals in this society has atrophied to such an extent that we are just no longer up to it. The cause, however, is ultimately irrelevant to the situation and the lesson it teaches. The lesson is we must simply look elsewhere for our justice."

She eyed him. "In other words, we must look to you and your Eumenides Project."

He nodded amiably. "Yes, precisely so."

"You're a man with a mission," she observed dryly.

"In part. But foremost, I am an entrepreneur. My partner, Dr. Hofmann, whom you have not met, may pursue the grail of pure science, but my own quest has been more mundane: to identify and then respond to a niche in the marketplace."

"And with so many ambitious prosecuting attorneys around, those niches must be popping up all over the country."

"Just so." Winston nodded.

"And LRA is merely a cover?" Sybylla asked.

"Oh, not at all. I'm surprised at you. How can you say such a thing after touring the facility upstairs? LRA is a thriving consulting firm, providing an array of profoundly effective services. From LRA alone, I could retire today, an extremely wealthy man. Now"—he leaned forward in his chair, his elbows braced on the desk—"if we have reached the end of your questions, I suggest we move ahead to the matter at hand."

Sybylla shook her head quickly. "It must cost a lot. I mean, to partake of the fruits of the Eumenides Project. Not for the underfinanced, am I correct?"

"You are correct, certainly. The services of the Eumenides Project are available to or, more accurately, reserved for clients who meet certain criteria. They must, if you will, be our friends. They must have substantial political potential. And of course the cases in question must also meet set standards. We do not waste our subjects on trials that are likely to receive little attention or have negligible legal implications. We are interested in setting legal precedents that will resonate in future interpretations of the law. And, naturally, we are interested in investing in promising careers."

"Ah yes. All those future senators and governors. Maybe even a President or two."

"In time," Winston agreed, "maybe so."

"And what do these favored few get for their money?"

"A conviction, of course," he said amiably. "Technically we guarantee only a mistrial, but in over four hundred trials, our subjects have very rarely failed to persuade their juries to convict. Our client gets a prospective juror who looks good to the defense, a person who appears intelligent and compassionate and avows that he knows nothing about the case at hand and has an entirely open mind. What our clients get, my dear, is a kind of legal virus, capable of entering a cell and replicating its information until the cell is transformed. Our subjects are well briefed about the case they will be observing. They are given a range of persuasive arguments and cogent personal insights. Finally, they are precisely instructed in the fine art of strong-arming their fellow jurors. It takes a rare panel to continue deliberating when one member remains unbudgeable."

"Failure to deliberate is grounds for a mistrial."

"Of course, but before declaring one, a judge will send the jurors back again and again. Overwhelmingly, our juror's obstinacy in conjunction with his eloquence will result in a conviction."

She frowned. "How do you get this . . . *subject* into the right voir dire in the first place? How do you get their name drawn from the drum?"

Winston nodded. "As you know, we have no unified practice of providing jury panels to voir dires in this country, but always there is some randomizing practice in use. Some jurisdictions use a drum, others a computer. There are probably courthouses where they throw the cards up in the air, for all I know, but however the randomizing is accomplished, we concluded long ago that interfering with that process left us too prone to exposure. We couldn't go paying off court officers to pull our jurors' names in every courthouse in America, after all—not if we hoped to remain undetected. So we turned our attention to what happens next in the selection process."

Sybylla frowned. "I don't understand. Do you mean the voir dire itself?"

"No. Court records must show that those names drawn for a particular voir dire must present themselves for that voir dire. We merely approach one of those prospective jurors en route to the courtroom—we call them aside, by name—and tell them they have been excused and may leave."

Dimly, she waited for him to continue. "You're kidding. That's it?"

"That's it. It never fails. People are thrilled to be able to go. We watch them as they arrive, you see. We take note of the ones who are especially argumentative with the clerks, those who complain to the other potential jurors. Then, if they are called for our trial and if they match the gender of our prepared subject, we call them aside. 'Didn't you ask to be excused? Well, the judge has just authorized us to release three individuals from the panel, so you may leave without penalty.' They hand over their slips, we inform the subject of his or her new name, and so it goes."

"And this works?" She was awestruck.

Winston smiled. "Never underestimate the eagerness of good citizens to shirk their civic duty."

And she blushed, remembering her own frustration at not being allowed out of the Old Spice voir dire, so imponderably long ago.

"What happens then? You tell your DA to look out for a tall woman with a rose behind her left ear and warn him that when this person comes up for voir dire, he should just ignore the fact that she subscribes to *Mother Jones* and let her on the panel?"

Winston sighed. "We merely give our client the juror's name. He does the rest. These are not stupid people, Sybylla. They have, after all, already achieved the position of district attorney."

It was overwhelming, she thought, the sheer scope of it, the audacity of it, and the fact that it had actually been working. She shook her head. "So much for 'a jury of his peers.' "

" 'A jury of his peers,' " Winston mused. "At best, a troublesome notion; at worst, downright absurd. Let me ask you something, Sybylla. Who are the peers of a criminal? Other criminals? Shouldn't we, by rights, be trawling the prisons for juries to judge their comrades? And where do we stop? If the defendant is poor and black, then surely those who sit in judgment of his actions should know how it feels to be poor and black. Child molesters should be judged by those who know the agony of desiring to harm children. Wife beaters should be judged by those who have beaten their own wives and can therefore best decide whether the victim 'deserved it.' Yes, you look horrified. It's a horrific notion, isn't it? Because the truth is that we have no peers, not really. We have always had to summon within ourselves the arrogance that resides there if we wish to judge our fellowman. I am merely honest about that arrogance. 'A jury of his peers.' " He sighed. "Only the most archaic aspect of our rotting trial system."

"What happens to the subject when it's all over?" She was blunt. For the first time in their interview, Winston seemed reluctant.

"We learn a good deal from debriefing them," he said finally. "We are constantly engaged in refining the treatment by which subjects are prepared for trials. We try new subtleties in their character backgrounds, in their way of speaking, their personal appearances, and naturally in the arguments they employ in the jury room."

"I meant after that."

"Depends," he said shortly.

"Ah," she said. "On what?"

"On whether the subject can be refitted, as it were, for another trial

Some subjects have successfully gone on to do one or even two more trials. Most, however, are no longer useful to us after their first."

"Sad," she commented. "All that work."

He smiled at her and shrugged. "As I said before, money is not our primary motive in this endeavor. We reap our rewards in other ways."

"Let me guess. You like getting invited to the best parties in Washington."

He pursed his lips. "Perhaps, something like that. And now, enough digression. Not that I haven't enjoyed our talk, but our time together grows very short. If you do not tell me where my implant is, Sybylla, I shall be forced to surrender you to the efforts of Mr. Kolb, who is very able in these matters. I urge you to avoid this. I do not think I would be able to face your father afterward."

Sybylla turned. The hulking man was still leaning back against the door. Expressionless, he nonetheless managed to communicate a pure and persuasive malice. She forced herself to face Winston again.

"Since you mentioned my father, I should tell you that I'm supposed to be meeting him for dinner tonight. If I don't show up, I'm sure he'll wonder where I am."

This seemed not to produce the desired effect. Winston merely nodded pensively at the mess of detritus and ephemera before him on the desk, then told her that she needn't worry, since he was sure Dermot knew precisely where his daughter was.

She felt a numbness ascending her legs from the frigid stone floor. Then a rush of even colder air hit the back of her neck as the office door opened and a small figure rushed in.

"Robert," a little voice said, "we need Kolb."

Winston's displeasure was plain. Irresistibly, Sybylla turned to look. The interloper was wiry and short, with surprisingly diminutive hands, and it took her a long moment to recognize him as the fourth, unidentified figure in her parents' photograph. He stood in the open doorway, visibly vibrating with tension, his jaw set in what seemed an unintended parody of rage. He glared at Winston, who took a moment to respond.

"Mr. Kolb is required here, Philip."

"Mr. Kolb is required in the garage. An unauthorized car's just entered the tunnel."

Winston scowled, first at the man in the doorway, then at the desktop, and finally at the StairMaster man himself. "All right, Kolb. Check it out, but come right back. We have to finish this tonight."

Finish *me,* Sybylla thought. Her mind raced. Behind her, the door snapped shut.

Winston said her name, then added, "I would like to introduce you to Philip Hofmann."

The small man walked forward, making an arc around her place on the couch as if she were something that might contaminate him with proximity, but staring at her as he went. He took a seat on the opposite side of the room and crossed his thin legs stiffly, his gaze still burning into her face.

"Technically, Philip should be doing the honors here," Winston said helpfully. "Not only are we in his office, we are also very much in his domain. This place"—he spread his hands—"this facility, is Philip's world, you see. His creation, even more than my own. It is his specific genius that has made possible the breakthroughs of which we are both so proud."

"Nice to take pride in one's work," Sybylla commented.

"You must forgive him for staring," Winston told her, an edge of amusement in his tone. "He hasn't seen you since you were a very small child, still a baby. Isn't that so, Philip?"

The small man didn't bother to nod. "It's amazing, the resemblance." He leaned slightly forward in his chair. "Your mother was a beautiful woman, too."

"You forget," Winston said tightly, "Sybylla never knew her mother." She was looking at the man's hands. They were remarkable, delicate, almost childlike. She easily understood how she might have mistaken one of them for one of her mother's all these years.

"I remember the first time I met Nuala," he said, pointedly ignoring Winston. "Your father brought her out to dinner with Robert and me. Some dive near MIT. We had to be careful around Dermot, not to offend him, you see. Because it was his occasion that night. He was bringing this woman to meet his friends, you understand, and he didn't want her to see that he couldn't pay for the meal."

His partner glared at him. "I've just been informing Sybylla that we are somewhat pressed for time, Philip. She was about to tell me where she has hidden our implant when you interrupted us."

Sybylla found her voice. "And I *will* tell you," she heard herself say. "But first, if you don't mind, I'd like to hear a little more. About your work." She turned to Hofmann and offered a fawning smile. "It must have taken you years to perfect the implant." She made herself hold his gaze as he seemed to weigh her sincerity against his own self-regard. Then, with the delight only a rare opportunity for a favorite activity can provide, Hofmann began to speak.

"I was chief resident in psychiatry at a hospital in Cambridge when Robert and I first met," he told her. "It was the early sixties, though the period really had more in common with the decade just past than with what we generally think of as 'the sixties' today. By that time, the CIA had been working with LSD in earnest for about a decade, after trying their luck with cocaine and a few other, even more colorful drugs. All part of an effort to refine interrogation techniques, create a kind of truth serum for the next world war. They didn't have much success—the drugs they were using made any kind of hypnosis impossible—but when LSD turned up, hopes were running pretty high. This was the first drug they'd seen that required extremely small doses to be effective, and one that seemed to produce no significant aftereffects. They were quite taken with the notion that a few drops of such a substance in, for example, an enemy's water supply could conceivably render a considerable amount of the population helpless, and needless to say, they were equally concerned that somebody else might have had that same idea before they did."

"But what did any of that have to do with you?" she asked. "Didn't you say you were a psychiatrist? What did you care about interrogation techniques?"

"Me? I couldn't have cared less." He smiled at Sybylla. The smile looked strange on him, as if he had been misinformed about what smiles were supposed to signify. "But a lot of money was being thrown around for research at that time, and some of it came my way. The government didn't know where the breakthrough was going to come, so they provided LSD and funding to anyone and everyone who might learn something by working with it. Some of it came my way." He straightened in his chair. As if he's uncomfortable, Sybylla thought. Then she understood that she was seeing pride, not discomfort. "In fact, mine were among the very first experiments."

"*Experiments,*" she said, an unwisely caustic edge to her voice. "By which you mean, of course, the administering of this hallucinogenic drug to people incapable of informed consent."

"The results were fascinating," he went on, swept up in his own nostalgia. "Erratic, naturally, as befits early, primitive research. But it was clear to us that the drug's potential as an effective therapy for schizophrenia and other delusional illnesses was profound. Government labs all over the country were labeling LSD a psychosis-inducing agent. 'Instant madness'! But before our eyes, we were discovering this extraordinary property."

"You mean the government was giving acid to sane people to make them crazy and you were giving it to crazy people to make them sane."

Hofmann sighed: the scientist's grudging tolerance for the layperson. "I suppose. It was only the beginning for us. We had opened a door, and what we could see beyond was vastly promising. I began a series of experiments with"—he paused to sneer his displeasure—"rather substantial government support."

"And you didn't care what the government wanted to do with your research?"

For an instant, Sybylla saw rage—an intense, withering rage—cross his features. Then it was gone. When he spoke, his voice was tamped down—a hiss.

"I cared about my work. I have always cared about my work, above anything else. The world goes on in its own madness. I can do nothing for it. I can only press forward with my own individual road. I do not expect adulation, or even recognition. I merely ask to be left alone to do what I am called to do."

She swallowed, then bit her lip.

"I began to work with LSD in combination with other drugs—scopolamine, for example, which seemed to enhance the sense of serenity in those schizophrenics who received the LSD doses. I tried different behavioral therapies, such as sleep therapies in combination with tape-recorded messages. I also developed a therapy called 'depatterning,' which utilized electroshock in conjunction with LSD. I began to refine the sizes and frequency of the doses. My results were extraordinary. Through the network of scientists who were working with lysergic acid, I became very well known, and even those psychiatrists and neurologists who were not experimenting with the drug heard of my work. I understood that this work was my purpose, and that I was fulfilling it, each day moving closer to an end of the suffering of mental illness."

He stopped. His passion lingered in the air.

"So?" Sybylla gave in to her suspense. "Then what?"

Winston stirred. "Then it stopped," he said helpfully. "It just stopped."

She frowned. "I don't understand. What about all that promising research? Isn't that what the government wanted?"

"I thought it was." Hofmann spoke with real bitterness, as if the ax had fallen only on him and only this morning, rather than three decades before. "LSD had begun to evade government containment almost from the beginning, and now it was becoming widely known among the public that the drug existed and had what were being described as 'consciousness-raising' properties. Suddenly, people were clamoring for the very same compound that was being groomed as a madness-inducing agent. It all came to a head at the first international conference devoted to LSD. There were a few researchers there who reported that their subjects who had had LSD therapy had found it useful, even rewarding, and they were anxious to take the drug again. This, as you know, was the line that would be taken up a few years later by Dr. Leary at Harvard, and subsequently by a significant fraction of the American population under the age of thirty, but at that time, such a notion was scandalous. There was a schism, of course, and shortly afterward the government found itself forced to commit to only one appraisal of LSD. Not surprisingly, they chose the road they'd been on all along: that LSD was a dangerous drug that made people crazy. The hoopla about personal growth and mind expansion was an aberration. Naturally, they couldn't be seen to be working with a drug that they would be vociferously condemning by the end of the decade, so they began to terminate their research endeavors. The money dried up, and my work, the work that held so much promise for so many mental patients, was simply abandoned."

"Must have been a blow," she said carefully.

Hofmann studied her. "A blow. Yes."

"More than that," Winston interjected. "Philip was at a critical moment in his research. He had just begun to formulate the concept of lysergic acid administered in implant form. It was clear to me, if not to those philistines who had previously funded his work, that Philip's research could have a profound impact on a range of societal arenas. The CIA was interested in assassins. That was their business. I was a lawyer, so my interests ran in a different direction. When I began to underwrite the work that would evolve into the Eumenides Project, Philip moderated the direction of his research without moderating his scientific goals."

She decided to try a different tack. "What about Trent? Would you mind telling me how my client served this noble goal of scientific enlightenment?"

"Trent," Winston said shortly, "was an error. An error from the very beginning."

"Whose error?" she asked.

"Your friend Cleve Rivera's. He presented himself to us as someone who knew the shelter system and the street scene intimately, who could help us pick up prospective subjects without attracting undue attention. One of our team members found Trent for us. Then we sent Cleve to pick him up. I don't know what happened. The team member still insists that the man he observed was a highly delusional schizophrenic."

Sybylla felt herself nod. "He was. He still is. But he wasn't Trent. The resemblance, I'll admit, is striking, but I'm sorry to tell you that your chosen 'subject' is right where you left him under the Queensboro Bridge. I believe his name is Paul."

Winston mulled this over. Then he shook his head.

"So when he screamed and yelled, you just thought he was acting like the loony he'd been billed as. Very nice."

"As I said," Winston muttered shortly, "an error."

"And all the time he spent here, you still didn't pick it up. I'm sorry, Dr. Hofmann. I'm not a scientist, but it seems pretty sloppy to me. Didn't you think it was strange when the LSD implant didn't calm him down?"

"We did," Hofmann said stiffly. "We thought it was very strange. But by then, we had other things to ponder, more pressing things. Like the fact that he had somehow gained possession of a scalpel and slashed one of the research assistants. After that, he somehow managed to get himself out of the complex."

Winston's long finger tapped the desktop. "The rest I think you've gleaned, Sybylla. We quickly discerned that your Wild Man and our missing subject were one and the same. The attention focused on Trent made things quite tricky for us, and we elected to sit back and wait to see what ensued. If, as we hoped, the implant remained undiscovered, then it seemed desirable merely to let the situation play itself out. Trent was obviously unfit to stand trial, and the issue would disappear with him into whatever hospital the city saw fit to house him in. Unfortunately, the implant was indeed discovered, but even then we elected to wait. Your involvement played a part in that decision, certainly. We did not wish any harm to come to you, Sybylla."

"I appreciate your concern," she said, as if it was still true.

"Naturally, we took pains to recover the implant. We did not make those decisions lightly, nor without regret, but we could not permit the possibility that the disk would be analyzed and that analysis publicized in any way. When we did not find the implant in your friend's lab, we searched your apartment." He smiled. "But of course you know that."

"Mr. Kolb was not subtle."

"People are strange," he mused. "Who would imagine your Dr. Patel would entrust an item of such significance to her aerobics instructor?" Winston frowned, abruptly somber again. "I want you to know that even when the trial began, we still had hopes that the matter would not require our further intervention. Your intention of pursuing an insanity defense had been established, and we were content to let that play itself out. In fact, I've little doubt you could have pulled off an acquittal—you're a potent advocate."

"Why didn't you just put one of your *subjects* on the jury? Then you needn't have worried about an acquittal at all."

"But we weren't worried," Winston corrected. "That is, what happened to Trent was not an issue for us. We were only concerned with what might be said about Trent's condition in open court. And accordingly, when I learned that you were questioning the psychiatrist about LSD, I became alarmed. I understood that you had misled us, Sybylla. At that point, it became imperative that the trial not proceed."

"So you provided a little emergency for Greer. And an assassin for Trent. Mr. Kolb again?"

"I'm sure you understand," he said simply.

"How did you kill him?" Winston was silent. "Just curious." She shrugged. "The pathologist said natural causes. Pulmonary embolism, I think."

He sighed, as if the topic was inexcusably boring. "*Air* embolism. Very simple and very neat. A syringeful of air, directly into a vein. A few minutes later, it ends up in the lung, causing pulmonary embolism, or in the brain, causing a major stroke, and that's that. Mr. Kolb uses a vein between the toes. It's extremely clean. Sometimes you get a little bruising near the site, but if you don't know what you're looking for, you tend to miss it."

She shut her eyes and, with a powerful rush, the image of Trent's unlaced shoe materialized before her.

"I still had the implant, though. And I still had Patel's lab report on it. Why didn't you come after me again?"

Winston smiled sadly at her. "I should have. I see that now. But at the time, I was betting on your letting the matter drop. Your father's hearings were under way; I assumed you'd be distracted. Finally, I hoped you had gotten the message that we took our security seriously. You hadn't, obviously. When you rang me at LRA to ask for a job, I was truly prepared to give you the benefit of the doubt." He nodded pointedly at her. "You are a gifted liar."

For a long moment, they stared at each other.

"Which brings us here." Winston's voice was newly soft. "Which brings us to this moment. My dear Sybylla, I'm sorry to say that I have no more doubt to give you the benefit of. Your purpose in coming to Washington was to expose the Eumenides Project, and you'll understand that I cannot allow that to happen. Now"—he set his jaw—"shall we wait for Mr. Kolb to return, or will you take this last opportunity to tell me without benefit of his encouragement?" He gave her a moment to consider these equally unappealing options. Sybylla tried to swallow, but her throat had ceased to cooperate. Vaguely, she wondered if she would ever breathe again.

Winston shook his silver head. "My dear, what a strange woman you have grown into. Your heredity, your upbringing . . . It's such a mystery." Ruefully, he smiled down at her scattered belongings on the desk before him. Then, without warning, his elongated finger parted the objects with an appalling inquisitiveness. She watched with a sinking heart as he found and extracted the red condom packet, then, in sickening slow motion, held it up to the desk light. "When I was your age," Winston said thoughtfully, "it was the gentleman who carried these."

Sybylla grimaced. "Those were the days, eh?" she managed. "*Kinder, Küche, Kirch* and all that." Her hands were clasped in her lap. They felt icy and wet.

He was staring at the condom. He frowned at it, then, with an almost-respectful nod, took hold of one corner of the foil and peeled it back. From his chair, Philip Hofmann sighed audibly.

"I see we will not have to wait for Mr. Kolb after all," Winston said thoughtfully. He got to his feet.

Sybylla's head was throbbing. She felt sweat break across her forehead. Winston put the implant in his breast pocket.

"My father kept a list," she said. Surprised, she sat up straight. She hadn't planned it, and she was far from sure what it meant, but it obviously meant something to Winston. His eyes widened, then narrowed.

"A list."

"A list of all your cases," she sputtered, gaining momentum. "A list of the entire Eumenides Project. He had it this morning in Washington—in his jacket pocket. I'm well aware that he's been covering for you for years, but do you really think he'd let the murder of his only child pass without any response? Fairly high risk, wouldn't you say?"

"A list." He seemed still to be grappling with the very concept. Smoothly, as if to belie the significance of the action, he took his seat again. "Tell me, Sybylla, what sort of list would that be?"

"Case titles—from a few months ago to way back in the early seventies. I have no way of knowing whether it's complete." She grinned. "But it's damn long. Enough to make a lot of current and former DAs pretty uncomfortable. Enough to make you as famous as G. Gordon Liddy."

"I don't believe you."

She frowned in mock concern. "Well, that is certainly your privilege, Mr. Winston. It seems unwise to me, is all."

"Tell me some of the names from this list," he challenged.

She nodded. "Happy to oblige. The last name was *New York* v. *Larry Randolph Jackson.* Ring a bell?"

The change was subtle, but she noted it nonetheless. A slight acceleration of breathing.

"And the first name?"

She closed her eyes. It came to her. "Dunay. *Louisiana* v. *George Washington Dunay.*"

Suddenly, everything changed. Winston relaxed into his chair. His grin was easy again, and wide, showing his ridiculously bright teeth. "I'm sorry to have to tell you this, Sybylla, but Dermot's record keeping has been unaccountably sloppy. The Eumenides Project's first case was not *Louisiana* v. *Dunay.* It wasn't a Louisiana case at all. It took place a few miles from here, in the District of Columbia. It was called *United States* v. *Fentano.*"

Ten seconds later, it hit. The tears had reached her neck before their coldness against her skin alerted her that she was crying. She felt the pain of it descend, twisting through her, spreading the awareness that it was true. It was true.

"Oh, don't look so disappointed, my dear." Winston was smugly soothing. "You must understand how things stood at the time. Your father was drinking himself to death in New York. He would trundle into work around noon, sit at his desk for a few hours, pretending he wasn't dying for a shot of whiskey, then dash out at four. He hadn't tried a case in nearly two years when they finally let him go. I'm sure you were too young to remember this time, but I can tell you that it was extraordinarily painful to watch my friend self-destruct. It was the pain of your mother's loss that began it, of course, but over the next three or four years, he never managed to pull himself together. His situation was desperate, Sybylla, but he was our friend. Philip's and mine. And so we helped him, and in helping him, we helped ourselves. That is the nature of friendship, I think."

Winston leaned back in his chair, serene. He pursed his lips, as if remembering something pleasant.

"We were ready to proceed with our first jury plant. Or we thought we were. But we were not yet in a position to offer a client any real confidence in our service, let alone the guarantee that we wished to give. We needed to work with someone who was intimate with the details of what we had done, someone who understood how the procedure would work. And that had to be a person who could afford the kind of risk we were asking him to take."

"You mean someone with nothing to lose," she heard herself say, in an approximation of her own voice.

"I do. Fortunately, they took him on in D.C., at my recommendation. And when the time came, our maiden subject performed beautifully. She single-handedly won over the two holdout jurors on the panel, and the jury reached a verdict in under eight hours on an extraordinarily complex case. It was a dual victory, my dear—for Dermot, who rebounded in his career by riding the Fentano victory, and for us. With our battle stripes earned, so to speak, we were able to launch the Eumenides Project in earnest. We are grateful to your father, and"—he nodded meaningfully at Sybylla—"I know he is grateful to us." He paused, pursing his lips. "You'll forgive me, then, if I decline to feel threatened by Dermot's so-called list. He can't destroy us without destroying himself, and I don't believe that he would ever do that. Particularly at this moment in his life, with all he has worked for so nearly in his grasp. You understand why I am so confident in this."

"He kept it for a reason," she managed to say. "Obviously, to use it against you."

"Quite possibly," Winston agreed, looking downright unperturbed. "And yet I maintain my confidence. Shall I tell you why?"

She looked up at him.

"It isn't only his professional life that your father owes to Philip and me, Sybylla. It's something else, as well. Something I feel is equally precious to Dermot. Can you guess what that something is?"

Her thoughts tumbled. She could barely shake her head.

"How did your mother die, Sybylla?"

She felt her lips part to speak, but nothing came.

"Hemorrhage, was it? A few days after your birth?"

She finally managed to make her throat work. "Yes. Something happened. I . . . I don't know exactly what happened."

"Nor could you, my dear. I always told Dermot, 'One day, Sybylla will ask. She'll want details. And will you be prepared to give them to her?' "

"What are you talking about?" she gasped. "What do you know about my mother's death?"

Sitting stiffly in his corner, Hofmann spoke. "It isn't a question of her death," he said fiercely. "It's a question of her life. That she was capable of bearing a child was remarkable in itself. No one should understand that better than *you*," he said accusingly.

She looked back and forth between them, suspended in horror.

Winston was smiling, his white teeth alive with reflected light. "Nuala was lovely and intelligent. Her affection for your father was very clear, and there was every reason to believe that the marriage would be extremely happy. But after the first year, she began to withdraw. Depression, your father thought. She had been trying to conceive, you see, and had not been successful. He brought her to a psychiatrist. Not Philip. He did not want Philip to examine her, but no matter. The psychiatrist diagnosed schizophrenia. Dermot did not like the diagnosis, so he took your mother to another psychiatrist. Schizophrenia again. By this time, the episodes were becoming more pronounced and more frequent. She spoke to the air, Sybylla. There were memory lapses. She became fearful, and aggressive, and when she was not in one of her spells, she was desperately unhappy. Finally, Dermot allowed Philip to examine her."

Winston looked at his partner. Hofmann was ready to take up the thread.

"Of course, she was schizophrenic," he said happily. "Had been for years, though her condition had obviously degenerated, making her increasingly less functional. Dermot was being offered only one option by the shrinks he'd taken her to, and that was hospitalization—long-term, with no treatment plan. I had another option."

"An implant," Sybylla whispered, getting it at last.

"Not just an implant," he said avidly. "The first implant. Crude, certainly, but I knew what I was doing, and I knew I was right. When he gave me his consent to proceed, it was the first time since Robert had assumed patronage of my work that I truly felt I would succeed. Because it was a stunning success, young lady. Oh, at first your mother became quite lethargic. Sleeping fifteen, sixteen hours a day and drowsy the rest of the time. But cogent, and not unhappy. I redesigned the implant and tried again. And it was better. She got onto a normal schedule, and she was calm. And no more psychotic episodes. Not a one! Dermot was beside himself. He could barely contain his gratitude. Especially when she became pregnant a few months later."

Sybylla shook her head, stunned and repulsed. "Are you telling me my mother was receiving LSD all through her pregnancy?"

"Of course not," Hofmann snapped. "We removed the implant as soon as Nuala became pregnant, and she did surprisingly well, though whether because the LSD had had a lasting effect on her condition or whether the hormonal changes of the pregnancy had some curative effect, I can't really say. And you were perfectly fine when you were born. Absolutely normal. Well, you had a small defect, but nothing significant."

A small defect? She peered at them, speechless. Winston shrugged.

"A deformity of one of your earlobes. Entirely irrelevant as far as your development was concerned, and hardly compromising of your ultimate beauty, if I may say so." His tone was proprietorial, as if she were his handiwork. "We don't even know that the ear had anything to do with your exposure to the drug. It may have been a random defect, or perhaps not. But in either case, it does not seem to have harmed you in any way."

Beneath a heavy layer of bitterness, Sybylla found her voice. "But what about my mother? What happened to her then?"

Hofmann took over the narrative again. "The plan was to wait till the birth and then see how things developed; if she needed to be reimplanted, then so be it, and if not, so much the better."

"Well?" Sybylla asked. "Which was it?"

"It was neither." Winston sighed. "There is abundant literature, of course, concerning temporary psychosis in the postpartum period in mothers with no previous psychiatric histories, and one can only assume that the occurrence in diagnosed schizophrenics must be higher still. I'm sorry to tell you, Sybylla, that your mother was institutionalized within a few weeks of your birth. To my knowledge, she remained institutionalized until her death." He frowned, then turned to the little man. "When was it, Philip? Sixty-eight? Sixty-nine?"

Hofmann shrugged, untroubled.

The room had become so still, Sybylla thought. The force of gravity seemed to have surged and was holding everything down with a renewed vigor. Her feet, in particular, felt leaden, and the muscles of her face were being yanked toward the chilly floor of the room. I will never be able to move them again, she thought dimly. But then again, there would probably never be a reason to move them, anyway.

"A few years later, we might have been able to do much more for your mother, but as I said, she was really our commencement. What we learned from her was precious to us. And"—he nodded at Sybylla—"you were precious to your father. So you see how, in the end, we were bound together, Dermot and ourselves. Our fates were tied beyond even the force of our professional ambitions. When we approached him about Fentano, he felt duty-bound to accept our offer, for reasons that had nothing to do with his faltering career. He knew he owed your very existence to us."

Sybylla closed her eyes.

"And isn't it strange now that you, of all people, should appear to challenge our work. You, who have benefited perhaps more than any other person in this world from what we have done, and from an achievement, remember, that our government saw fit to strangle in its infancy. It is almost like a Greek tragedy, isn't it, Sybylla? Like Oedipus, who sets out to investigate the cause of his city's woes, only to find that the trail of blame leads irresistibly to the fact of his own existence."

"No," she heard herself whisper.

"And now, I'm afraid, I really must leave you. I'm already late for my cocktail party, even by Washington standards." He chuckled. She couldn't bear to look at him. Behind her, dimly, there was a knock at the door, a slow squeak as it opened.

"*Finally,*" said Winston. "Sybylla, you'll go with Mr. Kolb now. He'll—" He glanced up, and it seemed as if the words themselves had been knocked from his throat. "Well," he managed to say finally.

"Well," said another voice, a familiar voice. Sybylla turned.

He came in gravely, his face slack with fatigue, wearing the same clothing she had seen him dressed in hours earlier. It seemed to take him only an instant to reduce the situation to its essence, but then, that had always been her father's particular skill, Sybylla thought. Even now, she had an overwhelming urge to embrace him.

Dermot stepped inside, sweeping past her. He walked straight to the center of the room.

"I knew it would come to this," he observed. "All these years. It was only a matter of time before it all blew up. It's blown up now, my friend. The whole world is about to find out how you've been amusing yourself down here."

Winston's face stiffened. He looked as if he were teetering, unsure of where the solid ground began. "Dermot?"

Sybylla gripped the cushion of her couch to keep her balance.

"Dermot?" he said again. "You'd do that?"

"I'd do that." Her father's voice was even, disconcertingly calm.

The tall man's eyes were locked on Dermot's. "But why?"

"*Why?* Because this morning I told my daughter she was in no danger. I thought I was right, but I wasn't right. Why wasn't I right, Robert?"

"I'm sure you are capable of working that out, my friend," Winston said tightly.

Dermot smiled a tepid smile. "Wasn't it enough that you've made my career your plaything? How could you think I would tolerate your doing this to me?"

"*To* you?" He snorted. "I think you mean *for* you, old friend. For your life. For your goal. For everything you ever told me you wanted. And it's yours now, Dermot. It's in your hands. Now, quite naturally, this problem about Sybylla gives us all great pain, but I think we have always been in agreement on where our primary obligation lies." Disarmingly, he smiled. "I can remember when you used to argue that the responsibility of the law was to society at large, and its principles inevitably had to favor the interests of the community over those of the individual. Does it ring a bell, Dermot? Or have you merely elected to betray everything you've set your course by?"

Her father was shaking his head. "You really *don't* get it, do you? You know, for years I've wondered about this. Deep down, I always thought, Robert must get his—I don't know—human *contact* somewhere. He must *connect* with some person, sometime, somewhere. Except that you don't, I think. You lack even the most rudimentary understanding of what people can mean to one another."

"Fascinating." Winston was humorless. "Do you mind if I ask what this psychobabble has to do with our situation?"

Before Sybylla's eyes, her father exploded in outrage. "She's my *daughter,* you piece of shit. She's my child, my flesh. She will *always* be more important."

The tall man stared, uncomprehending. Sybylla felt her mouth fall open, heavy as lead.

Dermot was struggling to get himself under control. "So now it's over. Are you hearing this, Robert? I was there when we started and I'm here to see it end."

Winston seemed to recover first. He shook his head crisply. "The nomination."

"Over," Dermot snapped.

The tall man took this in with an expression of raw disbelief. "I am sorry to hear that—for both our sakes. I respect you far too much to attempt to dissuade you, however, if that is indeed your decision. But I'm certain you understand my own resolve, Dermot. If you are determined to deny yourself the rewards of all our hard work, then it must be so." He leaned over and retrieved a slender black case from the floor by his chair. Then, without turning his head, he spoke to Hofmann. "Go find me an orderly," he said shortly. "I'm not waiting for Kolb."

The little man got to his feet. His small head turned to consider the two men, first one, then the other. "And then I think I'll step out, if you don't mind." His voice was high and fragile with tension. "This isn't much in my line, Robert."

This, Sybylla thought, being what was about to happen to Dermot and herself.

Hofmann stepped out into the hall. She heard his voice, high and whiny and barely perturbed: "You. Orderly. You're needed here." Sybylla heard an approach of feet.

Winston was concentrating on the black briefcase, feeding in its security code. "I want you to take these two subjects to the retention area," he said without looking up. "They're lucid but very dangerous, so I'm going to give you my own gun."

A hand fell authoritatively on Sybylla's shoulder. She looked up.

"Fine," said Sam.

Sybylla got unsteadily to her feet. He stood beside her, bitterly familiar. The shine in his cursedly lovely black curls caught the greenish subterranean light, and he looked utterly at home in his orderly whites. The swirling pain of recent revelations did not quite obliterate this fresh new anguish. I was right, she thought, taking no pleasure in the fact. From the beginning. From the start, he was part of this. It tore at what was left of her heart. Now, too, it was more than her own life in question. Whatever horror she felt toward Dermot, she still rebuked herself for bringing him into this disaster. But for her, he might now be before the committee, defending his way into legal history.

"If they try to run," her father's old friend was telling Sam, "you'll need to use this." He handed over the gun and Sam took it. "You don't have a problem with that, do you?"

"No problem," Sam said, looking it over.

Then, with slow and deliberate care, he pointed it at Winston.

CHAPTER

THIRTY-NINE

—◆—

One long, airless moment later, it was Winston who broke the silence in a voice shot through with almost unimaginable rage. "You must forgive me. I don't believe we've met."

"You're forgiven." Sam's voice was tight. "Come on, Sybylla. Judge Muldoon. We're going to leave."

Sybylla continued to stare at him. *We're going to leave.* It sounded unreal—as if she and Sam and Dermot could just pass through the tunnel and up to the pure air above and it would all be over. But it wouldn't be over. They couldn't just walk out the door and expect to be left alone forever after; it didn't work that way. "No," she heard herself say, her voice stilted from lack of use. "We need to finish this now."

Bafflingly, this seemed only to amuse Robert Winston. *"Finish* this? What right do you have to pass judgment on me, Sybylla? I'm as much your parent as Dermot and your unfortunate mother—more perhaps. You cannot divide your existence from mine, no matter how you might wish to."

"Shut *up.*" There was a whine of hysteria in her own voice. She hated it, and Sybylla pressed her hands over her ears to make it stop. Inevitably, the fingers of her right hand found the notch—his mark. There was no escape from herself, Sybylla realized, frantic. She wanted to obliterate him; for the moment, she did not care that they were interfused, that she could not negate him without negating herself. Sybylla felt her hand reach for Sam's, for the gun he held, but another hand got there first and another voice spoke.

"You are not responsible for this, Sybylla. Sam, give the gun to me, please."

Wordlessly, Sam handed it over. As Dermot looked down at it, his expression altered from a grimace to a frown of near amusement. Then, thoughtfully, he raised the gun to the level of Robert Winston's head and aimed.

"You find this diverting, Dermot?" Winston spoke harshly.

"Diverting?" He gave a thin smile. "Not precisely, no. But odd. It's all to prevent *this,* you see? Taking a gun and settling up. That's what the law is supposed to do, isn't it? But even with all your talk about civilized justice, it still comes back to this."

"This?" his friend sneered.

"Blood justice. Vengeance. Primitive stuff, isn't it?"

"And may I ask what all this vengeance is for?"

"I'm not particular," Dermot said a little sadly. "My life, my wife's, my daughter's. My career, too, naturally. I might as well throw in the poor people you've been using, since no one else seems to be speaking for them. You have so much to answer for, Robert."

"No more than you, old friend," he said stiffly.

Dermot nodded slowly. "I told the President as much when I withdrew from the nomination a few hours ago," he said. Sybylla, watching him, felt herself reach for Sam's arm. He gripped it tightly. "When Mr. Larkin phoned me this afternoon, I tried to reach Sybylla at home. That's when I knew what had happened, and I made my decision then. Do you understand, Robert? *I made my decision.* My friends from the Justice Department are waiting for us out in the garage, you see."

Winston was staring at him. For the first time, Sybylla thought, he seemed to understand that disaster was imminent, and she watched his face grow chalky white.

"The . . . garage?"

"Passing the time with Herr Kolb, I believe. I asked for a few minutes. I said it was a private matter. As an almost Supreme Court justice, I suppose they felt inclined to give me the benefit of the doubt."

"Well . . . fine." Disconcertingly, Winston appeared to rally. "Let's go, then. I'm happy to discuss our work with the Justice Department. Indeed, if memory serves, I even have some former clients in the ranks. Certainly"—he gestured with his hand—"let's go. I'm looking forward to clearing this matter up."

Dermot shook his head. "Unfortunately, that is no longer an option, Robert. The law cannot deal with you; you've shown us that by your own efforts." He sighed. "Perhaps if you had been less successful at subverting our system of justice, I might be more willing to entrust you to it. But by your own argument, there's every chance of your being acquitted by some juror too dense to comprehend your specific evil. No, Robert," he said, pursing his lips. "I cannot trust the system to do what needs to be done. I think that responsibility must fall to me."

A heavy clack—the unmistakable sound of a bullet filling its appointed chamber.

Audibly, Winston gulped air. "I don't believe you're capable—"

"Unfortunately, I am capable, yes."

Sybylla's ears took the bullet's crash and made it into a great numb silence. What a gyp, she thought, because nothing was happening, unless you counted the red hat Winston had suddenly pulled over his head. He leaned forward heavily in his chair. It was a special kind of hat, she observed, made of a magic yarn that pulsed and trailed its long silky fibers onto the floor. She heard Sam's voice, thick with dread:

"Let's go, honey. Please." Sybylla was nodding yes, but she hung back because she wanted to see. The rich crimson of the new hat shimmered and expanded over his features, making a dense red mask through which the absurd white of Winston's teeth still glinted. Sam had pulled her to the office door before she was able to tear her eyes from the spectacle. Painfully, Sybylla uncurled her arm from his and reached out for her father.

Dermot stood with the gun lowered to his thigh. He showed no inclination to move.

"Daddy?"

He put up his hand but didn't turn.

"I think we should go now."

His shoulders shook. Amazed, she understood that he was crying.

"I need a minute," Dermot said.

She was still touching him. Her hand was on his shoulder.

"I just . . . I need a minute alone." He reached into his jacket and removed the sheets of folded paper. She had to remind herself what they were. "This is yours. I kept it for you, all this time. For myself, too, of course, but mostly for you. To protect you." Unaccustomed to weeping, he paused to swallow. "I'm sorry it didn't do a better job."

"That's okay," she said stupidly. She took the list.

"I almost got you killed. Sybylla, I'm so sorry. For everything, I'm sorry."

"Daddy, it's fine." She bit her lip. She didn't want him to turn because she didn't want to see him cry. "Are you all right?"

"I'm fine." Dermot patted the hand on his shoulder. "Just give me a minute now, all right? I'll meet you in the garage."

"All right." She stepped back. Sam was by the door. "We'll wait for you there."

Sam pulled back the door for her and they both stepped through, blinking in the bright and sterile light of the empty corridor. His hand searched for her fingers. "Can you walk?"

Sybylla nodded. She took a step, and then another one. Behind her, the world exploded.

His arms were around her waist, tight like a vise and rooting her to the spot. So much strength, she thought disjointedly as she flailed against him, straining for the door. And his voice, so strangely gentle. "Don't look," it was saying. "Sybylla, don't look."

CHAPTER
FORTY

—∿∿—

It was midafternoon by the time she finally made it to the tiny post office, climbing in her now-well-worn sandals over the white chalky cobblestones. Even after all these weeks, she could not quite believe that those brown toes belonged to her. They gripped and pushed at the leather beneath them, unconfined, bare to the warm breezes.

Happy toes, Sybylla thought sardonically. O happy me.

It was a little amusing, this business of exchanging nods with the locals as she passed along the main street of the town. It had begun only in the last week, as if they reserved anything but their falsest pleasantries for those few who stayed on after the first euphoric burst of beachcombing and late boozy nights. Already there were two or three of the men who nodded with a special avidness at her approach, whose greetings of *yia sas!* were perhaps a touch louder and more enthusiastic, and the women seemed a mite more suspicious.

Not to worry, ladies, she wanted to announce to the crowded open market. I couldn't be less interested.

The soft white fabric of her skirt moved lightly around Sybylla's legs as she climbed, passing souvenir shops and open cafés. Her first days here, she had returned to the room each night exhausted, her calf muscles throbbing from the simple strain of navigating the town, which some genius had laid out centuries before on the side of a steep hill. Overhead, an ancient fort kept watch for the Turkish ships that hadn't come around lately, but her maiden climb to see it had left her so wrecked that she hadn't returned.

But I'm not a tourist, she thought, excusing herself, intent on banishing guilt. I'm not here for cultural enrichment.

She wasn't really expecting mail, she told herself, climbing the last few yards to the whitewashed post office. It was indistinguishable from the lines of structures that stretched above and below it, carpeting the hillside, except for the seal over its door that marked it as an official link in the barely reliable Greek postal chain. Only one person knew where she was, and she had gone out of her way to tell him he didn't have to write. Still, people could never entirely be trusted, and the thought of a letter languishing here, this close to her and yet unclaimed, was troublesome. So she came every few days. More would mean that she was eager, and Sybylla wasn't entirely eager to hear the news from home.

The old man stood behind the counter, a faded postal cap affixed to his small head either by exceptional balance or some kind of glue. He knew her by now. He smiled, showing three greenish teeth.

"*Yia sas.*" She nodded. Then said deliberately, "Do you have a letter? For Sybylla Muldoon? Muldoon—M-U-L-D-O-O-N."

He put up one blackened finger. With his other hand, he reached below the counter and extracted a small box crammed with postcards and blue airmail letters. Sybylla's heart sank. It would take him an hour to pick his way through all those foreign names. She sighed, but even as she did, her eye fell on the protruding corner of one envelope, gripped by the familiar design of its return address.

"Sir?" She pointed at it.

The old man looked up, perplexed.

"There?" She pointed again. "Muldoon."

He nodded and let her extract it herself, turning it over to her only after a lengthy examination of the address: "Sybylla Muldoon. General Delivery. Molyvos. Lesbos. Greece."

"Okay?" She smiled and nodded. "Okay. *Ef charysto.* Thank you."

She took it outside and put it in her bag. It was not only a letter—that much she could feel. There was the telltale frayed thickness that could come only from supplementary material. Clippings, most likely, and plenty of them.

That should not have surprised her. All this time she'd been away, Sybylla had understood that events—rather significant events—were continuing along without her. And it was all right, she told herself reassuringly, gazing down over the orange roofs to the cool glittering arc of the Aegean. She was ready for this now.

She checked her watch and set off back down the hill. Late for lunch and early for dinner, but Yorgos would give her a table and a coffee, she was sure—one of the benefits of almost exclusive patronage. Over the past weeks, indeed, she had put her nutritional needs almost entirely in his hands, checking the taverna's kitchen to see what looked good on the stove, or letting Yorgos himself choose her meal whenever he seemed at all eager to do so. Yorgos had also provided lodging by leading the way to his sister's guest house, an establishment she would never have found otherwise, since it declined to make itself obvious to tourists in any way, and even if she had, somehow, come across the address, the place was so fiendishly difficult to locate that she'd been tempted to leave herself a trail of crumbs for the first few days. He waved now when he saw her descending the street, confident of her destination but a little distracted.

"Miss Sybil. You are welcome."

She thanked him and took one of the outside tables.

"I know you're not really serving food, but I'd love some coffee."

He turned. "Yannis!" he screeched. "Café for Miss Sybil."

"*Ef charysto*, Yorgos."

"*Paraka lo.*" He went back to wooing less certain customers from the taverna's entrance.

The coffee came quickly, stirred with milk and steaming. She had been trying to curb her habit, cutting back first to four cups a day—one at each meal, one late at night—hoping ultimately to get down to two or three, but when they were this good, Sybylla didn't see how she could possibly deny herself. Even she, a confirmed addict, had never experienced this sheer a pleasure from coffee before. Strange how her own urban culture should so fuel itself with the stuff and still insist on such a lifeless version of it. This little cup, however, seemed a veritable elixir. Curative. She smiled, raising it to toast the bay beneath her; then she reached into her bag for the envelope and slit it open.

The letter came first, scrawled in his familiar hand on the office stationery—two pages.

A restorative sip and then she began.

Dear Syb,

All right, so sue me if I guessed wrong. You send me this postcard saying everything's all right and I shouldn't write, but then you squeeze in your barely decipherable address at the top, where it's made even more indecipherable by some postal stamp. So I say to myself, of course she wants to hear from me. Of course she wants to know what's happened. Everything that's happened, knowing her. I aim to please. I've been clipping things for you since you left, and here they are. I don't know if they will make you happy, but I truly hope they will not make you more sad.

You say you don't know when you'll be back, and that when you do return, you don't know if you're coming back to work here. All right. I'll tell you the truth—it seemed strange to me that you were here as long as you were. There's no shame in needing a change, you know. It doesn't make you any less of a lawyer, or a human being. I feel certain that, whatever you decide, whether you choose to remain in this blighted profession or not, you will always bring to your work the compassion and effectiveness that are your inescapable qualities.

And you needn't worry about us, Syb. By which I mean, you and me. I know that we will always be a part of each other's lives. I care for you too deeply to see that change.

So take the time you need and make sure you come back tanned and relaxed and laden down with ouzo. (I'm told that Lesbian ouzo is some of the best. . . .) Call me when you get back. The cats are fine. Much love.

It was signed with his usual illegible scribble.

She shook the envelope and the slips of paper fell out, shiny magazine stock and smeary newsprint. She paged through them quickly once, confirming to her vast relief that the subject matter did not include her father. "Thanks," she said, surprising herself by saying it aloud. She was too busy mourning Dermot to handle eulogies of his false life or speculation about his shockingly abrupt death.

Sybylla was not at all certain about how much of the Eumenides story had been released. In the days following the terrible endgame in the laboratories beneath LRA, she had told everything she knew to tell to the very gentle interrogator from the Justice Department, as well as handing over her father's list of cases. That, she was assured, was the end of it for her, and in exchange for leaving her own and Dermot's names out of the ensuing fallout, she agreed not to publicize what she had found. It had not been a difficult decision. Sybylla was sick to death of thinking about what Winston and Hofmann and their team had done. With its prime movers gone, the demise of the Eumenides Project was both abrupt and final. Those subjects who had already moved through the system were naturally beyond being helped, but the handful currently in the retention area were to be transferred to appropriate hospitals. These helpless citizens included in their number one particular old woman, whom Sybylla had last seen sleeping beneath her blankets and pitifully guarded by her hungry cat. She did not know specifically where they were taking Annie, but, she told herself, it could hardly be any worse than what that stalwart and piteous person had already endured.

It was decided that Dermot's body be quietly moved the short distance to his own home, where his suicide would be officially "discovered." This grisly duty had fallen to Sybylla. The sudden, baffling death of a shoo-in Supreme Court nominee would attract mournful, tragic speculation. That much could not be helped. But records declaring a newly diagnosed health condition—terminal—were also arranged to dull at least some of the curiosity. Beyond that, the problem of what to do with upward of four hundred tainted convictions, some of which had set precedents, and the people who had contracted for those convictions fell to the Justice Department. She did not know what they would decide to do about the problem, and at that moment she did not particularly care.

With her official role in the drama complete, and her fierce but unfocused wish for revenge thwarted by death, Sybylla had returned home to New York and promptly fallen apart. The phone rang off the hook with calls from reporters who wanted an explanation for her father's suicide, and there were memorial services in New York and Washington, interminable tributes to the lie Dermot had lived. She sat through them both, enraged, devastated, and numb. When she tried to go back to the office, hopeful that work would distract her, Steiner physically removed her from the Lafayette Street building, took her to lunch, and demanded that she take some time to decompress. That was when she told him everything, spilling it out over her untouched bowl of brown and wilting salad as he stared at her, amazed and repelled. He was the only person she had told—the only person she would ever tell.

Slowly, she began to sift the clippings, holding them up one by one to the sinking afternoon sun. An *American Lawyer* article used the sudden closure of Legal Research Associates, previously thought to have been a thriving concern, to question whether the trial consulting business was turning from boom to bust. An article from *People* showed Amanda Barrett gazing into a silver hand mirror after her first round of plastic surgery. The scars were fainter, but the smile was still sad. "I didn't do anything to him," the article quoted her as saying. Two or three of the *New York Times* pieces concerned Dermot's replacement, a bland middle-of-the-roader from Tennessee who looked likely to pass muster because virtually all of his important decisions were appropriately vague. There was a clip from the "Metro" section about the new security measures New York University had established for its laboratory complexes following the death of one of its chemistry professors, and a brief "Intelligencer" item about the demise of the Hyperion Club. In readying the great limestone mansion for sale, apparently, it had been discovered that one of the club's artworks, a painting entitled *The Furies*, by the Swiss painter Arnold Böcklin, was on a list of artworks missing from various European owners since World War II. No former members of the club were available for comment—indeed, *New York* magazine noted archly, no documentation of club members was being made accessible to the press even now—but officials of the Bavarian State Picture Collection in Munich were delighted with the news, claiming that the painting, along with various other canvases and sculptures, had been removed by unknown persons from a cave on the outskirts of that city during Allied bombardments in 1945 and not heard of since. No one had come forward to contest the return of the painting, which would therefore take place within the month.

By far the largest portion of the clippings, however, concerned the resignation virus that had suddenly emerged to plague both district attorneys and former district attorneys all around the country. The *Washington Post* was first to spot the trend, and the story jumped from its law page to the national section within a week. Naturally, reasons for the resignations were widely ranging and seemed terribly subjective—ironically, Sybylla thought, burnout apparently ranked first among them—but the DAs' new employment prospects, where they were indicated at all, were uniformly in the private sector. From Maine to California, people seemed to be fleeing public office in droves; men who had spent years proclaiming that they lived to serve were now abruptly discovering the joys of private firms and announcing that, contrary to any past indications, higher office held no appeal for them whatsoever. A few of the resignations came from men who, oddly, appeared to have no particular career plans at all. The entire group included three senators, three governors, and over ten higher-court judges.

But this phenomenon—extraordinary as it was—did not bring Sybylla a fraction of the satisfaction she derived from one *Daily News* cover story. This featured Andrew Greer delivering a strained smile to the press corps and announcing to "my city, the city of my birth and the city it has been my privilege to serve," that he was resigning his post immediately to spend more time with his family. His family, arrayed behind him as he spoke, looked fairly stunned at this news. Did the move have anything to do with next year's gubernatorial race? one of the reporters asked, confident of an affirmative response.

He would not be running for governor, Greer responded. Indeed, the popular DA went on, he would not be seeking public office of any kind at any point in the future.

"Go figure." Sybylla chuckled at the article. She folded it and stuffed it back in the envelope with the others.

Philip Hofmann, like his late partner, was absent from the clippings of course, having clearly managed to evade the media searchlight scanning the Eumenides fallout. Or else he was shielded outright, Sybylla admitted grimly, forcing herself to wonder whether the devoted scientist had somehow managed to find a new niche in which to employ his skills—perhaps, even, a niche not unknown to those government authorities he had so despised. They had trained him, after all. They might well be capable of finding some small use for his irrefutable talents. She hated the cynicism she could hear in her own thoughts—a final gift to her from Robert Winston.

But still, it was over. Trent and Susu and Cleve . . . and Dermot himself, whose deep love for her she had never quite believed in until she watched him lay it down with his own life at her feet—there had to be some peace, and it seemed to Sybylla that she had a responsibility to find it. She had found it here, certainly, and yet it was strange that she had never once entertained the fantasy of not returning to her real life in New York. Through the worst moments of loss, Sybylla had understood that her wish to serve as an advocate for those who had nothing remained unchanged, but she had ultimately come to realize that the form such an advocacy took was merely a detail. Perhaps it was time to find a less wrenching form.

She left some money on the table and set off again up the steep street toward the guest house, her breath beginning to accelerate. The sinking sun gave the whitewashed houses a rosy hue and glinted off the windows. As fantasy escapes went, she thought, it was hard to imagine a better one than this little town at the tip of Lesbos, which seemed unapologetically devoted to pleasure and not terribly judgmental about how it was achieved. She had spent the first week lying flat on the beach, pale as a sand dollar, her brain still and empty. The second week, her skin browning slowly, she sat up and started to think. Only by the third week had she begun to feel the worst of her bitterness pass.

Yorgos's sister waved at her from the table in the courtyard. She was sharing a bottle of retsina with two guests—newly arrived in paradise, judging from their white complexions and shell-shocked expressions—and she held up the bottle to Sybylla, who thanked her but declined. The smell of the lemon tree in the courtyard followed her inside and up the stairs to the blue-tinted wood of the bedroom door. She opened it and leaned in to peek: a white coverlet was draped over the mound of a body, rising and settling in its heavy sleeping rhythm.

There's a man in my bed, Sybylla thought.

Quietly, she shut the door behind her.

And not just any man, but a card-carrying member of the American Civil Liberties Union.

Before her eyes, he stirred and woke.

"Oh, hey," Sam said. "It's you."

She raised her eyebrows. "You were expecting someone else?"

He patted the coverlet beside him. "Come here immediately."

Sybylla obliged.

"Where you been?" He yawned again.

"Post office, to see if I had mail. Then I went for some coffee."

"Mail? I thought nobody knew where we were."

She shrugged. "Just Steiner. I sort of sent him a postcard with the address."

"I see." He smiled. "So, what's up?"

Sybylla crossed her legs. "Some newspaper stories. Nothing we didn't anticipate. There's curiosity about the resignations, but nobody appears to be asking very probing questions. I don't think we'll be bothered when we get back."

"Oh?" Sam asked. "You mean we're going back?"

She smiled. "I'm the sole support of two cats. I can't stay here forever."

He leaned back against the pillow, his arms folded behind his head. "Well, I guess if you put it that way. I suppose that means I'm going back, too, eh?"

"I kinda hoped."

"Did you?" He grinned. "Kinda?"

She sighed. "Well, you know how it goes. Knight comes to damsel's rescue; damsel darns knight's chain mail for the rest of her life."

He reached up for her. His hand was still warm from sleep.

"Because you *were* sort of wonderful," she considered.

The hand paused. "Only sort of?" She said nothing. "Sybylla, I claw my way onto the shuttle, nearly get myself arrested by the Secret Service when I try to get through to speak with your father, and then, after these not inconsiderable feats, I go and rip you from the jaws of certain death. What do you *mean* I was only sort of wonderful? I was *extremely* wonderful."

"You *are* going on about it, aren't you?" she observed. "I've already offered to darn your chain mail."

"But I don't *want* you to darn my chain mail." He was nearly shouting. "I would never *expect* you to darn my chain mail."

She leaned forward slowly, reaching to brace her arms on either side of his neck, leaning close until she was sure that he was sure that she was about to kiss him.

"All right, then. When your chain mail wears out, I'll just have to run downtown and pick up a new set for you." Sybylla grinned. "I only hope they carry it at Brooks Brothers."

ACKNOWLEDGMENTS

I am beholden to many who generously offered me the benefit of their expertise, critical skills, and sustenance.

In matters medical and pharmacological, C. Wayne Bardin, M.D., Dr. Richard Noviok, Dr. Carl Tisch, and Linda M. Bonnell, Pharm.D., were enormously helpful. In matters legal, Joanne Legano Ross and Henry Deutsch of the Legal Aid Society of New York gave of their time, advice, and secrets. Elissa Krauss of the National Jury Project answered my questions about trial consulting, and Tom Munsterman of the National Center for State Courts helped crack a niggling problem. In matters mythological, I am so grateful to Robert Fagles, who would certainly wish the Eumenides to receive more just treatment than they do here. I thank Anton Hajjar, who carted me around the back roads of Great Falls, and Brendan Cassidy of Princeton University's Index of Christian Art.

Among the many friends who read the manuscript at different stages and gave excellent suggestions, I am particularly indebted to Mary Jo Salter, Paul Muldoon, Belinda Haas, and Kathryn Watterson, as well as to Joyce Carol Oates, whose essay "I, The Juror" was also very helpful. Stuart Paley and Ron Konecky nudged the project along its way, and Pam Bernstein and her assistant Donna Dever brought it happily home. At Crown, Betty Prashker and Cressida Connolly threw great ideas into the pot and generally showed themselves to be members of that rarest and most admirable breed, editors who edit.

Any acknowledgment I might make to my parents, sister, husband, and daughter, to Chris Fahland and to Sally Kahler Phillips, must ultimately be inadequate, but that doesn't stop me from trying. Finally, my most profound gratitude is to Deborah Michel, who was involved in this novel since its inception and whose guidance, judgment, and friendship are on every page.

AUTHOR'S NOTE

It is well known that lysergic acid diethylamide was tested on a variety of subjects, willing and unwilling, during the 1950s and '60s. According to Martin A. Lee and Bruce Shlain, authors of *Acid Dreams; The Complete Social History of LSD: The CIA, the Sixties, and Beyond*, these included military personnel, prisoners, mental patients, foreigners, the terminally ill, "sexual deviants," ethnic minorities, and drug addicts. Central to the CIA's quest was the desire to "break down familiar behavior patterns" as an aid to reprogramming or brainwashing a subject. "If LSD temporarily altered a person's view of the world and suspended his belief system, CIA doctors surmised, then perhaps Russian spies could be cajoled into switching loyalties while they were tripping. The brainwashing strategy was relatively simple: find the subject's weakest point (his 'squeaky board') and bear down on it. . . . LSD would be employed to provoke a reality shift, to break someone down and tame him, to find a locus of anonymity and leave a mark there forever."

Pursuant to this goal, some CIA funding found its way to Dr. Ewen Cameron, a psychiatrist at the Allain Memorial Institute attached to McGill University in Montreal. Authors Lee and Shlain describe Cameron's LSD treatment of 53 schizophrenics:

> The so-called treatment started with "sleep therapy," in which subjects were knocked out for months at a time. The next phase, "depatterning," entailed massive electroshock and frequent doses of LSD designed to wipe out past behavior patterns. Then Cameron tried to recondition the mind through a technique known as "psychic driving." The patients, once again heavily sedated, were confined to "sleep rooms" where tape-recorded messages played over and over from the speakers under their pillows. Some heard the same message over a quarter of a million times.

This therapy, a more detailed discussion of which is included in John Marks's *The Search for the "Manchurian Candidate," The CIA and Mind Control*, failed to achieve the desired results, and the CIA ultimately gave up on LSD as a brainwashing agent. Nine of Cameron's test subjects, however, have sued the U.S. government for one million dollars each, claiming that they continue to suffer the effects of this research.

Not all of the experimentation involving LSD and the mentally ill was so dubiously motivated, however. In an October 1992 article in *Omni*, A.J.S. Rayl notes that by the time LSD testing was halted in the 1960s there had been over two thousand studies and articles, in respected journals, on the drug's effects on various psychiatric disorders. Interestingly, researchers are now beginning to readdress LSD's poten tial for treatment; in Switzerland, the drug is currently being used in conjunction with psychotherapy to treat patients with anorexia and obsessive-compulsive disorders, though not as part of a controlled scientific study. For thirty years restrictions have prevented all testing of lysergic acid on human subjects in the United States, but as of this writing the first human experimentation since the 1960s is in the planning stages and has received government approval; by the winter of 1996, this trial of LSD in the treatment of substance abuse may well be under way at the Orenda Institute in Baltimore, Maryland. The change in policy is welcomed wholeheartedly by most scientists in the field: "LSD was the new technology of psychiatry, and it remains untapped," said Dr. David Nichols of Purdue University in a December 1990 issue of *American Health*. "That the research was stopped—and not the abuse—is tragic."

Drug or hormone delivery implant systems are currently being widely used for contraception, as well as for some types of hormonal replacement therapy, especially in chidren (e.g., in congenital adrenal hyperplasia of the salt-wasting type). Uses for which implants are currently being tested include hormone replacement therapy for menopause and the treatments of prostate cancer, benign prostatic hypertrophy, pituitary tumors, endometriosis, and myomas of the uterus.

Die Furien ("A Murderer Pursued by Furies") was painted by the Swiss artist Arnold Böcklin in 1870 and purchased one year later by the Bavarian State Picture Collection in Munich. It has never since had another owner.

In the spring of 1993, when the first draft of this novel was well under way, an apparently psychotic homeless man stabbed a child on the Upper East Side of Manhattan. His case languishes in the system.

And in April of 1994, the following letter appeared in the *New York Times:*

To the Editor:

As a citizen occasionally caught up in the New York State jury system, I welcome Chief Judge Judith S. Kaye's initiative to remove some of the pain from the process. But I despair of any success. The lawyers who own and run the courts know a good thing when they see one, and their labor union is as unlikely to welcome change as the teamsters.

So I suggest another approach: professional jurors. We already have professional judges, lawyers and criminals, so this final step should be easy. If Judge Kaye can just jack up the fees, many of New York's panhandlers might find this a worthwhile profession. The hours are attractive, the courtroom is warm, and sleeping through the trial would insure complete ignorance of the facts and promote the rendering of impartial justice.

A. Sock, New York, April 7, 1994